Born in Essex, ~~~~~~~~~~ still lives in a village in the north of the county. Married with two grown-up children, she began writing thirteen years ago. Her first novel, *Spider's Web*, was published in 1980 and was followed by *Molly*, *A Fragile Peace*, *The Rose Stone*, *Sweet Songbird*, *The Hawthorne Heritage* and *Tomorrow, Jerusalem*.

GREEN AND PLEASANT LAND

Teresa Crane

Fontana

An Imprint of HarperCollins*Publishers*

Fontana
An Imprint of HarperCollins*Publishers*,
77–85 Fulham Palace Road,
Hammersmith, London W6 8JB

Published by Fontana 1992
9 8 7 6 5 4 3 2 1

First published in Great Britain by
HarperCollins*Publishers* 1991

ISBN 0 00 647250 8

Set in Trump Medieval

Printed in Great Britain by
HarperCollinsManufacturing Glasgow

PART ONE

1928

Chapter One

'If you can't beat them,' standing naked by the tall window, sunshine gilding wide shoulders and an elegant line of back and lighting his tousled hair to gleaming gold, Toby Smith yawned and stretched, 'nobble their best man, I always say.' He turned, eyes narrowed, smiling a little. 'Good wheeze?'

Lady Fiona Paget stirred sleepily. 'Sounds like a perfectly rotten trick to me.' Her tone was mild. 'It is a cricket match you know, my dear. Not the Battle of Waterloo.'

Toby's grin widened. 'Don't you want your husband's team to win?'

Fiona's mouth twitched to a faint smile. 'I'm not sure that's quite the way James looks at it.'

Almost imperceptibly the quality of the young man's smile changed. '"And it's not for the sake of a ribboned coat?"' he enquired gently, blue eyes mocking, '"Or the selfish hope of a season's fame?"'

Fiona, suddenly fully awake and wary, pursed her lips exasperatedly.

'I knew a Captain who quoted that shit the way the Padre quoted the Bible,' Toby said, amiably. 'The voice of a schoolboy rallies the ranks: "Play up! Play up and play the game!" What tommy rot.'

'What happened to him?' She was watching him now, interested. Toby, like so many survivors of the debacle of the Great War – indeed like Fiona herself, who had nursed in those filthy trenches, had seen a friend's blood soak into the soil of France – rarely spoke of it, would never be pressed. The 'war to end wars' may have been over for almost ten years, but the scars that it had inflicted remained, some more obvious than others.

'Who?' The deceptive, forget-me-not eyes were innocent. 'The schoolboy?'

'The Captain, you ass.'

He shrugged, losing interest. 'What do you think happened to him? The same as happened to most. So much for blue blood, the playing fields of Eton and Sir Henry bloody Newbolt.' He turned back to the window, his eyes on the lush green of the parkland, the square, solitary tower of the church, the distant cluster of tiled and thatched roofs that were the village of Breckon Parva. As it had been for the past two days, the wide East Anglian sky was pale and brilliant with sunshine. The sound of birdsong came to him with the drift of the summer air through the open window. A clock struck, musically, in the distance.

'It's poor Gideon I feel sorry for.' Fiona said, reverting to the original conversation. 'He won't like it, you know. He won't like it at all.'

'Then he'll have to lump it, won't he?' Toby's voice was flat. 'He'll get his day of glory; he'll just get it playing for the House instead of the village, that's all.'

Fiona said nothing.

He glanced at her across his shoulder, his face in shadow. 'You don't approve?' The question was light.

She lifted neat and well-marked brows. 'Does it make any difference if I do or not?'

He shook his head, smiling gently.

'Then there's not a lot of point in making the effort one way or the other, is there?' she asked, the words tart. She leaned on one elbow, watching him, unselfconscious in her nakedness. The short, dark red hair was rumpled, the narrow eyes pensive. 'Why does it mean so much to you? It doesn't seem like you to care so much about a game of cricket.'

'I don't give a damn about the cricket. I just don't like to lose, that's all. James has had the good sense to appoint me Captain – I intend to deliver a victory. It's that simple.'

Fiona chuckled in sudden real amusement. 'You already have a Cambridge Blue playing for the House. Why subvert poor Gideon, whose only claim to fame is his ability to knock a regular century each year for the village?'

He turned again, his long, spare frame outlined against the light. Fiona watched him with affection and the eye of a connoisseur; there was no doubt that Toby Smith, however uncertain his origins, was one of the most attractive young men she had ever known, from the shining crown of curly hair to the neat and narrow feet. That he was at least ten years her junior disturbed her not at all. If taxed she would never bother to deny it; she liked younger men, and considered it her great good fortune that a good many of them were ready to return the compliment.

'For your information so far as I can discover your young Hugo Fellafield only ever once got beyond twelfth man,' he drawled, the impeccable upper-crust accent exaggerated just enough to bring an answering glimmer of laughter to her face, 'and though I'm sure he's a jolly good chap and all that he's a bowler, old thing. A bowler. He's about as useful with a bat as you would be.'

She refused to be deflected. 'He's a good bowler?'

'Of course he is.' He reverted to his normal, pleasant tone.

'So,' Fiona tilted her head, watching him, shrewdly, 'poor Gideon loses out both ways? If he's as good as James says he is – and he's often said that the man would be County material if he weren't who and what he is – then wouldn't he appreciate the opportunity to test himself against a really good bowler?'

Toby moved to the tallboy, picked up a flat silver cigarette case, extracted two cigarettes with long, deft fingers and lit them both. 'Possibly.' His voice was cool.

She accepted the cigarette, lay back on the pillows, blew smoke to the high, ornate ceiling. 'But you aren't going to let him?'

'No.' He sat on the bed beside her, almost idly ran his fingertip between her small breasts then spread his flat hand upon her belly, her skin warm and smooth beneath the palm of his hand. 'Gideon Best is playing for the House this year. Whether he wants to or no. And this year – with Toby Smith as Captain – the House is going to win this bloody silly match for the first time, I gather, since 'twenty-three.'

'And none of this nonsense about it being only the game that counts?' she grinned, amused and caustic.

The hand moved. She drew a sudden breath, sucked her lip, watching him.

He smiled, that warm, angelic, dangerous smile that lit his face like sunshine and had been, she knew, the undoing of more than one innocent soul. 'Well of course not,' he said, mildly reproving. 'Whatever do you take me for, Lady Paget? Some kind of gentleman?'

She laughed aloud at that. 'Perish the thought.'

He leaned towards her, relieved her of the cigarette, kissed her with unexpected gentleness upon the mouth, then with a typically swift and fluent movement stood up, stubbing the cigarettes into a cut glass ashtray and reached for the clothes that were draped across the back of the chair. 'Come on you lazy loafer. Tennis before tea.'

'Oh no! Don't be such a brute!' Fiona rolled onto her stomach and buried her face in the pillow.

Toby grinned as he pulled on a crisp, white shirt, immaculate flannels, slung his pullover around his shoulders. 'Three minutes,' he said.

'Or what?' Fiona cocked an interested eye from beneath the fall of red hair.

'Or I cart you downstairs as you are.'

'You wouldn't dare!'

'No?' He slapped her buttocks none too lightly as he passed, still grinning. 'Try me.'

Groaning melodramatically Fiona rolled from the bed, walked to the door of her dressing room, stood for a moment before the rows of drawers and cupboards then shook her red head firmly. 'No. It's no good. I've given Benson the afternoon off, and she's positively the only person in the world who knows where the hell anything *is* in here! Anyway,' she began to rummage through a wardrobe, her voice muffled, 'you mustn't make an old lady overdo it, you know. Go and find Rachel, or Flip. They'll play with you. Rachel might even beat you. And serves you right. I'm going to have a bath. A long one.'

She found a pale silk wrap, hauled it from the cupboard,

slipped her arms into it, belted it with quick and determined movements about her lean waist.

Toby was back at the window. He had lit another cigarette and was leaning against the deeply shuttered window frame, his eyes on the ancient square tower of Breckon Parva church, stranded within the parkland of the Hall almost a mile from the village it served. 'Did James' grandfather really move the village to improve the view?' he asked, with sudden and interested curiosity.

Fiona joined him at the window, slipped an arm about his waist, laid her head upon his shoulder. 'He did. The houses were his. He decided to move them. And – Bob's your uncle – the village reappears over there.' She nodded her head towards the roofs.

Toby offered his cigarette. She drew upon it, gave it back to him. Toby tilted his head, eyes narrowed and thoughtful.

Fiona slanted a sly glance at him. 'What is it? Gives you ideas, does it? Fancy having a view of your own to improve? I'm not sure the locals would be quite so cooperative nowadays.'

Toby said nothing. A tall dark girl, bobbed hair swinging, was approaching the house across the wide sweep of lawn. Even from this distance the athletic grace of her carriage, the challenge in the lift of her chin was apparent. She was dressed in an outfit that looked as if it might have been left over from the making of *The Sheikh*. Ruby silk edged with gold glimmered in the sunshine, clung in the faint breeze to her long legs.

Fiona laughed, reached up to kiss the smooth-shaven cheek. 'What you need, my love, is a wife. A very rich and doting wife. Would you like me to arrange one for you?'

Toby smiled a little absently. 'As a matter of fact that's all in hand. I meant to tell you. What in hell's name *is* that Rachel's wearing?' Faint irritation had sharpened his voice.

Fiona was staring at him. 'What do you mean?'

'Rachel. Why the devil can't she dress like a normal person?'

'Not Rachel,' Fiona said, carefully. 'The wife. In hand? How in hand?'

He brought his eyes to her face, stubbed the cigarette out briskly in an ashtray on the windowsill. 'Oh, just that. I think

I've found her. She's rich. She seems amiable enough. And her father doesn't care that I'm not exactly top drawer. Seems he scrambled out from a fairly insignificant drawer himself. Self-made man. Underscars. Heard of them?'

Fiona, still regarding him, clear-eyed and thoughtful, considered for a moment. 'Underscars. The chemist shops? That have started to sell these fancy electrical gadgets and things?'

'That's the one. I've been doing some legal work for him. The old man lost his sons in the war. There's just one girl. Daphne.'

'And – you're going to marry her?' Fiona's voice, to her own surprise, held a slight acid edge.

'Probably.' He might have been discussing the price of fish for all the real interest shown in his voice. 'If I suggest tennis to Rachel do you think I could persuade her into something civilized or will she insist on dressing like some character in a panto?'

If she thought you really cared, Fiona found herself thinking, her understanding and sympathy for Rachel, as so often, surfacing at the most inappropriate of moments, she'd dress fit for Wimbledon's centre court. She shrugged. 'Who knows? Depends how she feels.'

'That's true. Never let it be said that our Rachel would ever allow other people's preferences to interfere with her own.' He walked to the door.

'Dare I say hark who's talking? Being brought up together has made you two more like brother and sister than any brother and sister I know. Wait for me. I'm going to use James' bathroom. It's much sunnier. Mine's such a dark little hole.' She sauntered to her dressing table, picked up a hair brush, a small perfume bottle, a box of powder.

Toby turned and leaned against the door jamb, watching her, his bright eyes warm. They had been friends long before they had become lovers, and their affection for one another was genuine and based on more than the excitement and physical pleasure each afforded the other in their lovemaking. Fiona was one of the few women with whom he did not play-act. She knew him and accepted him for what he was. And if she did not always approve of his attitudes and actions – and he knew she did not – then neither did she condemn.

'Oh, damn it – wait a minute – I've forgotten my comb.'

Toby strolled into the corridor and stood rocking on his heels, hands in pockets as he waited, looking at the paintings that hung upon the long panelled wall of the landing. In a moment Fiona joined him. She stood beside him, her eyes, too, upon the pictures. A landscape lit with sunshine, a riot of flowers, the lucent glimmer of a brilliant sea had all been depicted with a loving eye and an undeniable talent. Fiona's face was suddenly shadowed with sadness as she looked at them.

'Madeira, isn't it?' Toby asked.

'Yes. James's eldest son Peter painted them. He loved the island. Well – they all do, of course, but he really adored it. He painted it often. He was very talented, as you can see.'

'They're certainly good. He copped it at Passchendaele, didn't he?'

'Yes. October '16. Ralph – the younger boy – survived that one but was lost at Verdun a year later.' She shook her head. 'What a waste. What a bloody waste!'

A tragedy repeated, she knew, in homes and families throughout Europe. Fiona let her eyes move from picture to picture, trying as she so often did to imagine the young man who had painted them, straight and strong, the pride of her husband's life, dead before he reached his twenty-first birthday. James rarely spoke of either boy, but knowing him as she did she guessed how he must have suffered from such a crippling blow. His family and his hopes for the future wiped out within one brutal year. Yet still, she had kept royally her part of the amicable bargain they had struck when they had married seven years before. James once again had boys in the Breckon Hall nursery, to carry his name and eventually to take on the responsibilities of Breckon Parva and of the family business. Yet she could not help but ask herself, occasionally, if he did not sometimes hanker for those two young men cut down so young in the fields of France and Flanders – the grim fields she had herself known all too well. Had she ever nursed those two? Often she had wondered. She never would have known. All different, yet –

broken, shocked, half-drowned in mud – all so very much the same, she would have had no reason to remember them above the others.

Toby was surveying the pictures, his fair head on one side. 'Is it really as good as it looks?'

She smiled a little. 'Madeira? Yes, it is actually. It's –' she shrugged, spread her hands, '– just beautiful. Like an enormous, lovely garden.'

They turned and strolled to the head of the curving staircase, stood for a moment leaning upon the magnificent sweep of banister looking into the hall below. 'It's an enchanting place.' Fiona was smiling a little, her eyes warm, remembering. It had been during a visit to the island of Madeira that James Paget, nearly twenty years her senior, had in his own bluff and honest way courted and won her, initiating a marriage that in its own idiosyncratic way was as successful as any she knew.

'The climate is virtually perfect – a temperate warmth all year round. It never gets too hot and it never gets too cold. It's a kind of self-perpetuating paradise – the rain falls on the mountains, the water is carried down to the fertile ground around the coast, so it's green and beautiful all year round. You can grow almost anything there. The sun shines almost all the time – it's a magical place.'

'Young Hugo Fellafield's family runs that end of the business, don't they?' Toby had turned and was leaning against the banisters, his eyes once more upon the paintings.

'Yes. The Fellafield estate is just outside Funchal – that's where the cruise ships call, of course. In fact, it's just about the only town of any size on the island. The Fellafield side of the partnership has always been rather more actively involved in the business than James' family have.'

Toby raised gentle eyebrows. 'Gentlemen and players?'

She grinned, easy and unembarrassed. 'Something like that I suppose, to begin with. Though I doubt Spencer Fellafield would appreciate hearing either of us say so now. The two families have been in partnership for generations.'

'The production and shipping of Madeira wine being counted a cut above common or garden trade?'

'I suppose so, yes. And having the added charm of being a part of a truly lovely setting.' Fiona moved forward again. 'See – that's Funchal, and the bay. This is the view from the grounds of the Quinta do Sol, the Fellafields' place. It's a wonderful old house. Hugo's mother lives there virtually permanently. She's created the most marvellous gardens around the house. She's quite passionate about them.'

'And rather less than passionate about her unbeguiling husband? That sounds like an eminently sensible lady,' Toby interjected drily.

Fiona flicked lightly at his arm with the towel she carried, then drew him towards another painting. 'The Fellafields have owned the Quinta do Sol for over a hundred years, and of course because of the business connection between the two families, the Pagets have been involved with it for just as long. That's how Peter came to paint these over the years. There, that's it –' she pointed to a small painting of an attractive, rambling, white painted house that was built into the slope of a green hillside, its tiers of windows flanked by dark green painted shutters, the almost pagoda-like roofs a warm terracotta against the canopies of the surrounding trees and the clear blue of the sky. Lawns, shrubberies and terraced flower beds sloped away from the paved garden that surrounded the house. Flowers were everywhere, overgrowing steps and walls and surrounding gleaming pools and streams, a riot of growth and colour. 'It's truly like that. One of the loveliest places I've ever seen.' In the sunlit, musty corridor she was suddenly assailed by the evocative memory of a scent of mimosa upon mountain air, a diamond clarity of light, a glow of bougainvillaea in the warm dusk. She stood for a moment, lost in the recollection of it.

'I was up at Cambridge with the older of the Fellafield boys – Charles.' Toby's voice interrupted her thoughts.

'Why of course you were. I'd forgotten.' She laughed a little at his boyish grimace of distaste. 'Charles is so very like his father, isn't he? They're both the kind of people you can't imagine having been young! But don't let that prejudice you against young Hugo. Believe me, they're absolutely nothing alike. It astounds me sometimes that they're brothers – they're like chalk and cheese. Hugo's the one who's taking over the Fellafield side of the wine business. James adores him and he's quite one of the nicest young men I know.' She laughed again, affectionately. 'A bit weak, I suppose. And totally daft sometimes. Yet—,' she stood, considering for a moment.

Toby glanced out of the window at the sunshine and the wide fields.

'He hasn't had an easy time of it, really. He's been dominated by his father and that dreadful prig of a brother, virtually abandoned by his mother—' She glanced again at the picture of the house, nestling in its tranquil, beautiful gardens. 'Who can blame him if he isn't the strongest of characters? But he's a dear. I'm very fond of him.' She caught Toby's sly, slanted glance and laughed aloud, 'In the most motherly possible way! Wait till you meet him. Then you'll see.'

'All I hope is he can bowl as well as he's cracked up to.'

'I'm sure he can.'

He rapped at the banisters with his knuckle, full of energy, dying to be off. 'Right, then. See you later.' He ran down the first flight of steps, long hand trailing the banister rail.

Fiona leaned forward. 'Toby?'

He stopped, looked up. 'Mmm?'

'What's she like?' Despite her efforts her woman's curiosity could not be contained. 'This Daphne you think you'll marry?'

He looked a little surprised. Thought for a moment. 'Plain. Sensible. A year or so older than me.' He stopped, obviously casting round for any other snippet of information that might be of interest and, failing, grinned like a boy. 'That's about it. See you at tea.' She watched him run down the wide, shallow stairs, whistling. He did not look back.

Plain. Sensible. And nearly thirty years old.

Good God. Poor woman. Did she know what she was taking on?

A small thoughtful line bisecting her usually smooth brow, Fiona made for her husband's luxurious bathroom and a long, cool soak.

*

'Why do you keep the pheasants' eggs but give the partridges' back? It doesn't seem very fair.' Philippa Van Damme ploughed sturdily through the short, moist grass of the ride, almost running to keep up with the long-legged strides of her companion.

Gideon Best, dark face shaded as always by his battered keeper's hat, hitched the canvas bag he carried higher onto his shoulder. 'Told you before, didn't I? Partridge is a good mother, pheasant a bad. Damn flighty things'll abandon a brood if they're scared off. Partridge'll stick with 'em.'

Philippa stumbled, caught herself. Gideon did not ease his pace.

'But why do you take the partridges' eggs in the first place then? If you give them back when they're pecking or whatever you call it—'

'Chipping.'

'Chipping, then – why not leave them in the nest for the whole time?'

They had reached the clearing where the coops were situated. Around each coop was a small pen where the young pheasants pecked and scratched. The hens that had been set to hatch and adopt the alien brood crooned and clucked

Gideon strode to the lean-to where the heavy copper stood, stirred the glowing embers of the fire he had lit at dawn that morning, poured fresh water into the copper. 'Varmints,' he said. 'Rats. Crows.' He tipped the measured rice and wheat into the water and stirred it. 'They'll clear a nest as fast as a bird can lay.'

'So, you take the eggs and give them to a broody hen, then just as they're hatching out you put them back in the nest?'

'Tha'ss it.' The man cast a sardonic glance at the young, earnest face. 'Thinkin' of applying for a job?'

Philippa giggled. 'Of course not. I just wanted to know, that's all. You put wooden eggs in the nest, don't you?'

'Pot eggs.'

'Pot eggs. Doesn't the partridge guess?'

'If she does she's never let on.'

'But you leave the pheasant eggs with the hens and they hatch them.'

He straightened. Long, lean, shabbily dressed. 'Tha'ss right.'

'And you feed them and look after them until you can take the coops into the woods—'

'Coverts.'

'Coverts. And then you *still* have to look after them for a long time.'

He grunted. He was rolling the wheat mush into small pellets with stained, dark-skinned fingers.

Philippa considered. 'It does seem like an awful amount of trouble to go to just so that Sir James and his friends can shoot them.'

Gideon cocked one black eyebrow.

She grinned, slid her finger across her own throat, rolling her eyes ghoulishly. 'Whoops. High treason? A hanging offence?'

'Near enough.'

'Sorry.' She sounded not the least repentant. 'Can I help you feed the chicks?'

They worked in easy silence for ten minutes or so – an oddly assorted pair, the man tall, broad shouldered and rangy, the angular, Romany face in repose guarded and impassive as a shuttered window and the girl smallish for her fifteen years, stocky, clear-eyed and smiling, the bright cotton of her flowered summer frock a splash of colour in the sunlit clearing. Their acquaintance but a week old yet they were friends, these two, of the truest order. Not many could say that of Gideon Best.

They sat afterwards upon a fallen tree trunk, drinking strong tea brewed upon the fire and sharing Gideon's bread and cheese in a friendly quiet as they watched the young birds eat. A family of rabbits hopped cautiously to the edge of the clearing, then satisfied with the peace sat unconcerned, nibbling.

'Shoosi,' Gideon said.

Philippa cocked her head. 'What?'

'Shoosi.' He jerked his head. 'Rabbit.'

Philippa grinned. 'Shoosi. I like that.' She lifted her voice a little, calling to the rabbits. 'Sar shin, shoosi?' She giggled. 'Gosh, that's hard to say!' The rabbits had disappeared, white tails bobbing in alarm. 'I did get it right, though, didn't I? Sar shin – how are you?'

'Aye.'

She thought for a moment, then counted upon her fingers, 'And kushto is "good" and wafodu is "bad"—' She glanced at him enquiringly. He nodded. 'And dordi, dordi means "dear, dear!"' She glanced at him again, thoughtfully, as the faintest of smiles touched the austere line of his mouth. 'I'm not too sure about that one; I suspect it's lost something in the translation. But you wait – I'll go back to school speaking a whole new language! My friends will be pea green with envy!' She bit into a lump of cheese with enjoyment.

The sun was sinking. Gideon eyed the shadows that had cre across the coops and pens. 'You not expected at the Hall?'

Philippa shrugged offhandedly. 'There's an army of people up there. They won't miss me. If I show my nose Toby'll dragoon me into playing tennis or something. He's such a bundle of beastly energy.'

Gideon slanted a glance at her. Rumours of Toby Smith – and of Toby Smith's intentions with regard to the annual cricket match – had, as is the way of such things in a small community, already reached him. He bit into a doorstep of bread and cheese. 'He's your brother, this Toby?'

Philippa, ravenous after her day in the open air, was matching him bite for bite. 'Oh, Lord, no.' She spoke with her mouth full. 'Well – not my real brother, that is. I suppose sort of – adopted.' She hesitated, aware that rather than answering his question she had created another. She took another bite, hoping he would not pursue the slightly uncomfortable point. When she glanced at him, however, he was still watching her, waiting. She fidgeted a little.

The somewhat odd relationship between herself, Toby Smith and Rachel Patten, whilst never seeming over-complicated to them could, she knew, confuse outsiders. Not related by blood, their ties were emotional. Each born into very different backgrounds through force of circumstances they had been brought up together in the London orphanage run by Rachel's father and grandfather, and Philippa, her own father dead before she ever knew him, had considered them to be her family for as long as she could remember. Why Gideon, who usually never showed the slightest interest in her chatter about the guests at the Hall, should pick on Toby as an object of interest she had no idea; what she knew with certainty was that there were things in Toby's background that he would be less than pleased to have disclosed.

'Toby and Rachel and I were all brought up together,' she said. 'My mother—' she stopped. She could hardly tell even Gideon that Toby Smith had been found, a homeless urchin, wandering the streets of London, '—adopted him when he was very young. Quite a long time before I was born. We lived with the Patten family – that's Rachel's family – in London. They ran an orphanage – Aunt Hannah and Uncle Ralph still run it – they aren't my real aunt and uncle of course, though I think we must be vaguely related because Mother married Aunt Hannah's cousin—' She let her voice tail off, took another hefty mouthful of bread and cheese, uncomfortably aware that Gideon, uncharacteristically, was watching her still, waiting for her to go on. Again she wondered what it might be about Toby that had aroused this unprecedented and somehow vaguely hostile curiosity. 'Toby and Rachel fight a lot,' she offered, hopefully, a neutral comment that might satisfy, 'they always have. And—' she pulled a resigned, half-resentful face, '—they both treat me as if I were still ten years old.'

'But you aren't actually related?'

Philippa shook her head. 'No. Well – as I said – only a bit. Rachel's father is Ben Patten. He's quite a famous doctor – he's done a lot of research into gangrene, and infections and things. Rachel's mother lives in the country somewhere.' She gestured, vaguely, with her sandwich. 'I was born in Belgium just before the war. In Bruges. My father was Belgian. I never knew him – he died at the beginning of the war while I was only a baby. He was killed in the defence of Brussels. Uncle Ben – Rachel's father – came to sort of rescue us. He got us back to England on a troop ship. I don't remember any of that, of course. Now I live in the north with my mother and her husband Eddie – he's a pet – and Rachel and Toby live in London. Not together, of course,' she added, grimacing, half laughing. 'They'd scratch each other's eyes out in no time. Toby went to Cambridge after the war. He's some kind of lawyer – company law – and Rachel – well, Rachel doesn't actually do anything, I don't think.' Uncomfortably aware of something close to disloyalty she added hastily, 'Not that she isn't awfully clever – she's terribly artistic and clever with her hands. She makes the most gorgeous clothes – designs them and everything. But I don't suppose there are many jobs going in that sort of line. She's a bit—' she hesitated, searching for the word, '—eccentric.' She was pleased with that. Rachel herself, she knew, would have approved.

'So where did this Toby Smith come from, then?'

Floored, Philippa looked at him blankly. Gideon was a listener, not a questioner and she was certain she had diverted him from the awkward subject of Toby's parentage.

With deft fingers Gideon tucked paper, mugs and left-overs into his bag. Lifted his sharp, dark eyes that gleamed like cut topaz in the sun.

Philippa to her own disgust found herself stammering awkwardly. 'He – well, I'm not sure exactly who his parents were. My mother found – that is adopted – him when he was very young—'

Philippa was no dissembler. Never having had any problems with her own mother's somewhat obscure origins – explained to her meticulously and with love as soon as she was old enough to understand – she knew from experience that Toby, for all his ease and his laughter, for the most part guarded his past with understandable care and she had the sure and uncomfortable feeling that he would not take kindly to her discussing his improbable background with Sir James Paget's gamekeeper. And anyway, despite occasional disturbing misgivings raised by the quite appalling heartlessness – not to say ruthlessness – he could sometimes display to others, to her he had always been the big brother she had never had, and she loved him dearly. He deserved better from her than gossip to an outsider, however much a friend she might consider that outsider to be.

Gideon, with sure instinct, sensed and understood her dilemma and chose not to press her. With an easy movement he stood, swung the bag onto his shoulder, waited, offering no hand as she scrambled from the huge trunk onto the ground. He had heard enough. These past years spent in the protective shadow cast by Breckon Hall had taught him much about his so-called superiors. Toby Smith did not, after all, sound like a man too hard to handle. An upstart, meddling lawyer throwing his weight about. As a matter of pure pride Gideon Best was determined not to wield his bat for the House. He never had. He wouldn't start now. Not even to himself did he admit how much the brief glory, the belonging, the admiration of his peers, however grudging, each year on the occasion of The Match meant to him.

Philippa was scurrying along beside him again, face bright with curiosity as she looked up at him. 'What about you? Did you have any brothers or sisters?'

He grunted an affirmative.

'How many?'

Her cheerful persistence brought one of his rare smiles. 'You wouldn't believe me if I told you.'

'I would. Of course I would!'

'Eight brothers. Six sisters.'

The dark eyes opened, saucerlike. 'There were –' she calculated quickly '– *fifteen* of you?'

'Tha'ss right.'

'Where are they all now?'

He shrugged.

'You mean – you don't know? Not any of them?'

'Tha'ss right.'

She contemplated this for a moment in silence. 'That seems dreadfully sad. Didn't you like each other?'

The flicker of his grin this time was different – knife-sharp and dangerous. 'Some did. Some didn't.'

Philippa detoured around a pile of horse droppings, came back to his side again. The sun flickered, a shower of golden coins through the bright leaves of the trees. A startled, bright-plumaged pheasant rose, chattering its fright and vexation, almost from beneath her feet. 'And did you all live in a caravan? A proper one, with a horse and things?'

He nodded. 'A vardo. Aye.'

The practical Philippa frowned a little. 'But how on earth did you all get in? It must have been awfully big to take fifteen of you!'

'There were others. Always somewhere to sleep. Other vardos. A bender or a tan – tents or shelters, I suppose you'd say. A fire to sit by.'

'Uncles and aunts and things you mean? A proper –,' Philippa hesitated a little over the word, aware of uncomplimentary connotations, but with it on the tip of her tongue could not prevent its coming, '– tribe?'

He slanted a dark glance at her. Nodded.

She considered for a moment. 'You must have missed them awfully when you left?'

He said nothing.

'I mean – living all on your own the way you do – isn't it lonely? After living with such a big family?'

Hardly discernibly he lifted a shoulder.

They had emerged from the woodland onto a track that skirted the trees and edged an open field of lush green corn, young and tender-looking, the sun bringing to it just the first fragile touch of gold. A scarlet splash of poppies drew the eye, dazzling in the brilliance of light after the dimness of the woods. Ahead of them, nestled between the cool shadows of the trees and the sea of waving corn stood a small wooden shack, neat, dark and square, shutters and door closed against the sun.

'Did they mind?' Once started upon a subject Philippa, like a terrier with a bone, was loath to leave it until it had been well and truly stripped of its meat. Just a day or so before, Fiona – affectionately exasperated – had been heard to wonder aloud if young Flip might not be the reincarnation of a Spanish Inquisitor.

'Your family, I mean. When you left?'

For a moment she thought he would not answer. They had almost reached the hut. He swung the bag from his shoulder. 'Yes. They minded.'

Romany turned gawje. Poacher turned gamekeeper. Traitor. His mouth twitched grimly. Oh yes. They had minded. Still he watched his back.

The brittle edge to his tone caught Philippa's not insensitive ear. 'Oh. I see. So that's why you don't see them. Or – why they don't see you?' She neither expected nor received an answer. She watched as he unlatched the door. The inside of the shack was cool and dark, neat and spare as a hermit's cell, the narrow pallet bed made and tucked in as tidily as an envelope, the table bare, the single wooden chair pushed neat and square beneath it, the tall cupboard in which guns and traps and the other paraphernalia of Gideon's calling were kept, padlocked shut. Neither picture nor photograph decorated the walls, no curtains softened the square, shuttered windows, no carpet lay upon the rough floorboards. The only welcome was in the lifted head and soft brown eyes of a spaniel who sat, alert and eager at her master's coming, waiting for the gesture that would release her to greet him.

Gideon snapped his fingers. The dog, tail waving like a frenzied flag, bounded up to him, sat almost upon his feet, looking up into the dark face with single-minded devotion. Philippa thought – but could not be sure – that Gideon's eyes softened a little. He bent roughly to ruffle the long, soft ears, then straightened. 'Tea?'

Reluctantly Philippa shook her head. 'I s'pose I ought to be getting back really. And I don't think I'll be able to get away to help feed the chicks this evening. Can I come again tomorrow?'

He nodded brusquely. 'If you want.'

She flashed her ready, infectious grin. 'Good. I'll see you then. 'Bye Kili.'

The dog lifted her handsome head but did not leave Gideon's side. Gideon nodded goodbye, watched the sturdy figure as she turned and tramped back along the rutted track in the direction of the Hall. After a moment he took off his hat, shrugged out of his multi-pocketed jacket and hung both up on a nail banged into the back of the door. Then he plunged a hand into one of the capacious pockets and pulled out a slip of paper. He had nearly asked Philippa to read it to him – scrawled as it was in speedy if elegant handwriting, the deciphering of it had been difficult. Not that he couldn't read. Printed lettering he could manage perfectly adequately. But this—.

He spread it out, laid it upon the table. Toby Smith. The name was clear enough. And a time – six o'clock. Gideon shrugged, stuffed the note back into his pocket. Dordi, dordi! Whatever Mister Toby Smith wanted with him or of him at six o'clock would have to wait. The chicks needed feeding – as anyone on the estate should know. And - as anyone on the estate from Sir James down to the humblest assistant keeper equally should know – at this time of the year the chicks came first. Everything else took its turn.

Gideon opened the cupboard, pulled out a bottle of whisky, poured a small measure into a glass that stood upon the wooden draining board, meticulously stoppered the bottle, put it back upon the shelf and closed the cupboard door. He picked up the glass, meditatively swirled the liquid around it for a moment then in a quick and easy movement tilted his head and tossed it back. He stood for a moment of quiet enjoyment as the tot warmed throat and belly.

The silence of the woodlands and the fields – of his life – closed about the little hut like a companionable and sheltering hand.

The hard-drawn, sombre lines of his face relaxed a little. From somewhere within the rustling woodlands a cuckoo called. The dog stirred at his feet. He bent to pat her, thinking of the girl who had just left. Normally he had very little contact with guests at the House, except in the winter during the shooting parties that were Sir James' favourite pastime; and then the relationship could never be anything but between patron and trusted and competent servant. This girl was different. She had turned up at the coops a week or so ago and, in the straightforward and engaging way that he now recognized as typical of her, had introduced herself and launched into a spate of questions in the same breath. His monosyllabic answers had appeared not to daunt her in the least. He answered her questions; that was all she required. He had surprised himself. Her sunny smile and friendly nature had been unexpectedly hard to resist; despite himself he had found himself drawn to her and while, as always, he had made no great effort to respond to her uncomplicated friendly overtures neither had he, as he normally might, made any positive effort to deflect them. And so she had attached herself to him. She popped up by his side at any odd time of the day, sometimes escaping the house in a misty dawn to tramp through the dew-laden grass by his side or – as today – waiting in the ride at the time she knew the chicks must be fed to accompany him to the coops. He found her almost childlike candour amusing and in a strange way touching. 'I absolutely adore Aunt Fiona, and it's so kind of her to have me for the summer while Mother and Eddie are in London, but I can't help it, I do find the Hall and all those servants most dreadfully intimidating. Parks looks at me as if I'm a rather scruffy dog who ought to be kept in the gun room. And all those blessed knives and forks – golly, it's enough to take one's appetite away!' She had laughed then, her sudden, infectious giggle. 'No, now I shouldn't exaggerate. Nothing does that, worse luck!'

Her mother, it seemed, was a close wartime friend of Lady Fiona's, her stepfather a politician. Clever, self-educated and ambitious, he was one of the new breed of Labour men who had tasted power in the brief Administration of 1924 and who had every intention of tasting it again in larger measure.

'I'm glad Mother married him. They're good for each other,' she had said, and then with another of those grins, 'though no one could accuse them of seeing eye to eye all the time.'

Her frankness and trust was refreshing, her lively curiosity concerning all that went on about her appealing in the extreme in a world where jaded disinterest was considered the thing. Almost Gideon had come to look for the small, sturdy figure; her laughter and that blithe and splendid smile were hard to resist. A pity, he thought now, with the reassuring and accustomed edge of cynicism, that the next couple of years would see her emergence from childhood to young womanhood. That would put paid to those attractive, straightforward qualities if nothing else did.

Gideon Best filled his battered kettle from the pump outside the door and set it upon the hob to boil for tea.

Toby had handled stubborn and wordless insubordination often enough to recognize it when he saw it.

'That's settled, then, Best,' he said, easily. 'You come in at number three for the House. Shame about the mix up, but there you are – we're short a man, and yours was the name that came out of the hat—' He faced the dark unbelieving gaze with imperious confidence. Gideon it was who looked away.

Toby perched upon the corner of the desk in the deserted Estate Office, swinging one elegantly flannelled leg. Around them, ledgers and account books, papers, bills and old agricultural or field sports magazines cluttered every surface. 'Should be a good day,' he said, pleasantly.

Gideon hesitated long enough for insolence before he said, 'Aye – sir.'

Toby's smile did not flicker. 'That will be all, Best. See you on Saturday. Match starts spot on eleven. You've got that?'

'Yes, sir.' The saturine face was absolutely expressionless. In the past ten minutes, Gideon had been forced to reassess his too quickly formed opinion of this young man, an experience he had not enjoyed.

'We don't want another mix up about time, do we?' It was eight o'clock. The shadows stretched long across the lawns outside.

'No, sir.' Gideon turned to leave.

'Oh – and Best?'

He stopped. Waited.

'Get someone to take over your duties for Friday night, would you, there's a good chap? Get yourself a good night's rest. I've heard some splendid reports of you.' The clear eyes were level and friendly. 'Are they exaggerated?'

'I wouldn't know, sir.'

'Well we don't want to disappoint Sir James, do we? He's quite set his heart upon winning this match. Pleased as punch he was when I told him who we'd drawn—.' Toby let his pleasant voice trail off. His eyes were very sharp. 'It would be a shame, Best, if you weren't on form. Don't you think?'

The harsh line of the gipsy's mouth crooked sardonically. 'Aye, sir.'

Quiet as a shadow he left the room. Toby sat for a moment looking after him, leg swinging, eyes thoughtful as he reached into his breast pocket for his cigarette case.

'But, Toby, you *can't*! You don't understand! This is the *only* time that Gideon does anything with anyone! *For* anyone! Oh – you know what I mean!' Almost incoherent with outrage Philippa faced Toby. Her small, square, suntanned face was bright with anger, her brown shoulder-length hair a bird's nest.

Toby was regarding her with a combination of astonishment and irrepressible amusement. 'Flip, sweetheart, what are you talking about?'

Philippa came as close to stamping her foot as she ever had. 'You know very well what I'm talking about, Toby Smith! Gideon Best! *That's* who I'm talking about. You've fiddled it! Don't deny it, Toby, I *know* you – you fiddled it! To make Gideon play for your side because he's the best batsman. Well, you can't! It isn't fair! Gideon always plays for the village. He always wins the match for them. It's the only time that anyone ever *talks* to him – the only time any of them admit he *exists*!' She threw up two small hands in exasperation. 'Can't you *understand* that?'

He was laughing outright now, adding fuel to the flames of her anger. 'Flip – for heaven's sake! – it's a *game*. That's all. We were a man short. I put the names in a hat – Gideon Best's was the one that was drawn –'

'How very convenient!'

'– and I'm absolutely sure that the man doesn't care one way or another which team he plays for –'

'You're *wrong*. Wrong! He *does* care. But he'd never say so. Oh, Toby, please –!'

Toby assumed an expression of angelic patience.

'– please choose somebody else. Don't make poor Gideon play for the House. The village will never understand – they'll think he volunteered or something, to suck up to Sir James – and he'd never try to explain. Toby, he's a gipsy. An outsider. And a gamekeeper. A good one. Half the village spend half their lives trying to get the better of him. And fail. They resent and dislike him. He hasn't a friend. Not a single friend –'

'Oh?' Toby's blue eyes crinkled. 'Small brown-haired girls with dirty socks don't count?'

She ignored that. '– except for the cricket match. He's a brilliant batsman – everyone says so – and since he came he's always won the match almost single-handed—'

'You can't win a cricket match single-handedly, Flip. There are another ten men on the pitch.'

'I *know* that. But he's head and shoulders above everyone else. It's the only time the village want him. The only time he goes into the pub and someone buys him a drink. The only time people smile at him and pat him on the back—'

Toby lifted himself from the chair, towered above her, smiling still. Philippa fell silent, biting her lip. 'Did Best send you to talk to me?' The soft voice was cool.

'No! No, of course not! He wouldn't!'

Toby let the silence lengthen. 'I'm inclined to agree with you. So – would he be happy, do you think, to hear you doing battle for him?' He paused a moment to let the question sink in.

'I – I wanted – it just didn't seem fair—' She knew how weak that sounded, how childish. She flushed to the roots of her hair.

He relaxed, reached a brotherly hand to tug at her hair. 'Lame dogs again, Flippy? A less likely one I can't say I've ever come across.' He smiled suddenly, coaxing her, his eyes warm, 'And anyway, how come you know so much? Only here a couple of weeks and you're knee-deep in village politics already? You really are the most terrible old gossip you know.' His voice too was warm, edged with affection and amusement. Normally she would have been lost.

She stepped back from him, clasping her hands before her, face stubborn. 'You fiddled it,' she said again, obstinately. 'You want to win this beastly silly match, and you fiddled it.'

He sighed.

'And poor Gideon has to pay for it.'

'"Poor Gideon" as you so inappropriately call him will be playing alongside a Cambridge Blue and an ex – a very "ex" I

29

have to admit.' Toby was laughing again. 'Fifty if he's a day – an ex-Middlesex County player.'

'He'd rather play against them.'

Abruptly, Toby lost patience. He turned away, reaching into a box on the table for a cigarette. 'Don't be boring, Flip. Run away and play.'

She stared at his back for an outraged moment, then without a word turned and marched straight-backed out of the room, cannoning into the tall, bright-garbed figure who was coming through the door as she did so.

'Lordy, Flip, whatever's wrong?' Rachel's voice was light; surprise widened the vivid eyes. Philippa did not look at her. It had taken her an hour to screw up the courage to face Toby, to risk his wrath and his laughter, both so rarely used against her. And she had made a mess of it. To make things worse she suspected that Toby had been right; Gideon himself would think the affair none of her business and would certainly not thank her for poking her nose into it. Fighting tears she mumbled something to Rachel and fled.

Rachel watched her go, faintly bemused, then sauntered into the salon, eyed Toby a little caustically. 'Not another broken heart?' she asked, lightly. 'Honestly, Toby, I thought better of you than that. The child's all but your sister.'

'Shut it, Rachel.' Toby strolled to the tall window, stood looking into the golden summer's afternoon. From the tennis court came the sound of racquet and ball, raised voices, laughter.

'Drink?' Rachel had gone to the vast and ancient side table where stood a silver tray gleaming with bottles, decanters and glasses.

'Yes. Please.'

'Whisky?'

'Mm.'

'And?'

'Soda, please.'

She splashed the whisky into the heavy glasses, syphoned the water, carried the glasses to where he stood by the window. She was tall and slender, her movements graceful, her colouring startling. Her bobbed hair and the clear curve of her brows were jet black, her eyes, in contrast, the deep and velvety colour of violet petals. In the new fashion she had courted the summer sun and her skin was tanned to an even gold. Had she smiled a little more often she might have been called beautiful, but smile or no smile no man could ignore Rachel Patten when she entered a room with her swinging, provocative walk, her brilliant, unconventional clothes and the cool challenge of those long-lashed eyes. No man but Toby Smith, who had known her since childhood and who, she sometimes thought, would not truly have noticed her had she stood naked before him. 'So —', she handed him a glass, 'did I or did I not just see her flee this place in tears? What was wrong with her? If I didn't know the depths of your devotion to each other I'd have said you'd had a barney?'

He rolled the glass between his hands, still not looking at her. 'Storm in a tea cup. This ridiculous match tomorrow. The child's taken it into her head that some desperate injustice has been done to an underdog. You know Flip.'

'Indeed I do.' She eyed him, astutely. 'And has it?'

He turned at that, smiling a little. Despite herself she warmed, smiled back. Knowing as she did that her smile meant nothing to him. 'To be honest with you, I've never met less of an underdog than Gideon Best. He's James' pet gipsy. A gamekeeper. Built like a barn, ugly as sin, black as Satan and insolent as hell.' His voice was mild, a little injured. 'And here I am doing him a favour.'

'And is he duly grateful?' Rachel's voice was dry.

Toby tossed back half of his drink in a mouthful. 'It would seem not.'

'Well, well. Sounds like a uniquely independent minded gentleman to me. I look forward to meeting him.' Rachel reached to take the cigarette from Toby's fingers, drew on it, handed it back. She was dressed in Turkish trousers of a vivid emerald green and a peacock blue silk bolero. Glittering green and blue bangles clashed musically upon her wrists and matching, swinging, slender earrings emphasized the long and elegant line of her throat. The outfit was — she knew — exotic and infinitely enticing, her tanned skin warm and smooth where the short jacket lifted above the waistline of the trousers. She had met young

Jason Bentley halfway up the stairs and, gratifyingly but far from unexpectedly, he had all but keeled over at the sight of her. Her warm, deliberate smile had tied his tongue and activated his prominent Adam's apple until she had actually thought he might choke. Equally satisfying had been the reaction of the elderly Sir Charles Fulmore. It had been the alarming if amusing possibility of bringing about some kind of seizure that had led her to abandon that old and eager gentleman and sent her in search of Toby and, if possible, mischief. She threw herself into a chair, long legs in the diaphanous silk stretched, crossed, before her. 'I hear,' she said, over-sweetly, unable for her life to keep the acid edge from her tone, 'that the dainty foot's been found that fits the crystal slipper?'

He looked, for a moment, uncomprehending.

'Cinderella,' she said, witheringly. 'The love of your life? A wife.'

'Ah.'

'A plain and elderly lady, Fiona tells me. That should be fun.'

He refused to rise to her malice. 'Daphne is a couple of years older than me, yes. She's pleasant and she's –' He hesitated, clicked his long, well-shaped nail against his glass.

She sipped her whisky, eyes sparkling, wilfully mischievous, over the rim of the glass. 'Yes?' she asked, interestedly. And then, as he did not continue, 'Rich?' she suggested, gently.

He lifted cool, bright eyes to hers, held them levelly. 'Yes,' he said. 'Very. Of course.'

She tried to hold steady against what she saw in those eyes, and could not. This was a dangerous game she played, and so often she lost. She dropped her gaze to her glass. 'I hope you'll all be very happy,' she said, suddenly and quietly savage. 'You, she and all the little tenners.'

He said nothing.

She tossed back the remainder of her drink, rose from the chair with a studiedly graceful movement, so searingly aware of his eyes upon her and in such a pure anguish of need that she was suddenly truly afraid that it might, this time, get the better of her; that she might drop to her knees before him, grovel, howl, weep, plead – the brief and awful image sharpened further

her acrimonious tongue. 'I hope the lady knows she's marrying a cheat and a bounder?'

His eyes widened. 'Sorry?'

She sauntered to the tray, put her glass back upon it, glanced back across her shoulder, the old, barbed, challenging look. 'I'm with Flip. I don't believe for a moment that you pulled Gideon Best's name out of a hat.'

He spread innocent hands. 'I swear it.'

She continued to the door, paused, draping herself for a moment to picturesque effect about the doorjamb. 'One day, Toby Smith, the Good Lord will get you with a thunderbolt when you lie in your teeth like that. I hope to God I live to see it.'

'Best not stand too close, then.' His voice was light.

She slid from view. Her voice floated back, clear and sardonic. 'Not on your life, Smith. Not on your life. Take more than a common or garden old thunderbolt to get me.'

Chapter Two

Hugo Fellafield was pretty well content, a state of mind not too unusual in a young man as easy-going as he. The morning was lovely – fresh, sunny and full of promise. The roads were clear, the Essex countryside sped past at a satisfying clip as he drove with pleasure the smart two-seater Alvis that had been his twenty-fifth birthday present from his mother. Behind him lay a difficult week and the latest battle – lost as usual – with his father. Ahead lay a pleasant weekend in what he knew were lovely surroundings and in what he was quite certain would be agreeable company; it was not in his nature to look much further than that. He liked Breckon Hall, tucked into its picturesque curve of river on the Suffolk/Norfolk border, adored Sir James and Lady Fiona – rather especially, he thought with daring, Lady Fiona – and was looking forward to renewing old acquaintances and making new ones. The cricket match was a bonus. He hoped there'd be some pretty girls to cheer him on. He drove fast and with some skill, whistling into the wind, his straight, straw-coloured hair whipped from his face, his striped silk tie streaming over his shoulder.

Two hours later, on the dot of 9.30, the handsome green car turned into the long, tree-lined drive of Breckon Hall and hurtled through the dappled sunshine to pull up at the front door in a spray of gravel. Parks, the Pagets' butler was in the hall to greet him, Davies the young manservant who valeted for him when he stayed at the Hall was cheerfully at hand to take charge of luggage, boots and cricket bat. 'I'll give it a good oiling for you, sir. Lovely day for the match.'

'Indeed it is, Davies. Where are you in the order?'

'Number Five, sir. Just after you.' The young man grinned. 'Don't suppose I'll be needed!'

'Where is everyone, Parks?'

'In the Breakfast Room, Mr Fellafield. The family and their guests are all up and about early this morning. Have you breakfasted?'

Hugo grinned engagingly. 'I did, but it seems like three days ago. I'm as hungry as a hunter.'

'I'll have a place laid for you, sir.' Parks had always had a sneaking affection for the Fellafields' younger son; a feeling that had never in any way extended to the young man's elder brother.

Hugo turned towards the stairs, swung in practised fashion about the great newel post and took the first few stairs two at a time. 'I'm in the usual room?'

'Yes, sir. The Blue Room.'

'Righto. A quick wash and brush-up and I'll – oh, I say – I'm most terribly sorry—!' In turning to continue his dash up the stairs he had collided with a young woman coming down in the opposite direction. A dream. An hallucination. A vision in svelte pale silk morning pyjamas, long of leg, slender of waist and with the most startlingly beautiful eyes he had ever seen. He stood, gaping like an idiot.

'That's perfectly all right.' Rachel side-stepped gracefully, treated him in pure mischief to the warmest of smiles and carried on down the stairs, crossing the wide hall unhurriedly with her swinging, long-legged stride, perfectly and wickedly aware of the young man's astonished eyes upon her back.

Davies, from the bottom of the stairs, bag, boots and bat in hand, caught young Mr Fellafield's eye and winked, broadly, behind Parks' back.

Hugo pursed his lips in a silent, admiring whistle. Then he turned and leapt on up the stairs, two at a time, grinning.

The prospects for the weekend were quite evidently very good indeed.

It was a perfect day for the annual cricket match – a bonus well appreciated in a part of the country where the weather was not always so kind, even in summer. It was an event of some importance both for House and village, a fête looked forward to, planned for, talked about for all of the preceding year. In The

Bird in Hand the talk was of spinners and yorkers, square legs, slips and gullies, the need for strategy, a good eye and a straight bat. And, this year, with some grim satisfaction, the defection of Gideon Best. In the tiny front room of Mrs Parsons' cottage – where stood one of the only modern sewing machines in the village – no attention was paid whatsoever to the intricacies of a game that would take all day and – to an unpractised and uninterested eye at least – be played at such leisurely pace that one could easily, between one ball and another, forget which side was batting. Here, there were far more important decisions to be taken, subjects to be discussed: the blue skirt or the green? Daisies or roses in the brim of a wide straw sunhat? Hair up or hair down? And didn't that Betty Sandham look an absolute tart in that awful bright red lipstick that she'd taken to wearing? What was her mother thinking of to allow it? This last rather more than half-enviously; in a village still very rural and relatively untouched by the stirrings of change being felt in city and suburb, Betty Sandham was the only girl who somehow managed to flout parental authority and get away with it. She would, most agreed, with sagely nodded heads, come to no good end.

If the subject least discussed as the girls queued up for their turn at the precious machine for last minute alterations was the game that was supposed to be the centrepiece of the day, then surely that the most on all their lips was the far more important event that was to take place in the evening – the Cricket Dance. For months minds had been made up and changed, dresses had been sewn and endlessly altered, others' choices had been eyed with well-disguised satisfaction or with even better disguised envy. This was the social event of the year; this was the night when a girl might sparkle brightly enough to catch the eye and the interest of her – or, as had been known to happen more than once, of someone else's – chosen swain. The night when the glamour and romance tasted usually only second-hand at the Odeon in Diss or through the pages of a magazine actually came to Breckon Parva. The night dreams might come true – why not? Certain it was that many a courtship had begun on a warm June night as the young couples wandered from the lamplit barn where the dance was held into the summer woods and fields.

Many a speedy village wedding too could be traced back to the festivities of the Cricket Dance, with smothered smiles and counted fingers. So the little room buzzed with excitement as the girls came and went, every chair, every surface cluttered with cottons and scissors and bright scraps of fabric as, gossiping and giggling, curlered heads tied in turbanned headscarfs they laid their battle plans and strategies and dreamed their private and innocent dreams of conquest.

Rachel, in contrast, had given very little thought to what she should wear that evening. Although she knew that Fiona had hired a popular London dance band to play for the evening – a band she had herself recommended – she could not persuade herself to take anything but a passing interest in the festivities. In truth, now, she heartily regretted her impulsive acceptance of Fiona's invitation – an acceptance she was honest enough to admit, to herself if to no-one else, had only been prompted by the fact that she had known Toby would be at Breckon Hall this weekend. A fat lot of good such idiocy had done her. As always his proximity had thrown her into an even more perverse mood than was usual with her; and the news that he was to marry had, oddly unexpectedly, been a blow more savage than she had been prepared for. Now she was restless and edgy, unable to settle down to anything. Even the books of Islamic designs she had found in the library could not hold her attention for more than half an hour at a time. Her suspicions that something was going on between Toby and Fiona would not be stilled; and the sympathetic look she sometimes surprised in Fiona's green eyes was insupportable. Oh, damn and blast Toby Smith! All of her life he had been there, and for all of her adult life she had wanted him with a fierceness and strength that bordered on the obsessive. No distraction, no effort, could, it seemed, ease the pain of his indifference to her. Handsome Toby. Clever Toby. Heartless Toby. Toby, whose presence could goad her into even wilder and more wantonly mischievous behaviour than could his absence. Toby, whose life had been so inextricably linked with hers for so long yet on whom she had no claim, in whom she could have no trust. She wondered, often, if he truly cared for anyone. Charming certainly, affectionate sometimes, yet

37

always he was guarded, a soul shuttered and locked away from any depth of emotion. Except where Philippa was concerned. Often Rachel found herself puzzling about that, as she puzzled about his relationship with Sally, Flip's mother, the girl who had found him, fed him, fought for him and then – in Toby's eyes at least, Rachel knew – abandoned him to go to Belgium to marry Flip's father. Rachel had watched often the meetings between these two, had seen his pleasant and merciless disinterest, her hurt. When she had married Eddie Browne a few years before Toby had found some excuse not to attend; he had, however, presented the newly-weds with the most spectacular Persian rug Rachel had ever seen. Complicated Toby. And there lay the rub; always the possibility, however faint, that that guarded soul would open up, and if it ever did, why not to Rachel Patten? Beautiful Rachel. Wild Rachel. The only fitting mate for him; why could he not see it? Why did almost every other man she laid her disinterested eyes on fall at her feet whilst he still treated her as a grubby, grizzling ten year old tagging at his shirt tails? Why did she care? The news of the coming marriage had, ridiculously, hurt and enraged her – and again, as so often, she had provoked him to temper. No, this had not been a good weekend for Rachel, and it concerned her not one whit what she might wear for The Dance.

Philippa on the other hand had over the past week had every item of clothing she had brought with her out of her wardrobe at least a dozen times, and each time had decided in despair that she might as well go straight to bed with a book after the match. Her well-worn cotton dresses, her two 'best frocks' were humiliatingly childish. She would be better off, she told herself gloomily, wearing her school uniform. In unusual discontent she gazed at herself in the mirror; plain brown face, plain brown eyes, plain brown hair – oh, golly, it really wasn't fair! No-one would want to dance with her – well, she supposed Toby in his self-imposed brotherliness would, but what on earth good was that? She didn't suppose for a moment that Gideon would dance with anybody. And who else would take any notice of her?

It had been in this mood that Fiona had found her, a few days before the match, and had in her own brisk and inimitable way taken things in hand. A soft cream silk shirt of Fiona's own, a trip into Diss that had, magically, produced a pale green skirt prettily braided at the hem with a matching scarf, and Flip's world had been set entirely to rights. She had tried on the outfit at least half a dozen times, turning and swirling, adjusting the scarf, pulling her hair forward, pushing it back. On the last occasion, eyes bright, hair freshly washed and shining she had decided with some surprised satisfaction that she would not, after all, look an absolute fright, and so she faced The Day with pleasure and anticipation. She had been in the thick of the preparations all week, helping in the kitchen, popping up beside gardener or groundsman, busying herself in the visitors' wing amongst freshly aired sheets, vases of flowers and harassed maids.

She was surprised and delighted when Toby called her out on to the pitch to toss the brand new half-crown whose spin would decide which team would take to the field first. The coin glittered in the air, fell into the short, springy grass, the village captain – who was also the blacksmith – declared his team's intention to bat, and the day was well and truly started.

Fiona, her fair, creamy skin protected by a wide-brimmed, flower-trimmed hat that James had told her made her look like Marie-Antoinette playing at milkmaids, sat at a table outside the small pavilion and surveyed the scene with some satisfaction. The day was glorious, the grounds looked truly beautiful, well-kept and cared for, the specimen elms, oaks and beeches spreading shade upon cropped green grass, the river and the distant lake dazzling in the sunlight. Young men dressed in cricketing whites and blazers sat upon the pavilion steps or sprawled upon the grass. A scattering of spectators was spread all about the long boundary, rugs and blankets bright upon the grass, picnics already out. Not far from where she sat, her own two small sons, in matching white suits with blue sailor collars, played a miniature cricket game of their own with some of the village children, indulgently supervised by their Nanny, a nursemaid and one of the young undergardeners. Closer at hand, around her at small tables and in deckchairs, women and girls in pretty summer dresses and shady hats sat and gossiped quietly, barely pausing for breath as they pattered applause for the first two batsmen – the wheelwright and the baker's son – who strode with determination across the greensward whilst, awaiting them, young Hugo Fellafield stopped swinging his arms like a windmill and, expectantly grinning, started to polish the ball on his trousers.

'Let battle begin.' Rachel had slipped into the seat beside her, looking cool and very pretty in a simple drop-waisted white dress, a pale lavender sash about her narrow hips that somehow echoed the colour of her eyes. She wore no hat, her hair shone smooth and blue-black as the sleek feathers of a raven, the flawless skin of her face and arms was golden brown. She put her chin upon her cupped hands and pulled a rueful, comical face. 'Roll on lunch!'

It was not a good day for the village. By lunch four wickets had fallen for only twenty runs and Gideon Best's name was mud. Even those with the most minimal interest in the game knew that for the past four years his stands had been the mainstay of the village innings. The eye that made him a deadly shot, the athleticism that allowed him to move so swift and fast in pursuit of a poacher, the strength and balance that enabled him to sit the most capricious of horses combined to make him a natural batsman. Even faced with Hugo's fiery bowling everyone from the smallest child upwards knew that with Gideon at the wicket the stumps would have stayed put and the runs would have come. Gideon himself, fielding at long leg, close to the boundary, stood shoulders hunched, glowering blackly – his usual expression. As the fifth wicket flew with the last ball before the lunch break he turned and walked, solitary, in the direction of his hut.

Toby Smith, blue eyes narrowed speculatively, watched him go for a moment before turning to slap Hugo on the back and escort him to the pavilion and lunch.

By two o'clock the House team was batting, chasing a total of eighty-two, Toby himself and the head gardener's lad opening. They stood sturdily for fifteen minutes, Toby bringing off a couple of spectacular fours before being caught trying it again.

Grinning and good tempered he tucked his bat under his arm and set off towards the pavilion. As he did so Gideon moved out of the pavilion, padded up, his skin copper dark against his borrowed whites, the heavy bat looking like a matchstick in his big hands. Rachel, who had been laughingly applauding Toby, stopped abruptly, her face suddenly still, a gleam of undisguised interest in her eyes.

'And – just who is that?' she asked Fiona, through the applause as Gideon strode past them.

Fiona leaned close. 'James' pet gamekeeper. An absolute wizard, so he says. Appeared from nowhere four or five years ago. A Romany, James thinks.'

'He's the one all the fuss has been about? Flip's—' Rachel hesitated a moment, her face drolly disbelieving '—little friend?'

'That's the one.'

'Does he always look that grim?'

Fiona rolled expressive eyes. 'Always.'

The two men, both of a height, the one wheat-fair and relatively lightly built, the other from a distance looking black as a Moor and for all his leanness hugely built, were approaching each other across the outfield.

'Light and darkness,' Rachel said suddenly, half amused, wholly intrigued, 'Day meeting night.'

'Sorry?' Fiona cocked her head enquiringly.

Rachel, her eyes still on the two men, shook her head. 'Nothing. It doesn't matter.'

Both had slowed a little. Brilliant blue eyes clashed with and held the harsh and hostile dark gaze. 'Good luck,' Toby said.

Gideon Best, face impassive, said nothing, but lengthened his stride, bat swinging, as he made his way to the crease.

Rachel Patten, who had never shown the slightest interest in a game of cricket in her life, except perhaps to jeer, leaned forward, chin on hand, her eyes absorbed.

The result was a foregone conclusion, and the match was over by a slightly delayed teatime. With a face expressionless as granite rock Gideon Best knocked the village bowlers for six –

at least half a dozen times quite literally – apparently impervious to the chill atmosphere that had overtaken the field around him. Whilst bowler, wicket keeper and close fielders joked and grinned with the other batsmen, who came and went with a regularity that gave the village team at least some satisfaction, Gideon was ignored. But if he noticed, and he certainly gave no sign of it, he gave not an inch. Any ball that asked to be cracked to the boundary got the treatment it deserved. The closest he came to dismissal was a driven six that whistled like a bullet past the ear of a fielder so close that the poor lad dived not towards it but away, unwilling to risk life and limb even for the glory of dismissing Gideon Best.

Rachel Patten, during almost the whole of the long innings, hardly stirred. Eyes intent and thoughtful she watched not the game but the one man, who stood in lone and vivid defiance at the wicket. She hardly glanced at Hugo as, his own modest innings brought to an end by an unwarily hooked ball neatly caught, he cleared his throat hopefully beside her.

'I say – sorry – but is this chair free?'

Rachel nodded, her eyes still on the play. Fiona had long since departed to dispense small talk to her guests, an exercise in which Rachel had flatly refused to join.

Hugo, prematurely elated at this apparent success and understandably deceived by Rachel's apparent interest in the game, promptly launched into a detailed analysis of the play, to which Rachel paid no attention whatsoever. Not until his enthusiasm was turned towards the prowess of the man wielding the bat at that moment with such savage and productive skill did she turn her head to look at him.

'– a natural batsman if ever I saw one. Look at the way he moves –'

Rachel's lips twitched a very little.

'He's seeing the ball like a football. Lord, I should have liked to have had a go at him.' He grinned at the faint questioning lift of her brows. 'Bowling, that is. I'm a bowler.' The grin slipped a very little as he realized that the fascinating cricket watcher beside him should have known that, had she noted his feats of the morning as studiously as she was watching the unknown batsman. 'I'm Hugo Fellafield.' He added, a little lamely, 'I'm sorry. I should have introduced myself before.'

Rachel relented, amused by the boyish charm, the earnest admiration in the wide-set hazel eyes. 'Rachel Patten,' she said. 'Hello.' Her eyes flickered back to the man at the crease as the sound of leather on willow cracked out again and applause lifted as the ball skidded off for another four. 'Fellafield,' she added, smiling, her eyes still on the play, 'that's a name you hear a lot of around here.'

Hugo laughed. 'The Pagets and the Fellafields have been in business together since 1783. My – oh, great-great-great-grandfather, I think it was and Sir James' great-great-grandfather started the firm together.'

'And you've been shipping Madeiras ever since.' Rachel spared him a glance, and the sudden regard of those stunning eyes set a pulse bumping in a peculiarly uncomfortable way in his throat.

'Yes.' Not the most scintillating of replies. Cursing himself he cast about for something to keep her interested. 'Do you like the wine?'

'Very much.' Rachel's attention was wandering again.

'Have you – have you ever been to the Island?'

'No, I haven't. But the Pagets have some rather beautiful pictures—'

'On the landing upstairs. Yes. Peter painted them a year or so before he was killed. The house in the small painting is ours.'

That did catch her attention, quite gratifyingly. She turned, cocked her head, the provocatively lovely face interested. 'Really? It looks very beautiful.'

'Oh it is.' There could be no mistaking the true enthusiasm in his voice. 'It's absolutely splendid. When I was little I used to think it the most wonderful house in the whole world,' he laughed, a little self-consciously. 'My mother lives there for most of the year – looking after the Island end of the business, though I'm due to take that over in the next couple of years. My father's in the Civil Service, you see, and doesn't have much time.' He was unaware of the odd note of wistfulness that threaded his voice. 'Mother isn't terribly enthusiastic about business I'm afraid. She's a gardener. She has the most wonderful garden at the Quinta. She's collected trees and plants and things from all over the world and is most tremendously knowledgeable. Father always says she spends more time on that than – oh, I say, is that it?' The batsmen were walking towards the pavilion, bats swinging, the fielders drifting along beside them. Hugo, together with most of the other spectators stood, clapping enthusiastically. 'Oh, well done! Well done indeed.'

Rachel too stood, watching. She saw Sir James slap Gideon Best jovially upon the shoulder, bluff and hearty, his kindly face beaming. 'Well played, old lad, well played! What a bit of luck for us, eh, your name out of the old hat? Couldn't have done better if I'd pulled it out myself! Owe you a drink, Best, owe you a drink! See you later.'

Gideon's face relaxed a little, and he nodded. Then, turning, he found himself face to face with Toby Smith, hand extended, bright face open as the day. 'Jolly well done, Best. A splendid innings. Rumour didn't lie.'

But *you* did. Rachel, fascinated, wondered if anyone else read those words in the undisguised contempt in the dark face, wondered with an unexpected tightening of the nerves if Toby himself read them. Around them the crowd jostled, moving towards tea and cakes, talking and laughing. It seemed to the watching Rachel that the two men stood alone, with only her eyes upon them. She saw clearly Gideon's refusal to take the outstretched hand, saw too, with a strange, small stirring of excitement, the sudden venomous flash of anger in Toby's cornflower blue eyes.

'Rachel, darling – look who's here – late as usual. Have you seen Flippy anywhere?' Fiona's voice distracted her from the scene. She turned. A tall, lean woman in slacks and shirt, a scarf slung about her shoulders, her light brown hair a short halo about her head grinned widely.

'Sally!' With more enthusiasm than she would show to most, Rachel flung her arms about Philippa's mother and hugged her hard. 'We were expecting you this morning! What the devil happened?'

Hugo Fellafield, aware that for the moment his luck had run out, philosophically slipped away to congratulate Gideon.

Tea over, and necessary socializing set aside for an hour or two at least, Sally Browne and Fiona had settled themselves in a couple of battered leather armchairs in the long and lofty library of Breckon Hall, a fresh pot of tea and a plate of fresh-cooked scones before them. The library was a lovely room, the worn leather furniture comfortable, the deep-pile rugs softly faded in the two hundred years they had lain upon the polished floors. Tall windows opened upon a vista of parkland and water. It was a room of books – they lined the walls, and filled the shelves that stood at right angles to those walls, forming booklined alcoves. As this time of year there was no fire in the great soot-blackened fireplace, and a huge bunch of roses in a copper pot sat upon the hearth, filling the room with their scent.

The two women had talked almost non-stop for an hour, catching up on family, friends and mutual acquaintances and discussing the affairs of the MacAdam Trust, a charity which helped young unmarried mothers that they and Sally's husband had been instrumental in setting up after the war and which still flourished ten years later. This was an unlikely friendship, between an abandoned bastard child of the London streets and the elegant Fiona MacAdam, daughter of one Baronet, married to another; but it was a true friendship nevertheless, based on mutual regard and shared experiences. A friendship that both took for granted would last forever. That Fiona's conscience was not entirely clear concerning Toby Smith, the young man whom, however he might feel about her, Sally looked upon as a son, was demonstrated by the fact that she had studiously avoided mention of his name. Sally it was who brought it into the conversation, easily as always, but with that undercurrent of wistful eagerness that invariably made Fiona want to wring Toby's strong young neck. 'Sounds as if he's doing very well at Wellingale and Parker, doesn't it? He seems very much in demand?' Sally's voice, always one of the most distinctive things about her, was husky and pitched low.

Fiona poured more tea. 'So it seems, yes.' She flicked a quick look at her friend's face. 'You know he's thinking of getting married?'

Sally's hands stilled for a moment, then reached easily for the cup. 'Good lord! No, I didn't. Who's the—,' she paused, grinning, '—lucky lady?'

'Daphne Underscar. Heiress to the Underscar shops. You know, the chemists that have branched out into electrical goods? They've popped up in most High Streets over the past few years.'

'So they have.' Sally's voice was thoughtful, her strong face gave nothing away. 'What's she like?'

Fiona shook her head. 'Haven't met her. Amiable, Toby said.' She grimaced.

'And rich?' Sally's voice was quiet. A small look of understanding passed between them.

'Yes,' Fiona said. 'Very rich indeed I should imagine – at least potentially.'

Sally said no more. She lifted her head for a moment, her eyes on the sunlit distance of the park through the open window. Images flickered; a small, grubby cherub of a child curled upon her pallet bed. 'Tell me a story, Sal – Aladdin's Cave and all them jewels—.' A mischievous urchin swinging on her hand. 'A ha'penny toffee apple, Sal – oh, go on! Just a ha'penny one!' And then a tall composed youth, eyes and voice cool, nursing a hurt he would neither admit to nor discuss. She sighed.

Fiona, watching her, resisted firmly making the comforting gesture that would indicate that she understood the root of that sigh. 'Flip seems to be having a whale of a time,' she said.

Sally relaxed, smiling. 'Oh, yes. Fee, I can't thank you enough for having her – she does so hate London, and I couldn't leave her alone in that big house in Manchester with no-one to look after her but Mrs Malone – the poor kid would have gone out of her mind.'

'Don't thank me – she's a pleasure to have around. She's wonderful with the boys, and they adore her.'

Sally smiled. 'She's always been good with little ones. As you probably know she made up her mind at the age of ten that she was going to teach small children, and she's never changed it. A teacher she'll be, and that's that.'

'She'll make a good one. People like her. She's made friends all over the estate.'

'I do hope she doesn't get under everyone's feet? She is a terrible one for poking her nose into anything that interests her.' Sally pulled a rueful face. 'Can't think where she gets that from.'

Fiona laughed. 'She's a delight, my dear. She can stay for ever as far as I'm concerned.'

'And Rachel? She's just down for the weekend?'

'That was the original plan, yes.' Fiona put her cup back on the tray, stretched long legs before her, 'When I tried to get her to stay for a few more days she said she'd die of boredom away from London. But as a matter of fact she seems to have changed her mind.'

'Oh?'

'Something she said at tea. Sounded as if she'd decided to stay for a few days after all.'

Sally grinned suddenly, a flashing grin that, like her daughter's, lit her thin face like sunshine. 'Nothing to do with that nice young chap who's so obviously smitten, I suppose?' she asked, only faintly hopeful.

Fiona chuckled. 'Hugo? I shouldn't have thought so. He's hardly her type, I'm afraid. Still, you never know – stranger things have happened – we can only live in hopes! There must be someone, somewhere, that can tame our Rachel.'

'Does she see anything of her mother, do you know?'

Fiona shook her head. 'I don't think so. From all accounts she can't bear to be near her. Can't say I blame her, mind.' She added, with typical candour, 'The couple of times I've met Charlotte Patten she's given me the creeps – her and that—.' She pulled a face, '—"companion" of hers! God, if they weren't so crushingly respectable I'd have my doubts about those two!'

Sally stood up, brushed the creases from her slacks. 'Well, I just wish that Rachel could find whatever it is she's looking for.' Her hands stilled and she lifted her head to look directly at Fiona, 'Does she know about Toby? About his getting married?'

Fiona did not pretend to misunderstand. 'Yes.'

'How did she take it?'

'Not well. By which I mean that she made some very flip

47

remark and changed the subject. I think she then went and wound Toby up thoroughly—'

'—and has been leading your young Hugo Fellafield a merry dance ever since,' Sally finished for her. 'Poor Rachel. Will she ever settle, do you think?'

Fiona stood, they strolled towards the door. 'If she did she could do a lot worse than Hugo. He's a splendid young chap.'

'Which is more than can be said for his father,' Sally said, drily.

Fiona shot an amused glance at her. 'You've fallen foul of Spencer Fellafield?'

'Eddie has. Mr Fellafield doesn't take kindly to these upstart Socialist MPs, you understand. Eddie asked a question in the House that our esteemed friends in the Foreign Office didn't take kindly to. Eddie and Fellafield had words.'

Fiona, wordless, shook her fingers as if they had been burned.

'Quite. Eddie isn't one to be treated like an over-opinionated stable lad, as you know. Letters were exchanged.' Again that flashing grin. 'It was all very entertaining.'

Fiona, in sudden, laughing affection, slid an arm about her waist. 'Oh, Sal, it is so very good to see you! Are you sure you can't stay for longer?'

Sally shook her head regretfully. 'Honest, Fee, I can't. I was lucky to be able to manage today—I'll have to be back in London tomorrow morning.'

Fiona dropped a light kiss on her cheek. 'You can tell Sergeant-Major Browne from me that he's a damned slavedriver, and I won't have it! You must make time to come and stay—a week, perhaps two, later in the summer.'

'I will. I promise. And now I'm going to go and jump in a bath. Flippy tells me that this dance this evening is the event of the year—even us old ladies ought to do our best, don't you think? Wouldn't do to let the side down.' Almost at the stairs she stopped. 'Fee? Thanks again. Not just for having Flippy, but for all you and James have done for Toby. Clever he might be, and charming, but without your recommendation and backing one of the oldest law firms in London wouldn't have taken him, Cambridge or no. He—we—owe you a lot.'

The unusual and uncomfortable pricking of conscience made Fiona brusque. 'Don't be daft. Toby's success is his own. We oiled a few wheels, that's all. James likes him. We all like him. Now – off you go and make yourself beautiful. God, girl, since your silly husband's decided to let you away for the night, you might as well make the most of it!'

Philippa was dressed and ready a full half hour too early. Too excited to stay alone in her own room she slipped along the corridor to her mother's, a huge, old-fashioned room with a claw-footed bath behind a red silk screen. 'Oh, Flip – do go away! I'm not out of the bath yet and I'll never get myself done if you start nattering at me! Off you go. I'll be with you in half an hour or so.'

Flip ran to the tall wardrobe, twirled in front of the mirror, pale skirt swinging. 'Don't you want to see my outfit?'

'Of course I do. Later.' Sally was laughing, but firm. 'Out.'

The long bedroom corridors were empty of guests. Maids scurried, towels over arms, crisp ribbons streaming behind them from waist and cap as they sped from floor to floor. From the garden came the sound of talk and laughter as some of the older guests still sat over pots of tea and glasses of lemonade, faces gilded by the brilliance of the evening sun. It was a perfect evening, warm and still, though in the southern sky, almost imperceptibly, a dark low ridge of cloud heralded a possible change in the weather. The tennis courts were in use by several young men still in cricket gear. Others, also in whites and blazers, strolled the lawns or sat on the grass. Some few girls, bright and pretty in gay summer dresses, were gathered in knots about the gardens like so many bunches of fresh-picked flowers. She saw not a single face she recognized. Hands in pockets she wandered on, smiling at anyone who caught her eye, shamelessly eavesdropping.

'And it was Rodney Menton, of all people. You know, the Kensington Mentons—'

'Well, only half way to Nice my dear I realized what a terrible mistake I'd made.'

'Jolly fine fist that keeper chappie made of the innings this afternoon—'

'—quite the best restaurant in Town, of course.'

'—and just *guess* who was dancing with him at the Silver Slipper last Friday—!'

The barn where the dance was to be held was the scene of much activity. A farm cart stood outside the vast open doors whilst several young men wrestled barrels of beer into the shaded interior of the ancient building. Philippa stood patting the big, handsome head of the huge shire that stood with stoic patience between the shafts. A group of laughing girls, dressed ready for the party, watched and commented as the lads, stripped to shirtsleeves and braces manhandled the enormous casks. From within came the sound of a piano tuning up, and then a trumpet, braying a brief, experimental scale. Philippa slipped into the barn. It was decorated with swathes of green, the high, ancient beams draped with evergreen branches and gay with ribbons and paper lanterns. At one end of the vast structure two huge farm wagons had been turned into a stage upon which the five-man band, elegant and citified in their tails and black ties, carnations in their buttonholes, arranged chairs and music stands and tinkered with their instruments. The beaten earth floor had been swept clean and improvised benches and seats set about the walls. In front of the 'stage' a large dance floor had been laid. At the opposite end of the barn were plank tables and chairs, gay with every tablecloth the village could provide and with jars of flowers set at intervals along them. Here too was the bar; barrels and crates were stacked in the corner. Beer and lemonade provided free and by the gallon, Philippa knew. Champagne for the House guests and a blind eye turned to the odd bottle of spirits acquired at The Bird in Hand and tucked into a pocket.

Gideon Best was already there.

He had changed from his borrowed whites and was dressed in his normal corduroys, cotton shirt and neckerchief, his only concession to the occasion the fact that the shirt was white and clean and the neckerchief a brilliant splash of red and blue. His boots and gaiters were dark with water and stained with mud; Philippa guessed he had been to the coops to feed the chicks. He leaned, wide shoulders against the wall, long legs crossed before him, hands in pockets, unsmiling and black browed. He looked, Philippa thought suddenly, oddly out of place, oddly solitary in the bustle of preparation about him. It came to her that she had never before seen him in a crowd of people. It did not suit him. He looked awkward, strangely graceless.

'Hello.' She perched on the table beside him, ignoring his lack of greeting. 'You batted tremendously well today.'

He grunted.

'I like your scarf. What do you call it? Wait a minute – I know – a "diclo", isn't it?'

His eyes flickered to hers. She grinned. 'Do you like mine?'

He moved his head in what might have been taken for a nod.

'Good Lord.' Philippa smiled beatifically, swinging her legs, 'Are you going to grump all night? It is supposed to be a party, you know.'

'Damn daft business,' he said. But the gleam in his eye was reluctant amusement.

She grinned. Testing the acoustics the band had swung into the first few bars of *Bye, Bye Blackbird*. Philippa hummed happily.

'Shove over.' Gideon dug a hard elbow into her side. Obligingly she moved, happy to see the softening of his expression as he joined her on the table. In their own easy, companionable silence they watched the last minute scramble. The girls who had been standing outside had begun to drift in, standing about in subdued, giggling groups, more than one eye, Philippa was interested to note, cocked provocatively in their direction. Gideon ignored them. A couple of the House team, young men still in their whites and blazers, breezed in to 'bag a glass of beer', greeting Philippa in friendly fashion, nodding to Gideon. He ignored them, too. A tall dinner jacketed man, hair like black paint slicked against his head, a megaphone in his hand, clambered none too elegantly onto the 'stage'. The band were playing quietly *I'll See You in My Dreams*.

A girl carrying a large tray filled with glasses of lemonade stopped beside them. She was a pretty thing, dressed in a brilliant red dress, her neat waist encircled by a wide white sash. Ostentatiously ignoring Gideon – who did not in any case glance at her – she struggled manfully with the awkward tray, setting it upon a nearby table, rearranging the glasses, picking it up again, all but begging to be relieved of it.

Philippa slanted a look at Gideon. 'Aren't you going to give her a hand?' she asked, helpfully.

Gideon's dark eyes moved from her to the girl and back again. Then, his face impassive as ever, he pushed himself up from the table, leaned with no word to the girl, took the tray from her and, utterly ignoring her brilliant smile and fluttering eyelashes, strode across the barn with it, the startled girl all but running to keep up with him. With a movement so abrupt it rattled the glasses he deposited the tray upon the table and was back with Philippa in a matter of seconds having stayed for no word of civility or thanks.

Philippa eyed him exasperatedly. 'Honestly, Gideon, you are the limit. It's a *party*. You're supposed to *talk* to people.'

He drew up his long legs, rested his elbows on his knees, clasped long, none-too-clean fingers loosely, regarded her thoughtfully. 'Aye? That's the idea, is it? Dordi, dordi! I wondered.'

'You're impossible. Oh, look – here comes Aunty Fee and everyone. There's my mother, do you see? In the yellow dress. I like Aunty Fee's outfit – and, I say, doesn't Rachel look *stunning*? I thought she said she wasn't going to bother?' This last a little aggrievedly as she took in Rachel's drifting chiffon, a shimmering creation of violet and blue artfully cut to reveal a seemingly endless length of leg. '– Why don't you come and say hello to everybody? Gideon? – I said –.' She turned.

Gideon Best had disappeared. Craning her neck she saw him, solitary still, his back once again to the wall. In his hand he held a bottle. Catching her eye he grinned a little, toasted her sardonically, then pulled the loosened cap from the bottle with his teeth. She made a ferocious face, scrambled from the table and skidded across the dance floor to her mother.

Gideon, the taste of the whisky strong, warm and beneficent on his tongue, watched her go. The big barn was filling up. The sound of talk and laughter clattered upon the air, strident and to an ear tuned to the silence of the coverts, offensive. Normally he would have a couple of drinks and leave; today to do that would in some obscure way be to admit defeat, to submit to the scourge of his unpopularity. The story, inevitably, had got about that his defection from the village team had been a deliberate currying of favour with his master. He'd see the whole damned village in hell before he'd deny it. Poachers all. He hefted the bottle in his hand. The band had swung into another tune, the doll-like crooner lifted the megaphone, *'Yes, sir, that's my baby—.'* Someone shrieked with laughter. Near him a bunch of young men – all of them known to him, all of them much his own age - were getting down to the serious business of drinking. None of them so much as glanced at him. Poachers all.

He lifted the bottle, let the whisky trickle, a heartening friend, down his throat.

Across the barn Flip had disappeared into the crowd around Fiona and James Paget. Toby, damp blond hair immaculate, stood head and shoulders above them all, laughing and talking easily. The magnetically beautiful dark-haired girl in blue chiffon was Charlestoning playfully and with wanton grace, hair swinging, jewel-like eyes bright, encouraging the other members of the group to join her on the floor. Provocative bitch.

Poachers all.

Gideon tilted the bottle again.

'The trouble with champagne,' Rachel said, eyeing her empty glass in mild surprise, 'is that there's never quite enough of it. Hugo, be a darling – go and steal us another bottle.'

Reluctantly – the band after an hour or so of frenetic Charlestons and Black Bottoms had slid into a quiet and romantic rendition of *Always* and he had been very much hoping to take advantage of the change of mood – Hugo went.

'What a very obliging young man he is.' Rachel stubbed out her cigarette, upended her glass, stared into its empty depths thoughtfully. 'I rather like obliging young men. Which reminds me – ,' she lifted wide, intransigently innocent eyes to Fiona, '– where's Toby?'

Fiona shook her head, unruffled. 'I've no idea.' In fact she knew perfectly well where he was, having some little time before watched him stroll into the warm darkness with a very pretty girl on his arm. She was not, however, about to impart such dangerous knowledge to Rachel. Nor was she about to admit – to herself or to anyone else – that Toby's quite obviously deliberate defection had been brought about by her own refusal to have him in her bed whilst Sally was a guest in the house. 'Circumspection I can understand, Fee,' he had said, 'hypocrisy I can't.'

Rachel stretched long arms above her head. Bracelets jingled musically. 'It's really too bad of him to disappear like that. I want to dance.'

Sir James laughed gruffly. 'My dear young lady, you've been dancing all night. And very prettily too, I might add.' His eyes beneath the thick and curly grey growth of his eyebrows were twinkling. 'And as for needing young Smith as a partner – why look around you – every man in the place would be happy to oblige!'

Rachel, despite herself, let her eyes flicker to a figure, alone, who stood leaning against an empty beer cask, dark eyes in an impassive face watching the revels. 'Not quite,' she said, very softly. Not once in the evening had she managed to catch his eyes upon her; yet she knew – somehow she knew – that he was watching her. That he was as aware of her every movement as she was of his. And the knowledge, absurdly, excited her.

'Here we are.' Hugo, triumphant, had reappeared brandishing not one but two bottles of champagne. 'I hope you don't mind, Lady Paget, but I took your name most frightfully in vain.'

Fiona extended her glass. 'In that case you'd better let me have some before Rachel drinks it all.'

'I'll be loving you – Always.' Couples dipped and swooped or shuffled by, according to their prowess, the village lads in their Sunday best or still in cricket gear, other young men in dinner jackets and black tie; girls in cotton frocks, bright as summer butterflies, girls like Rachel dressed in shimmering and expensive materials that gleamed in the light of the oil lamps and candles, carefully coiffed hair wispy now and clinging to neck and forehead, faces flushed. It was extremely warm. The air was still and humid. In the past hour the clouds that had been building in the south had crept across the sky, threatening the summer night. Very faintly, thunder growled in the distance.

Restless as ever Rachel was on her feet again, hand extended. 'Come on, Jeremy, let's dance for heaven's sake – oh, damn!' Just as she spoke and as the young man she had addressed had eagerly reached for her hand, the music had died.

'Ladies and Gentlemen –' The tailor's dummy with the mega-phone held up a hand, 'A Ladies' Excuse Me – come along all you lovely young ladies – a chance to get the gentlemen on their feet or, who knows, on their knees?'

The drum tapped gently into waltz time. For a moment the girls stood around in giggling knots on the edge of the floor, then, gradually, amidst much laughter and protestation young men were dragged to their feet and propelled onto the floor.

Rachel, to Jeremy's open disappointment dropped her hand and turned, a small, dangerous smile on her lips.

Hugo watched her in an agony of hope if not expectation. Fiona, noting the sudden gleam in the violet eyes, the subtle excitement in that smile watched her too, intently and with amused curiosity. Whatever Rachel was about to do – and Fiona had no idea what it might be – it was certain to be interesting.

'Come on, old thing – isn't the best looking woman in the room going to ask her old man to dance?' James took her hand. Affectionately she squeezed it. As she stood she heard Philippa.

'Oh, golly! What on earth does Rachel think she's *doing*?' the tone a comical mixture of disbelief and admiration.

Fiona turned. Rachel had left the group at the table and was walking with studied grace across the floor towards the door. The swinging beads that edged her dipping skirt moved and clashed about her slim legs. Heads turned as she passed. A man whistled, low and with feeling. Her steady gaze did not flicker. Toby, a moment before, had appeared in the doorway, a pretty fair girl clinging to his arm, her hair a little rumpled, her eyes over-bright. He watched Rachel's approach with a faint frown upon his handsome face. She passed him without so much as a glance.

Gideon saw her coming. Deliberately he did not move. Long

of leg, wide of shoulder, almost defiantly shabby in this festive gathering he lounged easily against the great door frame, a freshly opened bottle in his hand.

Rachel, smiling, stopped directly before him, those remarkable eyes wide and challenging and lit with an excitement that any experienced man – and certainly Gideon Best – would know as perilous.

'Dance with me?' she said, and only the faintest lift of her voice at the end of the sentence made it a question.

'I don't dance.'

The unchastened smile did not falter. 'I don't believe you.'

He lifted a shoulder, the insolence calculated. Gideon Best had had enough of these irresponsible, privileged golden children, and had drunk enough whisky to show it.

The noisy group at a nearby table had fallen silent and were openly watching them.

For a long moment Rachel studied the dark, unfriendly face, the black, gold-glinting eyes. Then, unsmiling now, she stepped close to him, so close that she had to tip her head back to look up at him and the heavy cap of hair swung back from the flawless face. She slipped her narrow hand into his. 'Please,' she said. 'Dance with me.'

Until that moment he had been determined to stand against her. All night he had watched her, had seen the capricious tricks and changes of her, watched the dance she had led those young men who had clustered about her like ants around honey. He had known, the moment she had set off with that challenging, insolent confidence towards him what she had intended. Until that moment it had been his own intention to humiliate her, to send her back, rejected, upon that long walk across the floor back to her friends and her shoddy games.

She knew it. And the knowledge excited her. It showed in her eyes, oddly disturbing.

'Please, Gideon,' she said, softly, smiling; and with no warning, desire for her struck in his blood and his bones like the swift awakening of a sleeping animal.

He pushed himself away from the wall, stood the bottle upon a table. Still she held his hand, and like a lamb she led him to the dance floor, turned to him, moved into his arms. Her narrow body was light and supple; despite her height her shining head barely topped his shoulder. In the heavy heat of the smoky and overcrowded barn her skin was cool, and perfumed. She neither spoke nor lifted her head to look at him as they moved together to the music, uncaring of the eyes upon them. Rigidly he held her, grimly he fought her, as with no great expertise he steered her about the floor. Fool. Fool! To let this one get this close. Lovely – and worthless. Trouble and more trouble. His first instincts had been right. He should walk away from her now.

He knew she could feel his trembling, could sense clearly and with certainty the battle he fought. He saw as he looked down at her the demure sweep of lashes, the small, enchanting curve of her smile. Felt the reaction of her slender body.

The ordeal ended at last. The music stopped. She stood for a fraction of a second longer than was necessary in the curve of his arms, then stepped back, lifting her head, smiling brilliantly and with triumph into his face.

With no word he turned from her, leaving her to find her own way back to her table, shouldering his way through the thinning crowd, pausing only to collect his bottle from the table where he had left it before striding out into the sultry darkness. Thunder murmured, and above it he heard laughter. Her laughter, he knew.

'Well, well.' Toby Smith watched him pass with narrowed eyes. 'What was all *that* about?'

The girl who clung to his arm, and whose name he had forgotten, watched him with misty eyes and shook her head.

Rachel had returned to the table, grinning like an urchin, all tiredness gone, driven by the adrenalin of risk and success.

'Are you going in for lion taming next?' Fiona asked, drily, and was rewarded by the peal of laughter that followed Gideon Best into the night.

By midnight the band, prevailed upon by Rachel to play for half an hour longer than arranged, had finally played the last waltz. And the storm that had been muttering about the sky for most of the evening was almost upon them.

'The witching hour,' Rachel said as above the calls of farewell and the buzz of conversation the sound of the church clock rang against a background of muted thunder. She stood up, stretched, ruffled her hair, yawned theatrically. 'Well. The night, as they say, is young. I'm for a swim. Who's coming?' Composed, she reached down and slipped off her sandals one after the other, held them in her hand, swinging from the ankle straps.

'Swimming? I say! Where? Is there a pool?' A tall young man with a prominent Adam's apple who had been trying to catch Rachel's eye all night without much success positively bubbled with enthusiasm. Fiona, James and Sally had left earlier, dragging with them a protesting and exhausted Philippa. A small knot of young people had gathered about Rachel and Toby. The table was cluttered with empty glasses and bottles and full ashtrays.

'Who needs a pool when you've got a lake?' Calmly Rachel began to undo the tiny buttons of her dress.

'I say! What a topping idea!' A girl with a mop of red hair caught hold of her escort's hand, 'Come on, everybody! A swim in the lake! What fun!'

'Not altogether a good idea,' Toby said, easily. 'Isn't it a bit late? And there's a storm coming on.'

Rachel shrugged. 'Suit yourself. Go get under a table, darling, if you're scared of a bit of thunder. I'm swimming.' Gracefully she lifted the hem of her skirt, began to remove a stocking, disregarding the laughter and the wolf whistles as she ignored poor Hugo's obvious struggle not to stare. Stockings removed she straightened, and leaving shoes and stockings where they fell made with her long-legged easy strides for the door.

With a whoop a group of about half a dozen followed her. As they erupted, shrieking and laughing into the open a streak of lightning flickered some distance away and, seconds later, thunder rolled.

'It's going to pour in a minute,' someone said, giggling. 'Do you think Monsieur Worth made this dress waterproof?'

'Take it off, love, then it won't matter.' Rachel was unbuttoning her own dress as she strode, laughing, towards the lake. As they reached it the first heavy spots of rain were falling.

The redheaded girl hesitated, flinched as the lightning flared, suddenly violent, above them. Her escort reached for her hand. 'Come on, old thing. P'raps not such a good idea after all. Bye, all. Have a good swim.' They fled into the darkness.

The girl in the Worth dress, too, was hesitant. The young man with her picked her up and dumped her, fully clothed, into the shallows of the lake. Screaming and splashing she grabbed him and pulled him in after her.

Ignoring the pandemonium Rachel, her eyes upon the dark waters of the lake continued undressing, dropping her dress, her bra, her suspender belt and the wisp of her silk panties carelessly in a heap on the mud. Lights from the distant house glimmered upon the water. Huge, warm drops of rain splashed deliciously on her skin, landed like dropped stones in the water, rippling the surface. Naked she waded in, leaving her noisy, shrieking companions to their own diversions. Hugo, standing back from them all, saw the glimmer of her skin in the flicker of lightning, the long line of her back, the curve of her buttocks. Not for the first time in his life he cursed the fear of water that had prevented him from ever learning to swim. She waded until the warm water lifted above her thighs, caressing her body, taking her breath away. Then with a single graceful movement she slid like a fish into the water, striking out for the centre. The commotion on the shore had died. The girl in the Worth dress was crying. Voices murmured consolation, faded into the sound of the rain as the others began to drift back towards the house.

Rachel turned onto her back, floating, arms outstretched, rain pattering onto her upturned face. The water was glorious, warm and smooth as silk. Lightning split the sky. The lake lay flat and dark about her, silent, her movements barely rippling the water. She closed her eyes, lapped by darkness and the sensual feel of the water.

'Rachel?' Hugo's voice, anxious suddenly, and urgent. 'Rachel, are you all right?'

The roll of the thunder overtook the words.

'*Rachel!*'

The rain was getting heavier by the moment. 'I'm fine,' Rachel called above the sound. 'Get back to the house, you daft thing. You'll get soaked!'

Hugo hovered, a hesitant shadow on the bank. He had turned his jacket collar up and his straw coloured hair was plastered to his head, dark with rain.

'Go on! I'm perfectly all right. I'll come in in a minute. Get on in before the heavens open and drown you!'

As if to illustrate her words another vivid streak of lightning lit the landscape. Water drummed upon the surface of the lake. 'Don't be silly – I can't leave you –'

'Of course you can! Look – if you want to do something gallant, go get me a blanket and a golf umbrella. That'll stop me getting pneumonia.'

He fidgeted irresolutely for a moment more. 'You're sure you're all right?'

'I'm sure.'

'Right then. I'll do that.' Sodden and uncomfortable he grinned weakly. 'Don't go away—'

She rolled in the water, swam a few strokes, turned on her back again. The rain stung her skin. Thunder crashed. Exhilarated she laughed aloud. For a few more minutes she played in the water, ducking beneath the surface to the cool and peaceful depths, bobbing up, laughing, into the raging storm. At last, tiring, she struck out for the shore. Regaining her foothold in the soft mud she stood, slicking her hair back from her eyes, water streaming from her naked body. Slowed by the heaviness of her limbs after the weightlessness of the water she waded ashore, spreading her arms and lifting her face to the rain, shivering a little now as the air chilled her skin. She looked towards the house, and as she did so a flash of lightning revealed the distant figure of Hugo, umbrella up, dashing across the wide lawns towards her.

It revealed something else, too.

Not a hundred yards from the lake was an ancient stand of trees, oak and beech, lovely great trees that had been planted three hundred years before, when park and house were new. In the brilliance of light, silhouetted against them stood a man, bareheaded, drenched to the skin, apparently oblivious of rain

60

and storm, watching her. Tall, wide shouldered, well-formed and still as a statue.

Gideon Best.

The storm had reached its height. The flicker of lightning, the crash of thunder was almost constant. She tilted her head, lifted her arms to squeeze the water from her hair, each movement studiedly, fluidly graceful. The shadow moved. Stepped towards her.

'Rachel, for heaven's sake! You'll catch your death!' Hugo, umbrella, blanket and all tumbled upon her. 'You're mad! Absolutely mad!' He was laughing with her, admiration and a puppy adoration on his face. 'Quickly, cuddle into this! Oh, what an absolute *idiot* you are!' Carried away by his own enthusiasm he put his arm about her as he covered her with the blanket, dropped a swift kiss onto her wet hair.

She struggled free, giggling. 'It's no good saving me from pneumonia and then suffocating me!' Clutching the blanket around her she reached for his hand. 'Come on, share that umbrella. And run for it!'

For a long time after they had gone the man beneath the trees stood in the shadows, unmoving. Then he stepped out of their cover into the still steadily pouring rain. The centre of the storm had moved on, thunder rumbled more distantly, the lightning was less ferocious. Slowly he walked to the lake's edge, to where a small sodden heap of clothing lay, abandoned and forgotten. In the dying flicker of light he bent and picked up the ruined dress. It hung, a beaded, bedraggled rag, in his big hand. Rain dripped from his dark hair, his shirt, sopping wet, was plastered to his body. He lifted his head. In the distance the thunder still growled menacingly, and as he watched, one by one, the lights of the house went out. He stood for a long time, silent and still as some night-hunting animal watching for prey. Then in one swift movement he tossed the dress back into the mud, turned and strode back into the shadows.

Chapter Three

Daphne Underscar eyed her reflection in the tall mirror neither with any great degree of enthusiasm nor with any particular sense of disappointment. The plain and angular image that looked levelly back at her had been with her for all of her nearly thirty years; she had given up looking – or hoping – for change. The nondescript brown hair still frizzed unbecomingly around her long face, the eyes were still large and pale, the eyelashes so light as to be almost nonexistent, the teeth, though white and regular, were too big and too prominent. 'Tombstones,' Aunt Fran had always cheerfully called them. A fair enough description Daphne admitted now, baring them in a mirthless grimace that, appearing so suddenly on the prim face in the mirror, made her laugh aloud. The dress wasn't right, either. Something had happened to the hem – it dipped at the back and lifted most inelegantly at the front. She tugged at it, wriggled her shoulders and wished she had Aunt Clara's panache. Aunt Clara would never have fled upstairs to change the old gardening shoes and frock she had been wearing when their visitor had arrived. Aunt Clara was one of those formidable women whom one could imagine might sail into the Ritz in wellingtons and gardening gloves, asking the head waiter to look after her trug whilst she ordered a 'good strong cup of tea'.

Oh, the dear, dotty Aunts. How she still missed them.

Reluctant as yet to leave the sanctuary of her room she wandered to the window. In the long, walled garden the foreshortened figures of her father and his visitor wandered amongst her roses and her honeysuckle, cigar smoke as always wreathing about her father like a small, personal cloud. Toby Smith, she noted, was smoking a cigarette. She hoped he wouldn't throw it down on the neatly weeded York stone path. She allowed her eyes to lift for a moment, looking across the walls to the other gardens. She had lived in this house for as long as she could remember; this view was the most familiar in the world to her, its inhabitants and their habits and foibles as well known as her own. She knew for instance that the gardener at Number Six would have been in today to trim and tidy the tall hedges, and cut razor-sharp edges to the flower beds that lined up like regiments of soldiers beside them. She knew that Mrs Barber at Number Ten would be winding herself up into a nice state of fury, as she did every year, to see the best apples on her tree overhanging the garden of Number Twelve. In the other direction the nanny at Number Sixteen was playing in the garden with the three small Bartlett children. Any moment now one of the little beasts would push or trip one of the others and all hell would break loose; just as she thought it a child sprawled headlong and a wail split the quiet air.

Smiling wryly she brought her attention back closer to home; in the garden of Number Fourteen, Amos Underscar and Toby Smith talked earnestly.

She watched them, pensively, for a very long moment. That her future was being discussed in the garden whilst she looked on from a window three storeys up neither surprised nor particularly distressed her; Daphne Underscar had long ago learned not to waste energy and time fretting upon a situation that was beyond remedy, however aggravating it might be. Rather more important to her at this moment was that, unusually, her own attitude to this new threat to her comfort and her maidenhood was far from clear cut. So far, a combination of her own practical commonsense and her father's healthy attachment to the fortune he had made virtually single-handed had allowed her to adroitly side-step most of those suitors who had bravely – no doubt aided by the sight of an Underscars shop in every High Street of significance in the land – found themselves able to overlook her lack of physical charm. The one or two who had nearly slipped through her guard, in those early days when girlish dreams still lingered, had been very quickly seen off by the Aunts who, before retiring back into their idiosyncratic grey-stone Yorkshire farmhouse had had charge of her until her twenty-fifth year. Recently she had been left in peace, and had been thankful for it. She saw no virtue whatsoever in handing herself over lock, stock and fortune to a man whose interest in her began and ended at her bank balance. The older she got, in fact, the less important – indeed the less attractive – had become the idea of marriage. The chanciness of the bond, as illustrated by those of her friends and acquaintances who – for love or for money or for a convenient combination of both – had undertaken it, seemed to her quite clearly to make the game not worth the candle. She was perfectly all right as she was; what was so unnatural about that? The dotty Yorkshire Aunts, beyond doubt, were absolutely content manless; why not she? And – most telling argument of all – as the years had slipped by, her father had begun, bit by little bit, to see her not as a feckless and empty-headed young female not to be trusted with the key to a sixpenny piggy bank but as his own practical and even reasonably intelligent offspring. Not quite one of those tragically lost sons, but no longer, either, a useless dependant of a daughter.

And now – here was Toby Smith. A charmer if ever there was one, and with an astute head on his shoulders. Handsome, ambitious, Cambridge educated, and fly as an East End street trader. Amos Underscar, hardbitten and suspicious old campaigner that he was, had in a mellow moment described him as 'Tomorrow's man'. She had never known the old man so taken with anyone before.

Daphne turned from the window, went back to her dressing table. Tomorrow's man. Whose tomorrows? Hers? If so they were too precious to be squandered. And what of that disturbing undercurrent of self-centred ruthlessness that she so surely sensed in Toby Smith? How would that – how could it – serve Underscars?

She leaned her chin upon her hands, her eyes absent and unseeing upon that all-too-predictable reflection. She had heard Toby Smith speaking to Amos with an intense enthusiasm about the phenomenon of the thousands – hundreds of thousands – of small houses that were springing up, row upon marching row of them on the outskirts of the capital. Houses built, each one identical to the next, in the new suburbs that, advertised in the popular newspapers with free rail tickets and free teas for prospective buyers, boasted neat new shopping parades, daily milk deliveries and electric trains to London. Houses that needed cleaning and caring for, houses where from the doorstep to the chimney pot each proud housewife – often in possession of her own home for the first time in her life – was in open competition with her neighbours. Furniture and knick-knacks, carpets and curtains, all must be new, all must be smart, all must be up-to-the-minute. Vacuum cleaners and cookers and irons and the suddenly essential wireless. Saucepans and kettles, crockery and cutlery. The housewife who saw herself, bright and pretty in her shining new house, in the advertisements that covered the hoardings and filled the newspapers and magazines, demanded those things those same advertisements told her she needed. Underscars could expand and provide them. Daphne Underscar had been trying to say so by many devious means and to an exasperatingly deaf ear for the past couple of years. Now Toby Smith in a graceful and convincing voice was saying the same. And because he was a man, and a persuasive one, Amos Underscar was listening. Aggravating that might be, but Daphne, pragmatic by nature, practical by upbringing, was not a woman to be blinded by pique. That she, wrapped and parcelled and neatly bound by a band of gold, was part of the negotiations she had no doubt; this it was that was giving her cause for thought. Unless she much misread this Toby Smith he would never be satisfied with half a cake, no matter how large the slice. Danger and advantage were delicately balanced here; she wondered, for the first time, if her father realized just how delicately, and in wondering it fleetingly saw the man who had dominated her life for so long as fallible, and ageing.

A furrow appeared for a moment in the high white forehead. Sacrilege to think so of Amos Underscar. But then, he was seventy, had been a man full grown and vigorous when the century turned and the old Queen died. Twenty-eight years on, mind and body appeared as firm as ever – as did the Victorian values with which he had grown up – but sooner or later he would have to release the reins of power. In the past few years Daphne had allowed herself to nurse the small, growing, perhaps futile hope that by the time that day came he would have come to realize at last that, male or female, an Underscar was an Underscar and capable of running and expanding the business that was the source of the Underscar fortune. But alas, old prejudices, like old dreams, die hard and the uphill battle was far from won. And now Toby Smith had arrived upon the scene. Absently Daphne reached for her scent bottle, brusquely dabbed behind her ears, pulled the bell rope beside the dressing table.

'Yes, miss?' The little maid, brisk and pretty in black and white, bobbed at the door.

'Ah, Lewis. Tell Papa and Mr Smith that luncheon will be served in the terrace room in, say, five minutes.'

'Yes, miss.'

'Did Cook manage to get to the fishmongers?'

'Yes, miss. She said to tell you she'd got the Dover sole.'

'Good. We'll have the Chablis with it, please. Oh, and make sure the gentlemen are served the Paget and Fellafield Bual with the cheese. I believe Mr Smith is partial to his Madeira.'

'Yes, miss.' Lewis bobbed her cheeky curtsey and left.

Daphne Underscar, plain face falling into the pleasant, attentive expression proper to a proficient hostess followed the whisk of her white petticoat down the wide staircase.

Luncheon was an enjoyable meal, made more so by the attentions of an intelligent and attractive man. An unrepining spinster Daphne might be; a man-hater she was not. And Toby, at his best, was unnervingly likeable. Business was not discussed; the weather was, as was the delight of her flower-filled garden, the airiness and surprising size of the house, the merits and pleasures of living in Islington and the appetizing lightness of the meal. To his credit when Daphne, ignoring the lifting of her father's brows, introduced the subject of women's suffrage and the so-called Flapper Vote, just brought in, that at last put women voters on a par with men, he discussed that too with animation and enthusiasm. He had it seemed been brought up in a Suffragette household; spoke of female relatives – Daphne could not quite discover the degree of relationship – imprisoned for the Cause. If it were a test, and why, Daphne found herself wondering, a touch caustically, should she think of bothering with such things? – he passed it with flying colours. The subject of politics introduced he was ready to talk with a disarming and unpatronizing frankness; yes, he believed that times at last were changing. Given the war and its aftermath, they had to. The country was going to have to adapt to new ways and new thinking. Socialism, given the minimum concessions that the government of the day could manage would not tamely sit down and fade away. The system being what it was some other party would suffer, and it seemed to him that it would be the party most like the Socialists – the Liberals – who would be most at risk and who would in a very few years be likely to go to the wall. Conservatism was too deeply rooted in the British character for the Tories to suffer. The establishment, unless something unforeseeable might occur, would hold. No, he did not believe that the extremes of Communism would find hold in Britain – especially not now after the terror and upheaval of the Russian Revolution – but enough people, disillusioned and angry, subscribed to those extreme views to make it dangerous to ignore them. At Cambridge he had known that influential, intellectual and oddly exclusive group of young men, drawn from the very strata of society one would have expected to abhor the very thought of such ideas, whose Communist leanings were regarded in some circles as all but treasonous. Affected young poseurs, some of them, but not all. When two ends of a spectrum join together – well-educated intellectuals and dis-affected workers – then let those in the centre beware.

At this stage Amos decided his daughter had gone altogether too far and suspecting, Daphne knew, deliberate sabotage of his plans to marry her off to this affable young man, changed the subject determinedly. The rest of the meal was spent discussing the neutral and in Amos' eyes far more fitting subject of the new Madame Tussaud's building that had opened in London a month or two before. Over the Madeira he jocularly informed Daphne – as opposed to asking her – that she would greatly enjoy an outing suggested by Toby for the following Friday. Unfortunately he himself was unable to join them, but – heavily coy, this – the young people would no doubt enjoy the evening far more without him. On polite enquiry Toby said he thought she might enjoy an evening at the opera followed by dinner. Daphne expressed herself duly delighted with the idea and the arrangements were made. The preliminaries, Daphne thought as she smiled politely and shook her guest's hand at the front door, had been neatly dispensed with; the horse trading was now under way.

It puzzled her a little that still, as she supervised the clearing of the meal and ushered her father, protesting, to rest, she did not herself know what she wished from the outcome.

Toby himself could not have been better pleased. He whistled as he negotiated the crowded streets between Islington and the tiny flat he had acquired – with the help of an outrageously huge and expensive overdraft – behind Kensington High Street. With any luck at all Amos Underscar and his temptingly-sited shops were in the bag. That Daphne Underscar necessarily came in the same bright package did not now worry him as much as it had when first he had made her acquaintance. She was an intelligent, practical woman. Perfectly clearly she was going into this with eyes as wide open as his own. An arrangement. A convenience that, hopefully, would suit them both. He liked her wit, and her low, soft voice; liked the occasional flash of wry humour she displayed. True her physical presence was a little dismaying – a woman with her money and total lack of looks should surely, in thirty years, have been able to produce some kind of style? But one had to be philosophical about such things. Had she been beautiful – or even half-way good looking – she would not still have been on offer, and Amos Underscar would not in a million years be considering Toby Nobody Smith as a son-in-law. Arriving at his cubby-hole of a flat he flicked open his cigarette case, lit a cigarette and reached for the telephone.

The phone in Rachel's flat rang for a long time before a voice, high pitched and drawling, finally came over the line.

'Ye-es?'

Nonplussed, Toby hesitated. 'Hello. Is Rachel Patten there, please?'

''Fraid not, old thing. She's fled an over-amorous suitor and taken herself to the depths of the country again. Norfolk, or Suffolk or somewhere equally dreadful—'

'She's at Breckon Hall?'

'Some such place, sweetie, yes.' The voice changed a little. 'But tell me – can I help?'

'No. No, thank you. It's Rachel I want. I'll get hold of her at the Hall.'

Toby clicked the receiver with his finger, grimacing as he waited for the operator to answer.

The telephone at Breckon Hall rang for even longer than it had in Rachel's flat before Parks' voice, distant and very much on its dignity, answered. Toby grinned. It was an open secret that Parks abominated the telephone. 'Hello, there, Parks. Toby Smith.'

'Good afternoon, sir.'

'I gather you've got Miss Patten staying with you?'

'Yes, indeed, sir. You wished to speak to her?'

'Please.'

Full minutes later Rachel's voice, sharp and clear, came across the line. 'Hello?'

'Rachel, it's Toby. I need a favour.'

There was a small, acid silence. Then 'I'm fine, thank you,' Rachel said, pleasantly. 'The weather's been good – a bit breezy, but the sunshine's held out. You?'

'Stop arsing about. I wanted to know – can you use those weirdo theatre friends of yours to get me decent seats, preferably a box, at the Opera House for next Friday?'

He heard her long nails clicking against the telephone; he knew that habit of hers, had watched her flicking and drumming her nails on the receiver.

'Rachel? Oh, come on, love. It's important.'

Rachel relented. 'Just a sec. I've got the number here somewhere. Here we are –.' She read out a Covent Garden telephone number. 'Ask for Jaques. Mention my name. He owes me a favour.' Her voice slid into laughter. 'He owes me several actually.'

'Thanks. You're a chum. What are you doing down there at Breckon again? I thought you hated the country?'

'It has its attractions.' Her voice was breezy.

'Is Fee there? I wouldn't mind a word.'

'No, she isn't. She's gone off to Diss with the boys to do something unspeakable with ponies.' Her voice rippled with sly laughter again. 'James is here. Shall I get him?'

'No thanks. I'll ring later.'

'Right. I'll tell her. Bye—'

'Hey, Rachel?'

'Mm?'

'Who the devil *is* that staying in your flat?'

Rachel was airy. 'Oh – I don't know. A friend of a friend, you know? Needed somewhere to rest a weary head and all that.'

'Is it a male head or a female one?' Toby's voice was dry. 'I've just spoken to it and I'm damned if I could tell.'

Rachel chuckled. 'Why expect me to know? I actually met it and I couldn't tell. What difference does it make?'

'You're ridiculous. You'll wake up murdered in your bed one of these days.'

'I know. What a headline that'll make.' The line clicked and was dead.

Toby shook his head, looking at the lifeless receiver. Then he shrugged, re-called the operator and asked for the Covent Garden number.

Rachel stuck her tongue out at the inoffensive telephone before dropping it back into its cradle. For one moment there, when Parks had called her to the phone saying it was Toby, she had thought – what? That Toby had actually wanted to speak to her? That he'd actually missed her? What a joke.

She had taken the call in the library. Beyond the tall windows the park lay, trees and grass stirred by the warm summer wind, the surface of the lake rippling like shining silk. She glanced at her watch. Where the devil was Flip? She'd begged and begged that Rachel should cut her hair this afternoon, and then having extracted the promise had promptly disappeared. Rachel had not seen her since lunch.

The tall windows stood open, heavy curtains blowing in the breeze. Rachel walked out onto the terrace, stood, hands in the pockets of her slacks, looking out across the wide, rolling landscape. Not so very far from here the flat lands of Norfolk, spread with hardly a lift or change to the long, wild coast. But here in the small valley where nestled Breckon Hall the lines were softer, more interesting to the eye. Grassed and wooded slopes – they could hardly be called hills – provided pleasant contrast to the heathered heathland and the flat water-meadows. The tenant farms were neat and pretty – though Breckon was primarily a sporting estate and the woodlands given over predominantly to the birds, the agricultural aspect of the land was far from neglected and the village, rebuilt those generations before, was picturesque. And everywhere were the trees; beech and elm, oak and lime, chestnut, cedar, poplar and, by the lake and the river, willow. Most had been planted something like three hundred years before by visionaries who knew they would never see the full fruition of their efforts. Such altruism puzzled Rachel; she could not see herself spending time, effort and money upon a project from which only her children's children would truly benefit. Those early Pagets, she wondered – did they stand here looking out into a wilderness of raw, fresh-turned ground and tiny trees and see the magnificence that was to come? Or was there a Rachel Patten around to ask – what of me? What of today? Pensively she hunched slim shoulders to her ears, rubbing her cheek upon the smooth silk of her shirt. Now was what she understood; the feel of the silk against her skin, the touch of the warm wind upon her face, the light that danced and glittered upon the water. There was yesterday, and there was today. There was what you wanted, and what you could get. There was the life and the loving of the moment. That was all.

She lifted a hand to rumple the thick black thatch of her hair, the expression on her face suddenly sardonic. The man she had walked out on two days ago had not understood that line of reasoning at all. It was to get away from his obstinate and piqued attentions that she had fled once more to Breckon Hall. She truly did not understand it. Why did they all – all but the one who could actually have managed it – want to tie her down? Why couldn't they accept that what was done was done, and when it was over you walked away from it? It was a simple enough philosophy, surely – and one she never bothered to hide. It wasn't – it truly wasn't – her fault if people got hurt because they thought they could change her.

And, meanwhile, where the hell was Philippa and her wretched hair?

She sauntered down the steps and out across the lawns towards the lake. High clouds scudded across the sky; the sunshine came and went. The huge trees rustled and stirred, whispering secrets in the wind. She stood by the lake and watched a family of ducks busy among the weeds. Remembered the night a few weeks ago when she had swum here, naked, while the storm crashed about her and the man had stood beneath the trees, watching. She shivered, suddenly and unexpectedly, at the memory – a small chill of fearsome and purely physical excitement, swiftly suppressed, that despite the warmth of the day brought the roughness of goosebumps to her skin. She had, not unusually, drunk far too much champagne that night but not so much that she had not known exactly what she was doing; and certainly not enough to blur the memory. She knew what she had seen. And, oddly and exasperatingly, each time she thought of it she felt again that stab of deep excitement that stirred the pit of her stomach and set her skin crawling. Ridiculous. The man was a servant, and uncouth to boot. His looks were barbarous and his manners worse. She had not seen him again in the week that had followed the incident, though Philippa chattered on about him as if she spent half her life following him about. Rachel had come to the conclusion that the man was actively avoiding her; she had also come to the conclusion, with the uncompromising honesty that so characterized her, that she could not blame him. Her behaviour at the dance had been outrageous; a spoiled child taking advantage of her privileged position to make a fool of a grown man. It was surprising he hadn't socked her one. At one point, she reminded herself with a small grin, when she had insisted on him dancing with her, she had half thought he might. Whatever else, it made a refreshing change.

She turned and strolled around the lakeside, scuffing her unsuitably sandalled feet in the damp grass. At the far end of the lake a small stream carried the surplus water along a sandy, pebbled bed into the woodlands. A narrow, grassy path followed its bubbling progress. Wild flowers, purple and pink, that city-dwelling Rachel could not identify, grew riotously along the banks. Birds flittered amongst the branches and in the long grasses by the water, sang with piercing sweetness over her head. Flickering sunlight fell in golden splashes through the heavy, leaf-laden canopy of the woodlands. She wandered, deliberately unthinking, hands in pockets, her feet in the silly sandals wet as if she were paddling in the stream, taking a pure, physical pleasure in the colours, the sounds, the smells around her. Ahead she could see a clearing, a sunlit glade of dappled green and shadow. She stood still for a moment, breathing deeply, and heard voices.

She turned her head a little, away from the wind. At first she heard nothing, but then, again, came the sound of a girl's voice and a small shout of laughter.

Undoubtedly the missing Philippa.

Very quietly Rachel moved on down the path towards the clearing. Small wooden coops dotted it, each surrounded by a layer of cut brush and undergrowth. A man – tall, dark, his clothes so much the colour of the woodlands about him that at first, in the moving light and shadow it was hard to see him clearly, moved from coop to coop. In his hand he carried some sacks. As she watched he put his hand into one of the coops and brought out a squawking chicken. He straightened, deftly pushed the bird into a sack and tied the neck.

'How many are you going to take?' Philippa was sitting cross-legged on the ground not far from him, pulling idly at the grass and letting the little pieces drift into the wind.

'Every other one.'

'Why not all of them?'

'Need some still to call the chicks back. The young 'uns need protection till they start to roost.'

'When will that be?'

'Not long now.'

'And then what?'

The man straightened, sombre face lit with a grin of pure,

affectionate exasperation. 'Were you born asking questions, Rakli?'

Philippa laughed, a little ruefully. 'My mother says so, yes. Am I being a pain? It always worries me.'

Gideon stood for a moment, straight and tall, the sacks dangling in his hands. Then, with care for their living contents, he laid them upon the floor, approached the seated child, ruffled her head with an unguarded affection that, oddly, made the watching Rachel catch her breath in something ridiculously close to envy. 'Daft chavi. Of course not. After they start to roost then we still feed them – in the rides – corn mostly. That's when we have to fight the foxes, the buggers. And the poachers—'

'When you put the lights in the rides? Aunty Fee told me – she said they look so pretty, glimmering between the trees.'

Rachel, still and watching, saw a sudden swift movement. Liver and white. The dog's barking split the air. Intruder, it snarled. Intruder!

'Here, Kili!'

Two faces were turned towards her, the one open and expectant, the other closed and suspicious.

'Rachel! Oh, Lord, whatever is the time?' Philippa scrambled, ungainly, to her feet. 'Oh, I'm so sorry! I forgot – were you looking for me?' She scurried across the clearing, her expression all guilt. 'Gosh, I'm *always* forgetting the time!' She lifted helpless arms. 'Oh, Rachel, truly, I *am* sorry – how awful of me. Gideon – do you remember Rachel?' She turned. Stopped. 'Gideon? Where are you?'

The clearing was empty. Man and dog had disappeared. Philippa shrugged. 'He is funny. Like the pea in the nut shell trick. You know –,' she added at Rachel's questioningly cocked brow, 'now you see it now you don't.'

'You've spent three days nagging me about your bloody hair.' Rachel's voice was milder than the words.

'I know. I'm sorry. You will do it?'

'I might.' She put an arm about the sturdy young shoulders, smiled into the open, sun-freckled face. Realized with something of a shock that the roundness of childhood was almost

74

gone. The clear, strong bones stood fearlessly in the light. The dark eyes were steady, bright and warm. The child – no, not still a child though by no means yet a woman – exuded a trust and a confidence that won the world to her without effort. Vaguely, from childhood, Rachel remembered Philippa's father, Philippe Van Damme. It was from him she inherited her uninhibited charm; and from her mother her strength, of which she was as yet unaware, for it had never yet been tested. 'What will Sally think?' Rachel asked.

'About me having my hair cropped? Oh, don't ask silly questions. She'll *hate* it. Parents always hate it when their children change things, don't they? Oh, come on, Rachel – I'm *dying* to get it done.'

They were almost at the house before Rachel asked, very casually, 'What was it the man called you?'

'Sorry?' Philippa turned a genuinely blank face.

Rachel hesitated. 'Rakli. My rakli, he said.' She could hear as she said it the searing note of tenderness in his voice as he had spoken the word. 'What does it mean?'

'Oh, that. It means –', she hesitated, ' – gipsy girl. Well, yes, that's what it means, but with a bit more – you know – affection?' Her voice trailed to silence.

'Ah.' The sound was non-committal. 'Well,' Rachel leapt with long, easy strides up the terrace steps, two at a time, 'I hope your gipsy swain doesn't object to a rakli with shingled hair?'

Daphne Underscar hated shopping for clothes. In fact she hated shopping for anything, but clothes were her especial bugbear. The pert and pretty assistants who, she always felt, eyed her angular figure and plain face so superciliously made her feel awkward and uncomfortable. The shops were always too warm, she invariably became so hot and bothered that anything she tried on looked even more a rag than it might have done. She had no idea what suited her – suspected rather strongly that nothing did – and was far more at home in her usual shabby jumpers and skirts than in the inappropriate and skimpy fashions of the day. On the Thursday before her trip to the opera with Toby she did, however, make the effort, and before the day was through regretted it mightily. She trailed around the department stores of Oxford Street and Regent Street – the prudent amount allowed her by her father precluded the rather smaller and more exclusive establishments of Bond Street – and found absolutely nothing even vaguely suitable. In the short, flounced, black lace creation that the assistant in Peter Robinson's persuaded her into she looked, she decided, like nothing so much as a discarded lampshade. An afternoon dress in lime green velvet trimmed with monkey fur in Dickins and Jones looked so ludicrous that, catching the assistant's doubtful eye over her shoulder in the mirror she actually laughed aloud. At last, hot, tired and in desperation, having reached Piccadilly Circus and Swan and Edgar without having bought so much as a pair of gloves, she plumped for an apricot satin gown, sleek to the hips and then flaring about the knees – a garment that looked at least half-way decent in the shop, but that, when she got it home hung upon her like a pale and shining potato sack and was dumped with no ceremony into the bottom of a wardrobe already knee deep in such unsuitable creations.

So it was that when Toby called for her at seven the following evening she was wearing her usual nondescript black frock with beaded neck and sleeves, a jet slide pinning down her wiry, uncompromisingly bobbed hair and her dead mother's old-fashioned jet earrings in her ears.

Toby, she was very pleased to note, was not so crass as to tell her she looked beautiful; the last young man to make that mistake had been shown the door, politely but firmly, almost before the words were out of his mouth. Instead he presented her with a corsage of white camellias, commented on how very pretty and unusual were the earrings, expressed the hope that she liked *Cavalleria Rusticana* and *I Pagliacci* which were the programme for that evening, and with the minimum of fuss escorted her to a waiting taxi. They made very polite and very general conversation during the short journey, arrived in good time – something of which the well-organized Daphne approved wholeheartedly, for she detested latecomers and their excuses – and were settled into their box with the mandatory box of chocolates by the time the curtain swept up.

Daphne enjoyed herself thoroughly. She hummed the Easter Hymn, suppressed her desire to laugh at the idiocies of the plot and clapped as vigorously as anyone at the end of the one-act *Cavalleria Rusticana*. Then they drank the champagne that Toby had thoughtfully provided, debated a little on the quality of Turiddu's voice and then made themselves comfortable again as the curtain rose on the drama of the clown and his love and jealousy. Here was different stuff indeed, sung with feeling and passion, and Daphne found herself blinking away tears as the unfortunate Canio's voice soared and sobbed through the famous 'motley' aria. With the final, inevitably tragic end to the drama Daphne was not the only one in the audience to come to her feet, clapping and calling.

Outside on the crowded pavement, the excitement still with her, she stood by Toby's side marvelling still at the incredible emotion that could be engendered by the human voice.

'I thought we'd go to The Embassy,' Toby said, casually. 'A few of my friends are going to be there.'

She smiled pleasantly, her inner eye still dazzled by lights and colour and the excitement of spectacle. ' – in Old Bond Street,' Toby prompted. Surely even Daphne must have heard of the most famous nightclub in London?

She nodded. 'That sounds nice.'

He lifted a hand for a taxi. 'It is. Very nice.' He smiled a little at the inappropriate word. 'And not all that easy to get into since the Pragga Wagga adopted it as his latest watering hole.'

She frowned, puzzled, her attention at last fully on him. 'The what?'

He laughed, genuinely amused. 'It isn't a what it's a who.' They climbed into the taxi. 'The Pragga Wagga. The Prince of Wales.'

'Oh.' Startled, she turned her large, pale eyes on him. 'Why on earth do you call him that? And – I'm sorry – where did you say we were going?'

'The whole of London calls him that. And we're going to The Embassy.' He was patient, but a faint edge of irritation clipped his voice. 'It's one of the Prince's favourite clubs. He comes to dance. Everyone does. Ambrose and his band are there – now come on, Daphne, you must have heard of *them*?'

'Well – I suppose I have, yes.' The full impact of what he was saying had been slow to filter into Daphne's over-stimulated senses. 'Toby – I thought you said we were going out to dinner?'

'We can eat at The Embassy.'

'But—' Daphne stopped.

'Something wrong?' For the first time Toby was cool. He'd broken his neck to wangle this invitation to the most exclusive club in London. There were girls aplenty who would have fallen over themselves – and him – to accompany him. Daphne it seemed was not only unaware of her good fortune but was actually questioning it.

'It's just – I thought we'd be going somewhere quiet. I'm not dressed for—' She stopped again. Cleared her throat. Pure panic was bringing sweat to the palms of her hands and she could feel it trickling down her back. She could see it all – the smart, pretty girls, the smart, handsome men, the smart, stupid talk; everything she most disliked, everything most guaranteed to put her at a disadvantage. She glanced in the flickering darkness down at her rusty black dress. 'Toby, I don't think I'm dressed for somewhere like that.'

He sat back. So that was it. Odd. He had not somehow thought Daphne prone to such female fads and fancies. 'You'll be fine. Truly you will. Most people come on from other things – concerts, the theatre, that sort of thing.'

Daphne's dismay had settled like a lump of stone in her stomach. 'I don't dance,' she said, quietly.

Toby had been looking out of the window. He turned his head. 'Sorry?'

'I don't dance,' she said, flatly and much louder, exasperated with herself that she sounded as if she were admitting to some heinous crime. 'I've never learned.'

With an easy, and surprisingly almost affectionate movement he reached for her hand. 'It doesn't matter, really it doesn't,' he said encouragingly. 'The dance floor's so small one can barely dance properly anyway. I'll teach you. Don't worry.'

He did not, she noticed, let go of her hand; she was surprised and a little alarmed at the small stirring of pleasure that gave her. Vaguely now she remembered having read about this Embassy place in the papers, always in connection with the Hon this or that, or the young Lady the other, and always in relation to some finger-shaking sermon about the Bright Young Things and their disreputable doings. She obviously read the wrong papers.

Brow furrowed she sat back in the deep leather seat, ridiculously aware of their hands, linked casually together beside her.

The Embassy Club, haunt of the rich and the elegant, the glamorous and above all the blue-bloodedly famous was, as Toby had said, in Old Bond Street. Its entrance was through a long tunnel that ran between two shops, and was guarded by a well-set-up and impressively uniformed commissionaire who regarded Toby with no friendly eye as he approached. Daphne, beside herself with nerves she fervently hoped did not show, watched as the man, after a low-voiced exchange with Toby, sent for a dinner-jacketed waiter who then disappeared down the tunnel towards the club. Toby turned and strolled back to her, winking. 'Won't be a sec. Just checking. The silly blighters forgot to leave a message.'

A group of people drifted into the narrow entrance hall, greeted the commissionaire familiarly, talking and laughing loudly amongst themselves. A girl in high heels stepped on Daphne's toe and walked on, ignoring her. 'But, Jamie, my pet, what an absolute *scream*! Whatever did you do—?' She was dressed in drifting chiffon, her slim bare shoulders protected by expensive, snow white fur which, as she walked she let slip to the floor, pulling it behind her with a languid hand.

Daphne gritted her teeth.

The group moved on. A couple stepped from a taxi to be greeted with some subservience. The man was middle-aged, grey haired, portly. Vaguely Daphne recognized him. A politician, she thought – in fact, yes, a Minister, surely, in His Majesty's Government? And married, as she remembered, to a plump and worthy woman much given to good works and huge Edwardian-style hats. The slip of a girl at his side was too blonde for nature, excessively pretty, was possessed of a glittering smile and had a grasp upon his arm as possessive as a miser's upon gold. Daphne, uncharitably she felt, doubted she was his daughter.

The waiter returned, scurrying. The commissionaire received his message, turned to Toby, saluted deferentially. 'Sorry about that, sir. Have to check, you know.'

Toby acknowledged his apology with a slightly chill smile, took Daphne's arm and steered her towards the door.

Her first impression was of heat, smoke and noise. A dance band played. The tiny dance floor was crowded, as were the tables that, as her eyes adjusted to the dim light, she saw were clustered about the room. The decor was elegant; pale and restrained. The room was a kaleidoscope of colour – young women like exotic flowers in reds and yellows, blues and golds, jewels glimmering upon smooth skin, hair gleaming beneath diffused lights, the soft and colourful silks, chiffons and satins of their clothes in pretty contrast to the black and white of the masculine dinner suits. Mostly young, always expensively dressed and well-groomed, occasionally downright beautiful, the sons and daughters of London's elite and their hangers-on smoked and drank, flirted, danced and laughed, confident in that magic circle of birth, education and kinship that was so much their natural inheritance that they gave it not a thought. Until an outsider threatened it.

'Toby, old chap! Welcome. Pull up a pew. Beth, love, make way for Toby and his lady. My dear old Toby – where have you been keeping yourself? Long time no see—.'

Daphne accepted a seat, murmured acknowledgement of the introductions shouted above the sound of the band. Champagne was brought, and more champagne; she watched, fascinated, as with warmth and ease Toby became, within minutes, the centre of attention. With no apparent effort he slipped into the spotlight and held it, his smile brilliant, his eyes bright as sapphires. Women watched him, with a degree of interest that encompassed everything from the unobtrusive to the rapacious; but none, certainly, ignored him. Men slapped his back, roared with laughter at his slightest word, or so it seemed to Daphne. Sitting at the edge of the circle, watching, her large hands folded upon her lap beneath the table she found herself suddenly and uncomfortably aware of small, whiplash glances, of measuring, knowing eyes, of whispers as a couple of girls on the far side of the table leaned to each other, hair swinging to hide their smiles.

She could imagine as clearly as if she could truly hear them, the words.

'Whatever is Toby up to now?'

'My dear, she must be absolutely *rolling* in money—'

'If she is it doesn't show – just *look* at that rag she's wearing.'

She lifted her chin, feeling the rise of colour in her cheeks.

'I say – would you c-care for a dance?'

It was a moment before she realized that the words had been addressed to her. She looked up. A very large young man, pink faced and fair-haired and distinctly unsteady on his large, flat feet, towered above her.

'I – I'm afraid –.' She stopped as he staggered a little, steadied himself with a hand upon the table. One of the girls opposite giggled quite openly. 'I'm afraid I –'

'Come on, old girl.' He grabbed her hand, hauled her to her feet. In her mortification it seemed as if every eye in the room was upon her. 'Just a quick trot around the floor with good old Bertie –' Good old Bertie teetered, apparently on the verge of falling over.

'Not this time, old thing.' With an easy smile Toby was between them, a gentle hand firmly upon Bertie's chest so that the huge young man found himself propelled with no effort into the nearest chair, where he sat, grinning inanely. 'The lady's with me.' With an engagingly encouraging smile he crooked an elbow for her hand. 'Shall we?'

In an agony of embarrassment she allowed him to usher her towards the tiny dance floor. 'I told you!' she hissed between clenched teeth, 'I can't dance!'

He turned, slid his arm about her waist, shrugged gracelessly, teeth gleaming. 'Just shuffle your feet in time with the music,' he said, cheerfully. 'That's all that anyone else is doing.'

For some strange reason this patent untruth brought an unwilling, answering smile. Awkwardly and stiffly she held herself in his arms, trying to follow his easy movements, stepping on his toes, biting her lip, face blotched hotly with embarrassment. She could almost feel the eyes of the two girls at the table on her back; could almost hear their sniggers.

'Relax.' Toby grinned good-naturedly. 'Just relax.' He steered her to the middle of the floor where so jammed were the couples that anything beyond the minimum of movement was impossible. 'There. Now you could have two left feet and no-one would notice.'

'I'm afraid that's just about what I have got.' Her voice was rueful.

The bright blue eyes beneath the sweep of lash gleamed with amusement. 'It doesn't matter. Honestly it doesn't. I wouldn't have dragged you up, but it was all I could think of. A couple of rounds with Bertie and you would have been a goner, I think.' Again that engaging smile.

Gamely as she could she smiled back, willing the music to stop, aware only of her acute embarrassment, her dowdy dress, the plainness of her face and figure in this glittering gathering. As with the last flourish of the drums the tune ended she turned away in relief. Toby caught her up halfway across the floor, escorted her to her seat. Good old Bertie was sound asleep, head on the table despite the ear-splitting crescendo of talk and laughter around him. She slid gingerly around him, sat down, pushing her chair back into the shadows by the wall.

The music started again. 'Toby!' A shrieking girl, her blazing hair like a beacon, her dress a brilliant emerald silk that revealed a great length of slim, well-shaped leg swooped upon him. 'Oh, thank God! The only decent dancer in town! I'm *dying* for a dance, you wonderful thing –' She moved into his arms, head tilted, then turned to Daphne. 'You don't mind, my dear, do you?'

Daphne shook her head. Bertie snored. Someone proffered a large glass of champagne. Daphne took it, watching as Toby and the girl in green threaded their way through the crowds towards the floor. Toby bent to her and said something. She threw her head back and shrieked with laughter. They moved onto the floor, his arms about her, her head on his shoulder.

Daphne swallowed the cool, sparkling drink almost at a gulp.

'More?' asked a voice, helpfully.

'Yes. Thanks.'

The foaming stuff glittered prettily. She took another large mouthful. Suddenly she did not feel so bad. She studied the faces about her, animated in the dim, smoke-wreathed light. To her inestimable relief no-one took the slightest notice of her. She drank her champagne. The music had changed. Toby and the girl in green were Charlestoning, Toby with a style, and the girl with a frenetic enthusiasm that had drawn a clapping crowd around them. Magically, it seemed, her glass was full again. This time she sipped it, savouring it, quite happy in her self-imposed isolation. Toby escorted the girl in green back to the table, and, unable because of Bertie's sleeping bulk to sit next to Daphne took a seat opposite. A blonde girl in red draped herself across his shoulder and whispered in his ear. Toby caught Daphne's eye and winked. Astoundingly she found herself winking back. 'Do dance,' she mouthed the words across the table against the music and the laughter. 'I don't mind. Really I don't. I'm fine.'

He hesitated only a moment then nodded, grinning, and took the other girl's hand.

She never, afterwards, remembered the exact moment that she came to the decision. She could not even, for the life of her, understand why she should have made such a decision in such an uncharacteristically impulsive way and in circumstances that normally she would well have recognized as being anything but conducive to clear thinking.

The only indisputable fact was that at some point that night she knew with unshakeable certainty that she wanted Toby Smith.

As she watched him dancing, talking, laughing, standing easily, hands in pockets, rocking gracefully on his heels or half sitting upon the table, leg swinging, the audacious charm of the man was evident; yet it wasn't that. She knew it. How could it be? Daphne Underscar was too shrewd a character to fall for a pretty face and a pair of bright eyes. She wanted him, she told herself, for Underscars. She wanted that persuasive popularity. She wanted that sharp brain, that cavalier, almost callous charm,

83

that unquenchable energy channelled into the business. A breath of fresh air. And, she suspected, a ruthlessly strong hand beneath that easy-going façade. Her father was right, bless him. This was the man for Underscars.

That she might have hoped that this, too, was the man Daphne Underscar had unconsciously been looking for through all these long years never entered her head, or, if it did, it was a thought quickly and scornfully dismissed.

Chapter Four

Discreetly muted talk and laughter, mingled with the chink of cutlery, the occasional clatter of china and the bland and quiet notes of a piano lifted to the ornate ceiling of Harrod's Restaurant. Beyond the windows the wet roofs of Kensington gleamed, red and grey, beneath lowering late summer skies.

Rachel sipped her sherry appreciatively, glanced round with mischievous eyes. 'I adore this place. It's so screamingly stuffy.'

Fiona raised sharply-drawn eyebrows. 'Speak for yourself, young lady!'

'Oh, don't be daft, I don't mean you! But honestly – just look around.' Rachel's face screwed itself into an expression of comic disbelief.

Fiona's green eyes flicked to the next table where sat a plump dowager with her two even plumper daughters, and she smothered a grin. 'You have a point. But the food's good. And it's really terribly convenient.'

Rachel drained her glass, set it down, grinned. 'Convenient if you've got any money to spend, you mean. Me, I'm stony broke, as always. I can't think what's happened to my allowance again this month, honestly I can't. I do hope you aren't expecting a Dutch treat?'

Fiona laughed. 'Of course not. Lunch is on me.'

'Good. Then I shall eat everything in sight and take home what I can't manage. I'm starving.' Cheerfully Rachel waved her glass at a hovering waiter. 'Might I have another, please?'

Fiona watched her with real if exasperated affection. 'What do you do with your money? Ben surely doesn't keep you short?'

'Of course he doesn't.' Rachel waved an airy hand. 'It just seems to go, that's all.'

Fiona played with her own glass, turning it in her narrow

hand, watching the play of light on the amber liquid. 'Ever thought of getting a job?' she asked, mildly.

'God, what an idea! Of course not.' Rachel's tone was still light, but her eyes had sharpened. 'You haven't brought me here to lecture me, have you? Because if you have, dying of hunger as I am, I shall have to decamp and leave you to it.'

Fiona could not help laughing. 'Of course not. It's just, sometimes I wonder, you're such an intelligent and talented person –'

'Thank you kindly.' Rachel was pertly and resolutely frivolous.

'– it seems a shame not to do something.'

'What should I do?' Rachel's mouth was drawing into its habitually mutinous line. 'Follow Flip's worthy example and teach school, perhaps? Be honest, Fee – would you want me teaching your kids? Be some boring businessman's doting secretary? Sit on his lap and let him grope me while he dictates boring letters to boring clients? No, thank you. Are you going to eat those cheesy bits?'

Wordlessly Fiona passed the plate.

'You should know more than most –' Rachel nibbled, rolled her eyes in not altogether assumed ecstasy, '– gosh, these are good! – that opportunities for "talented and intelligent women",' ironically she emphasized the words, 'are few and far between. Mind you,' she slid another maliciously mischievous glance in Fiona's direction, 'I do get offers from time to time.'

'I should imagine you do.' Fiona was dry. 'That's what worries me.'

'Oh, God, now you sound like Pa.' With a small, restlessly irritated movement Rachel pushed the plate from her and picked up her glass again.

Fiona, sensibly, decided to accept the opportunity to change the subject. 'How is he?'

'He's fine.' All trace of mockery, of the brittle gaiety she so often affected, had left Rachel's voice. 'He's great. As always.' She fell to silence, her eyes pensive upon the flowers that graced the centre of the beautifully laundered white tablecloth.

Fiona waited.

After a long moment Rachel lifted her eyes; eyes that were

shadowed with some emotion that Fiona could not fathom. 'I must be a dreadful disappointment to him, I think.' The words were level, matter of fact.

'Oh, don't be silly.' But Fiona's brusqueness carried little of conviction, and they both knew it.

Rachel shrugged, tinkering with the silver cutlery, straightening and rearranging it, her long, slim brown fingers with their scarlet nails steady. 'Of course I am, Fee. We both know it. I adore him, you know I do. I love him more than anyone or anything in the whole world. But Pa and I – we're chalk and cheese, aren't we? There he is – brilliant, dedicated, entirely selfless – what is it Sally's often said of him – "building Jerusalem in England's green and pleasant land"?' Her voice was edged with an affectionate mockery. 'But he doesn't get much fun out of life, does he? All those campaigns – better conditions for the workers, better schooling for their children, better support for the old man and the sick –' Her mouth twitched wryly, '– it doesn't leave a lot of time for anything or anyone else, does it?' She watched her own fingers as they caressed the heavy metal of the cutlery, then shrugged, the graceless mockery back. 'And what does he get as –' she smiled a small, dry, humourless smile, '– offspring? Poor Pa. A worthless flibbertigibbet of a daughter who squanders his hard-earned money, consorts with layabouts and ne'er-do-wells and spends her time designing ridiculous clothes that no-one but she will ever wear—.'

'You do yourself an injustice I think,' Fiona said, quietly, watching her, intrigued as always by this girl's perilously complicated character.

'No. I don't.' The words were flat and did not invite argument. 'I know what I am. In more ways than one.' Rachel had pulled a rose from the vase and was shredding it methodically onto the table cloth. 'No-one else in the world knows better than I what I am.' Again that small, disturbingly caustic smile.

'Your father loves you dearly.'

'I know.' She raised dark, unfathomable eyes to look directly into Fiona's own. 'It doesn't help.'

Fiona leaned back to allow the hovering waiter to place her soup carefully before her. She waited until Rachel too had been served before she asked. 'And your mother? What of her? Do you ever see her?'

Rachel, distracted from her contemplation of a large plateful of smoked salmon let out a quite genuine splutter of laughter. '*Mother?* Don't make me laugh! I haven't seen her in years. Not since just after Uncle Peter died. Her or that –,' Rachel hesitated, caught Fiona's repressive eye and grinned, '– ladyfriend – of hers,' she finished, mincing the word.

'Does Ben see her?'

Uninterestedly Rachel shrugged, attacking her smoked salmon. 'Not often. Pa tries – he would – Mother simply isn't interested. It was Uncle Peter she loved.' Her voice still showed little or no emotion – genuinely, Fiona thought. 'If she ever loved anyone but herself, that is.' Rachel applied herself to her salmon.

'And what about you? Have you ever considered getting married?'

Rachel lifted her head, violet eyes innocent. 'Get married? Why ever should I do that? Why limit yourself to one cake on a plate if you can have them all?'

Fiona, unable to repress her laughter, dipped her spoon into her soup. 'You're impossible.'

'I try.'

They ate in silence for a moment until Fiona laid down her spoon, put her chin upon her narrow hand and surveyed Rachel thoughtfully.

'Now what?' Rachel asked, suspiciously.

'Hugo Fellafield's very smitten, you know,' Fiona said, composedly.

'Hugo? Oh, Fiona, come on! You must be joking?'

Fiona neatly finished the last of her soup, dabbed her lips with her napkin. 'You could do worse. They're an old family, and very well connected –,' she grinned. '– not least with us. There's quite a bit of money around. His father may not win the prize as the most popular man in the world but he's very highly thought of, one gathers, in quite high places. He's something very big and rather hush-hush in the Foreign Office, and heading for even bigger and better things. The older boy, Charles –'

'Another pain,' Rachel interjected, succinctly.

'– is reckoned to have a brilliant political career ahead of him, so the Madeira business will be Hugo's.'

'By default?' Rachel asked, sweetly and innocently malicious.

Fiona ignored that. 'And honestly, Rachel, Hugo's such a thoroughly nice boy –'

'Exactly! Fiona – what in the world would I do with a thoroughly nice boy?' Rachel spread her hands in an exaggerated gesture.

Laughing, Fiona held up her own hands in a gesture of surrender. 'All right! I give in! Perhaps you're right. Hugo's no Daniel. I'll never mention the subject again!'

Rachel eyed her in smiling mistrust. 'Fee, you didn't get me here to soften me up on Hugo Fellafield's behalf, did you?'

'Heaven forbid, of course not! It's just that he's one of my favourite young men and I don't like to see him down in the dumps.'

Demurely Rachel placed her knife and fork side by side upon her empty plate. 'And can't you think of some way to cheer him up?' she asked, with faultless innocence.

Fiona's laughter pealed through the restaurant, turning heads. 'My dear, it would be like going to bed with my own son! How scandalous! No – I got you here to help me choose the most becoming – and possibly the most expensive – dress in London. And to persuade you down to Breckon for the party.'

Rachel stilled. 'No. I'm sorry, Fee. I told you. I'm busy that weekend.'

'I don't believe you.'

Their eyes met, levelly, Rachel's at first flashing anger, and then, suddenly, dropping. There was a long silence.

'You have to face it sooner or later my dear,' Fiona said, very quietly.

'Face what?' The words were childishly defiant.

'Toby's marriage.'

Quiet fell again.

'It's nothing to do with me,' Rachel said.

Fiona did not answer. As the main course was served they sat

89

in silence, and in silence they started to eat. Rachel fiddled with her food, head bent. Fiona watched her.

'How could he?' Rachel burst out at last, disgust in her voice. 'How *could* he?'

'What?'

'Marry for money.'

Fiona stared at her in genuine astonishment. 'But Rachel – Toby would never marry for anything else. You know it.'

Rachel shrugged dismissively, still playing with her meal.

'I would have thought –' Fiona hesitated, then plunged on, '– that you would have been pleased.'

'*Pleased?*'

'That he wasn't marrying for love.'

'Toby Smith couldn't love anyone if he tried.' Viciously Rachel stabbed at a piece of chicken.

'Yes. I'm very much afraid that you may be right.' Fiona had spoken very quietly.

Slowly Rachel lifted her head. 'I love him,' she said, suddenly, her face tight with pain. 'I always have.'

'I thought that might be the way of it.'

'You're too clever by half.' Rachel nibbled at the chicken.

Once more Fiona let the silence stretch between them. 'Rachel, my love, Toby is going to marry Daphne Underscar. It's signed, sealed and all but delivered. It's going to happen. On top of that he's the one man you can't have. He thinks of you as a sister –'

'Huh!' The snort was venomous.

'Are you sure that isn't it?'

'What?'

'The one man you want. The one man you can't have.'

The gleam in Rachel's eye was sarcastic. 'I haven't noticed Rudolph Valentino knocking on my door.'

'Rudolph Valentino's been dead two years.'

'Ah.' Rachel smiled, angelically. 'That must be it.'

'Rachel!'

Rachel put down her knife and fork, picked up her chicken with her fingers, smiled sweet as sugar at the dowager's outraged glare. 'All right. You're right. I don't give a damn for Toby Smith.

I'm just being perverse.' She gleamed an intransigent smile over the chewed chicken. 'I still won't come to your party.'

'It isn't my party. It's James'. And it isn't me who wants you to come. It's Philippa. It's her last weekend before she goes back to school and she's just dying to see you.'

'Oh, Lord!' Rachel said, disgustedly, shaking her head, 'here come the big guns.'

'To say nothing of poor, pining, thoroughly nice Hugo Fella-field,' Fiona added, straightfaced. 'Oh, and I can't recall if I told you that the firm that was supposed to help with the decorations has let us down? I had some vague hopes that you might step into the breach and help us out – poor old Breckon does rather need jollying up for a party this size. Still – if you're otherwise engaged –' She sipped her wine, pulled an over-rueful face. 'Flip and Hugo and I will have to stem our tears and look elsewhere, I suppose.'

Very precisely Rachel finished her piece of chicken, set the bone upon the plate, sucked her fingers and then wiped her fingers on her napkin. Smiled again at the dowager, winked at one of her plump, giggling daughters. 'Lady Paget,' she said, crisply, 'you are the most diabolical woman for getting your own way. You beat me into a cocked hat.'

Fiona smiled serenely, applied herself to her duck. 'I know,' she said. 'Disgusting, isn't it? James is always telling me about it.'

Sir James Paget's sixtieth birthday celebrations were, as his wife had intended, an occasion to remember. Breckon Hall was packed with visitors, old and young. Picnics, riding and boating expeditions and games were organized, there was food and drink for an army. The centrepiece of the weekend was the party, to be held on the Saturday evening. Rachel, with her own special and usually neglected flair, had turned Breckon's small ballroom into a brilliant, flower-filled garden. Philippa, excited almost – but not quite – to speechlessness, was to wear her first grown-up ball gown which, Fiona told Sally in a splutter of laughter, had already been tried on so many times that it might well wear out before the party ever started.

On Saturday afternoon Fiona, the job of organization done so neatly and efficiently that she knew the whole affair was running absolutely according to plan and, barring accidents, could now manage without her constant supervision, sat in one of the deep leather armchairs of the library, a pot of tea on the small table before her. This was perhaps the only quiet place in the house. Through the tall windows, open to allow the warm September air with its autumnal smells to drift into the room, came shouts from the tennis courts, laughter and conversation from a tea party spread upon the lawns.

Toby stood, shoulders hunched, his back to the room, looking out into the mellow afternoon. He was dressed in a crisp and spotless open-necked white shirt, the sleeves rolled negligently to his elbows, and white flannels. His tennis racquet he had tossed onto a settee.

'You really mustn't sulk, darling. It doesn't suit you at all.' Fiona's voice was light, her eyes unusually intent. Apparently relaxed she poured tea, picked up the cup, sipped it, watching. After a moment's silence she added, faintly and acidly humorous, 'Since I can't believe your heart is broken, I can only assume the cause of this unexpected tantrum to be the fact that the suggestion came from me rather than from you. If you like we can start again, and you can be the one to make the break. Would that be better?'

He did not accept her gentle invitation to laughter, nor did he rise to the affectionate sting in the words. Impatiently he swung from the window. 'I simply don't see why the break has to be made at all! We're perfectly all right as we are. What's changed?'

'Your situation has,' she said, immediately and crisply. 'Whether you like it or not, you are engaged to be married. Quite apart from the fact that, as you very well know, it's my absolute rule that my –' her lips twitched a little, '– young friends should be unattached, it happens too that I very much like your intended. I don't enjoy deceiving people I like. And your Daphne neither deserves nor, I think, could cope with such a situation. Come and drink your tea, there's a pet.'

'You like Daphne?'

'Don't sound so surprised. Yes, indeed, I like Daphne. I think she's an exceptionally intelligent and amiable person. You must have noticed?'

Toby chose to ignore the gentle sarcasm. 'Well – yes – of course.' He dropped into the chair opposite, picked up his teacup, his handsome face still fallen into faintly scowling lines.

Fiona watched him with real fondness, and no small regret. 'We'll still be friends,' she said. 'More than ever if I'm a judge. Come on, Toby my dear – isn't it better this way? No tears, no recriminations, no broken hearts, no flaming rows.' She smiled, warm and affectionate, and this time, despite himself, Toby found himself suddenly smiling back.

'You're an absolutely impossible woman.'

She shook her head. 'No. Just sensible. You surely can see it?'

For a moment he held to his ill-humour. Then, wryly, he shrugged. 'Yes. I suppose so.'

'Good. Now – enough of that –' The subject dismissed with typical brisk despatch she kicked her shoes off and tucked her feet up beneath her in the wide chair. 'Tell me your plans.'

He regarded her with exasperated blue eyes. 'Well thanks for being so devastated by the end of our affair!'

'Oh, don't be silly, my dear. And don't be stuffy either. It isn't your style. Come on. Do tell. What's the deal?'

Toby shouted with laughter. 'Fee, what a way to put it!'

'A spade's a spade and always has been,' she said, composedly. 'Now, come on – pander to a nosey old woman. I'm dying to know.'

He relaxed. 'Underscars is a family firm, as you know. Amos has the controlling interest, of course. Daphne already has some few shares, that she inherited from her mother, and so have what she calls the "dotty aunts" up in Yorkshire –'

'The ones who looked after her until a few years ago?'

'That's it.' Toby had time to register the fact that Fiona's contact with Daphne, whom she had met for the first time the evening before, had certainly been more than just a passing one if she had already elicited this information. 'They're Amos' spinster sisters – Daphne's very fond of them – but their holdings are very small, and Amos virtually controls them. What's more

93

he's got their disposal fairly well tied up – the aunts can't sell them without offering them to him first –'

'Ah—' Fiona's eyes were sharp, and the sound was questioning.

'Until now Amos has held seventy-five per cent of the stock.'

'And now?'

'He's giving us thirty per cent as a wedding present. I'm to have a seat on the Board – which doesn't please old Beringer, Amos' stuffed shirt accountant one bit – and the brief to modernize the shops and their merchandise.' Suddenly excited Toby leaned forward in his chair, long hands loosely clasped before him. 'Fee, the potential is almost unlimited! Underscars have some of the best sites in the best High Streets in the country. Amos has piddled around with some small expansion, but he's really got no idea of what's actually possible. Electrical goods, furniture, crockery, linen – all modern, all designed for the small suburban house, of reasonable quality and at reasonable prices. There's a fortune to be made!'

'And to be spent, first, from the sound of it?' Fiona murmured, over-innocently.

Toby leapt to his feet, strode to the fireplace, turned, jabbing a long forefinger into the air. 'The money's there! Mouldering away in the bloody bank! You have to invest to make money – everyone knows that –'

'Hence Amos' Mr Beringer's unease at your rather rapid Board appointment?' Fiona asked, shrewdly.

Toby laughed, eyes bright. 'I should say so. We've had a few dust-ups already. We'll certainly have some more before this is through.'

'But you really believe it's possible? You've thought it through?'

'Backwards, forwards and upside down. Fee, we can't lose. Refurbish the shops, revamp the image, advertise, get Mrs Suburbia breaking her pretty neck to get to our stuff before her next door neighbour does—'

'That's more or less what Daphne said.' Fiona chuckled a little. 'In rather more ladylike terms, of course.'

Toby blinked. 'She did?'

Fiona's smile flickered again. She had come away from a determinedly manoeuvred and extremely interesting hour-long chat with Daphne Underscar last night with the growing and amusing feeling that Toby Smith had perhaps, in this surprising young woman, taken on rather more than he was aware of. Not to say bitten off more than he could chew. Now, however, could hardly be thought the appropriate moment to tell him so. 'She did. She also mentioned that her father, though enthusiastic, is not quite as committed to sudden change as you are.'

Toby was airy. 'He wants to take things a little slower than I'd like, yes. It's natural, I suppose. I'll talk him round.'

'I'm sure you will.' Fiona, thoughtfully, applied herself to her cooling tea.

'Toby! There you are! You said you'd make up a doubles – oh, sorry, Fee—' Flip, unceremoniously, almost fell through the open french windows. 'Am I interrupting?'

'Not at all. We'd finished.' Fiona unfolded her long legs, stretched a little. 'I think I can squeeze in a rest and a bath before the high jinks start. Off you go the pair of you.' She lifted her pale, bright face to Toby, smiling.

He hesitated for a moment, then, gently and oddly tenderly he bent to kiss her cheek. 'Thanks, Fee. For everything.'

She reached up and squeezed his fingers. Flip did a war dance of impatience upon the priceless rug, swatting at a fly with her tennis racquet.

The serene smile remained upon Fiona's face until they had gone. Then it faded, leaving an expression of pensive sadness. A little wearily she ran her hand through her short, dark red hair, ruffling it. She would miss him. Oh, how very much she would miss him.

She leaned back in the chair and closed her eyes. Outside the world played, strolled, laughed in the sunshine. She sighed. She was getting too old to play these dangerous, damaging games. Perhaps the time had come to call a halt. It had been a long, long time since her heart had ached so. Longer than she could remember.

Her eyes flew open. Mooning. By God, she was mooning like any silly schoolgirl!

With a small, tart grimace of self-mockery she drained the last of her tea, stood, stretched a little tiredly, and marched briskly from the room.

Rachel Patten enjoyed the party that evening rather more than she had anticipated. Possibly due to a fairly steady intake of the generous supply of the Pagets' excellent champagne the unaccustomed sight of Toby anchored to Daphne's side did not, she was pleased to note with what was, perhaps, a dangerous lift of confidence, disturb her as much as she had thought it might. They made an ill-matched enough couple, she thought with some pleasurable malice as she danced past them in Hugo's eager arms. Where on earth had Daphne acquired that truly awful dress?

'I say – would you care for a stroll in the garden?' Hugo asked as the music stopped. He looked like an eager schoolboy, the wide-set hazel eyes in a face fresh-skinned as a child's, straight straw-coloured hair slicked to his head.

He could not believe his luck.

For two dances running he had held this goddess – this dream of beauty in shimmering silver-blue – in his arms. Not once had he stumbled, not once found himself tongue-tied. She had answered when he had spoken. Had laughed at his favourite joke (the only one he could ever remember, actually, though he hated to admit it) And now she cocked her lovely head on one side for a moment of suspense before she said, 'Why not? It's beastly hot in here, isn't it?' Then, as if it were the most natural thing in the world she casually linked her hand into his crooked arm and allowed him to steer her from the dance floor towards the open windows that led onto a paved balcony beyond. As a waiter passed with a full tray Rachel adroitly acquired a tall glass of champagne. The waiter stopped, offered the tray to Hugo. Hugo opened his mouth to refuse – he had had rather a lot of the heady stuff already – then changed his mind and accepted. Together they strolled into the darkness, stood for a moment leaning against the stone balustrade looking out over the dark mass of the parkland, mysterious in moonlight, sipping their drinks. From behind them music drifted and the sound of

voices. Their shadows were thrown long upon the lawn in front
of them. The sky was pitch black and starless, the air fresh.

'Are you warm enough?'

Rachel nodded, rubbing her hands upon her bare arms.

Gallantly Hugo slipped his dinner jacket off, laid it about her
shoulders, feeling the cool silk of her skin against his warm
hands, smelling the exotic perfume that always wreathed about
her hair and her body. It took a physical effort to remove his
arm from about her strong, narrow shoulders. Unbidden, as so
often, he saw again in his mind's eye the way she had looked
the night of the storm, naked, her body shining and streaming
with water ... Suddenly thirsty he gulped his champagne.
Rachel balanced her empty glass on the balustrade. 'Let's go for
a walk.' Not waiting for him to answer she was off, slipping
noiselessly down the wide, shallow steps and fading into the
darkness. Hugo hastily finished his drink, stood his glass next
to Rachel's, turned to follow her and all but fell over the shoes
she had discarded upon the terrace.

'Rachel?'

'Here.' Her quiet voice was amused.

He caught a glimmer of silver in the darkness. When he joined
her she slid a friendly arm about his waist, laid her head upon
his shoulder. He wondered that she did not hear the thunder of
his heart. 'It's a super night.' He was proud of the evenness of
his voice. 'I like it cool like this.'

'Me too.' They wandered into the darker shadow of a tree.
The music was faint, now. Streamers of light lay across the
lawns and the gardens, faded enticingly into the still night. A
waterfowl clucked sleepily on the lake. Rachel stopped walking,
lifted her head. 'Smell.'

All Hugo could smell was that tantalizing, not to say totally
distracting, perfume. 'Mm,' he said, intelligently.

'Autumn's coming. You can smell it. Wonderful. It's my
favourite time of year.'

Hugo, who had always rather fancied summer himself, made
some rapid mental adjustment and found himself saying, 'Me,
too,' and believing it. Had the girl said she liked eating broken
glass he would have agreed as wholeheartedly. Never in his

young life had he been so spellbound. The girl beside him radiated a magnetic attraction he had no power to resist. She was, quite simply, the most beautiful woman he had ever seen, let alone held, and the bright glow of her beauty and her capricious intelligence lured him like a moth to a flame. The inevitable fate of that bemused insect bothered him not at all; at that moment and in the first flush of infatuation no sacrifice would have been too great to lay before her. When, quite naturally, she turned towards him, snug in his jacket, leaning against his chest, the length of her slim body burning his like a brand, he trembled.

She felt it, and laughed a little, quietly, not unkindly. Narrow, cool hands slid up his chest, took his face, brought it down to meet hers. Her mouth, at first, was soft, and tasted of champagne, the kiss almost casual. The perfume enveloped him, the fragrance of enchantment. Young, and fierce with love he could not control himself. He crushed her to him, feeling with astonishment the litheness of her body as it moulded itself to his. Her mouth opened, her hands were in his hair, painful, long nails cutting, fingers tangling as, fierce as he, she kissed him back very thoroughly indeed. He was swamped by a wave of physical desire stronger, more irresistible, than he had ever experienced in his life before. Surely, surely, she – this wonderful, adorable woman – must feel the same?

Rachel, with a deftness that had he had eyes to see it would have spoken of much practice, slipped from his arms, retrieved the jacket that was slipping from her shoulders and rumpled her dark hair with her hand, laughing. 'Goodness. That was nice.'

His face was flaming. 'God, Rachel – I'm sorry –!'

'Whatever for?' She was genuinely astonished.

His heart still thundered. His body was horribly, uncontrollably aroused. For an awful moment he felt close to tears.

She sensed his sudden distress with sure instinct. Calmly she stepped close to him, lifted her arms, cradled his head against her. Clinging to her as a drowning man might cling to rock, he slid to his knees. 'There, there.' She touched his hot face gently with long, cool fingers, stroked his hair as if he was a distraught child.

Gradually the demeaning trembling eased. Ashamed he sat back on his heels, his head bowed. With a quick, graceful movement she sat beside him on the damp grass, leaned to him, kissed him upon the lips, softly and gently. He closed his eyes and his mind, suspended in darkness, his only contact with reality the touch of those soft, perfumed lips.

Rachel sat back, drew up her knees beneath his jacket. He caught the gleam of her urchin smile. 'Better?'

'Yes.' He reached a hand to her.

She took it, squeezed it lightly in friendly camaraderie.

'I'm sorry,' he mumbled.

'Don't be. I enjoyed it.' The words were simple, and utterly honest. And desperately easy to misinterpret.

He lifted his head. 'Really? You aren't angry with me?'

'Of course not!' Her laughter was music in his ears. Heart suddenly singing he jumped to his feet, held out a hand to pull her up after him, held her close for a moment before she pulled away, laughing. 'We'd better get back. If we aren't there for the cake-cutting God only knows what rumours will circulate!'

Let them. Feeling at least ten feet tall he slipped his arm about her shoulders, holding her against the chill of the air. Her long legs keeping perfect rhythm with his they strolled back towards the lights and noise of the house. From somewhere in the darkness as they passed the shrubbery came a scuffle, and a giggle, hastily hushed. In the dappled light Rachel grinned. 'Someone else who's going to miss the cake-cutting if they aren't careful.' She drew away from him a little, smoothed her dress, expertly rearranged her hair with her fingers. Slipped her narrow feet into the discarded, sparkling shoes. Every movement was a poem, an aria, the glow of a rainbow in a summer sky. He could not take his besotted eyes from her. They stepped back through the open windows and into that other world – of heat and noise and colour, of faces smiling, laughing, talking. Bemused, Hugo stood for a moment reorientating himself. And in that moment Rachel was gone. He found himself standing, his jacket hanging from his foolish hand, watching her as she slipped into the crowd, greeting friends, throwing back her head to laugh, patting a cheek here, a shoulder there, carving a glittering path through the ballroom. He saw her stop at the group where stood Toby Smith and his tall, awkward-looking fiancée. Here she settled for a moment, like a gleaming dragonfly upon a leaf, accepting a glass of champagne, turning her back upon Toby, engaging the plain, shyly smiling girl in conversation. In vain he waited for her to turn, to look back at him, to signal in some way, however small, that like him she still felt the magic of the darkness, the thrilling excitement of that kiss—

'Hugo, for Christ's sake, where the hell have you been?' The voice, normally well-modulated and cool was threaded with sharp impatience, as it most often was when it spoke to Hugo.

Hugo turned. His brother Charles jerked his head towards the open door. 'The pater's waiting in the library. He has to go – he's in the middle of a crisis – you are a fathead! He's waiting to give you your instructions for Madeira.'

'But I don't leave for a fortnight.'

'It's the only chance he has. I told you – there's a crisis on –'

'There always is.' The muttered words were mutinous. Charles ignored them.

'– Do look sharp, there's a good chap. I'm running him down to the station to catch the last train and it goes in less than an hour.'

'I still don't see what's so pressing if I'm not leaving for two weeks—' Hugo, reluctantly, allowed his brother to usher him towards the door. 'Surely there's nothing so bloody important about the Madeira trip that it can't wait?'

Charles smiled a small, tight smile. He was a large young man, darker than Hugo and inclined to paunchiness. His square, heavy-browed face habitually wore an expression of humourless and portentous earnestness that made him look older than his years and illustrated his character exactly. Since the nursery the two brothers had had about as much in common as have winter and summer. 'I told you,' he said now, with the long-suffering and insulting patience he always employed to indicate that in his opinion his younger brother, although being naturally half-witted, could at least sometimes try to overcome that dis-ability. 'The pater wants to talk to you. He's waiting.'

How many times had Hugo shuddered at that? How many

times had his father waited for him; exacting, critical, relentlessly severe? There were no beatings now – though the memory of them, brutal and humiliating, still remained – but any encounter with his father was still enough to bring a faint sheen of sweat to his skin, an unpleasant queasiness to his stomach. He had all but forgotten the planned trip to Madeira, when he was to start his true apprenticeship in the family business – for heaven's sake, it was two weeks off, why think of it yet? Feet dragging, shrugging his jacket back onto his wide shoulders, he followed Charles' important, heavily purposeful strides to the library door, stood for a moment smoothing his hair and taking a deep and steadying breath before entering.

From the jacket, a drift of perfume lifted to his nostrils. A distant drumbeat echoed faintly in his blood. He grinned, suddenly and jauntily, a kind of defiant happiness almost defeating the childish apprehension. But he rearranged his features carefully to a semblance of soberness before, from long habit, he rapped quietly on the door and waited for the summons to enter.

Rachel, with some relief, had seen him go. From across the room she had seen the encounter with Charles – whom she detested – and watched as Hugo with obvious reluctance had followed him out of the room. A summons from that martinet of a father, no doubt. Poor old Hugo. She had dismissed him from her mind almost before he had left the room.

The band was playing ragtime. She allowed herself to be swept onto the floor by a fair young man in a white dinner jacket, a red rose drooping in his buttonhole. With some malice she watched covertly as Toby stood, foot tapping, beside Daphne, watching the dancing. Daphne turned to him with her quiet, toothy smile and said something. He shook his head, courteously.

God in heaven, what kind of a relationship was that? Suddenly incomprehensibly and savagely angry she threw herself into the dance. The fair young man, whose name had completely escaped her, delighted, matched her step for step. A circle grew about them, clapping, urging them on. The band, sensing a spectacle, played a little faster, a little more urgently, sweat pouring down reddened faces. Rachel's long legs flashed, her night dark hair tossed, she laughed aloud.

Toby turned away, uninterested, almost the only person in the room not watching. Fiona and James, accompanied by Sally and her husband Eddie Browne had joined the group. Toby was talking to Eddie, apparently absorbed in whatever he was saying. Damn him! *Damn* him!

All her good intentions crashed about her. She danced as if possessed, lifting her skirt, tossing her head, gleaming a challenge from those violet eyes at any man who cared to see it.

Toby found Sally, tall and quiet, by his side. 'Doesn't Rachel dance wonderfully? She's one of the few people I know who can actually make this silly ragtime stuff look like real dancing.' The words were light.

Toby smiled politely. 'Yes.'

Eddie had moved away, leaving them a little separated from the crowd. Sally was watching him levelly, hazel eyes narrowed in a way he remembered better than he ever would have admitted, even to himself.

'Toby?'

He waited, still polite, still unwarmed.

'I wanted – to wish you luck.' Sally shook her head a little, sharply, impatiently. 'No. How silly. More than that. Happiness. Success. All the things you want. All the things you've always wanted. I wanted you to know—' She stopped.

'Yes?' His face, without moving a muscle, had closed infinitesimally. Her saw her recognition of it, of that expression no one else would have noticed. Had they not, after all, for so many years, been as close as – closer than – mother and son, brother and sister? Until she had left him. Even now he felt the childish hurt, the desolation, of that; and hated himself for feeling it. It was the only hurt he had ever suffered. He could not have forgiven it if he had tried.

'I wanted you to know how proud I am of you,' she said, steadily, her distinctive, husky voice low. 'And that I do hope you'll be happy.'

'Toby!' Rachel was there, eyes sparkling, the restless energy of her blazing like a torch. 'Dance with me! Come on, for heaven's sake – are you going to stand there all night? You'll take root!'

Irritated, Toby shook his head.

Rachel caught his hand. 'Come on!'

Sally, smiling sociably and with total lack of meaning, stepped back.

'Do dance, Toby.' Daphne, gauche in a purple frock that, displaying bony shoulders and long, skinny arms, made her look the best part of a decade older than her years, smiled her good natured smile.

He allowed himself to be led onto the dance floor. Two good and natural dancers, they smoothly swung into a quickstep. Rachel hummed lightly as she danced, *'Why do I love you, why do you love me –?'* Her body was supple and strong, moved with his as if by instinct. For a moment he allowed himself to relax, to enjoy the sheer and unexpected pleasure of the fluent movement. The perfume she always wore drifted about them pleasantly. She tilted her head back, teeth gleaming between parted lips. 'Are you looking forward to getting married?' She pitched her voice just above the sound of the music.

'What?' He was taken by surprise. 'Why yes. Of course.'

Rachel's eyes flicked with graceless and obvious implication to where Daphne stood, awkwardly, glass in hand. 'Why yes. Of course,' she repeated, the emphasis of the words entirely changed.

Toby, long practised, ignored her. They whirled into a spinning turn, moved smoothly out of it.

'Very good.' Rachel, apparently and as far as Toby could see typically, determined upon provocation, grinned sarcastically.

Still he said nothing.

She sang again. *'Maybe that's because you love me, Maybe that's why I love you –* So – what's the deal, then?'

Almost he missed a step. 'Deal?'

'With Daphne's pa. Don't tell me you're eloping over his dead body with not a penny piece between you?'

He guided her expertly across the crowded floor. 'Bloody women. You're as bad as Fee.'

'She asked too, did she?' Rachel threw back her head and

laughed. 'We're interested, that's all. It's only because we love you, darling.'

'It's none of your business.'

'Ah. So there *is* a deal?'

'Not exactly. Amos is giving us a share of the company as a wedding present –'

'– but not a controlling share,' Rachel finished.

'No. Of course not.'

Rachel's smile took on an extra edge. 'Amos Underscar isn't stupid, then?'

'No, Rachel. He isn't stupid. He could hardly have done what he's done if he had been, could he?'

'And his daughter?'

'What of her?'

'Is she stupid?'

'No.'

She leaned away from him, looked him straight in the eye, waiting for a moment for his full and undivided attention. 'Are you sure?' she asked, very sweetly.

They finished the dance in silence.

The evening wore on. The cake was cut, the speeches made. Hugo returned and sought out Rachel. Rachel – blow hot, blow cold – kissed him lightly and insisted that he lead the line for a rowdy ballroom version of *In and Out the Windows*. The line snaked around the room, winding in and out of chairs and tables and about laughing groups of older people who clapped and sang aloud. *'In and out the windows, in and out the windows, in and out the windows, as we have done before –'* In passing Rachel snatched at the flowers she had so painstakingly arranged in the hours that had led up to the party, flinging them at the others in the line. In a moment the air was full of flowers, tossed and flung in all directions.

'Stand and face your lover, Stand and face your lover, Stand and face your lover, as you have done before –' Mockingly she bowed to Hugo, refusing to be caught and kissed. Hand strong in his she propelled him – he apparently still leading – through the tall windows and out into the dark gardens. *'In and out the*

windows –' Shrieks and laughter patterned through the singing. Voices were a little slurred. Over the lawn, round the tree, through the rose garden – dismayed squeals as thorns caught at silks and fine chiffon – up the steps and back into the ballroom. *'Stand and face your lover –'*

And once again, Rachel had gone. At some point, hands linked, hands dropped, she had disappeared. She was nowhere to be seen. Oddly philosophical – or perhaps not so very oddly considering the extremely large brandy to which he had helped himself in the library after his father, all disciplined silence and tight lips, had left – he accepted the enthusiastic kiss of a bright-eyed girl in red and black and joined a group of friends about to broach one of the last bottles of champagne.

Rachel sat in the shadows, beyond the lights, a half-full bottle of champagne on the steps at her feet. Distantly she heard the laughter. Distantly she heard the music. Light and shadow danced, mingled, blurred. She dashed a tired hand across her eyes, for a moment bowed her face into her hands, then lifted her head, looking into the darkness.

Far off, will o' the wisp light glinted, infinitely mysterious; came and went, wraithlike, inviting. Near where she sat, perched upon the top step of a flight that led down through a paved garden then on through a little wooden gate into the copses and woodlands of the estate, a woollen picnic blanket lay discarded upon a chair. She picked it up, draped it about her shoulders against the chill of the night air. The lights glimmered again, vague and distant as a promise unfulfilled.

She picked up the bottle and drank from it, pensively. A gust of music and laughter; voices singing, *'Should auld acquaintance be forgot?'*

She stood, kicked off her shoes and, bottle in hand, stepped into the cool September darkness.

The woodlands were eerily still. The small stream rushed and rippled, even that sound, of its moving waters, muted in the darkness. A sleepy bird stirred and chirruped as she passed, then settled again to sleep. Something rustled in the undergrowth, and was still. Ahead the rosy, dimly-gleaming lights glimmered alluringly, flickering like firelight through the trees as she walked. The grass was soft and chillingly cold on her feet. She stopped, drank from the bottle again, a pale, ghostly figure in the darkness, the silver-blue beaded silk pale as moonlight. As she approached them the lights steadied, resolved themsleves into a line of lanterns, set along the grassy ride where she had seen Philippa and Gideon, that was now strewn with straw, the coops gone. The young pheasants, not yet roosting, rustled and stirred, made small, trustful, sleepy noises. The ride, the lantern-light flickering upon the surrounding trees, looked like a glade from a fairy tale. Ogres and elves and lovely fairy maidens. Witches and bears and handsome princes . . .

The sudden footstep behind her startled but did not frighten her. When a hard, ungentle hand fell upon her shoulder, however, she yelped, as much in anger as in fear, and swung round to find herself looking into a dark and bearded face under a battered keeper's hat. The man appeared in the dim light to be as taken aback as she was herself. At the sound of the small scuffle the birds, disturbed, chucked alarmedly.

Rachel wrenched herself from the bruising grip. 'What the hell do you think you're up to?'

'I might ask the same of you, miss.'

Disconcerted he might be, but the man's pale eyes were narrowed suspiciously. His eyes flicked over her.

Rachel drew the picnic blanket about her and lifted her chin. 'I came out for a walk, if it's any of your business.'

'The birds are my business, miss.' He had a strong, Norfolk countryman's accent. The light, suspicious eyes did not flinch from her furious glare.

'You surely don't believe that I intended any of your wretched birds harm?'

''Tis hard to say, miss, what people's intentions are. At the very least 'tis a foolhardy thing for a young lady like yourself to be wanderin' the woods at this time o'night.'

'Why?'

'Varmints.' The word, soft and sharp in her ear, made her jump almost from her skin. A tall, black shape had materialized apparently from nowhere at her side. 'Unpleasant things, varmints. An' they come in all shapes and sizes.' Gideon Best slung the long barrelled shotgun he carried across his shoulder, tilted his wide-brimmed hat lower over his eyes. Kili stood poised, a small, dark shadow, at his heels. 'Like Gummer here says, 'tis no place for a – young lady.' Faint, unexpected and undoubtedly insolent derision threaded the last words.

'I – came out for a walk –' Rachel recognized the almost childish defiance in the reiterated words. Suddenly, as the champagne-induced confidence that had carried her here drained away she was nowhere near as sure of herself, suddenly the darkness and the flickering shadows were oppressive. Dangerous.

'I'm perfectly capable of taking care of myself. Unfortunately your friend here seems to think I have some kind of designs on your charges.'

'If you had you wouldn't be the only one,' Gideon said, drily grim. 'All right, Gummer. I'll handle this. Thanks, Mush. You did well.'

The other man grinned, suddenly relaxing. 'You sure you can manage? This 'un look a pretty desperate character to me.'

Gideon hitched the long gun higher on his shoulder. 'I'll yell if I need you.'

'Right.' Teeth gleaming, the man faded into the darkness.

Rachel, in silence, faced Gideon. Lantern-light flickered upon his face, shaded by the wide brim of his hat. She remembered, suddenly, the still, tall figure who had watched as she had stood naked by the lake and despite herself her cheeks grew hot. 'I'll go then,' she said.

'Not alone.'

'Why not?'

He shrugged.

'You think there are poachers about?'

'Could be.'

'They wouldn't hurt me. They wouldn't dare.'

Gideon clicked his tongue, muttered a word she did not know.

'What's that? What was that word you used?'

He turned his head. 'Dinli,' he repeated, shortly.

'What's that supposed to mean?'

'It means "fool".' The words were very soft and very clear.

'I think you're insolent.' Her teeth were clenched so hard against temper she could barely speak.

He eyed her levelly. 'And you know what I think of you. We're both probably right. Come.'

Wordlessly, the dog at his heels, he led the way through the ride, past the straw in which the birds nestled snugly, to a dark path that struck off at right angles. He moved, she noticed, almost without sound. Big as he was, booted and gaitered, he made less sound than she did with her bare feet upon the grass. 'Wait –.' She caught her breath abruptly and stopped. Something sharp had cut into her foot. Bending she peered at it. Black in the darkness, blood welled. 'Damn it!'

He stood a little way from her. 'What is it?'

'Nothing.' She gritted her teeth, put her foot to the floor.

'Let me see.'

'I told you. It's nothing.' She still held the almost empty bottle of champagne. Defiantly she took a mouthful, then bent and tipped the rest over the cut foot. 'There. All better.'

'Show me.'

'It's nothing, I tell you.'

He knelt beside her, picked up her foot in his hard, warm hand. She grabbed his shoulder to steady herself. A small light flashed. 'It's not much. But it's deep.' Gideon straightened, pocketed the small torch, took the bottle from her and tucked it beneath a fallen log by the side of the path. 'It needs cleaning, and covering.'

Feeling quite as foolish as he thought her she put her foot gingerly to the floor, hobbling on her toe, trying to keep the damaged heel out of the dirt.

'I'll carry you.'

'You won't,' she said, smartly.

He did not bother to reply. She felt his hand upon her shoulder, a strong arm beneath her knees and, unceremoniously, she was in his arms, not gently or comfortably. She struggled to free an arm and then, having done it, realized the only sensible place to put it was about his shoulders. He hefted her a little higher settling her in his arms, she thought, like a sack of turnips, then

108

set off in silence with long, easy strides along the path, Kili padding along behind.

'Where are we going? This isn't the way I came.'

'You expect me to carry you all the way back to the house?' he asked, very drily.

She chewed her lip, angry as much with herself as with him.

Within a very few minutes they were at the edge of the wood. Rachel sensed rather than saw in the darkness the beginning of the open fields. A square shape loomed. With no warning Gideon swung her to the ground. Rachel hopped uncertainly on one foot. The cut heel was hurting badly now, and she could feel the stickiness of blood. Gideon threw open the door, slid a strong arm about her waist and all but lifted her across the threshold. 'Stay still. I'll light the lamp.'

She waited, the injured foot lifted, steadying herself by the doorjamb. A match was struck and flared into life. Gideon bent above the lamp. She watched him as he lit it and replaced the globe of smoky glass about the flame. In the hard, steady light the harsh, oddly foreign-looking planes and angles of his face, the hawk nose, the grim line of jaw were thrown into uncompromising relief. He looked, she thought, with a sudden stirring of unease, a savage, an exotic and dangerous beast of prey. Then he stood, and turned, and the dark face was back in perspective, withdrawn as always, the eyes, a flat slate-black now that the lamplight no longer caught them, guarded. 'Sit,' he said brusquely to Rachel, and as brusquely gestured to the dog, who trotted obediently to her corner and curled up with a small, thankful grunt upon a threadbare blanket.

Containing an exasperation that, oddly, she suspected might at any moment turn to slightly hysterical laughter, Rachel hopped to an uncomfortable-looking wooden armchair and sat. As Gideon busied himself pouring water from a jug into an enamel basin and rummaging in a small cupboard for a doubtful-looking jar of ointment she looked around, taking in the monastic neatness of the place, the utilitarian maleness of it. No small frivolity brightened the atmosphere, no small comfort spoke of home.

Gideon brought the bowl, the ointment, a roll of bandage and a scrap of clean towel to her. His brown, competent hands moved with precise care. He lifted her foot. It looked gratifyingly nasty – the lips of the small wound gaped, blood oozed and dripped blackly.

'I'm sorry, I'm afraid I'm dripping on your nice clean floor.'

He shrugged dismissively, not looking at her, his eyes on the wound as he bathed it, none too gently. 'It's only blood.'

Rachel gestured to an unseen onlooker. 'It's only blood,' she confided. 'My blood. No problem.'

Gideon's lips twitched a little. He glanced at her with those odd, dark, gold-shadowed eyes. Then he stood and went to the cupboard on the wall.

At sight of the whisky bottle Rachel smiled her most practised and beguiling smile. 'That's the best idea you've had all night.' The sentence ended on a small, undignified yelping scream as, with no warning he tipped the raw, stinging alcohol onto the wound. 'Gosh,' she said after a moment, blinking away the tears of pain, 'what a waste of good liquor!'

Again that small, tight, almost reluctant smile.

'Don't you ever laugh?' Rachel asked, flippant to the end, her foot feeling as if it were being chewed by tigers.

'When there's something to laugh at.' He had opened the tin of ointment and, this time with more gentleness than he'd shown all night, was smoothing it over the wound.

'Try me.'

Dismayingly, the words did not come out anywhere near as lightly as she had intended. The moving, soothing fingers hesitated, then worked on. Rachel, to her confusion and horror felt the humiliating prick of tears behind her eyes.

Silence fell. Suddenly enwrapped in self-pity she watched him as he bandaged the foot, then unravelled his length to stand, towering, beside her. She sat, utterly still, not looking at him, her lovely face set, oddly empty.

He moved about the room in that easy, silent way of his. She looked into the distance; remembered the look on poor Hugo's face, remembered Daphne, angular, unlovely, corrosively envied, remembered Toby's fair, handsome face. 'Are you looking forward to getting married?' 'Why yes. Of course.'

'Here.' A tumbler, half-full, was thrust at her. Gideon sat on the pallet bed in the corner, hunched forward, elbows on knees, as far from her as he could get, a mug nursed in his hands.

She sipped the whisky. Hot and harsh it scorched her throat. She swallowed a cough.

Gideon tilted his head and swallowed, easily and, she thought, with some relief. He splashed more whisky into the mug. 'We'll have to fit you out with a pair of my boots to get you home.' His speech, and the accent upon the words, like his looks, were oddly alien, outlandish, as were those occasional slips when he used the words of his mother tongue.

'That'll be fun,' she said.

He lifted his head. 'Why did you come to the coverts?'

It was the first time she could recall his actually asking anything close to a personal question.

'I don't know,' she said, lightly. 'Do you know? *Someone* must know?' She took a mouthful of whisky, held it, swallowed it, did not choke. 'I expect I was drunk.'

'You're not drunk.'

'I know.' She suddenly felt desperately, overwhelmingly tired. She toasted him with her glass. 'Hellish, isn't it? I do try.'

'Why?'

There was a very long moment's silence. Kili on her blanket stirred, rolled onto her back, blissful in sleep.

'Because –' she watched him for a moment – stranger, outsider, priest of silence, '– because I'm not what people think I am.'

The shadow of a smile flickered. 'Who is?'

She laughed a little, thinking still of Toby. 'True.'

They drank in a suddenly easier silence. Rachel's foot throbbed. 'And you?' she asked.

He lifted enquiring brows.

'Are you what people think you are?'

'Who knows? Who knows what they think I am?'

'And who cares?' she prompted, gently.

His smile this time glinted like sunshine on water. He did not reply.

'You're lucky,' she said.

He shrugged, face closing again.

Rachel drained her glass. 'I ought to go. If they miss me they'll worry.'

'Aye.'

Neither moved.

'I'm sorry to have been such a bother,' she said.

'No bother.'

She laughed. 'I can't remember the last time I apologized to anyone. It isn't a habit of mine.' She set down the glass, stood up. 'I really should get back to the house.'

'Wait.' He brought a pair of boots from the cupboard, comically large and heavy, clown-sized upon her slim feet. She stood in them, laughing, fell a little towards him, knowing well what she did. He caught her, balanced her, stepped back, untouched. She took a couple of awkward steps, held out her hand. He took it, but stood no closer. 'Stay,' he said to Kili, who at the sound of movement had stood, alert and ready. The dog looked at him reproachfully, then curled into her blanket again.

They left the hut, walked the well-trodden path to the lawns before the still brightly-lit house. Car doors slammed, farewells echoed on the chill air.

'Thanks,' Rachel said. 'I can manage now.' She slid her feet from the ungainly boots, held them out to him. He took them with no word, turned.

'Gideon?'

He stopped. Turned back. Watchful. Wary.

'Thanks,' she said again.

He lifted a hand, melted into the shadows. She stood for a moment before, gingerly, she walked across the smooth grass to the stone balcony that led into the all but wrecked ballroom. 'Rachel!' Hugo galloped to her like an over-affectionate puppy dog, 'Where on *earth* have you been? We've been looking absolutely *everywhere*!'

In the shadows beyond the lawn a stiller, darker shadow stood for some minutes, watching the house. Then with no sound Gideon Best turned and melted into the darkness of the woodlands.

Chapter Five

'Winter weddings are miles more romantic than summer ones, aren't they? Do you think it might snow? It would be super if it did. Oh, golly, just look at my hair – whatever am I going to do with it? Rachel, do come and help –' Philippa groaned melodramatically, eyeing her reflection in exaggerated despair. 'Whatever are you looking at out there?'

Rachel turned from the window. 'Nothing much.' She was wrapped in a pale crêpe de Chine dressing gown much envied by Philippa who, in her sensible wool, found the temperature in this pretty room of Rachel's, with the fire roaring up the chimney almost unbearable. Hanging on the wardrobe door was a suit of fine wool, a deep cream colour trimmed with burgundy, the long, narrow jumper-style top belted low upon the hips with a wide burgundy leather belt; Rachel Patten's stylish outfit for the wedding of Toby Smith and Daphne Underscar.

Philippa dragged a comb through her hair, which crackled and flew, lifting from her head as if invested with a manic life of its own. Despite herself Philippa giggled. 'Just *look* at me! I look like a hotchi witchi in a fit!'

Rachel paused in the act of fitting a cigarette into a slender ivory holder. 'A what?'

'A hotchi witchi. A hedgehog. It's what Gideon calls them.' She tugged again. 'Rachel, do help! I can't go to Toby's wedding looking a perfect fright!'

'For heaven's sake!' Good-naturedly Rachel took the comb from her hand. 'Don't go at it like a bull at a gate! It's hair, not wire wool – here –' She tipped a little water from a jug into a bowl on the washstand, damped her hands, flattened the recalcitrant hair, then with competent movements combed it smooth.

'Gosh, thanks.' Thoughtfully Philippa eyed Rachel's own sleek, shining cap of blue-black hair. 'Do you think perhaps I should dye it?'

'Good God, no!' Rachel was startled into a spurt of laughter. 'Whatever for?'

'Well – it's a bit nondescript, isn't it? Sort of – English brown. Yours is much nicer.'

Rachel, standing behind her, laid two long, narrow hands each side of her head, looking at her in the mirror. 'Flip, my love, your hair is perfectly nice the way it is. As is the rest of you.'

'There. You see what I mean?' Philippa pulled a gloomy face.

'What?'

'Nice. Perfectly nice. What kind of a person is that to be?' Unable to sustain the gloom she grinned, pulling a face at herself in the mirror. 'I bet no-one ever called Pola Negri "perfectly nice". Or Mata Hari.' She tilted her head back, looking up at Rachel. 'Or you for that matter. "Perfectly nice" is hardly your style, is it?'

'Oh?' Rachel drifted back to the window, stood looking out into the darkness of the December morning. 'What do you think is my "style", then?' Her voice was indulgent still, yet once again, as so often in these past days, Philippa had the strange impression that Rachel's attention was not on what she was saying; not, indeed upon the world around her at all. Not that she had not been a most amiable and benign hostess, accompanying her young guest on her energetic frontal assault upon wintry London's galleries, museums, shops and parks with scarcely a murmur; it was simply that, every now and again, she seemed to slip into some private, distant world of her own.

'Perfectly fascinating?' Philippa essayed now, watching her with a grin. 'Perfectly – 'ow you say it? – irr-es-ist-ible?' She swooped from her chair, flourishing her hair brush, her finger under her nose like a moustache. 'Ma'mselle – you are the verree vision of lerveliness and pulchritude!'

'*What!*' Her clowning had the desired effect. Rachel turned, laughing. 'Oh, Flip, you are a fool! Where in the world did you get that from?'

'E. M. Hull.' Cheerfully Philippa tossed the brush on the bed, then threw herself, bouncing, after it. 'Matty Burford's got every one of her books. She hires them out to read under the bed-clothes.'

'Hires them out?'

'Yes. You know – cakes from home. Toffees from the tuck. She's a perfect pig.'

'But an enterprising one.' Rachel, smiling, picked up the cigarette holder again, lit the cigarette, drew in smoke on a long breath.

'I suppose so.' Philippa propped her head upon her hand. 'Rachel, it was awfully good of you to suggest I came and stayed with you and your father for these few days. I do hope I haven't been a pest?'

'Of course you have. The most pesty person I've ever come across. I shall most certainly never invite you again.'

Philippa grinned. 'It was jolly good of the Doc to put up with me, too. This is a super house, isn't it? I can't think why you don't live here all the time, instead of in that poky little hole of a flat,' she added with the brutal candour of true friendship.

Exasperated, Rachel reached for the bedspread, pulled at it sharply so that Philippa rolled almost to the floor. 'That poky little hole of a flat is my home,' she said. 'Believe it or not, I like it. Harley Street smells of antiseptic. It hits you every time you come round the corner. Yuk. Now –.' She tugged at the bedspread again. Philippa squealed, clinging to the edge of the bed, giggling. 'Out! You may be going to this tiresome wedding in your dressing gown but I most certainly am not. So shoo!' She slipped the dressing gown from her shoulders, stood in lace-trimmed ivory crêpe de Chine camiknickers, leaned towards the mirror, eyeing herself critically, pushed an experimental finger into the heavy cap of hair.

'Loveliness!' Philippa faked a swoon, hand upon heart. 'Pulchritude!'

'Murder!' Rachel pounced on her, dragging a pillow from the bed. 'Mayhem!' She fetched an inexpert swipe at the breathlessly laughing Philippa, who dodged it with ease and fled to the door, poking out her tongue and waggling her fingers on the end of her nose.

'Pillows at ten paces. I'm an expert. Dorm champion. You wouldn't stand a chance.'

'I don't doubt it.' Rachel tossed the pillow back onto the bed. 'But if you value your life, young lady, I should scarper. Now. The others will be here in an hour or so.'

'Yes, miss. Of course, miss.' Philippa sidled out of the door, popped her head back round it. 'Can I borrow some scent? Anything'll do. As long as it's expensive and classy.'

'Pest! Here –' Rachel tossed a small bottle. Philippa caught it one handed. 'Now go!'

An hour later they assembled in the pleasant sitting room – Rachel, Philippa and Rachel's father Ben Patten – and eyed each other appreciatively.

'You look absolutely stunning, my darling.' Ben Patten, a big man, his shock of hair iron grey, kissed Rachel's cheek lightly, the austere lines of his square-jawed, craggy face softening, as always, as he looked at her. 'And as for our Philippa –' He spread big, bony hands. 'A transformation! My dear, you look perfectly lovely!'

Philippa blushed a fiery red, smoothed the russet velvet of her dress. The dropped waist, decorated with a russet satin sash and bow and the short, swirling skirt were, she knew, flattering to a figure that had lamentably still not shed all of its puppy fat. The colour suited her well, her hair and eyes shone like fresh-peeled chestnuts against its autumnal glow. Flushed and excited, even she had to concede that the face she glimpsed in the mantel mirror seemed almost a stranger's – a grown up stranger's. The only fly in the ointment of her happiness was that Matty Burford was not here to witness the transformation; she made a mental note to make sure she got into the photographs. Matty would be puce with envy.

'You're looking pretty snazzy yourself.' Rachel patted his wide shoulders in the well-fitting morning suit. 'When are the others picking us up?' Sally and Eddie Brown had arranged to pick them up by taxi before going on to St Mary's in Upper Street, Islington for the ceremony.

'Any minute now.'

Rachel walked to the table where stood the sherry decanter

and glasses. 'Time for a quick one then. Dry or medium?'

'Medium,' Philippa said, smartly.

'We don't have any medium lemonade.'

'Oh, come on, Rachel – don't be mean –' The doorbell rang.

'It's Mother!' the grown-up Philippa squealed without taking breath and shot from the room like a bullet from a gun.

Ben laughed, softly, and Rachel smiled in return, pouring sherry. By the time Bartlett, Ben's housekeeper ushered the newcomers into the room she was standing, tray in hand, like any well-trained footman.

'Ben.' Eddie Browne held out a slim, strong hand. 'Good to see you again. And Rachel.' He turned, smiling widely. He was an attractive man of wiry build and jaunty bearing, dark skinned and dark eyed. 'Lovelier than ever, by golly.' He kissed her cheek with quite openly more than avuncular enthusiasm, the intelligent eyes gleaming amusement. His voice was broadly and bluntly Yorkshire.

She grinned back at him. 'Drink?'

'I'll say. But none of that lady's eyewash if you please. You've whisky?'

She jerked her head, amused. 'In the decanter.'

'That'll do me, then.' He turned away, reaching for the decanter.

Sally, behind him, rolled her eyes to heaven before leaning to kiss Rachel warmly. 'Rachel, love – you look absolutely marvellous. And what about Flip – doesn't she look the bees' knees?'

Philippa, stuck like a burr to her mother's side, blushed and pulled a silly face.

'Thanks so much for having her for these past few days. She's obviously had a marvellous time.' The years had not erased the traces of London from Sally's husky voice.

'It's nothing. I've enjoyed it. I wanted her to come. I wouldn't have suggested it otherwise.'

Sally, knowing Rachel as she did, accepted that as the simple truth. 'You're a braver man than most. She'll talk the hind leg off a donkey one of these days.'

'Mum, honestly!'

Ben had moved over to them. Sally turned, and politely they kissed, barely brushing cheeks. 'Sherry, Sal?'

'Yes. Thank you.'

'You're looking well.'

Eddie joined them, an arm about Philippa's shoulders. Rachel took a glass of sherry and sipped it, watching. Painful childhood memories, long and savagely suppressed, stirred. Voices heard through a wall. Her mother's – cool, controlled, contemptuous. Sally's name, thrown at her father like a sharpened blade. And other, more terrible things, that even now Rachel could not think of without anguish.

She tossed back the sherry. Replenished the glass. Carried the decanter to the others. 'Refill, Sally? Pa?'

They were talking of the exciting new discovery made by the British bacteriologist Alexander Fleming. 'Please God, this is the way through –,' Ben was saying, '– it's got to be the most important medical breakthrough of the century.'

Rachel topped them up, smiled at Eddie's conspiratorial wink, replaced the decanter. Outside the sky was darkening. Perhaps Flip's wish for snow might yet be granted. Restlessly Rachel wandered to the window, stood looking down at the waiting taxi, only half listening to the ebb and flow of the conversation behind her. Like a tongue returning to a sore tooth the recollection of that awful night twinged painfully in her mind and not for the first time she allowed herself to wonder – had her mother's accusations been true? Had Ben Patten and Sally Van Damme as she was then, been lovers? And if they had – where had it gone, that love? How could they stand now, like polite strangers passing the time, talking of penicillin, of the obscenity trial at the Old Bailey that had brought such notoriety to the lesbian author of *The Well of Loneliness*, of the death of Emmeline Pankhurst – did nothing last? Was it true that the purest and most violent of passions could be whittled and worn away by time? The depressing thought settled on her heart like a stone.

Philippa was talking now, rattling away like a machine gun, words and laughter tumbling together breathlessly. Rachel turned. Philippa had her arm about her mother's waist, half leaning upon her in an easy, affectionate way. As Rachel watched

Sally lifted a hand and smoothed a wayward strand from her laughing daughter's face.

The twist of jealousy that suddenly gripped Rachel was like a physical pain. 'Time to go.'

To Philippa's delight it began to snow just as they reached the church. The building was cold, the smell of flowers sweet on the chill air. Rachel sat straight and still, her smooth face expressionless as, beside her, Philippa fidgeted and craned her neck to inspect the other guests. At the front of the church Toby sat unmoving, awaiting his bride. Watching the back of his fair, curly head Rachel to her surprise at first felt nothing, just a chill emptiness that matched the atmosphere of the cold and slightly forbidding building in which she sat. Perhaps, then, the day would not be such an ordeal as she had thought? Perhaps the very finality of what she was about to witness would cauterize that wound that had bled for so long and leave her free and whole at last? Her eyes fixed upon the flower-decked altar she found herself praying for the first time in many years. Please. Let it be so.

Daphne arrived exactly on time, walked, with long, slightly awkward strides, but smiling composedly, down the aisle on her father's arm, followed by two self-consciously giggling little girls in pale blue, low-waisted dresses and little Dutch-style caps who clutched posies of blue and white flowers. The bride's own dress was simple and paid only lip service to the fashions of the day, its waist a little lower perhaps than was natural, the hemline a little higher in front, balancing the graceful train at the back. The sheened satin glowed softly white in the light of the candles. As she joined him at the altar Toby glanced down at her with a smile.

In that moment Rachel knew that an uncaring deity had not heard her prayer. She stood, cold and still as a statue, her eyes upon the carved head of a cross-eyed cherub that decorated the end of the pew in front of her; concentrating on it with every ounce of strength she possessed. It was an ugly thing, ill-executed and quite disturbingly unchildlike. One ear was higher than the other and the eyes squinted alarmingly. The service had begun. She stood and sat, obediently, with the rest of the congregation. She neither sang the hymns, glanced at the Order of Service nor watched the celebrants. The cherub's ugly little face grinned vacuously at her. Deliberately she emptied her mind, let her eyes wander to the brilliant stained glass window above the altar. She had never experienced such unutterable, painful misery.

The ceremony was mercifully short, though by its end, oddly, she was fighting a desire to curl beside her father and sleep; to drift into that dreamless, secure sleep of childhood from which his familiar face had so often woken her and which had eluded her now for almost as long as she could remember.

By the time bride, groom and guests spilled out to where the cars awaited them in the road outside it was snowing hard. Rachel stood back as, in a shower of confetti, the newly-weds ran to the leading car. The temptation to turn and walk away, to refuse to take further part in this farce was almost overwhelming. She shivered.

'Hey, what's this?' Her father took her by the arm, ushered her towards a car. 'You'll catch your death standing there in the cold.'

The reception was held at a nearby hotel. She ate nothing and drank far too much. She sat through the interminable speeches, answered when spoken to and as far as was possible kept her eyes from the tall, ungainly figure of the bride and her new husband. Her congratulations were brief, the kiss she deposited on Daphne's cheek was as cold as the snow that drifted past the windows. She herself felt frozen – frozen in a misery she could share with no-one. Frozen to death, and no-one to notice. The noise about her hurt her head. Her face, rigid as ice smiled and smiled, a smile empty as a harlot's promise. She drank glass after glass of heady wine, desperate for the help it might offer to see her through the next few hours. Oblivion would be better – *anything* would be better – than this canker of pain that she could not show. She spoke inanities to the young man next to her, laughed too loudly and too long, herself heard the steadily increasing note of hysteria in her blurred voice. At last she could stand it no longer. Excusing herself brusquely she stood, a little unsteadily. The room tilted. Toby was on his feet, speaking easily and with humour, his smile engaging. He caught her eye as she struggled to extricate herself from her chair, the feet of which were embedded in the soft carpet. A deferential waiter stepped forward to help. The shadow of a frown flickered in Toby's eyes. Faces were turned, politely enquiring. Gritting her teeth against the sickly shifting of the room about her she walked in what she hoped was a composed straight line to the door. Toby's voice resumed. There was appreciative laughter. A waiter opened the heavy door for her and then shut it behind her, cutting off sound. She was in a long, deeply-carpeted corridor, lofty, much embellished, all gilt and mirrors and crimson drapes. Huge chandeliers glittered harshly, the light blurring in her tired eyes. She leaned against the wall for a moment making a determined effort to still the awful swimming of her head, the faint queasiness of her stomach. A bit of peace and quiet, that was what she needed. And a brandy. A large one, to settle her beastly stomach and clear her head. That would do the trick. Taking a deep breath she pushed herself away from the wall and walked, slowly and carefully towards the discreetly curtained bar at the end of the corridor.

A half hour later she knew in that clear, ice-cold part of her brain that still almost jealously nursed her pain, that she was very drunk indeed. Practice and concentration had schooled her tongue as she had ordered first one and then another large brandy. Now, with bladder bursting and stomach rebelling she was not certain she could summon the reserves to get her from her seat at a secluded table to the door marked 'Powder Room'. She could not for the life of her remember what she had done with her handbag. Had she brought it with her when she left the reception? She did not know. All she knew was that with every passing moment a trip to the sanctuary of the ludicrously named Powder Room became more imperative. Gingerly she eased herself up, holding to the table. The room spun, settled a little. She saw the barman glance at her enquiringly. She took a deep, steadying breath, headed, she hoped in a straight line, for the door.

The Powder Room was very pink, over-luxurious and hot as a tropical night. She stood for a moment, dizzily, her reflection swaying in the many mirrors that gleamed endlessly about the walls. Deep chairs were set before tables and mirrors. She stumbled to one, sank into it, dropped her face to her cupped hands.

The world spun like a top.

She only just made it into the cubicle in time to be wrenchingly, miserably sick. She leaned above the soiled bowl, hating the acrid smell, hating the mess, hating herself. She pulled the chain, and heaved again as the water gushed. It was long minutes before she could muster the strength to make it to the bowls and taps that lined the wall. She ran cold water, rinsed her mouth, splashed her face and hands, drenching the front of her suit as she did so. She picked up a towel and buried her face in it. At least the dizzying movement had stopped and her stomach had settled. She felt utterly empty and, even in this overheated room desolately chill. She was trembling. She stood for a long while, fighting weakness, fighting tears, but it was too much. Trailing the towel still in her hand she went back to the chair, dropped into it, surveyed her reflection in the mirror in despair. Her thin face was pale as clay, her eyes were dark-ringed, her hair tousled. The tears which streaked her face had made her mascara smudge and run. She looked like a clown. Exhausted, utterly wretched, she laid her head upon her arms, making no attempt now to stop the painful sobs. Only gradually did they die; long after the alcohol had taken its effect and she had slipped into a sleep that was almost unconsciousness her breath caught and hiccoughed in her throat and tears slid damply through her untidy hair onto the towel on which she had laid her head.

It was Fiona who found her; at least, it was Fiona who made the attempt to wake her – God alone knew how many other startled and no doubt disapproving guests had come and gone in the meantime about her all-but-unconscious form. Rachel pulled away from the insistent hand upon her shoulder, turned her head, muttered incomprehensively.

'Rachel! Oh, Good Lord! – Rachel!' Fiona shook her again.

Far, far away, from the comfort of oblivion, Rachel heard her, and with all her might resisted the concerned voice, the urgent hand on her shoulder. She turned her face into the towel. Her mouth tasted foul, her head rang like a gong, her eyes were sore and swollen from crying; she refused to open them. Determinedly she tried to slide back into the darkness.

The door banged. There was a moment's quiet. Then it opened again. This time there were two voices. 'Rachel, love – wake up. Do try –' Sally's cool hand rested upon her hot forehead, the words were quiet.

'Help me get her on her feet.' Fiona's nursing voice, crisp and cool. 'She's already been sick by the look of it. 'Come on now, Rachel, open those eyes.'

Rachel stayed slumped over the table, a dead weight upon their hands. She did not want to open her eyes. She wanted to die. Right there and then, she wanted to die.

'Perhaps I'd better get Ben?' Sally asked, uncertainly.

'No!' That opened Rachel's swollen eyes. She grabbed at Sally's arm, her long, blood red nails scratching painfully. 'No! Don't tell him! Please, Sally –' She stopped, flinching as the light speared into her confused brain. Maudlin tears had started again. 'Please don't let him see me like this. I couldn't bear it. I couldn't!' The words were slurred, her voice edged with hysteria; she could not control her tongue.

'All right. All right.' Fiona again, quiet and reassuring. 'We won't tell him. Calm down, Rachel. We won't let him see you. I promise.' She exchanged a look with Sally over the sobbing girl's head, eyebrows raised in exasperation. 'James,' she mouthed.

Sally nodded, turned and slipped from the room.

'Now then.' Fiona slipped a strong supporting arm about Rachel's shoulders. 'Try to stand, love.'

Rachel, crying uncontrollably again, shook her head.

'Try.' Firmly Fiona heaved her to her feet. She stood, swaying.

'Oh God! I'm going to be –' She clapped a hand to her mouth.

Fiona propelled her at great speed into the cubicle and left her to it. When, pale and shaking, she finally emerged Fiona handed her a clean, wet towel with no comment. Rachel staggered back to the chair, put the towel over her head and sat, elbows on the table, her aching head supported in her hands. She was still crying as if she would never stop.

'I never cry,' she said.

She felt the touch of Fiona's hand upon her shoulder.

'Never.' A little calmer she pressed the towel to her face and roughly rubbed the smell of vomit from her hair. Then she emerged, flinching, into the light again. 'Jesus!' she said, 'look at me!' She turned then, directly to Fiona for the first time. 'Fee, please, help me get past Pa? I can't – I *can't* – let him see me like this.' Her tongue felt thick and furred as a dog's pelt, it refused to enunciate clearly. 'I'm sorry. I'm so sorry. But please, just help me get back to the flat.'

The door opened and Sally slipped quietly into the room. 'He's outside,' she said to Fiona, then, 'How are you feeling?' she asked Rachel.

Rachel's head jerked back. 'Who? Who's outside? Not Pa?'

'No, no. James,' Sally said soothingly. 'But Ben is asking for you. Toby and Daphne left half an hour ago. Everyone's leaving.'

'Tell him—' Rachel stopped, her brain all but paralysed.

'Tell him she met an old friend,' Fiona improvised swiftly. 'And she's gone off for a few drinks with him.'

Rachel winced.

'Tell him – oh, come on, Rachel, what would you say?'

Rachel struggled. 'Tell him – tell him I've gone off to celebrate the fact it's Toby who got married today and not me.' The faintest and weariest of smiles flickered. 'He'll believe that. Tell him I'll go back to the flat. I'll be in touch in a day or two.' Exhausted at the effort her head dropped forward.

'Right.' Sally turned. 'You can manage?' she asked Fiona.

Fiona nodded, dropped a quick kiss on her cheek. 'Off you go. Try to get Ben out of the way. Tell James we'll be out in a moment or two.'

Fifteen minutes later, halfway across the dark, snowy car park, Rachel's knees buckled and but for James' arm about her she would have slid to the ground. Puffing a little he hauled her tall form into his arms. 'Just get her to the car,' Fiona said, unruffled.

'But Fee – we can't just dump her back at her flat in this condition!'

124

She eased the girl's nodding head onto his shoulder. 'We aren't going to. We're taking her home. To Breckon.'

Daphne Underscar Smith looked out of the train window into the snow that swept past like a dazzling, dizzily streaming white curtain, blocking any view. It had been a tiring day. Exciting, too. She glanced at Toby, sitting opposite. Unexpectedly, as if sensing her attention he caught her eye and smiled. Absurdly embarrassed, she smiled back. They had already, when first they had boarded the train at Victoria, exchanged comments upon the day – rather, she had thought, like acquaintances exchanging pleasant gossip about a party they had both attended. Since then they had travelled in a not uncomfortable and occasionally broken silence. The rest of the first class carriage was empty. She suspected that her father had reserved all half dozen of the seats – and the warmth, the regular, rhythmic click of the wheels and the rocking movement was making her sleepy. She longed to kick off her shoes and tuck her feet up onto the seat beside her, but could not summon the nerve. Toby, neat and relaxed, looked fresh and alert as he had throughout the long day. He was looking out of the window again. She eyed him covertly. Odd – not to say totally unbelievable – that this man, this all but unknown man, would now have such an influence on her life. Would he disapprove if she took off her shoes and put her feet up? She did not know. In fact she knew very little about him altogether; since he had joined Underscars some months before he had spent a great deal more time with her father than he had with her. Not that that had surprised or disappointed her – she had known from the start the basis upon which this marriage was founded. And now here they were. Man and wife, and travelling to Brighton on honeymoon. A small worm of unease uncurled and stretched in the pit of her stomach. She cleared a throat that had suddenly become inexplicably dry.

Toby glanced at her, smiling. 'Not long now.'

She did not for a moment misinterpret his meaning. She knew with absolute certainty that he could not have guessed her thoughts. Yet nevertheless she felt embarrassed colour flood to her face. She nodded, reached for the magazine that Toby had bought for her at the station. Looked at its shining pages as she turned them apparently idly with sightless eyes. The text might have been written in Arabic for all the sense it made. Something ridiculously like panic had set her heart thudding uncomfortably, her face, she knew, was still flushed and blotchy. Heartily she wished the week away. Why hadn't she *told* Toby that she didn't need – didn't want – a honeymoon? Why had she allowed the silly plan to go ahead? And above all why, oh why, had she bought that ridiculous nightdress? In the shop it had looked so splendid – ravishing, the shop assistant had said. A nightdress for a honeymoon. How absurd. How utterly absurd. Shopping for her trousseau had been a nightmare; the nightdress, she thought with a certain tart humour had been the logical outcome. Peppermint silk indeed! Whatever had she been thinking of?

The train swayed as it streamed around a curve. Daphne shut the magazine, looked out into the darkness again. It had almost stopped snowing. She could see her own reflection; long, plain face, prominent teeth, a stylish hat perched on the frizz of her hair like a bird on an ill-trimmed bush. She looked hastily away, down at her gloved fingers that were laced in her lap. She would have been perfectly happy to go straight to the house they had bought in Bayswater, the house she had spent the last months decorating and furnishing, the cost of it her father's personal wedding present to her. But the conventions must be observed in such things, and a week in wintry Brighton it must be. Relaxing a little, and good sense asserting itself again she almost found herself smiling, albeit wryly, at the recollection of waspish Aunt Clara's comment, 'In this weather, indeed! I can't think what you're going to do with yourselves!' Aunt Clara, she reflected, was not alone. The bride herself had absolutely no idea of what they were going to 'do with themselves'. It was a thought that had become more and more obtrusive as the weeks had gone by. She had even, blushing, enquired at the library for a book that might enlighten her, but the tome that the stone-faced assistant had produced from the top shelf of the Biology section had done nothing but confuse her more. It had all looked unexpectedly ridiculous and quite demoralizingly undignified. There could be no doubt about it; being brought up by three maiden aunts had left certain gaps in her education.

Thinking of the dotty aunts she found herself glancing at the smart pigskin suitcase that bounced in the netting of the luggage rack above Toby's head. She had been changing into her going-away outfit in the bedroom provided by the hotel when a tap at the door had presaged the entrance of Aunt Clara, always spokeswoman for all three. The old woman, straight as a rod and thin as a whippet, had eyed the blue velvet coat and matching hat with approval, tidied the angle of the hat, inspected the soft new leather gloves and handbag and pronounced herself satisfied that her erstwhile charge had turned herself out in a creditable way for the occasion. She had then slapped a long brown envelope on the dressing table. 'Present for you.'

'But Aunt Clara – you bought us all that lovely china!'

'That was for both of you. This is for you. The shares.'

'What shares?'

Her aunt had tutted impatiently. 'Use your head child. Underscar shares.'

It had taken a further moment to sink in. Then 'You mean – your shares?'

'Certainly. Some of them were your mother's. Only right you should have them now. And then I – we – thought why not the lot?' The old eyes had twinkled shrewdly. Not for nothing had this elderly spinster watched and listened over twenty-five years.

'But I thought – isn't there some kind of legal requirement that my father gets first refusal of Underscar shares?'

'We aren't selling them. We're giving them to you.' The old woman cocked her head a little. 'To you personally, that is. It's all perfectly legal and above board. I checked.' Briskly she had pecked at Daphne's cheek, standing almost on tiptoe to do so. 'Right. I suppose that young whippersnapper will be waiting for you. You'd better be off.'

With no time for thought Daphne had taken the envelope and tucked it into her case. Only as she had sat, rocking to the rhythm of the train and thinking over the excitements of the day had the full significance of the gift hit her.

'Here we are.' The train had slowed, come to a halt with a hiss and shriek of steam. Toby stood up and reached for the cases, swinging them easily from the rack. Courteously he opened the door for her and helped her down from the carriage. The platform was cold, wreathed in steam, small flakes of snow drifted in the foggy yellow light. Toby lifted his hand to a porter. 'We'll take a taxi to the Grand. It isn't far, but it's too cold to walk and anyway it's much easier with the luggage –'

The hotel was warm and glittered with light. The lobby with its sweep of staircase and its grand chandelier was busy. In the distance a dance band played.

'Mr and Mrs Smith? Certainly, sir. If you'd like to follow me?' They followed the pleasant, smartly dressed young man up the stairs, murmured answers to his comments and questions concerning the weather and the journey, stood back while he opened a wide panelled door with a flourish. 'I trust you'll enjoy your stay with us. Your luggage will be up in a moment.' Smiling – knowingly, Daphne thought, though perhaps, she was ready to admit, in her hypersensitive state, unfairly – he withdrew.

Toby tossed hat and gloves onto the glass topped table beside a huge arrangement of hothouse flowers and a bottle of champagne in an ice bucket and looked around. The room was large, and lavishly furnished. Impressive double doors, standing open, led into a bedroom; through them Daphne caught sight of quite the most enormous bed she had ever seen. Toby nodded, satisfied. 'Looks fine, don't you think?'

'I – yes.' Daphne stood, awkwardly clutching her fine blue leather handbag, her feet throbbing in the matching and equally new shoes. Suddenly all she wanted in the world was to throw off her clothes, crawl into that huge, soft bed and sleep. Alone.

Toby had moved behind her. She stood, rigid. 'Here. Let me take your coat.' Clumsily, her fingers all thumbs, she undid the buttons, allowed him to slip the coat from her shoulders. The dark woollen dress she wore beneath it had bunched at the knees. She made a great show of straightening it. Toby slipped his own coat off and walked into the bedroom to hang them in the wardrobe. Daphne reached up to take her hat off and dropped her handbag, which burst open, spilling compact, lipstick, purse, and assorted hairgrips onto the carpet.

'Blast it!'

She was still on her knees when Toby came back into the room. Blessedly, he did not offer to help. 'Why don't you tidy yourself up a little while I open the champagne?'

She fled into the bedroom. There were flowers here, too, on the dressing table. The perfume was heavy. She pulled off her hat, tossed it on the bed, sat on the stool before the dressing table mirror, dragged a comb through her untidy hair. Through the open door she heard the pop of the champagne cork. In a moment Toby appeared, carrying a tall glass of the pale pink, fizzing stuff. The mere sight of it made her feel faintly sick. She smiled, caught sight of the prominent teeth in the mirror, looked away. 'Thank you.'

As he set the glass beside her there was a tap at the door. 'Ah. That must be the luggage.' She watched him through the door, heard the murmur of voices. With a hand that shook very slightly she carefully tipped half the glass of champagne into the flowers. Toby reappeared at the door. 'They want to know if we want to go down to dinner or to eat here? What do you think?

The thought of food had much the same effect upon her stomach as had the sight of the champagne. She hesitated. The bed loomed, big as a house, beside her. 'Let's eat downstairs,' she said, hastily.

'Fine.' He went back into the other room.

Trying to ignore the tiresome and perceptible trembling of her hands she powdered her nose, renewed her lipstick, stood up, smoothing her dress. Pondered for a wild moment upon the possibility of suggesting that they forget about dinner altogether, get the ridiculous and nerve-racking business of the marriage bed over and done with as quickly as possible and with the minimum of fuss and get a good night's sleep. With a quick movement she picked up her glass and drank the sparkling stuff like medicine; almost jumped out of her skin as a big, soft-footed man carrying their cases and followed by a neatly uniformed, smiling maid entered the room.

'Righto.' Cheerfully Toby bent over her shoulder to eye his

reflection in the mirror, running a hand over his curly hair. 'Come and polish off the champagne while they unpack. Then we can change for dinner.'

The evening was a pleasant one; or would have been had Daphne been able to forget or ignore what was to be the logical end of it. They dined well, danced a little, discussed the spate of anti-war books, the ugliness of the Eton crop, and agreed that the latest Noël Coward, *This Year of Grace* looked worth a visit. The tables, and the dance floor, began to empty. The clock ticked on. At last Toby made a great show of looking at his watch, stretching a little in his chair. 'Well. It's been a long day. Time to turn in, I think.' He did not look at her.

It came to her with sudden, blinding clarity that he, too, was nervous. For a terrible moment she found herself wondering if he might not be as ignorant as she; a thought quickly dismissed when she remembered the hints and rumours that had trickled to her ears during the months of their engagement. With a bright, false smile she stood up. 'Absolutely. Oh, absolutely. It's been a terribly tiring day.'

She took his arm, allowed him to escort her out into the lobby and up the stairs. The smell of the flowers enveloped them, heavy and sweet, as he opened the door. 'I thought I might –.' He stopped.

She turned. 'Yes?'

He waved a vague hand. '– might go back down for a nightcap. Leave you to—' He cleared his throat, '—you'll have – things to do?'

Embarrassment hung in the air, heavy as the perfume of the flowers. 'Oh,' she said. 'Yes. Thank you.'

He nodded. Turned. Closed the door quietly behind him.

She stood for a long time, absolutely still, where he had left her. Disappointment and relief warred within her. What had she expected? That he might sweep her from her feet, carry her across the threshold? Murmur sweet nothings about the delights of love? Overwhelm her with passion, brushing aside her girlish protests? What tommy-rot.

Tiredly she kicked her shoes off, leaving them where they lay, and walked into the sumptuous bedroom.

Rachel opened her eyes. Groaned. Shut them again. A hangover surely couldn't last this long? God! she felt truly awful still. She rolled onto her stomach, buried her face in her folded arms. She had only the vaguest recollection of the long car journey into Norfolk; the most vivid and the most mortifying memory was of being very sick again into a ditch, the freezing wind cutting through her like an ice-cold knife. James. Kind James. James had carried her somewhere – where? To the car? To this room? She did not know. She was not even sure of the day. The wedding had been Saturday. They had arrived at Breckon Hall, she supposed, in the early hours of Sunday morning. Sunday – yesterday? She hardly remembered. She had woken, wept, slept again. There had been trays, and cups of tea, and visits from Fiona; but through it all she had refused to open her eyes. It was as if something had collapsed within her, given way. The world was not a place she wanted to see; not a place she wanted to live in. Until that moment when Toby had turned and smiled into the face of his bride – his plain bride, his rich bride – she had never acknowledged even to herself how much she loved him. How much she wanted him. She knew him, oh how well she knew him; knew his faults and his failures. But she would take him, surrender herself to him she knew – even now – on any terms. How she always had despised women who acted so. How she despised herself.

She curled up beneath the bedclothes, arms hugging herself, knees drawn almost to her chin; but there was no comfort. Nothing could contain the pain. She felt weak tears rising again.

With a sudden movement she threw back the bedclothes, swung her legs gingerly to the floor, wincing at the crashing pain in her head. She was dressed in a cotton nightgown – presumably Fiona's – and though a small fire glowed in the grate the room was very cold. She shivered miserably. On the chair beside the bed lay, neatly folded, a pair of heavy woollen slacks, a shirt and a thick jumper, all, again, presumably Fiona's and put there for her use. Dejectedly she pulled them on, grateful for their warmth. Then she sat for a long time on the edge of the bed staring emptily into space, trying to summon the energy to do something. Anything.

At last she stood and walked to a small dressing table upon which lay a brush, a comb and a small hand mirror. She picked up the brush, glanced in the mirror and stopped, brush poised, looking at her reflection. She looked awful. Her eyes were puffy and darkly ringed, her face colourless, her hair lank and untidy. In the plain, unfamiliar clothes she looked a stranger. She turned away, walked to the window, leaned her forehead against the cold glass, stood for a long time looking into the gathering darkness of the winter's afternoon. The bitter bleakness of the landscape suited her mood exactly. The leafless trees stood as if dead, as if no hoped-for spring could ever bring them to life again. The hedges were dark and lifeless too, the earth bare, rigid and frozen as she herself felt. Dark clouds scudded across a windswept sky.

Her bare feet on the wooden floor were painfully cold, but at least now she was up the throbbing in her head was receding a little. She was suddenly desperate to escape, to escape this room, to escape the house, to feel the wind, to walk the frozen, rutted earth. To lose herself.

She slipped from the room into the quiet hallway outside. She knew where she was, knew too that from here she could slip down the back staircase in the east wing. She prayed she would meet no-one. The house was very still and quiet. Reaching the dark stairway, soundless on her bare feet she ran swiftly down into the stone-flagged hallway below. A dozen or so pairs of boots were lined up neatly by the wall. She chose a pair that looked the right size and slipped her feet into them, grabbed a man's battered leather jacket – one of the many that hung on the rows of hooks by the door – and shrugged it onto her shoulders.

Outside the rising wind gusted, blowing her hair across her face. She turned up the corduroy collar, hunched her shoulders against the cold, shoved her hands deep into the pockets of the jacket.

From the library window Fiona watched the solitary figure stride off across the lawns into the darkening afternoon and sighed. Desperately as she wanted to help she knew she could not. Rachel's wounds were not of the kind that could be treated. Only time and her own strength could heal them.

Rachel trudged the woodland path unseeing, all but unfeeling. Images danced in her tired brain, and she knew, suddenly, where she was going. Knew why.

There was rain in the wind now, and small spiteful pellets of sleet that stung her face. She put her head down and strode on, hair whipping about her head. When she reached the hut she neither hesitated nor knocked. She pushed open the door, walked in, slammed the door behind her against the weather and leaned against it, wearily, looking at the figure who sat at the table.

Gideon Best lifted his head. Stilled like an animal that scents danger. His finger still marked the place in the book he had been so painfully slowly reading. After the sudden noise of her entry the quiet drummed in the ears. Kili had scrambled to her feet, stood now pointing, one paw lifted, waiting for her master's command. He clicked his fingers and immediately she curled back onto her blanket. Gideon's eyes had not left Rachel's face, nor hers his. She felt wetness on her cheeks and was mildly surprised to realize that she was crying again, had indeed been crying all through that wild and windy walk. The tears ran into her mouth, salty and strong. She tilted her head back, resting it on the rough planks of the door.

'What do you do when you want a woman, Gideon Best?' she asked.

He still had not moved. Now, very slowly, he stood. In the small room he looked even bigger than she remembered. Darker. His harsh features were expressionless as he watched her. Still the hot tears spilled onto her cold cheeks. She did not move as he came softly towards her, but stood, head tilted, waiting. The room was warm. Silence hung between them, primitive, a communication beyond words. He lifted a brown hand, brought it to her face, laid its strong back against her wet cheek. She turned her head a very little, so that her lips grazed his skin. He bent his head. She felt his tongue warm on her cold, tearstained face. She closed her eyes. She could feel the power of him, the overwhelming strength. The promise of oblivion. Outside the wind buffeted the hut. Draughts scurried, the lamp on the table flickered. She stood like a doll as he undressed her. He still had not spoken. Only as he lifted her to the bed did he say, 'Come, my Rakli.' Softly, the words almost lost in the sound of the wind.

Their loving was swift, and not gentle. It was as she had hoped. As she had expected. And afterwards, for a little while at least, she rested at last, drained and at peace.

PART TWO

1929

Chapter Six

It was well into the dry, cold spring of 1929 before Daphne broke the news to husband and to father that she effectively held the balance of power between them. The reason that she waited so long was simple, and typical of her. She wanted to be sure of what she was doing.

Almost the moment they had returned from Brighton Toby had begun eagerly to draw up plans for the expansion of Underscars; only to discover that the rather less expansionist Mr Beringer, financial adviser to Amos Underscar since the opening of his first shop, had apparently gained the old man's ear in the meantime.

'Maybe he's right, young Toby. Times are hard, and getting harder. There's many a man without a job –'

'It isn't the men without jobs we're going to be selling to. It's the men *with* jobs. No – not even that – much more important, it's their wives! Amos, we've *been* through all this! All right, there's an element of risk – when isn't there? But the market is there. You know it. And it can't do anything but grow. If we don't get to it first, someone else will—'

Amos puffed on his cigar and said nothing, his face non-committal.

Daphne, quietly and with a minimum of fuss, took herself off on underground trains. She visited Dagenham and Becontree Heath, Golder's Green and Sidcup. She visited site offices, and sales offices, drank tea, ate buns and exchanged gossip with other prospective buyers, inspected built and half-built houses, struck up innocent conversations with builders and customers alike. She walked the High Streets until her feet were sore, comparing goods, comparing prices. Her unprepossessing appearance, her pleasant voice and smile were all, it seemed, positive advantages; she found no-one unwilling to talk to her.

She also discussed the company's affairs, at length, and without his ever suspecting it, with Mr Beringer.

At the end of this exercise – which no-one, she was amused to note, had even noticed that she had undertaken – she came to her decision. It was only then that she broke the news, first to Toby then gently but by no means less than firmly, to her father.

Toby was jubilant. Not for one moment, she saw, did it occur to him that she might ever use this unexpectedly gained strength against him; it did not indeed seem to occur to him, though she was at pains to make the situation quite clear, that, unlike the thirty per cent he had received from Amos, these shares, and the votes they carried – and the ten per cent she already owned – were not his, to be used solely for his advantage. That she had weighed and measured as precisely as possible the evidence before she had finally come to her decision did not impress him, for the simple reason, she knew, that it did not occur to him to think about it. She was backing him against her father, as was right and proper. He would take it from there. He opened champagne, kissed her soundly upon both cheeks, toasted the future and success for the expanded Underscars.

Daphne, for the moment, was happy to allow the matter to rest there. That night, aglow with excitement and champagne, they made love – an act, Daphne had to admit a little ruefully that was rare enough to be something of an event – and to both their surprise enjoyed it thoroughly. Daphne, amused and amazed at her own sudden lack of inhibition, lay for a long time afterwards listening to Toby's soft and even breathing beside her. When he stirred, turned, reached for her again, she was ready, and more than ready.

Telling her father that he had effectively lost control of his own company – albeit to a daughter who had been his right hand for the past many years whether he admitted it or not – was more difficult. The first explosion, understandably, was against the aunts.

'I'll have them certified, the lot of 'em!'

'Oh, don't be daft now, Father. They're as sane as you or I, and you know it.' Daphne was brisk. 'I gather that Aunt Clara rather thinks that if it's been accepted that I'm capable of voting in a national election then I should have a say in a few other things as well.'

'There's an agreement.' The old man was dogged. 'The shares have to be offered to me first.'

'They haven't sold them to me, Father. They've *given* them. You can't legislate against that, I'm afraid. It's all quite legal, open, above board. Aunt Clara went to a solicitor.'

Amos took out his cigar case, glanced about Daphne's small but elegant sitting room, shoved it back into his pocket again. 'Fine thing that is! Solicitors, in families!'

Daphne suppressed a smile. 'She was just checking, that's all. Father, listen – you don't fool me, you know. You never would have negotiated this whole business –' Business? Marriage. A tie for life. She swallowed a sudden, surprising and unexpected stirring of anger. '– if you hadn't thought that what Toby was suggesting, was ready to initiate, was the best thing for Underscars. You can't get cold feet now. I was in Dagenham last week. Dagenham and Becontree Heath. I think that's where we should start. They're saying it will be the biggest development of new houses in the world. Not mansions, Father. Small – very small – family houses. Thousands of them. Street after street of them. Bought or rented. But empty, Father, empty. Not a bed, a table, a chair in them. Not a stove, not an armchair. Nice, neat little rows of houses. With gardens. And inside bathrooms. Not slums. A house that a man – and a woman! – might be proud to own. Proud to furnish.'

Amos snorted. 'Pride doesn't pay a lot of bills, lass. What'll he pay with? Buttons? Where does the money come from?'

Daphne took a long, patient breath. 'Even you must have heard of Henry Ford?'

Amos said nothing, regarded her with bright, assessing eyes. He had pulled out his cigar case again.

'Oh, for heaven's sake! If you want one of those disgusting things, have one!'

Daphne strode to the window and threw it open, the sash sliding easily. Fresh spring air drifted into the warm room, sharpening her breath. Clumps of crocus splashed colour upon the lawn below and in the sheltered borders daffodils nodded in the brisk wind.

'In Dagenham I saw the site of the new car factory. It's huge – five hundred acres! It's marshland now, but they're building a blast furnace, a foundry, an enormous factory. They'll even have their own jetty.' She turned, as impatient and excited as her usually placid temperament would allow her to be. 'That place is going to employ an awful lot of people. They'll pay good, steady wages. And the Ford workers will live in Dagenham, Heathway, Becontree. They won't live in tenements, Father. It's all new housing. They're talking of more new estates further out too, towards Hornchurch. All on the electric line to London. All needing what we can sell them.'

She turned back to him, her voice uncharacteristically sharpened. 'Toby's right, Father. The market is there. We just have to take the chance.'

Leisurely, he lighted his cigar. Drew upon it with open enjoyment. 'You're probably right, girl.'

'What?'

His mouth curled around the cigar. 'An inelegant response, lass, to say the least. What d'you think your Aunt Clara would have to say about that?'

She half laughed. Watched him, very closely. 'You mean it?'

'Where else you been besides Dagenham?'

She shrugged. 'All over. South. South west. North – Enfield and beyond. There's a huge amount of development going on out there – mostly commuters. Father, they're building *everywhere*. Anywhere within reach of London –' She came to him, swiftly, 'Father, I've seen it. Believe me. Toby's right. The demand is there, and it's growing. We can fulfil it, I know we can. Give us the chance – you won't regret it.'

He drew again upon his cigar, lifted it to the light, surveying it as if it were the most important thing in the world. 'Don't have much choice, it seems?'

Impulsively she leaned to him, hugged him. 'Don't be daft.' She lifted her plain, warm face, grinned widely. 'If you'd shed tears I might have changed my mind.'

He pulled away from her, straightened, his face glimmering a small smile. 'Shed tears, lass? Whatever are you talking about? Long gone is the day I'd shed tears.'

There was a small, understanding silence. 'Me too,' she said, and dropped the lightest of kisses on his balding head. 'Me too. I hope.'

Rachel Patten had kept away from Breckon Hall all through the winter and through that chilly spring. In London she could, and did, lose herself in a never-ending round of parties, theatres, nightclubs, late nights and later mornings, flirtations, amusements, the attention of admirers. Protected by a shield of brittle gaiety she could forget that day she had gone to Gideon Best, forget or at least ignore what they had discovered about each other. There could be no relationship between Rachel Patten and a landless, penniless, uneducated gipsy. The thought was laughable, and laugh she did, a lot that winter. She laughed over cocktails, she laughed as she danced, she laughed at Hugo Fellafield's puppy-like devotion. When she heard, late in the spring, that Daphne Smith was pregnant she laughed until she cried.

All but unnoticed around her the world went about its business. In America, a strong, young country virtually untouched by the war that had shattered and all but destroyed its European competitors a decade before, a speculative boom made fortunes overnight, whilst in a Germany recovering at last from military and economic disaster National Socialism played on the fears and prejudices of a people determined to recover national prestige and pride. In Britain the dole queues grew; unemployment was the main issue in the first election in which all women over twenty-one years of age would be allowed to vote.

'I shall vote for the man that produces the most original cocktail,' Rachel soberly told the young woman who canvassed her in the street. 'That is unless Jack Buchanan is standing? I could be persuaded to vote for him – he dances so divinely, don't you think?'

Hugo Fellafield was dazzled by her. It had taken weeks for him to screw up the courage to contact her after he had returned from his trip to Madeira, and when finally he had managed it, it had been with no great hopes. He had been overjoyed when she had agreed to see him, devastated when she had casually telephoned an hour before the meeting to cancel it. Two days later she had turned up on his doorstep at eight o'clock in the evening, two young men in tow, on their way to a party. That had been the beginning. Willingly he was drawn into her world; theatrical, amusing, flippant, eternally restless; and as willingly he had once again fallen under her spell. It was early March when he proposed to her for the first time, strolling beneath the springtime trees of St James' Park in the rosy light of dawn. Sleepily she had giggled, tickled his ear with a long finger. 'God, Hugo darling – don't ask questions like that at this time in the morning! It's enough to make a girl's aching feet fall right off!'

'Rachel, I'm serious.'

'Well you shouldn't be. You obviously didn't drink enough of Vincent's divine White Ladies –'

'Rachel. Please—'

She stopped, turned to him, laid a finger on his lips. 'Darling, darling Hugo. If I were going to marry anyone I might well marry you. But I'm not, so I won't.'

With that he had to be content; but she had, intentionally or not, left him some shred of hope and he clung to it, resolutely ignoring the fact, that she never tried to hide, that he was far from the only man in her life. The next time he had tried had been after they had made love for the first time. Almost casually Rachel had invited him to her flat after a night's dancing at the Kit Kat Club. She had hardly spoken to him all evening, had danced with him only once, and his silence in the taxi had been a miserable one.

'Don't be morose, darling, it doesn't suit you a bit. You can come up for a nightcap if you like. But you have to smile first.'

In her flat she had put on a record whilst he mixed the drinks. As he turned she had drifted perfectly naturally into his arms, humming, swaying gently, her body brushing his. They made love on the floor, a little awkwardly, the record swishing rhythmically in its last groove above them. Overwhelmed once again almost to the point of tears he had again asked her to marry him – and that time, oddly, it had made her angry. 'What for, Hugo? To make an honest woman of me? You won't do that, you know, no matter how hard you try. No-one will. Now for heaven's sake go away. I'm exhausted.'

Capricious, confusing Rachel; he could not get her out of his mind. Nothing she did, it seemed, could break his growing infatuation.

What he could not know was that Rachel herself hardly cared what she did. In her efforts to armour heself against the canker of unhappiness and confusion that gnawed her she allowed herself no rest, no time to think. She surrounded herself with people, filled every waking moment with exhausting activity, but it did not work.

Fiona was frankly shocked when she saw her. 'Good God, girl, what have you been doing to yourself? You look like a wraith!'

Rachel shrugged. 'I've lost a bit of weight, that's all.' She picked at her lunch, reached for her wine.

'Weight you can ill afford to lose from the look of you.' Fiona eyed her shrewdly. They had met only once or twice since the, for Rachel, unfortunate day of Toby's wedding and Fiona suspected, in fact rightly, that on Rachel's part this was deliberate. She wondered, but had not liked to ask, if Rachel had heard the news of Daphne's pregnancy. She reached to cover Rachel's too-thin hand with her own. 'You look as if you need a jolly good sleep and some decent food inside you. Rachel, love, come to Breckon for Easter? It will be very quiet – just a few close friends – a country weekend.'

Rachel dropped her eyes, stabbed at her food with her fork.

'James was asking about you just the other day. We're all so very fond of you.'

Rachel gave up all pretence of eating, tossed down her fork and, sighing, rested her forehead for a moment on her hand. 'I can't think why.'

Fiona laughed. 'There doesn't have to be a "why", daft thing.'

Rachel shook her head. Disconcertingly tears had risen, taking her by surprise. She clenched her face against them, keeping her head down. More than anything, suddenly, she longed to be in the peace and quiet of Breckon. To walk the fields and the woods, to swim in the lake.

To meet and face Gideon Best?

God, no!

'I can't,' she said. 'I can't manage Easter. I'm—' She stopped, caught in her own lie, casting desperately about for an excuse. 'I'm—,' she stopped, lifted her eyes to Fiona's face, flushed at what she saw there. 'Oh, Fee, it isn't that I don't want to come –'

'Then come.'

'I behaved so badly last time I was there –' How badly, she found herself thinking, I pray you'll never know.

'Then come and behave well.' Fiona was brisk. 'It's no good my dear, I won't take "no" for an answer. You've been burning the candle at both ends for far too long. If you won't look after yourself then you'll have to let me do it for you. Unless of course you want me to run to your father with tales?'

Rachel looked truly shocked. 'Fee! That's blackmail!'

'Of the worst order,' Fiona agreed, cheerfully. 'So. That's settled?'

Rachel held out for a moment longer, then grinned back at her. 'Oh, all right, you great bully.'

'And no backing out at the last minute?'

'No backing out.' Rachel hesitated for one last minute then laughed aloud at the repressive expression on Fiona's face. 'I promise.'

'Good. James and the boys will be so pleased. Now, tell me what you've been doing with yourself –' she grinned swiftly at Rachel's snort of laughter, '– the bits that are tellable, that is.'

Easter was blustery, sunny and dry. The countryside around Breckon Hall was fresh with the year's new growth and bright with spring flowers. Fiona's house guests included a young couple, Martha and Henry Stewart whom Rachel had not met before and with whom she got on very well. She stuck with them like a burr. If they went walking she walked with them; if they did not she stayed at home. There was, she reasoned, safety in numbers. True to her word Fiona had organized the most relaxing few days possible. Her eight guests were free to come and go as they wished, dinner was served each evening by candlelight in the smaller, more intimate dining room.

Rachel saw no sign of Gideon Best.

A huge wooden jigsaw puzzle was laid out in the library, half done, waiting for anyone with an idle moment to tinker with it. On Saturday afternoon, when the wind died down a little, a light-hearted tennis tournament was organized. It was still cool enough in the evenings for the great fire to be lit in the drawing room and after dinner much time was spent by its warmth and light sipping a smooth and mellow Bual Madeira, the conversation spanning everything from the London theatre to the latest leap in the New York Times Industrial Average and the advantage of travel in the great airships the Germans were developing to circumnavigate the world.

Rachel began to relax. Why she had been so nervous of coming back to Breckon she could not now imagine. The ghost of that winter's day and its strange conclusion was laid. If she met Gideon Best, so what? She met – all too often – other men with whom she had made love, and without batting an eyelid. What was different about the gipsy? Uneasy recollections of tears, of distraught and humiliating self-abasement, of a total loss of self-control in the course of their savage love-making she suppressed fiercely.

On Sunday morning, the whole party ready to attend the small church in the park for the most triumphal service of the year, Fiona – one small sailor-suited boy clasped firmly by each hand – asked Rachel to find James, who had disappeared some minutes earlier. 'It really is too bad of him. He said something about rats and arsenic.' She pulled a face. 'He's probably in the Estate Office – do be a pet and fetch him. Everyone else has left for the service. It really would be too bad if we kept the whole congregation waiting –'

Rachel slipped around the side of the house to the office. The door stood open, and from it she could hear Sir James' bluff voice, ' – in Five Acre you say? Can't have that, can we? Be grateful if you'd clear 'em out.'

A man's voice murmured in reply. Rachel swung around the doorpost. 'Sir James? Fiona asked me –' She stopped.

Sir James turned, smiling. Gideon did not. As she stood, frozen to the spot, he nodded to Sir James, made a vague, polite, but somehow far from deferential gesture towards the wide, battered rim of his keeper's hat. Only then did he turn, though he must, she knew, have recognized her voice. Not the slightest flicker of recognition moved in face or eyes. She stepped back as he strode past her, nodding curtly, the self-same acknowledgment he would have awarded any other guest of the house, no more and no less.

'– to fetch you.' Rachel finished her sentence on an apologetic little laugh. 'I'm sorry. Did I interrupt something?'

'Not at all, my dear. Small problem with vermin up near the coverts. Rats. Damn nuisance. I'd hoped the cold winter might have killed them off. They'll have the eggs and the nestlings before you can say shoot if we're not careful. Right. Here I am, ready and waiting. Lead on, my dear.'

Walking across the parkland towards the little church whose bell tolled out its Easter message of salvation across the fields and woods Rachel saw, glimmering, the waters of the lake, ruffled by wind. A small, strange regret stirred, quickly stifled. Of one thing she was now sure. Gideon Best had been avoiding her these past days every bit as assiduously as she had been avoiding him.

Perverse as ever she discovered that the thought did not please her.

In the end it was she who sought him out.

Easter Monday was a fine, clear day, breezy and bright. The new-leafed trees of the woodlands tossed their heads like spirited girls asking to be noticed, the birds chattered and sang incessantly, a hymn to the day and to the renewal of life brought by the spring. In the woods the first faint blue sheen upon vivid green showed where the bluebells were beginning to unfurl their pretty heads. Sensibly clad in slacks, shirt, heavy jumper and headscarf Rachel, for the first time since she had arrived, set out to walk alone.

She knew where the coops would be, this early in the year – in the clearing behind Gideon's own hut. When she got there a tall, broad-shouldered figure who, with his back to her, was mending a nest box, turned with a wide grin. 'Mornin', miss.'

'Good morning.' She treated the young man to a dazzling smile. Glanced around. Tried not to acknowledge that what she felt at sight of the otherwise empty clearing could possibly be anything as strong as disappointment. She had, as always, acted on impulse. She would not admit even to herself that she had set out deliberately to find Gideon Best. She had not the first idea of what she would have said to him had he been here. 'It's a lovely day.'

'Certainly is, miss.'

She nodded, moved on past him, amusedly aware of his shy eyes following her. The wind gusted, catching her scarf. Sunlight flashed and flickered through the dancing treetops. She took a great breath of the fresh, chill air; the ground was soft with leaf mould beneath her feet. She followed the path on down to a small stream. Late primroses smothered the banks, pale and perfect within their rosettes of leaves. She picked a couple, tucked them into her buttonhole and strolled on. A fallen tree spanned the narrow water. She scrambled across it, stood for a moment, head cocked, listening – to the tinkling laughter of the stream, to the calling of the birds, to the depth of silence beyond those sounds. It was the most peaceful moment she had experienced for months. She tilted her head back, closed her eyes, felt the warmth of the sun on her face.

The crack of a twig breaking underfoot was like a pistol shot. It was not until later that she understood that the sound must have been deliberate. She turned, eyes wide with shock. He had materialized behind her, his big, rangy figure emerging from the shadow of the trees, shabby, unsmiling. He carried a gun in the crook of his arm, from his other hand dangled a brace of rabbits. The spaniel stood, the inevitable shadow at his heels. They faced each other for a long moment in silence.

'Hello.' Rachel's small laugh, to her own annoyance, was nervous.

He nodded.

'I – came out for a walk. It's such a lovely day.'

'Yes. I saw you.' A very small pause. 'I followed you.'

Rachel blinked. 'Followed me? I didn't hear you.'

He smiled at that. 'You wouldn't.'

She studied his face for a long moment. 'I thought you'd been avoiding me,' she said, bluntly.

'I have.' The answer was equally blunt.

Rachel half laughed again, the sound still not easy. 'What changed your mind?'

He shrugged. Wild horses would not have dragged from him an admission of the effect that the sight of her standing poised and still, her lovely face tilted and lit by sunlight had had upon him. Nor how often he had laid solitary through the dark winter nights with the memory of her body so perilously vivid within him that all rest and peace were shattered. He clicked his fingers to the bitch who trotted to lie in the shade of a tree. Then he tossed the rabbits down, rested the gun carefully against the fallen tree, hunkered onto his heels, gathering twigs.

Rachel watched in silence.

He reached into the capacious 'poacher's pocket' of his jacket, drew out matches, two small tin billy cans, one tucked inside the other, and in them two screws of somewhat grubby paper. He lit the fire, filled one of the cans from the stream, set it upon the flames.

She watched, torn between amusement and astonishment.

He jerked his head. 'Why don't you sit?'

She sat upon the log, hands tucked beneath her legs, the bark cutting sharply into her palms, her eyes following his movements.

He spilled the tea from one of the screws of paper into the second can, settled himself to watch the water in the other, his arms crossed upon his bent knees, as still as a carved figure. Kili watched his every move, her soft dark nose resting on her paws.

Not to be outdone, Rachel held her tongue.

Around them the busy silence of the woodland chirped and twittered, and the wind gusted, as if in play.

He lifted his head at last, the dark and gleaming eyes disconcertingly direct upon her. With difficulty she sustained the glance, held her own eyes steady.

'You were unhappy,' he said.

'Yes.'

'And now?'

She shrugged.

The water hummed upon the fire.

He made the tea in the second billy, produced a small tin cup. 'Sugar?'

'A little. Thank you.'

He poured the liquid, strong and golden, some into the cup that he handed to her, some into the billy that had been on the fire. 'Mutramengri,' he said, with a small smile. 'Tea.'

She took it. 'Thank you.'

He cupped the other can in his big, dirty hands and sipped it. Rachel held hers upon her lap. Sat looking down into it. Steam rose, fragrant and strong.

'So. You are still unhappy.'

That brought her head up sharply. 'I didn't say that. Anyway –' Something of the old caustic tone glimmered through. ' – don't worry. I'm not looking for consolation this time. You're quite safe. I won't eat you.'

He smiled at that, a smile that brought faint colour to her face. She looked back down at her tea.

'Why are you unhappy?'

She shrugged again.

His face changed, hardened, as if a shutter had been closed.

She saw it, and in seeing it only then realized that at some time in the past few moments guarded friendship had been offered and – as Gideon saw it – rejected. Impulsively she dropped to the ground beside him, reached a hand and then withdrew it without touching him. 'Oh, please. I'm sorry. I don't mean to be rude.'

His face relaxed a very little. He watched her, saying nothing.

She settled herself on the leafy floor, her back to the log, her head tilted back, the untasted tea in the small tin cup warm in her hands. 'I think,' she said after a long silence, 'that I've always been unhappy. Well – nearly always. Ever since I discovered—' She stopped.

'What did you discover?'

Without any conscious decision or thought she told him.

'That I'm not my father's child. That I'm – I suppose it must be the word – a bastard. Product of rape. My mother hates me. She always has. I once heard her say –' she hesitated, '– that she should have got rid of me.' She did not look at him; her eyes were fixed upon the tossing branches, and the clear blue sky beyond.

'How did you discover it?' His voice was very quiet, almost gentle. For the briefest of moments she could hear it, just so, the words different. 'Come, my rakli –' and she shivered.

'I heard them. They had a terrible quarrel – Mother wanted to leave Pa – she wanted to live with his brother, who'd been crippled in the war. Oh, it's all too horribly complicated to explain. But I heard. And I knew it was true.' She stopped, let her eyes drop to his intent face. A small, surprised frown drew her brows together. 'I've never told another living soul about it. Since that day I've never even spoke to Father about it. I sometimes think he must believe that I've forgotten.' She laughed, a small, harsh, painful sound, lifted the cup to her lips.

'Why does this memory, so old, make you unhappy?'

'What?' Startled, she almost spilled the tea. Her head lifted quickly, her eyes fierce. 'What do you mean, why? Didn't you hear what I said? My mother was raped – by a gipsy pig, that was what she said—' She threw the words at him, suddenly wanting to hurt. His expression did not change. 'I was the result. She hated me. "You should have let me get rid of her when I wanted to!" she said. I was eight years old –' She clamped her lips tight upon tears. Swallowed hard. 'Are you suggesting that I should be *happy* about it?'

He sipped his tea thoughtfully. 'Not happy. Not unhappy. What happened to your mother was not your fault. Your parenthood is not your fault. Your own actions are yours to answer for – but – the actions of others?' He shook his head. 'Does your father – the man who has fathered you for these years – make you suffer?'

'No!' She was shocked. 'No, of course not. On the contrary. He's bent over backwards to –' Her voice died a little as she realized what he had drawn her into saying. '– to make me happy,' she finished.

'Your mother, then?'

'I don't see my mother.' The words were curt. 'We don't care for each other.'

'So. You were unhappy as a child, and that I can understand. But now?' The dark, shaggy head shook slowly. 'You are a woman. A beautiful woman with many advantages.' The words were cool, and neither meant nor taken as a compliment. 'Why should childish hurts hurt you still?'

She sipped her tea, dark, clear and sweet, faintly herbal. 'I don't know.' She did not look at him. 'I just know they do.'

He made a small, dismissive noise, reached for the billy, poured more tea.

'You don't understand,' she said.

'No. I don't. Things are as they are. They cannot be changed. Why yearn for what cannot be?'

'It seems to be in my nature.'

The words were so sharply bitter that they caught his attention. He turned back to her, eyeing her intently, waiting. When she said no more he asked softly, 'So – now, perhaps we come to it? What is it you yearn for – that you cannot have – that makes you so unhappy?'

She drank the last of her tea, tossed the grouts into the grass. 'That really is none of your business.'

Gideon Best was far from stupid, and he knew the nature of woman perhaps rather better than she gave him credit for. 'A man,' he said, quietly, a thread of true surprise in his voice.

Her silence was an admission. She lifted her eyes to his, defiantly.

He shook his head, smiling. 'I find it hard to believe.'

'That I could love someone?'

'That a man could resist that love,' he said, simply.

'This one does.'

Something was working, now, in his eyes. A disconcerting glint of understanding; a sharp edge of disbelief. Of distaste? 'The night you came to me,' he said after a long, thoughtful moment's silence,' was the night of a wedding.'

Deep, furious colour suffused her cheeks; her face burned with it.

'Toby Smith?' he said, quietly. 'Surely not?'

'Why not?'

He scattered the small fire abruptly, stamping out the embers.

'Why not?'

He gathered the implements, stowed them in the capacious pocket. 'You were right in the first place. It's none of my business.'

The atmosphere had changed. Friendship and warmth had fled. In its place something dangerous growled, stalking them both. Mouth set she rammed her hands into her pockets. He straightened, facing her, watchful again and wary. Kili came to him, stood, head lifted, waiting.

'Tell me something,' he said.

'What?'

'Does it not occur to you that you are unhappy because you do nothing?'

'You mean if I had a dozen kids about my skirts I wouldn't have time to mope?' The brittle sarcasm did not somehow quite come off. For an odd and frightening moment she sensed violence in him. She stepped back.

'No,' he said. 'That was not what I meant.' And with no further word, the dog at his heels, he turned, scooped up the rabbits and left her standing alone, the trees whispering sibilantly around her.

Daphne Smith's pregnancy was, from the beginning, an uncomfortable one. She was sick not only in the mornings but throughout the day. Her energy deserted her. Her doctor, with professional cheer, assured her that this was not abnormal; but somehow, from the start, she did not believe him. Instead of putting on weight she lost it. Tired as she was she could not sleep. Uncharacteristically, disorientatingly, she became short-tempered, unable to care about or concentrate on anything that did not concern the coming child.

Initially Toby, if a little quite naturally abstractedly delighted at the news, apparently noticed nothing, neither her worries nor her physical ills. He was deep in the expansion plans. The first of the revamped Underscars was to open in the early autumn in

Becontree Heath. He worked long hours, both at the office and on site, insisted on checking every single supplier himself. 'I want no mistakes. Cheap, yes, if possible. Value for money. But never shoddy. That's the motto for Underscars. Our customer must know he can trust us.'

Daphne shifted in her chair. It was the first time she had seen him for three days. She did not even know where he had been.

'I've found a firm that specializes in garden equipment. Small stuff again. Nothing fancy. I thought we might think about putting in a small gardening counter.'

'Shouldn't we wait until we know how the household stuff is going?'

'Does no harm to think ahead.' Toby yawned. He was working hard. Playing pretty hard too. He stretched. 'Think I'll turn in. Coming?'

Restlessly Daphne fidgeted again in her chair. 'No, not yet. I can't seem to sleep. You go on up.'

The next day he was off again, with vague promises of an early return, even vaguer indications of exactly where he would be at any given time. Daphne handed him hat, gloves, scarf and briefcase. Watched him walk briskly away, back into a world where she could not reach him. She felt horribly ill, and with each passing day could not convince herself that the feeling was natural. Her disappointment was profound. Quite wretchedly so. When first she had discovered she was pregnant she had been ecstatic. It had seemed like the fulfilment of a promise. Over those few weeks before she had conceived it had appeared to her that, subtly and slowly, she and Toby had been building between them some semblance of a relationship; even, perhaps, some semblance of affection, enlarged and stabilized by a shared aim, shared interests. It had also become apparent, astonishingly, that he was ready to listen to her. Made wary by years of dealing with her father she had been sensitive to the dangers of appearing too overtly interested, too clever; but on many an occasion he had discussed the business with her frankly, had listened to her opinions and ideas with attention. Now, suddenly, all of that had stopped. And it was, she could not help but feel, her own fault. She could no longer keep up with him. Her one concern at the moment was the coming child; and her sickliness, her unspoken and all but unbearable fears had, far from bringing him closer, driven him from her. He was openly glad to get away. She shied from the thought that, simply, Toby – as most young men of his generation – felt this was the natural way of things. Somehow, inexplicably – for never would she have said that she, in the true sense of the word, knew her husband – she was certain that Toby, no matter how much she might try to hide it, was no subscriber to the blind view that women were in any moral or intellectual sense inferior to men. On the contrary she suspected – no, was convinced – that deep down, much as he would have been pleased to deny it, he knew as well as she what lunacy such an idea was. When exactly that conviction had taken root would have been hard to say, but certain she was that it was so. And certain too, in an intuitive sense for she most definitely had nothing more concrete to go on, that the source of this unacknowledged understanding of Toby's was the unpretentious, down-to-earth, energetic and, to Daphne, oddly enigmatic Sally Browne. Watching the handsome figure of her husband stride down to the wrought iron gate with no backward glance, dodge across the congested road to the park, his best route to the office, she found herself thinking, and as so often lately wondering, about the relationship between these two.

She knew very little, had gleaned here and there from the odd word, the odd inference – always from others, mostly, discreetly, from Fiona, never from Toby himself – that once, in his child-hood and youth, he and Sally had been extremely close. She knew Toby was an orphan, that Sally it was who had cared for him, had at one time been the only person in the world to do so. She knew too that somewhere, somehow, Toby felt himself to have been betrayed. The few times she had met Sally Daphne had found it hard to believe that she had ever been the kind of person to inflict lasting harm upon another; it was puzzling, and oddly disturbing, to see the almost calculated cruelty with which Toby treated her still.

She sighed, put her hand to her aching back, leaned for a moment against the heavy banisters. From the kitchen drifted the smell of frying bacon. Cook, once more, was steadfastly cooking breakfast for the mistress, insisting no doubt that she should eat for two.

Daphne put a hand over her mouth and bolted up the stairs.

It was a week later that she knew, with certainty, that all was far from well with the small, struggling life within her. She woke with a pain, nagging and persistent, in the small of her back. As it happened Toby was home that morning. She sat across the table from him as he ate steadily through breakfast, his eyes upon the morning newspaper, and tried to ignore the discomfort. She had had pain before. She would rest in a moment, and surely it would go.

'Will you be home tonight?'

'Sorry? Oh – yes – I think so. There's a meeting this morning – eleven o'clock – at the office. Firm called Petals or Betals or some such. Come up with some excellent fabric designs at a very reasonable price.' His eye was still on the paper. 'We'll probably use them.'

'Fabric designs? I didn't see any fabric designs?'

He glanced up. 'What? Oh – no – it's all been a bit rushed. I didn't think you'd –' he hesitated, and had the grace to avoid her eye, ' – have time.'

She sat back in her chair, trying to ease the steady, nauseating pain. 'No. You're probably right.'

She saw him off, closed the door, leaned quietly for a moment. Maisy, the shy young parlour maid, came out of the dining room door, looked at her in concern. 'Are you all right, madam?' She came to her, her young face worried.

The pale, plain face swam in Daphne's eyes. 'No, Maisy,' she said collectedly. 'I don't think I am all right. I think you should send for Doctor Oliver.'

She resisted sending for Toby until she knew there was no hope of saving the child. Then, when it became obvious that the short, ill-fated pregnancy was over almost before it had begun, in pain and desolation she agreed that he should be telephoned at the office.

He still had not arrived when the blood became a flood and the speck that had had no time to become a child miscarried.

Chapter Seven

Hugo Fellafield, untouched drink in hand, was staring moodily out of the drawing room window across the summer parklands of Breckon Hall. As Fiona, dressed for dinner, came into the room he turned.

'Hello again, my dear.' Fiona proffered a smooth cheek to be kissed. 'You've had a busy day! You've been closeted in that study for hours! Business finished?'

'More or less. Sir James asked me to tell you he'd be down in half an hour or so. He had a bit more paperwork to do.'

'Oh, that will be fine. I already sent word to the kitchen that we'd be eating a little later. Be a darling and pour me a drink, would you?' Fiona threw herself into a deep, shabby sofa and tucked her feet up beside her. A large black labrador immediately took station next to her, tucking his hindquarters in, leaning against the sofa, lifting his head, watching her across his shoulder, begging to be patted. Absent-mindedly she obliged, her eyes upon the tall, tanned young man who was pouring her drink. 'Well, at last we have a chance for a word. How long have you been back?'

'Oh – a couple of weeks or so.' That Hugo was not quite himself was obvious to anyone who knew him even moderately well. The easy, good-natured smile was strained, his manner abstracted.

'How was it?'

'The trip? Oh – it was fine.' Hugo made a noticeable effort to lift himself from the gloom he had so obviously been sunk in when she had entered the room. 'Business is booming. We've had a couple of excellent vintages. Last year's Bual is particularly good. And the weather this year promises very well so far.'

'And your mother?'

For the first time a genuine smile lit his face. 'She's in splendid health. She sends her love. Wants to know when you'll be visiting her again. There – hope that's how you like it?' He walked across the room, handed her a drink, sat down on the sofa opposite, still nursing his own glass.

'Thanks, that's fine. Very soon I hope. Perhaps when we come back from Nice? I remember our last visit with such pleasure. The gardens at Quinta do Sol must be looking wonderful at the moment.'

'They certainly are. Mother really does have the greenest of fingers.'

'It's because she loves it so much. Her garden must be one of the most beautiful in the world.'

He nodded.

Fiona sipped her drink thoughtfully, watching him. 'Your father – he doesn't visit the island very often?'

'What? Oh – no –' Hugo had slipped into his abstracted dream again. 'No, he doesn't. A couple of times a year is all, if that. Too busy, I suppose. And Mother hates London. She can't bear to be away from the Island and her garden for long.' His voice was disinterested.

The trouble, then, did not lie in that direction. Fiona had often wondered at the rather strange relationship between Spencer Fellafield and his calm, sweet-natured but far from submissive wife, but however things stood between them it was obviously not what was bothering their younger son. Rachel then. Who else? Fiona experienced a small stab of almost guilty sympathy for the boy. Whatever had made her think these two might have been good for one another? Now what had the girl done? There was, she decided, no tactful way to find out; if in doubt Fiona always favoured the straightforward approach. She sipped her drink, watching him. 'Have you seen much of Rachel since you got back?'

He made no attempt to hide the bleakness of his expression. 'Only once.' Abruptly he stood, walked back to the window, stood staring again into the fading light of the summer's evening.

Fiona waited, leaving it to him to elaborate if he cared to. He turned, his face in shadow, the light from the window gilding his smooth, blond head. 'I want her to marry me.'

'Oh, dear.' The words, wryly sympathetic, were out before Fiona could prevent them.

'She won't of course. She won't even discuss it. She gets angry. Or, worse – more often – she laughs.' He made a quick, despairing movement. 'Fiona, I love her so desperately! I can't live without her—'

'You wouldn't be able to live *with* her, my dear.'

He ignored the quiet words. For so long his feelings had been bottled up; he had no-one to talk to, no-one to confide in. The misery of the past two weeks had been all but insupportable. 'Now she won't see me at all.' He came back to the sofa, tossed back his drink. 'I say – do you mind if I have another?'

'Help yourself.'

He talked as he poured a stiff measure of whisky into his glass. 'I telephoned her when I got back, twelve days ago. I'd been thinking of her – oh, all the time. I'd – I'd told Mother about her. Mother suggested I might take her to the Island – a short holiday, you know? The cruise is a treat in itself, as you know. And – well – I suppose Mother wanted to meet her –' He surveyed his drink, sipped it, came back to sit on the sofa opposite her. The dog ambled to him and he rubbed the black ears. His open face was miserable. 'I suppose I had laid it on a bit thick. Mother certainly suspected there was more to it than a casual friendship. Anyway, Rachel said to go on round to the flat – we could have supper, she said, and I could tell her all about the trip.' A small, bitter edge had crept into his voice. 'So round I went – champagne at the ready, and roses –' He laughed, bleakly, '– only to find that at the last minute she'd decided to invite half a dozen of her blasted cough-drop friends to join us. And they stayed. My God, how they stayed! They drank my champagne, they poked fun at me. And Rachel encouraged them – you know how she can be –' He tilted his head and drank, quickly.

'You quarrelled?'

'And how. If she had gone out of her way to choose people I wouldn't be able to stand she couldn't have done better.'

'Perhaps she did.'

He lifted his head. 'Sorry?'

'Perhaps it was her way of showing you you're incompatible.' Fiona was affectionately patient.

'But we aren't!' Unable to sit still he jumped up again, strode to the fireplace and back again, the pent up energy of anger propelling him. 'Fee, we aren't! She must know it! When we're together – just the two of us – it's–' He made a helpless gesture, the whisky slopped in his glass. 'Oh, I know how corny it sounds, but it's wonderful! Bloody wonderful! She can be such a marvellous person – and then–' His voice cracked a little. He turned his back to her, leaned upon the ornamental mantel staring down into the huge display of early summer flowers that graced the hearth.

Silence fell; in the distant reaches of the house a telephone rang. Fiona took a long, quiet breath. 'Hugo,' she said, gently, 'I hate to say it but Rachel's showing more sense than you are, you know. It wouldn't work.'

'It would. I'd make it work, if she'd let me.'

Fiona shook her head. Said nothing.

'It's that damned crowd she goes around with–' His voice broke again, huskily. He stopped abruptly.

'That's the crowd she wants to be with, Hugo. Whatever you think about it – whatever any of us think about it – we can't change her.'

He spun fiercely to face her. 'I don't want to change her! I swear it! If she'd marry me, I'd do anything – *anything* – to make her happy!'

'And it wouldn't work!' Fiona swung her legs to the floor, came to him, caught his arm. 'For heaven's sake, my poor Hugo! Can't you see? You'd be utterly, utterly miserable! Rachel's right!'

'No! I don't believe it! I won't believe it! Fee, I'd be good for her – I know I would! She's such a wonderful girl – yet –' He shook his head despairingly, '– yet – look at the crazy way she acts! If she goes on like this she'll–' he hesitated.

'–destroy herself.' Fiona finished very quietly. 'You may well be right, my dear. But, believe me, until Rachel is ready to find her own salvation you can't force it upon her. You'll drive her to further and further extremes. It's you she'll destroy.'

He turned away from her, silent, his face set in stubborn and rebellious denial.

'Aunt Fee, that was Mother – oh, sorry, hello, Hugo – I didn't know you were here. Am I interrupting?' Philippa entered the room in a cyclonic rush, skidded to a halt as she saw Hugo.

'No, of course not.' Fiona dropped a swift kiss on her cheek. 'Sally? On the telephone?' She pulled a wry face. 'Don't tell me?'

'Yes. 'Fraid so. She sends millions of apologies of course, but she says she really can't get down here this weekend. There's a constituency meeting on Saturday and Eddie's going out shaking hands and kissing babies on Sunday –'

Fiona laughed. 'As long as he doesn't get it the wrong way round and take to shaking babies and kissing hands!'

Philippa, despite her obvious disappointment, laughed with her. 'If Mother weren't there to keep him under control I wouldn't put it past him. Anyway – she feels she should be there, with the election coming up and all. She feels that with the new women voters to convince she can be of some real help this time. But she promises – faithfully! – that she'll be down next month.'

'Well she'd certainly better.' Fiona sat on the sofa, patted the seat beside her. 'Now. Come and sit down and tell us about your day. Are you having a nice holiday?'

'Oh, marvellous. I've been out with Gideon today. Poor Gideon – I trail around behind him worse than Kili does!'

'If he minded he'd say so. Ah – the dinner gong – I wonder where James is?'

'He was in the library while I was on the phone. Shall I get him?'

'Yes, please, my dear.' Fiona watched the girl from the room with an affectionate smile. 'Goodness me, how she's grown in these past few months. She's really turning into a very presentable young lady, wouldn't you say?'

'Sorry?' Hugo lifted his head.

Fiona tutted exasperatedly. 'Oh, Hugo, do come out of that brown study! It doesn't suit you at all. And it certainly does no good to mope around as if you had lost a guinea and found sixpence!'

He shrugged. Sighed. 'I wouldn't mind if I'd even found the sixpence.'

'Hugo!'

He grinned a little. 'Sorry.'

'So I should think.' She held out her arm. 'Now – you may take me in to dinner, and as penance you must tell us all about Madeira – and smile as you do it.'

It was half way through the excellent meal, and having, without quite knowing how, landed himself the job of explaining to an openly sceptical Philippa the origins of Madeira wine, that Hugo decided that, good manners notwithstanding he was going to cut his visit short and return to London. He had to see Rachel, talk to her, alone. He had to convince her, had to show her how very much he loved her.

'– I don't believe it!' Philippa was shaking her brown head incredulously. 'D'you mean to say that it was an accident? That they found out by *chance* that the wine benefited from a trip to the tropics and back?'

Hugo made a gallant effort to concentrate. 'I believe so, yes. Certainly that's the accepted story. The movement of the ships – and the heat, of course, that's very important – transformed an ordinary wine into something quite splendid. Actually, though, the knowledge that that can happen to some wines wasn't new, even in the sixteenth century. I'm not awfully good at the history of the thing – you'd have to talk to my mother about that – but Pliny had something to say about it, or so I believe. And the Ancient Romans often treated their wine by heat, too.' Hugo paused. 'Fiona—' he began, diffidently.

'So then they actually used the wine as ballast – carried it backwards and forwards to the Indies – to make it into proper Madeira?' Philippa was intrigued, and paid no heed to Hugo's attempt to change the subject.

Creditably Hugo managed to turn at least a part of his attention back to the conversation. 'Yes. The wine is called *vinho da roda* – wine of the round voyage. A lot of old Madeiras are named after the ships they travelled in – *Wanderer, Rapid, Comet, Hurricane* – it was a method used right into this century. A thousand pipes were carried to India and back in – oh, 1906, I think, or '07 –'

'What's a pipe?'

'A pipe is the equivalent of between forty-four and forty-five dozen bottles.' Sir James was amused, whether at his young guest's cheerful persistence or her ignorance she could not tell. 'The island ships seven or eight thousand pipes a year I believe. Of course we've been hard hit by Prohibition – the States was always one of our largest markets. The original fashion for drinking Madeira in England was actually set by settlers who came home after the War of Independence.' He lifted his glass, regarded it with an appreciative eye. 'I wonder if those brave revolutionaries realized they were fighting for Prohibition?'

'Fiona?' Hugo said again.

'Shouldn't think so,' said the pragmatic Philippa. 'They're probably turning in their graves.'

'– I really think I'm going to have to go home tomorrow.'

Fiona glanced at him sharply. 'But Hugo! You were supposed to be staying until Wednesday!'

Hugo fiddled with his food, not meeting her eye. 'Yes, I know. But we've finished our business –' he turned to Sir James, '– that's right, isn't it, sir?'

'Certainly is. You and that mother of yours have done a very good job. The Funchal end has never run so smoothly.'

Hugo smiled a little at the compliment, but his heart was not in it. 'And I really should get back to report to Father. He was away when I got back from the Island.' He flicked a glance at her and then looked away. The green eyes left him in no doubt at all that Fiona knew well that his sudden return to London had little or nothing to do with his father.

'The boys will be disappointed. You promised to take them fishing, didn't you?'

'Yes. And I will. Next time I come. But – I really must go.' The boyish face was set into stubborn lines. 'There are things I must do.'

'Things that can't wait?' Fiona's voice was quiet.

He met her eyes squarely at last. 'That's right,' he said. 'Things that can't wait.'

He rang Rachel the moment he got home next day. There was no reply. He spoke to his father, agreed, reluctantly, to lunch with him at his club; rang Rachel again.

Still no reply.

He telephoned before he went to meet his father, slipped away during the, as always, dourly awkward meeting.

Rachel's telephone rang, distant and monotonous. He could picture it on the small, silk-draped table next to the armchair. Could hear in his head the number of times Rachel had said 'Leave it, Hughie – it won't be anything important.'

He went back to his father, finished the inevitable catechism. 'Yes – the old man died last winter but the son, Luis – is if anything even more knowledgeable than his father. He's very keen on modernization but not one to throw out the baby with the bathwater.'

Where was she? Where the devil was she? And – the gnawing, shaming question – who was she with?

'He's acquired that small patch to the south of the village from some cousin or other. It's high enough to grow sercial –.' And, later, after the all important wine business had been discussed. 'Mother? Yes, she's fine. The garden's looking wonderful. She's added a sort of conservatory to the house – tiled floor, full of plants – very colourful, very Portuguese –' He could stand it no longer. 'Look – Pa – I'm sorry but I'm in the most frightful hurry. Would you mind if I skipped now? There are quite a few people I haven't managed to contact since I got back. And –' Inspiration! '– I've been trying to contact the Americans about the wood for the new casks. You know how hard they are to get hold of – there may be a message.'

Spencer Fellafield nodded. No mention had been made, even obliquely, of the hard work Hugo had put in during this trip. No word of praise had been spoken. Hugo had been expecting nothing else, indeed such a thought scarcely occurred to him. He had not expected approbation from his father ever since he had been old enough to understand the meaning of the word. All he needed now was to get away. To find Rachel.

He stood, awkwardly, scraping the chair on the polished wooden floor. 'Right – I'll be in touch in a couple of days.' He was aware of the tentative tone of his own voice and despised himself for it.

'Very well. Be certain you attend to the business of the regular late arrival of the *Saint Agnes*. It really won't do. Schedules are to be adhered to, not ignored. Pottle and Walters don't like to be kept waiting for their shipments.'

'Yes, Father. I'll tell them.'

In the foyer he waited, impatiently, for the single discreetly panelled telephone kiosk to become free. The telephone rang, on and on. This time, grimly, he hung on. She must be there. She must be.

At last, at long, long last, someone picked up the receiver. 'Hello?'

'Hello? Who's that?'

'St Sebastian, waiting for martyrdom. Who's that?' The voice was amused. Hugo hated it immediately.

'I'd like to speak to Rachel, please.'

'Rachel? Rachel who?'

Hugo gritted his teeth. 'Rachel Patten. This is her number, isn't it?'

There was a muffled burst of laughter. 'Rachel, darling, is this your number?'

He heard her voice, heard her laughter. The telephone receiver clattered. After long moments Rachel's voice breathed into the phone, a little slurred, light with laughter. 'Hello?'

'Rachel, it's Hugo. I have to see you. Now.'

'You can't.' Her voice was suddenly guarded; laughter had fled. In the background he could hear voices, and music. 'I've got friends in.'

'Later, then. I'll come later.'

'Hugo, I don't know what we'll be *doing* later – we may decide to go out.' Her voice had dropped, the background noise subsided, as if she had turned her back on the room.

'I'll wait.'

There was a long, exasperated silence. He could hear her breathing.

'Hugo—'

'I have to talk to you.' Stubbornly he held to the conviction; if he could see her – speak to her – 'Rachel, I can't bear it that we aren't friends.'

'Of course we're friends, Hugo.' Her voice was still very quiet, the words brittly, deliberately light.

'That wasn't what you said the other night.' It was as if some demon had taken control of his tongue. Of all things, he knew, that was the last thing he should have said.

The silence this time was cold.

'Rachel. Please. I have to see you. Please.'

'All right.' The sudden, unexpected capitulation was brisk and cool. The uproar in the background swelled. Someone shrieked and there was the crash of glass. 'Tonight. Here. Say – ten o'clock?'

'I—' He stopped. She had hung up. He stood for a very long time, the heavy black receiver silent in his hand. The huge, quiet, brass-decked, highly polished revolving doors that led from the hushed, panelled hallway with its lofty ceiling and great sweep of stairs out into the bustle of Piccadilly swished and spun. He watched his father through the glass as he nodded in response to the Commissionaire's deferential greeting and climbed, elegant as always, into a waiting taxi.

Very, very carefully Hugo replaced the receiver. Tonight. Ten o'clock. So be it.

He was there at ten minutes to. He parked the car a couple of streets away, walked through muggy darkness to the small, unkempt cul-de-sac where Rachel lived. The houses at one time must have been fashionable; tall, narrow town houses, not inelegant, the front doors up a flight of steps directly from the pavement. Now only a very few had survived London's housing hunger intact. Most had been split into three, some even four, flats. Rachel's was on the second floor, the floor that, at the time of family occupancy, had been the main living area. The small combination dining/sitting room had a balcony overlooking the street. The kitchenette opened off the little, partitioned hall and the single bedroom, that had once been the dining room, led directly off the sitting room. She shared a tiny bathroom, on the landing, with the flat upstairs. From the outside the flat looked like any other run-down rented accommodation, two-a-penny in any street in London. Inside, Hugo knew, it was an Aladdin's cave. Exotic and glimmering fabrics decked walls and ceilings, lighting glowed eerily through draped silks. Cushions glinted with sequins, fringes of brilliant beads edged the curtains that screened the doors and windows. The enigmatic art of the Egyptians vied with the comparatively tawdry brilliance of the Indian continent and the evocative genius of Bakst costume designs.

Hugo stood in the dark street, head thrown back, looking for some sign of life, some glint of light. But there was none.

He was not surprised. Why should he be? She was perfectly capable of forgetting or ignoring the fact that he was coming and deciding to go on to some nightclub.

He mounted the dark, gaslit stairway, rang the doorbell, twice. Nothing happened.

He tried once more. Two giggling girls passed him, eyeing him, he thought, with open amusement.

He had turned, about to leave, when he heard movement. A moment later the door opened.

'Hugo!' She sounded mildly surprised. Silhouetted against soft light she was dressed in gauzy blues, gleaming golds and brilliant greens – her favourite colour combination – that set off the pale, creamy skin and startling eyes to perfection. Her hair was rumpled. One long earring dangled from her left ear, the other glinted in her hand as she stepped back and gestured, smiling faintly, for him to enter. 'Come on in.' She lifted her head, eyes and face shadowed in the low light. 'Join the party.'

'Party?' He looked around. The flat was dark, silent, apparently empty. He resorted to laughter, strained, much too loud. 'Where's the party?'

She looked at him levelly for a long moment. He walked past her into the sitting room. The lights were very dim, the heavy curtains drawn. The atmosphere was stale and very warm. A heavy, sweetish smell hung on the air. Glasses were everywhere, and bottles, most of them empty.

Very quietly Rachel closed the door, stood by it, not moving. 'Well?'

Something was wrong. Something was very wrong indeed. She stood too still, too warily. He glanced around.

'Well?' she asked again.

'I – Rachel, I wanted to talk to you. Needed to. If you'll just listen –'

'Don't ask me to marry you,' she interrupted, her voice suddenly harsh. 'Not again. Not now. It would be too –' She hesitated, moved her head in a small, negative gesture, making her hair fall across her face. '– too inappropriate.'

There was a long moment's silence, broken by movement. Somehow he wasn't surprised. Subconsciously, he supposed, he must have known that she might do something like this. When the tall, lean figure appeared in the bedroom doorway Hugo was able to turn, oddly calm, to face him. He was very dark and extremely handsome, the gleaming hair slicked back from a face that looked down from every hoarding in London. His expression was affable, his eyes, as he took in Hugo's slim build and boyish face, interested. He was stark naked; broad of shoulder, slim of hip, long of leg. 'Good evening.' The accent was very Gallic, almost ludicrously so. 'You 'ave come to join us? 'ow very pleasant.'

'This is Paul,' Rachel said, woodenly. 'He's French. He comes from Algeria. Via Paris. Don't you, Paul?'

Very slowly Hugo turned back to her. She held his eyes defiantly for a moment then she dropped her head, shrugged a little, reached for a crumpled packet of cigarettes that lay on a nearby table. 'I told you,' she said. And then again, the emphasis different, the tone oddly fierce, 'I *told* you!'

Hugo turned and made for the door. His mind, mercifully, was numb. Had she hit him, had she come at him with a knife or a hatchet she could not have been more brutal, the effect more shattering. Very carefully, very precisely he closed the door behind him, felt his way down the dark stairs, let himself out into the empty street. Every step rang loud in his head, echoed from the towering walls about him. He did not look up. He did not see the movement of the curtain, the faint gleam of light that fell across the pavement behind him.

Rachel stood at the window, holding the velvet curtain, watching. His footsteps died as he turned the corner without looking back. She leaned her head for a moment against the heavy, musty material, her eyes closed. She heard movement behind her, felt the nearness of the man, the warmth of him as he came to stand very close behind her. He slid his hands around her body, cupped her breasts gently.

'Go away, Paul.' Her voice was very even. 'Just get dressed and go away. Please. Even I can have enough of a good thing.'

He stilled. She felt his shrug. 'As you please, Madonna.' He waited, expecting her, she knew, to change her mind. He was not a man used to, or interested in, fighting for what he wanted. When she said nothing he moved away. She stood still, looking into the darkness, hearing his movements behind her. She felt his farewell kiss, light and friendly upon her neck, but still did not turn. She was still watching the street as he ran lightly down the steps and onto the pavement, lifting a jaunty hand to his lips, tossing her a kiss.

She stood for a very long time, ignoring the tears that slid, for a reason she could not fathom, down her face and dripped onto her peacock gown. The cigarette she had not lit was crushed in her hand, the tobacco smell strong. She dropped it onto the carpet.

At last, stiffly, she turned, went into the bedroom. The bed was used and rumpled. She pulled her earring off, tossed it onto the table, stood looking at the disordered bed. Then, without bothering to undress she crawled into it, gathering the bedclothes about her, pulling them over her head, curled like a child about the pillow.

Outside her window soft footsteps sounded, and voices. There was laughter, soft and intimate, and then a long silence.

Rachel cuddled closer to the pillow, put her fingers in her ears and closed her eyes tightly.

*

That seemingly endless summer vacation was a time that Philippa was to remember for the rest of her life; as a time of happiness, of dreamy contentment, of self-discovery. Always she looked upon it as the last summer of her childhood.

With her mother and stepfather almost totally involved in the forthcoming General Election she spent a great deal of time at Breckon, even whilst Fiona and James were on their annual trip to the South of France. The place had become a second home to her, and she loved it. She made firm friends with Fiona's two small sons, Jeremy and Jonathon, romping with them in the nursery, leading them around the paddock on their small, fat ponies, picnicking with them in the park. As she had the year before she fell into the habit of accompanying Gideon on his trips to the coverts, helped him as he nursed and fed his chicks, watched as the young birds grew and began to roost. Gideon himself, she knew, got very little sleep at this time of the year; his valuable charges, too tame for their own safety, had to be watched, day and night. Many times in the warmth of the summer's afternoon he would stretch full length beneath a tree, tip his hat over his eyes and drop off to sleep, soundly as if he were in a feather bed. She would sit beside him, in friendly silence, enjoying the quiet movement of the woodland about her, the rich smell of leaf mould, the copper gleam of the pheasants' plumage as they pecked about in the straw Gideon had laid along the ride. With him she explored the woodlands. He showed her the badgers' set in the bank on the far side of the woods, and the huge, canopied oak that was the favourite roost for a barn owl. She did not, however, spend every day in his company, nor in the company of the children. Often she would wander the parkland and woods quite content to be alone. She spent long, lazy days beside the lake reading, or lying on her back dreaming into the blue skies, or on her stomach watching the graceful swans and the busy moorhens and ducks. Sometimes, confusingly, she was restless, subject to those odd and disturbing swings of mood that characterize and haunt adolescence. One day, in shorts and shirt, skin browned by the summer sun and scratched by the woodland brambles she would run wild as any child; the next, demure in skirt and blouse she would wander, solitary, along the path by the stream or sit for hours contemplating the still waters of the lake, eyes distant and dreamy.

Gideon watched with amusement and with real affection. It was as if the child he had known the year before was growing up before his eyes.

One decision she took that year, and would not waver from. She wanted to teach. Ever since she could remember this had been her ambition and, as one long summer's day followed another the conviction grew that nothing else would suit her. Her mother, informed of her decision in one of their long and chatty telephone conversations was not surprised, neither did she try to deter her. 'If it's what you want, love, then of course it's what you must do. We'll discuss it next week when I come down to Norfolk.'

Philippa laughed. 'You really are coming this time?'

Sally's husky voice was firm. 'I really am. Fiona will kill me if I don't make it this time. I'll be down on Friday.'

Fiona too thoroughly approved the decision. 'You'll make a marvellous teacher, Philippa darling. And it's such a rewarding thing to do. I'm so glad you've decided.'

'I decided years ago, I think. I used to sit my teddy bears and dolls in a line and make them repeat their times tables.' Philippa laughed at the recollection. 'I don't suppose real teaching will be quite as easy as that!'

On the day that Sally was coming to join them for a short holiday Philippa, more excited than she would admit at the prospect of seeing her mother, could settle to nothing. She helped Gideon feed the chicks, went back to the Hall to beg a picnic lunch, ate it beneath the shade of the grove of trees beside the lake. It was another lovely day, warm, still and lazy. She lay back, her arms behind her head, gazing through the filigree lacework of leaves to the blue sky beyond.

All summer she had been aware of the imminence of change. All summer she had known that now, with her sixteenth birthday behind her, her life would change direction. There had been talk of finishing school, paid for by the money left to her by her father's family; talk that Philippa herself had firmly put a stop to. Whatever she wanted to be, a simpering, etiquette-bound, well-turned-out young Miss was not it. The mere thought made her shudder. Her mother had shouted with laughter and hugged her. 'Oh, Flip my love, thank heaven for that! Whatever would I have done with a lady for a daughter?' She smiled now, thinking of it. Oh, how very much she was looking forward to hearing her mother's voice, her ready laughter. She sat up, drew up her knees, linking her arms about them. In the distance she could see three mounted figures – Fiona on her handsome bay mare, the two small boys, backs valiantly straight, bumping behind on their plump little ponies. She watched them amble through the sunshine and into the shade of the trees. A swan sailed in stately grace across the lake followed by its small tribe of fluffy brown cygnets, almost now as big as their parents. A bee buzzed about the fat, crisp-looking clover flowers. She looked at her watch. Two o'clock. Sally was driving down from London and had promised to arrive between three and four. Time to bathe and change, and then she'd go down to the gatehouse to meet her. She loved sitting on the wall by the big, open gates. Sir James always said that if you sat there for an hour the whole village would come by; if you sat there for two you might even get to see a stranger.

Humming to herself she gathered the remains of her picnic and set off back across the lawns to the Hall.

An hour or so later, cool and refreshed, her damp hair that had grown now to a shoulder-length bob swinging about her face as it dried, she strolled slowly down the curving drive towards the gates, Ben the black labrador frisking about her as she walked. She was wearing a pale lemon blouse with a small, frilled collar and a brightly flowered cotton skirt that, openly delighted, she had had to belt tightly since the waist was decidedly too big. She had spent a long and critical time before the mirror; and could not in honesty say that she had entirely disliked what she had seen. Her skin, thank the Lord, was good, and showed no sign of the disfiguring spots so many of her friends seemed to suffer. Her eyes were big and dark in a face that had in the past year thinned to show cheekbone and jaw. Even her bosom, that she had truly thought might remain flat as a pancake for the rest of her life, was developing – although, disgruntlingly, nowhere near as fast or as shapely as that of Matty Burford – and her waist had certainly narrowed. All in all, though there was much room for improvement and she had to admit that there was little sign of her ever becoming a beauty that men might launch ships or do battle for, she wasn't entirely dissatisfied with her looks. One of the stable lads had whistled the other day as she had passed; an impudence she had, of course, ignored whilst filing it away to tell Matty the minute she saw her.

The tiny lodge by the gates was empty; Bill and Ethel Bartlett, who lived there, both worked up at the Hall during the day. Whistling the dog to her Philippa hitched herself up onto the wall, bare legs swinging. A farm cart passed, flat and ponderous on huge rubber-tyred wheels, the great Shire that pulled it plodding patiently, the driver calling a cheerful greeting. Miss Greenaway, the district nurse, prim and straightbacked on her bicycle, nodded a little frigidly, bumping awkwardly over the potholed lane. The butcher's van rattled into the drive and on, round to the back of the house.

Philippa jumped from the wall, settled on the grass verge, the dog companionably curling himself beside her. For a long time everything was still. She leaned her head back against the wall, listening. A small summer's wind had blown up and rustled in the leaves of the elms that sheltered the gatehouse. The sun was warm on her face. At last she heard the sound of a motor car. Eagerly she scrambled to her feet, stood leaning against the wall, watching the corner of the lane. But, disappointingly, it was not Eddie's battered old black Morris that came around the corner but a small sports car driven much too fast by a young man in goggles who waved in friendly fashion before zooming past and disappearing in a cloud of dust. She looked at her watch. Half past three. For a moment she was tempted to give up her vigil, go for a walk perhaps, or find Gideon. But then she thought of the pleasure she knew would light up Sally's face when she saw her. It wouldn't be long now.

She settled herself comfortably back on the grass and put her arm about the dog's neck.

It was a long, long time later that she heard her name being called. 'Miss? Miss Philippa? You there?'

She stood up, puzzled. Over the wall she could see one of the stable lads, a gangling boy of about fourteen, hurrying urgently down the drive towards her. She met him at the gates. 'You're looking for me?'

The lad had snatched his grubby cap from his head, stood twisting it in his hands. His young, dirty face was grim, unsmiling. 'Aye. You're wanted up at the house, miss.' He darted a quick look at her, then ducked his head.

Something very strange and extremely unpleasant had begun to happen in the pit of Philippa's stomach. Her heart too, thumped in a strangely irregular way. 'Is – something wrong?'

'Don't know, miss.' He would not look at her. 'They just sent me to get you. I couldn't find you. Gideon said 'e thought you might be 'ere.'

Philippa stared at him for a moment, every sense suddenly alert, sensing danger, sensing tragedy. The boy steadfastly avoided her eyes. All at once she turned blindly and began running in the direction of the house. Ben, scenting a game, leapt joyfully up at her, almost tripping her up. She thrust the dog away and pelted on. She ran up the shallow steps, her impetus taking her into the cool and shadowed hall. Voices came from the library. Someone – Fiona? – was quietly crying. Almost beside herself with fear she threw herself through the door, and stopped.

Fiona's face was tearstained, ravaged. Sir James, who had been standing with his arm about his wife's shoulders looked up as Philippa entered and a spasm of pain crossed his kindly face.

Philippa stood as if carved from stone. She felt deadly cold. There was a long and quite awful moment of silence. Then Fiona moved towards her, hands outstretched.

Oddly, Philippa found herself retreating a little, stepping back from the offered comfort. 'It's Mother, isn't it?' she said, very quietly. 'Something's happened to Mother.'

Fiona came to her then in a rush, enfolded the small, resistant and rigid figure in her arms. She could not speak. After a moment, gently but very firmly, Sir James drew her away from

Philippa, took the girl's hand. 'Come, child. Sit down. Yes – I'm so very sorry – you're right. Something has happened to your mother. And, Philippa my dear, you're going to have to be very brave – the news I'm afraid is bad. Very bad indeed.'

Chapter Eight

Toby heard the telephone ring, heard the new maid, Parker, answer it, warily holding the instrument several inches from her ear and shouting into the mouthpiece as if to convey her voice across whatever distance was required by sheer volume. 'The Smith residence, hello? Yes. I beg your pardon? Yes, she is. Who shall I say is calling?'

He stubbed out his cigarette, flattened and folded the newspaper to the financial page, reached for his whisky. The small study was cool and shaded, the windows open onto the garden that was bathed in late afternoon sunshine. The big leather armchair, donated, as so many other things, by Amos, was extremely comfortable. He was vaguely aware of Daphne's crisp footsteps in the hall beyond the half-open door. 'Yes, hello? Yes, it is. Why, Lady Paget, how very nice to –'

Toby ran his eyes across the columns. The speculative boom in America was reaching close to fever pitch. There were fortunes to be made for those with steady nerves and ready cash. If every penny weren't tied up in the business he'd—. He lifted his head, his ear at last caught by the hushed and urgent tone of his wife's voice.

'What! Oh, no! Surely not? Lady Paget – Fiona – I—' She stopped. The silence hung suddenly heavy. 'How – how did it happen?'

Toby laid aside his paper and came to his feet. He crossed the room, his footfalls silenced by the deep pile of the carpet, pushed the door open. Daphne stood, the telephone to her ear, an expression of appalled disbelief on a face that was drawn with shock. As the door swung open she lifted her eyes to his. What he saw in them had him across the hall in two strides, snatching the telephone from her fingers that had no strength to resist him. 'Fee? Toby. What is it? What's happened?'

Fiona was struggling with tears again. 'Toby – I didn't want to tell you on the phone – that's why I asked for Daphne.'

'Tell me what? *Fee! Tell me what!*'

'It's Sally.' Fiona stopped. Her voice through the tears that had begun again was deathly weary. 'Toby – I'm so terribly sorry – she's dead.'

In the long silence the tall grandfather clock ticked rhythmically, and then began to strike. One. Two. Three.

'Toby? Toby, darling – are you there?'

Four. Five. Silence.

'Toby?'

'How?' The single, harsh word was all that he could manage.

'A car crash. This afternoon. She was on her way down here. She skidded to avoid a dog – a damned dog – and hit a lorry coming the other way. I don't know any more details. Only that – they said – she was killed instantly.'

He was standing utterly still, exercising a savage control. 'Where's Flip?'

'She's here, with us.'

'How is she?'

'Almost demented.' Fiona caught her breath, could say no more.

Toby shut his eyes for a long second. Daphne moved to him, laid a hand upon his arm.

'She – she'll stay with us, of course – for a while anyway,' Fiona managed at last. 'Eddie's on his way. Oh, Toby, how on earth can such a dreadful thing have happened? Toby?'

His face expressionless, he had handed the telephone to Daphne as if he could no longer bear to hold it, and turned away. She took it, watching him anxiously. 'Lady Paget, it's Daphne – yes, yes, he is. What an awful thing – Yes – yes, of course –'

Toby walked back into the study, picked up his drink, swallowed it in one gulp. Stood with the glass in his hand, holding it like a weapon, as if he might hurl it from him.

'– you'll let us know? Thank you. And if there's anything we can do – anything at all – yes, I will. Yes. Thank you. We'll see you then. And – once again – I am so terribly sorry. I know how very close you were to Mrs Browne. Please give our love and sympathy to Philippa and to Mr Browne.'

Toby put the glass down, very carefully, on the table. He heard Daphne hang up the telephone, sensed her coming into the room behind him. He did not turn.

'Toby?' Her voice was tentative. 'Toby, dear – I don't know what to say. It's such awful news – I know –' She stopped. What did she know? Next to nothing. Only that she had never seen him look like this.

He nodded.

She came to him, stood beside him looking up into his grim face, her own a picture of concern and reflected grief.

He stood like stone, eyes blank and distant, not looking at her.

'Would you – like a drink?'

He did not reply. He seemed hardly to be breathing.

She splashed whisky into the glass, handed it to him. He took it with no thanks, tossed it back in a mouthful.

'I think perhaps you should sit down for a moment.' His stillness was frightening, a clamp upon violence.

'A sodding car crash,' he said at last in a voice so unlike his own, so raw with rage and grief that it startled her. His hands were clenched by his side. He threw his head back, as if in a sudden spasm of pain. 'A sodding dog. The stupid *bitch*! She always drove like a maniac!' His voice cracked harshly.

'Toby! Toby – please –' Truly worried now, Daphne tried to draw him towards the chair. 'Please sit down.'

He pulled away from her, walked to the mantel and stood, hands braced upon it, looking down into the empty grate. She stood in helpless silence and watched him. After a moment he turned, his face schooled. With obstinately steady hands he took his cigarette case from his pocket, extracted a cigarette, tapped it sharply upon the silver case before lighting it. The lighter flame did not waver. In its light his eyes were remote, inward looking, so full of pain that it wrenched Daphne's heart to see it. When he spoke, however, his voice was back to normal. 'Poor Flip,' he said. 'Poor little devil.'

There was a tap on the door.

'Come in.' As Parker obeyed the quiet command Daphne hardly looked at her. Her eyes were fixed upon her husband's face. In the time she had known him she had never known Toby show such emotion. Had never suspected he could. 'Yes, Parker?'

'Please, Mum, Cook says supper's ready to be served.' The maid's pale, slightly bulbous eyes moved interestedly from one to the other.

Daphne turned back to Toby. 'Toby?' she asked, gently. 'Could you eat, do you think?'

He was staring into space, the cigarette burning unsmoked in his fingers.

'Toby?'

'I'm sorry. What did you say?'

'Supper's ready. Could you eat a little?'

He seemed hardly to understand the words, so far removed from her was he. 'What? Oh, no – Daphne – look – I have to go out –' He stubbed out his cigarette, slipped off the blue velvet smoking jacket he had been wearing. His movements were abrupt.

'Out?' She was shocked. 'But – where? Whatever do you mean?'

He brushed past her, stood in the hall putting on his jacket. 'Out. That's all. I won't be long. At least –' He stopped, ran a hand through his hair. '– that is, don't worry about me.'

She hurried into the hall after him, catching his arm. 'But where are you going? Toby, my dear, you shouldn't go out at a time like this. You've just had the most awful shock –'

He shook his head, impatiently. 'Daphne, don't. Don't. Just let me go.' His voice was very low, the blaze of his eyes intensely blue. 'I'll be back, I promise. But let me go.'

She stepped back from him. Hatless and in soft house shoes he left; he who normally would never be seen anything but perfectly and appropriately dressed. And she was, she knew, helpless to stop him. At the door he paused, half turned. 'I'm sorry,' he said, and was gone.

She stood for a very long time unmoving and in silence, her hands clasped before her. When she turned Parker, eyes all but popping out of her head was hovering behind her. 'Tell Cook I'll take a little supper alone in the study, please, Parker,' Daphne said, pleasantly and steadily.

'Yes, Mum.' The girl hurried off.

Moving slowly, Daphne went back into the study, automatically bent to pick up the paper Toby had been reading, settled it back into its neat folds, laid it precisely upon the table.

Where had he gone? Where? And why? Why hadn't she been able to keep him here, safe, where she could tend to his hurt, ease his pain perhaps, just a little?

She walked to the window, stood looking out with unseeing eyes, her hands laid flat upon her stomach. She felt queasy again. She should have told him. She should have told him, weeks ago, that she was pregnant again.

Beyond the window swallows dipped and flew, graceful as dancers.

Bleakly she swallowed the faint rise of nausea. What if she had told him – now or earlier? He still, she knew with certainty, would not have stayed.

An out-of-key piano jangled in the next room; one or two none-too-sober voices were raised in song. The air was heavy with cigarette smoke. Beyond the open door a brightly-lit tram clanged by. Toby propped himself more comfortably against the dirty, beer-stained bar. He was dishevelled, his tie open at the neck, his curly hair wild. The barmaid, a well-endowed lady of indeterminate years with a head of what looked like improbably brilliant copper wire leaned across to him, revealing a cleavage of quite spectacular proportions. 'Want another, love?'

'Yes. Thanks. And a packet of Players.' He pushed his whisky glass across to her.

She picked it up. 'Another double?'

He nodded, his eyes on the crowded room. When she handed him the cigarettes he peeled cellophane from the packet, took a cigarette, lit it, blowing smoke to the darkened ceiling. His mouth tasted foul and there was a throbbing nag of pain behind his eyes. The woman came back, slapped his glass on the bar. 'Elevenpence 'apenny the fags, love, an' one and two the tot.'

He slid half a crown across the wet bar. She took it, returned with the coppers change, watched him interestedly as he pocketed it. 'Not local, are yer?'

He shook his head.

She grinned, gap-toothed. 'Out on the razzle?'

'You could say that.' Morosely he sipped his drink.

She laughed, caustically. 'That's what I like ter see. A feller 'oo knows how ter enjoy 'imself.'

Ignoring the friendly sarcasm he tossed back his drink, levered himself away from the bar. 'Thanks,' he said, tersely.

Outside the summer's night was warm, the light not yet quite gone. The tangled spars and masts of dockland, the huge mass of the cranes, loomed against a sky not quite darkened to night. He wandered the narrow streets, hands in pockets, shoulders hunched. At his side, shadows in the darker shadows, darted a mischievous and restless small boy, hand held firmly in that of a laughing young woman. A young woman, scarcely more than a girl, who had found him wandering these very streets, home-less and abandoned, who had fought for him, no blood kin of hers, with strength and with courage. Who had fed him while she herself went hungry, had warmed him with her body when the world would have seen him die of cold. Who had loved him. Who had, he knew but had never before brought himself to admit, never stopped loving him.

Light fell across the pavement in front of him. More music, more smoke, more lifted voices. Another pub.

With more violence than was necessary he pushed open the door.

The place was very crowded. He pushed his way to the bar, drawing scowls here and there as he shouldered his way through, jogging elbows and shoving backs.

''Ere – watch where yer goin', mate, will yer!'

He took no notice. He ordered his drink from the slovenly barmaid, drank it as he had drunk all the others in those endless hours since he had left his new world and returned to his old at one mouthful, ordered another.

'Wait yer turn, matey.' The words were not particularly un-friendly, but the glittering glance the man shot at him was.

'Piss off,' Toby said, very clearly.

'Yer what?' The man, a docker by the looks of him and built like a tank, surged truculently forward.

'Come on, Dusty, leave orf.' Another man caught his arm, swung him away.

Toby grinned, as nastily as he could contrive.

'I'll 'ave the little bleeder's guts!'

Almost happy, Toby straightened. 'You can try.'

The big man leapt like an ungainly cat, brushing aside the restraining hand and lunging at Toby. Toby side-stepped remarkably neatly considering the amount of liquor that blurred his brain and slowed his movements, and the man clattered into the bar, scattering glasses.

''Ere, you – what the 'ell you think yer playin' at?' The barmaid was outraged. 'George? George! Get yerself over 'ere! Trouble!'

The man turned to find himself eye to eye with a grinning Toby. With a roar he launched himself again and this time, inevitably, Toby was not quick enough. Arms like steel bands clipped themselves about him, trapping him, crushing the breath from his lungs. Almost reflexively he brought his knee up. He saw the man's face twist and gape with pain, smelled the beer and the stale tobacco on his breath, but the arms did not release their grip. Locked together they crashed to the floor.

The barmaid had come out from behind the bar with a broom. Amidst roars of laughter from the onlookers she belaboured them both as they rolled on the dirty floor in sawdust that had lain there for a week at least. She was shrieking like a demon. 'George! George, blast you! Someone get that bugger out here!'

Toby used teeth and head. The man beneath him grunted, the bear-like grip loosened and he struggled free. The broom caught him square across the shoulders. He rolled, taking his opponent with him, using him as a shield. Laughed outright as he felt the impact of the broom through the other man's body. 'Gawd!' the other gladiator groaned.

'George! There you are! Where the 'ell yer been? Back ter bloody Ireland? Get these two out of 'ere!'

Struggling, they had rolled again. Toby, big as he was, felt himself collared and all but physically lifted, shaken as a terrier will shake a rat. 'All right, then, young feller-me-lad. You want a fight? Try me.'

The hand released him. He staggered, righted himself. Found himself looking into a face like a metal plate atop a body that might have modelled for King Kong. The face, beneath a mop of carroty hair did not look friendly. Discreetly, hands spread before him, his most winning grin in place, Toby stepped back. The other man had surged to his feet, stopped dead at the sight of George. George swung his massive head. 'Well?'

The other man looked aggrieved. 'Don't look at me, Georgey boy. You know me. I didn't start it. It was this smart-arsed little bugger – '

There was a general murmur of assent.

A finger the size and strength of a jemmy pointed, unwavering. 'You, me boyo, had better get out of here. Now.'

Toby went.

The streets were quite dark now, lit at intervals by dirty, glimmering lamps that reflected in the mirrored mosaics of their curved shades. He brushed himself off, flexed his bruised body, wiped his hand across his face and found blood.

''Ere – Mister?'

He turned. A girl had followed him out of the pub. She was tall and skinny with a mass of dark hair that framed a face sharp-boned, bright-eyed and inviting. Her mouth was a brilliant gash, garish in the lamplight. She leaned against the wall. Her skirt was quite the shortest he had ever seen, drawn tightly across her buttocks.

'You look like a lad who could do wiv a bit o' – ' She made a small, calculatedly suggestive gesture. '– comfort.'

He said nothing for a moment, stood easily balanced on the balls of his feet, rocking a little, hands in pockets, watching her.

She pushed herself away from the wall, walked towards him on long, thin legs. By no stretch of the imagination could she be called a beauty, but she had something, and she knew well how to use it. She stopped a little way from him, tilted her head to look up at him. The lamplight shone through her tangled hair, lit the planes and angles of her face, sharp, predatory, infinitely carnal. The painted lips parted in a small smile. 'You got yerself a bit messed up in there.' Before he knew what she was doing she had stepped very close to him, in her hand a grubby wisp of handkerchief. She licked it, reached up, scrubbed at the corner of his mouth. He flinched a little from her rough ministrations. The handkerchief came away stained with red. She stood very close; and he knew she felt the reaction of his body. She grinned, languidly, lifted her long thin arms and laid them about his neck. 'I got a nice little place just round the corner. Fancy it?' She stood on tiptoe, darted a sharp tongue out to lick the corner of his damaged mouth. 'It'll cost yer. Plenty.'

'I'll bet it will.'

'Toff, ain't yer? Always fancied naughtyin' with a toff. You on?' Her voice was very quiet, husky. She lifted her arms; long, bony fingers crept up his neck, tangled in his hair.

He brought both hands up, took her narrow wrists in a grip harsh enough to be painful, forced them away from his neck, down, imprisoning them behind her back, clamping him to her. She did not resist him, nor did she protest. He saw the gleam of teeth between the scarlet lips before he kissed them, viciously, knowingly inflicting pain. The thin, strong, bony body ground itself into his.

From the nearby docks a ship's siren boomed melodically, twice, as it sailed upon the flood tide.

It was the following day, almost a full twenty-four hours after the accident before Rachel heard of Sally's death. Her father it was who telephoned her, his voice strained with a grief she could only imagine for the woman he had once loved. Yet even in this extreme, she noticed, he did not ask where she had been in that day and night he had been trying to contact her. Neither did she tell him.

'Oh, but that's terrible! Dead? Sally? I can't believe it!'

'None of us can.'

She kicked off her shoes. She was still dressed in the drifting gold and green chiffon — now much the worse for wear — that she had donned last night before leaving for the party, that had come, to no-one's great surprise, to something of a rout. She had missed arrest, she judged, thanks to a combination of instinct and a sensible pre-knowledge of possible escape routes, by about two and a half minutes; quite the closest shave to date. Her mouth felt like a sewer and her head ached. She glanced in the mirror. She had lost one of her earrings; she looked an absolute wreck. Shock had paled and drawn her face; for an awful moment she had a vision of herself as an old woman. She turned away. 'How did it happen?'

'Fiona said she swerved to avoid a dog, and hit a lorry coming in the opposite direction.' Ben Patten fought for and gained complete control of his voice. 'Apparently she was killed immediately.'

'Oh – Pa –' The sense of what he was saying was only now beginning to penetrate her bemused and over-stimulated senses. Tears welled suddenly. She could not speak. She shook her head, helplessly. 'Sally!' she said at last. 'Of all people –'

'Yes.' The word was very quiet.

The sound of her mother's voice came to her over the years; words she had never forgotten, words she had never repeated to a soul. She wondered if her father remembered them as she did, syllable by syllable, the very tone of the vicious and triumphant voice; 'I know! I know about you and Sally Smith! I can give you dates, and times –'

'Pa –' She stopped. Her father was not a demonstrative man. The reserve with which he had girded and protected himself over the years was not an easy thing to penetrate. 'Would you like me to come over?' she asked.

He hesitated for only a moment. 'No, my love. Thank you, but there's no need. I have to go out in an hour or so anyway. There'd be no point.'

'You're – you're all right?' It was the closest she could get to the question she really wanted to ask, the things she wanted, after all these years, to say.

In the smallest of silences that followed she had the sudden feeling that he was precariously close to breaking down. Yet when he said, 'Yes, my dear. I'm all right,' his voice was firm as ever, and the moment was gone.

She replaced the receiver, stood for a very long time, head bowed, her fingers pressed painfully hard into her eyes, face clenched against tears. In the days of her childhood Sally Smith had been a combination of mother, friend, big sister. Since Sally's move North and her consequent marriage to Eddie Browne the relationship had been far less close; but no child ever forgets easy kindness and laughter, especially a child burdened with knowledge too heavy for her to carry.

'Damn it!' Rachel said, miserably. 'Oh, Goddamn it!'

So many things never said. So many thanks never given. Too late now.

The thought spawned another that froze her, that paled her own unhappiness and shock to a shadow.

Toby.

Almost without thought she reached for the receiver.

The telephone rang several times before anyone answered. 'The Smith residence, hello?' The voice all but pierced her eardrums.

'Good afternoon. Is Mr Smith there, please?'

There was a slightly awkward silence. 'I'm afraid he isn't. No.'

Rachel held her patience. 'Mrs Smith then? Is she there?'

'Er – yes she is. Who shall I say is calling?'

'Rachel Patten.'

The receiver clattered, there were a few moments' quiet. Then Rachel heard Daphne's feet clipping fast upon the wooden floor. It sounded as if she were running. 'Rachel?' her voice sounded a little breathless, very strained.

'Daphne. Yes, it's me. I – you've heard about Sally?'

'Yes. It's just awful isn't it? Something you only expect to happen to other people.'

Or to oneself. 'Yes. Daphne – I just wondered – how has Toby taken it? Is he all right? He and Sally were very close at one time. He must be pretty cut up.' She waited for a long moment. 'Daphne? Hello?'

'I – don't really know.'

'I'm sorry?'

'I don't know how he's taken it.' Daphne's voice was very

quiet, Rachel could only barely hear the words. 'He left, just after Fiona phoned. He – hasn't come back.'

'What do you mean hasn't come back? Where is he?'

'I don't know. I thought – when Parker said it was you – that you might be ringing to say that he'd turned up at your place.'

Rachel's dazed brain was working slowly, but it was still working. 'You mean when he heard what had happened he went off – and hasn't come back?'

'Yes.'

'How long?'

'About this time yesterday. Oh, Rachel, I'm so worried about him –' Daphne had held steady for a night and a day. She had endured a nightmare of worry – worry for Toby, fear that her own emotional state might be putting the unborn baby of whom Toby knew nothing at even greater risk than the doctors had soberly pointed out existed already. She had not slept all night, but lain rigid listening to every sound in the street, aware of every movement, every minutest change in her own body. Her normally calm, pragmatic nature seemed during this precious pregnancy to have deserted her. The loss of that other child had affected her profoundly, but she had suffered alone. Her father and her husband had expressed disappointment and to some degree sorrow; the onus of real grief had fallen upon Daphne and she had suffered it in solitude. That, and the guilt. Over and over again the doctors had told her that the miscarriage had not been her fault; over and over she had smiled, and nodded, and disbelieved them. When she had discovered that a new perilously fragile conception had occurred she was ecstatic and terrified in turns. Neither extreme of emotion was one that Daphne Underscar had ever had to cope with before. So far, her secret jealously guarded and with life proceeding along its usual even and determinedly unadventurous way she had managed to contain her uncharacteristic lack of self-control. But this last twenty-four hours had tried her sorely. 'I –' she began, then clamped her mouth shut, aghast at the sudden rise of near-hysterical tears.

Rachel waited. Unwilling sympathy moved in her. How the

hell was this pathetic creature supposed to cope with the likes of Toby Smith? 'Daphne?'

She clearly heard the sound of a blown nose. 'Yes. I'm here,' the voice wavered, woefully.

'Would you like me to come over?' She had made the same offer to her father desperate for it to be accepted, desperate to break down the emotional barriers of years and share his grief. This time the same words, more casual but as honestly spoken, yet carried less substance. She did not for a moment expect to have to fulfil their promise.

'Oh, please – would you?' Daphne was grasping at straws. Since her marriage to Toby she had avoided Rachel Patten assiduously, so far as she could without being overtly ill mannered. The woman terrified her, with her long legs and her lovely face, her easy, arrogant confidence, her undisguised – and justified – assumption of intimacy with the odd, attractive, apparently invulnerable man who was Daphne's husband, and father of this unborn child. 'I'd be so grateful. It's silly, I know – but I've been so worried.'

'I'm sure he'll be back soon. But look –' the offer had been made, in honesty could not now be retracted, '– if you'd like I could come over in an hour or so.'

'Thank you. I really would be very pleased to see you.' Daphne replaced the receiver, leaned for a moment against the wall. Anything was better, at the moment, than being alone. Another solitary evening would drive her to the madhouse. Company would be good for her. And perhaps – the thought that had driven her to the telephone, running – perhaps, with her long-standing knowledge of Toby Rachel might be able to guess where he had gone. Almost certainly she would know why.

Daphne straightened, took a deep breath, marched straight-backed into the comfortable sitting room to order tea.

It was after supper and the long shadows of evening had faded into true dusk. They had conversed first in awkward niceties, then as the evening wore on and the wine bottle emptied in more open yet still guarded truths Daphne told Rachel about the baby.

Rachel sat in the shadowed room nursing her coffee cup. She had enjoyed the evening more than she was willing to acknowledge. Toby's absence – and Daphne's anxiety – she had dismissed. 'He's on a bender. What else would you expect? How else would he cope? He'll be back. Don't worry.'

Daphne, now in possession of rather more facts about her husband's past than he had ever himself divulged was inclined to agree, though still a little nervously. It was obvious that at every sound from the street outside she stiffened a little, listening. But Rachel had found unexpected pleasure in these few quiet hours talking of the past. Off guard, Daphne's shy confession hit her unexpectedly hard. A child. Toby's child. Contentment and incipient friendship faded. The old envy stretched sharp claws and teeth. She set down her cup, very carefully. Stood up. 'It's been a long day. I think perhaps I should go.'

'Oh, please don't!' Daphne clattered her cup onto a small table and jumped to her feet. Her wiry hair had straggled from its restraining clips, the hem of the shapeless skirt she wore dipped and crinkled. Her homely face was pale and worn. This pregnancy, Rachel suddenly realized, had not been any easier than the last. And Toby, obviously, had not even noticed. She clamped down upon unwilling and unwelcome sympathy.

'I really must. I'm fit for nothing.' She did not care to admit, for some reason, that she had not slept for thirty-six over-strenuous hours. 'I must get some sleep.'

'Please. Won't you stay? We have –' The telephone shrilled, startling Daphne into rigid silence. 'Excuse me.' She blundered away, out into the hall, reaching the instrument before the slow-moving Parker. 'Yes? Oh –'

Rachel, standing by the open door, detected at once the trace of disappointment in her voice.

'Lady Paget – hello. How are you?'

She listened for a moment. Rachel wandered back into the room, perched on the arm of a big armchair, listening. 'Right. Yes. Thank you for letting me know. No, he isn't actually – I'll tell him when he comes in –' Another bolt hole closed. Toby was not, then, at Breckon – a possibility that had occurred to her some time earlier. She heard the telephone receiver replaced.

Daphne came back into the room, her step heavy. 'That was Lady Paget. She's going north with Philippa and Mr Browne, to help with the funeral arrangements. Sir James has to go to London for a few days. She just wanted us to know what was happening.'

'She hasn't seen Toby?'

'No. She thought he was here.'

'He will be soon.' Rachel, despite herself, yawned. She was deadly tired. The excesses of the night before coupled with the shock of the news of Sally's death had combined now to produce a lethargy that threatened imminently to overwhelm her.

Impulsively Daphne came to her. 'Rachel, please, won't you stay for the night? We have a room ready – I have things you can borrow –' She looked suddenly, ridiculously shy. 'Not what you're used to – but just for tonight?'

Rachel shrugged. Suddenly and urgently she needed to sleep. Alone, and away from her own scented bedsheets, that had not been changed since Paul's last tempestuous and meaningless visit. 'All right. If you like.'

'You've made me feel so much better.' Still a little shyly Daphne reached a hand and took Rachel's. 'Thank you. And it's getting very late. I'd hate to send you off alone at this time of night.' She moved to the fireplace, pulled the bell pull firmly. 'Ah, Parker –' as the door opened. 'Have the bed in the front bedroom made up, would you? Miss Patten is staying the night.'

The bed was vast, old-fashioned and comfortable. The sheets smelled crisp and fresh. Astoundingly – unusually – Rachel fell asleep within a very few minutes, aware vaguely of the somehow comforting sounds of the household around her as it bustled its way to bed.

When she awoke, suddenly and completely, those sounds had stopped. The smallest gleam of light showed under the door, a night light presumably, left on in the hall downstairs. There was no sound. What had awakened her? She lay staring into darkness, ears pricked, every sense alert.

It came again. The creak of a stair. And this time accompanied by the breath of a human voice.

'Toby?'

The sound ceased. There was a moment of total silence.

Noiselessly Rachel slipped out of bed, moved to the door, opened it a crack. Her door was at the end of a deeply shadowed, half-galleried landing. The stairs, at the far end, and at right angles to the landing were illuminated by the dim night light. Halfway up them Toby stood, still as a statue, his head lifted, looking at his wife who leaned over the landing banisters, her feet bare, her hair awry, her shapeless nightdress making her look an untidy, overgrown child. 'Toby – where have you been?'

Toby's face, lit by the night light, was marked, exhausted and deathly pale. A dark bruise smudged his cheekbone, his lower lip was swollen. He wore neither tie nor jacket, his shirt was crumpled and dirty. He stood, swaying, his hand grasping the banister. Then, slowly, he turned and slumped onto the stair, elbows on knees, his dishevelled head buried in his hands. Rachel could see his shoulders shaking. Tears stung her own eyes. She ached to go to him, to hold him, comfort him, to ease the terribly racking sobs that were shaking him. She stood as if rooted to the spot as Daphne flew down the stairs to him, sat on the stair beside him, her arms about his shoulders. With a small sound, like a crying child, he turned to her, buried his head in her shoulder. Her hands caressed his hair, his wet face. 'There, there – poor boy, poor Toby,' she crooned to him – small meaningless, comforting phrases. His crying quieted a little. Daphne laid her cheek upon the curly head and closed her eyes. Very, very quietly Rachel turned away, leaning against the wall, head back, staring bleakly into darkness. She heard the calming of Toby's sobs, heard Daphne's voice, softly whispering, then heard the creak of the stairs as they mounted them at last, heard the quiet closing of the bedroom door behind them. Stiffly then she moved, going back into her empty room, climbing back into the big bed and lying, eyes wide, listening to the faint murmur of voices beyond the wall. Wondering if Toby knew how very much his wife loved him. Wondering if Daphne herself knew it. Wondering what to do to ease the pain, the desperate enraging pain that ached within her.

Two hours later, with the light of early morning filtering into the bedroom and with the house silent at last, she knew.

She arrived back at the flat in the middle of a bright and sunny morning. She had not seen Toby; making no attempt to hide her relief and happiness, Daphne had explained that he was sleeping off a merciless hangover.

'Where did he go?'

Daphne had shaken her head. 'I don't know. He didn't say. I didn't ask. It doesn't matter, does it? He's back. He'll be all right now.'

'Did you tell him?' Rachel had been unable to stop herself from asking, 'About the baby?'

Daphne had nodded, shyly. 'Yes. It – helped a little, I think. He was very pleased.'

Rachel flung back the curtains with unnecessary force. Light streamed through the none-too-clean windows. She turned and surveyed the room. 'Jesus Christ,' she muttered, grimly. The room was a mess. Bottles and glasses littered the dusty surfaces, ashtrays were full to overflowing, the fire was a heap of cold and untidy ash, the air was foul. She threw open the window, strode to the telephone, picked it up and asked for a number. 'Could I speak to Martin, please? Rachel Patten. Yes. Thank you.' She stood clicking her long fingernails impatiently upon the telephone, averting her eyes from the muddle around her. 'Hello – Martin? It's Rachel – yes, fine thanks. Martin – I've got a suggestion to make – what? Come off it, young fella me lad, you'd never manage it! No – it's rather more in the order of a swap I had in mind. You were moaning the other night you had nowhere to take that pretty little light o'love of yours away from Momma's prying eyes, remember? I've got the answer to your problem; my flat. That's right. In exchange for your car. Just for a couple of days. I fancy getting away. I need a car, you need a – ' she laughed a little '– a bit of privacy. How about it?' She paused, listening. 'Done. I'll get some booze in for you, you make sure there's petrol in the car. See you this evening. Have fun.'

She replaced the receiver, stood for a long moment staring into space, her face expressionless. The memory of Toby's shaking shoulders, of Daphne's awkward, whispered endearments lacerated her. Damn them! Damn them both, and their child with them!

Gideon Best moved silently through the rustling woodlands. Dark though it was he knew every step of the path, every obstacle. He was tired; he had been on the go since first light and now the long summer's dusk was done and starry darkness ruled the sky. He settled the long gun into the crook of his arm and increased his pace. Kili padded as silently along behind him. As they came to the field on the edge of the coverts where stood his hut there was a rustle of movement in the undergrowth. The dog stopped, one foot held high, head cocked and alert. A fox, perhaps, up and hunting for the young game birds. 'Find it, girl,' Gideon said quietly. Kili disappeared into the bushes, there was a small, snapping growl, something fled into the deeper woodlands, the dog following. Gideon stood for a moment, looking after her, his mind occupied as it had been on and off all day, with Philippa. Bad bok that such a thing should have happened to her mother. The child had been beside herself with grief. His heart ached for her.

He reached the door of the hut, one ear listening for Kili's return. He pushed it open, reached for his matches, walked in the darkness to the table where the lamp stood.

He smelled her perfume a fraction of a second before he struck the match. He stood quite still, the match burning bright and high in his steady fingers. She lay in his narrow pallet bed, the blanket drawn to her pale, bare shoulders, her eyes very bright as she watched him.

The match burned to his fingers. He shook it out, struck another, bent to the lamp. Lit, it flickered, then steadied in a smell of paraffin. On the table beside it stood a bottle of whisky. An expensive old malt, not his. He picked it up, unscrewed the cap, tilted his head and drank from the bottle, savouring the warmth and smoothness of it. Then he set the bottle back upon the table and turned.

Her eyes narrowed a little in the light, she lifted a hand. 'Come to bed, Gideon.'

'Get out,' he said.

She smiled a small, fierce smile. 'Is that any way to speak to a girl?'

There was a faint scratching at the door. Gideon opened it, roughly patted the dog's head, sent her to her corner. Her claws upon the wooden floor were loud in the stillness. The lamp hissed steadily. 'Have you no thought for others?' His voice was very quiet. 'No care for the damage you might do?'

She said nothing.

In a couple of strides he was towering above her. His anger was deep and unassumed. It glowed in his eyes and edged his harsh voice. 'If you should be found here? If someone saw you?'

'I won't be. No-one did. There's no-one at the Hall to see. They're away. No-one knows I'm here. What's the matter, Gideon Best – are you afraid?'

She saw the spasm of anger that tightened his jaw and his big hands. It excited her almost beyond bearing.

'Get out!' he said again.

'No.' Her heavy dark hair was spread about the thin pillow. There were shadows beneath her eyes and her face was thin. She looked exotic, wantonly beautiful, infinitely dangerous. With a swift and angry movement he reached for the blanket, dragged it from her.

She made no attempt to prevent it or to cover herself. She lifted her arms above her head, smiled to see the struggle within him.

He caught her wrist roughly, hauled her upright. 'Out, I say!'

She did not resist; on the contrary, with almost boneless grace she allowed him to pull her upright and then instead of pulling away she used the impetus of the fierce movement to carry her body against his, her own free arm tight about his neck, her lips at his ear. His clothes were painfully rough against her soft skin, his grip upon her wrist bruising. 'You're hurting me,' she whispered, her breath warm in his ear, 'hurting me!'

With almost superhuman control he put her from him; but he was shaking, from anger and from desire, and she could see it. A small smile curved her lips. 'What are you afraid of, Gideon? Don't you like what you see? You did before.' She ran long fingers over her own aroused breasts and his subversive body surged at the flicker of pleasure that lit her eyes.

'I choose my own women.'

'Not this time, Gideon.' Her voice was very soft. 'This time I choose. And I choose you.'

'No.'

She laughed a little, her eyes holding his, steady and certain.

'Lubnie!' he said.

She stepped close, wound her arms about him, burying her fingers in his thatch of hair. 'You really shouldn't use these words I don't know. That one didn't sound at all nice.'

'It means – whore.' He spat the word at her.

She tilted her exquisite head, smiled dazzlingly into his face. 'I thought it must be something like that. Now we're getting somewhere. Come now, admit that you want me, even if only to hurt me you want me – don't you?'

'There's madness in you.'

'There's madness in all of us.' She was unbuttoning the dirty, rough-textured shirt, slipped her hands inside, caressing his chest, sharp nails scratching, goading him beyond bearing. His fury exploded; he knocked her away from him, his hands were harsh on her body, turning her, forcing her not on to the bed but onto hands and knees on the floor. And this time, in uncontainable anger he did hurt her; used her quickly, bruisingly and with no gentleness and then flung himself from her, leaning on his hands upon the table, his head bowed, fighting to control his breathing and the trembling of his body. Behind him he heard movement.

'Gideon?'

He turned. She had slipped into bed, was lying exactly as she had been when he entered the room.

She smiled, wickedly cajoling. 'Come to bed?'

He shook his head bemusedly, reached for the bottle.

'And bring that with you, hm? It's good stuff – seems a shame to waste it. We've got all night, Gideon. All the lovely night. Come to bed.' She saw the sudden, grudging glint of laughter in his eyes, vanquishing anger, and knew she had won. For now at any rate; and who the hell cared about tomorrow?

Chapter Nine

Almost as if to balance the tragedy of sudden death Daphne's pregnancy, in the fourth month, unexpectedly became easier. She felt fit and well, the sickness all but vanished and the gynaecologist that Amos had engaged the moment he had heard of the coming child professed himself optimistic. Daphne was not, in childbearing terms, as she well knew, a young woman, but she was strong, in good health and had the best of care. Despite what had happened before he could see no reason why the pregnancy should not successfully run its full term. Her relationship with Toby, too, had subtly improved since the shock of Sally's death. Only once had he actually spoken of her, as only once had he wept, on that night after the crash when he had returned, battered, bruised and stinking of whisky. Much of what he had said had been ramblings that had meant little or nothing to her and had required no response from her but to listen, quietly and without comment; but one thing she remembered clearly, and pondered often. Through all his real pain and misery, all his regret that the time – until then taken for granted – left for reconciliation was now lost, still he had spoken of betrayal. He still did not, it seemed to Daphne, accept that it had been the young Sally Smith's right to take the opportunity to marry the man who loved her and leave the boy she had sheltered and cherished for most of her harsh life, albeit in the safest of havens. Toby, she was coming to realize, did not forgive easily, if at all.

Underscar's expanding business prospered; and in this too it seemed that Toby was ready for her to take her part. He listened to what she had to say, considered and answered as if her thoughts and suggestions carried weight. The Beacontree shop was doing well, another refitted store had opened in Enfield.

Those shops that they could not yet afford to extend had opened extra counters selling small electrical goods and labour-saving devices. And as Toby had predicted, the ever-increasing demand showed no sign of slowing down; and this despite rising unemployment and hints of a tough time ahead for an economy fragilely based upon a post-war boom that had long spent itself and a vicious circle of American loans paid to the vanquished European states in order that they might be able to meet their debts to the no less shattered victors. Toby and Daphne fell into the habit each morning over breakfast of discussing Underscar business; Toby to be sure doing most of the talking, Daphne coming up on occasion with some sensible comments and suggestions, based often and quite simply on her longer experience. For the most part Toby appeared to pay no great attention to her contributions, though often she noticed from later observation that he took good heed of them; but even Toby had to admit to being impressed when, having seen an article in a popular glossy national magazine for women upon the huge increase of 'owner occupancy' she approached and persuaded the editor to follow it up with another about the 'essential' furnishings and fittings such a home required. Jubilantly Toby counted the number of times the words 'available at Underscar stores all over the country' appeared and grinned like a schoolboy. 'Well done, old thing! Oh, well done! Quite a scoop!' He tossed the magazine upon the table beside a newspaper the headlines of which hinted that the glittering and insubstantial bubble of speculation on Wall Street had finally burst. 'Marvelous publicity! And right onto the breakfast tables of our customers.'

'And this?' Daphne picked up the paper, frowning a little despite her pleasure at his praise. 'Will it affect us do you think?'

Toby shrugged. 'Who knows? The market's just started to slide a bit, that's all. It was bound to happen. It'll settle.' He pushed his chair away from the table, rang the little bell that stood by his plate. 'I'm off then. I'm meeting Amos and Beringer in half an hour at the office. Mind if I take this?' He reached for the magazine, turned as Parker entered the room and bobbed her awkward curtsey. 'It'll make interesting reading. Especially for that old miser Beringer. My coat, hat and gloves please, Parker.'

'Yes, sir.'

'Take it by all means.' Daphne kissed him, as she always did, very lightly upon the cheek. 'Give my love to Father. Remind him he's coming to dinner tonight; he really is becoming so forgetful.' Amos Underscar, as he himself had been aware although not ready to admit for some time was at last showing his age. More and more he was coming to rely on Toby, and on Daphne herself. Still vigorous, and on his day shrewd as ever, nevertheless he tired easily and his memory was not what it had been.

'I will.' Jauntily Toby set his homburg at a becoming angle upon his fair head, pulled on supple leather gloves. Daphne watched him, smiling, aware – as she knew he was himself – of the dashing, imperviously elegant figure he cut. For one second she remembered how he had looked that night a few weeks before, hunched and shaking upon the stairs, his bruised face wet with tears. Remembered too how he had turned to her, leaned his head tiredly upon her shoulder; how they had lain and talked in the warm secrecy of the huge marriage bed. She walked to the window, stood looking down into the street below, saw him run lightly down the steps to the pavement and swing off across the road without looking back.

She stood for a long time, watching with eyes that did not see the buses, the automobiles, the horsedrawn traffic and the hurrying people that were making their noisy way through the morning streets to another day's employment. It was working. Astonishingly, her marriage was working. Admittedly there was little of passion, none of the conventional declarations or appearances of love and devotion that might normally be expected to attend a marriage of less than a year's duration. But – there was something there. A foundation was being laid upon which to build. It was too early yet to tell how substantial a structure it would support.

Astonishingly it came to her that she had never been happier. Almost superstitiously she laid her hands upon her stomach in an instinctively protective movement. Please God, let the child be born whole and alive. Fiercely she focused every atom of her body and her mind upon the prayer. Whole and alive. She asked nothing else. Nothing.

'Please, Mum – may I clear away now?'

She turned, smiling and pleasant. 'Of course, Parker.'

Whole and alive. It must be. This time it must be.

Rachel Patten, on the other hand, sitting on a train that carried her through a Kentish countryside that was just showing the first hints of autumn colour, was saying no such prayer. On the contrary for the thousandth time she was berating herself for her own stupidity. Fool! How could she have let this happen? Why hadn't she – usually all but paranoid about such things – taken precautions? How could she have taken such a lunatic chance?

The train curved, swaying, around a bend, chuffing vigorously. The lovely countryside, green and gold and richly brown, slid past the window; a patchwork of orchards, fields and parkland, neatly hedged and criss-crossed with winding lanes.

Rachel leaned back in her seat, tilting her head tiredly, closing her eyes. The last days – the last two weeks – since she had begun to suspect the unspeakable thing that had happened to her had been a nightmare. At first she had ignored the signs; now she had missed a second period. There could be no doubt. Three days before she had immersed herself in nigh scalding water and drunk a bottle of gin. The sickness was still with her. She had been so ill she had thought she might die of it. Had wanted to die of it. The memory still brought sweat prickling to her skin. And all to no avail. Nothing had happened. The monstrous thing still clung to life inside her. She had to get rid of it. She had to. She shivered a little despite the warm sunshine that streamed through the window and onto her face. The day after her grim, failed attempt with the gin and the scalding bath she had telephoned one after another of her shadier acquaintances, making oblique and dangerous enquiries; she had a friend, a friend in trouble, a friend who badly needed help. At last an address had been forthcoming. Yesterday she had visited that address; a tall, gloomy house in a Soho back street. She had been given warnings, an appointment, and a price. All she needed now was the money, and the courage to go through with it.

She turned her head, opened her eyes as the train pulled into a small country station. Ducks wandered about beneath the slatted wooden platform, roses rambled over the ramshackle waiting room. It all looked impossibly, ridiculously peaceful. Did anyone really live like this?

She knew from the rare visits of her youth that Ramsden Halt was the next station. She shifted in her seat, smoothing her gloves. She must be mad, utterly mad, even to think of approaching the mother she had not seen or spoken to for years. She should simply get off the train, cross the platform, take the next train back to London.

And then what? To whom could she turn for the money, that she must have, and must have immediately? Every day – every moment – was precious. She could not – would not – approach her father; her extravagance was already a bone of contention between them, and she could think of no reasonable excuse for asking for the sum she needed. And anyway, knowing him, loving him as she did, she could not for her life use his money for something that she knew was against every principle he had ever held or believed in. The same held true for Fiona – and she could not be sure that Fiona, learning what she intended, would not run straight to Ben to try to stop her. She had friends with money, certainly, but in no case did the friendship run deep enough to trust. What she intended was a criminal offence, and she knew well the malice that lurked beneath many an apparently friendly surface. She had lain all night, tossing and turning, forming and rejecting plans, knowing that with each day that passed the situation became more risky. And then it had come to her; who might understand the situation better than the woman who had been forced to give birth to a child she had not wanted? A child she had rejected, a child she had left, as she had left her husband, with no backward glance. Surely, somewhere, Charlotte Patten must have a conscience? Surely, sometimes, she must feel guilt, perhaps even remorse? Surely, now, she would not refuse to take the chance to help that daughter, to ensure that another unloved and unwanted child would not have the misfortune to be born into a world that cared nothing for it?

In the bright light of day Rachel now had her doubts. What had seemed rational and sensible in the desperate hours of night no longer seemed quite so logical. Yet here she was, and she must do something. Her mother could only say no. There must be an outside chance she would say yes. It was a chance she had to try.

The train hissed to a halt. Rachel straightened her hat and stood, waited smiling whilst the elderly man who had been eyeing her appreciatively all the way from London Bridge Station gallantly let down the window and opened the door for her, touching his hat at her murmured thanks. She stepped onto the platform. The train shrieked, steam billowed, buffers clanked and it was gone, running smoothly on shining rails, the thread of its smoke streaming like a fragile ribbon behind it. Rachel stood alone on the platform, still undecided. Oak Cottage had no telephone, so she was not expected. She could just as well simply catch the next train back to town.

'Can I help you, miss?' A portly, middle-aged man in a peaked cap, heavy watch chain strung across his big, waistcoated chest had come from the tiny ticket office to pick up a parcel delivered from the train and was looking at her curiously.

'Er – yes. I – I'm going to Oak Cottage. Mrs Patten. I can't quite remember –'

He beamed. 'Over the bridge, miss. Through the little gate and turn left. Oak Cottage'll be – oh – half a mile on, I'd say. On the right.'

She smiled her thanks, proffered her ticket, which he took and tucked into his pocket. She felt his eyes on her as she climbed the wooden steps to the tiny bridge that spanned the railway. She had dressed with care this morning in a pale blue linen frock trimmed with white and a matching printed linen jacket. Her hat, close fitting with a brim that shaded her eyes, was white with a darker blue ribbon, that matched exactly her gloves, small handbag and strapped shoes. She looked fresh and elegant, if a little pale. She felt awful.

The lane was narrow, rutted and little used. There were no pavements. She walked slowly, trying to absorb the peace and beauty of the countryside around her, trying to steady the sick thumping of her heart. The lane turned from the line of the railway, she passed a couple of farm cottages and then the road – more a track now – dipped into woodland. The trees met above her head, forming a sun-dappled vault of green. She could hear the sound of running water. As the lane emerged again into sunlight it bridged a small stream; beside the stream a neat house stood, a little below the roadway, its garden ordered and colourful. The front door stood open to the sunshine. A woman in pinafore and sunbonnet was weeding an already immaculate flower bed. She looked up as Rachel's shadow fell across her. She was of medium height, fleshless and fiercely freckled. Her hair and the lashes that fringed pale eyes were sandy. She stood up, brushing her hands together. A small frown creased her forehead. 'Yes?'

'It's Miss Hertford, isn't it?' Rachel asked politely.

The frown deepened. 'Indeed it is.' The words were a question.

Rachel held out a gloved hand. 'Rachel. Rachel Patten. We haven't met since I was a child.'

Something flickered in the woman's face. Shock? Dislike? Distaste? Rachel could not put a name to it. She refused to be disturbed by it. 'Is my mother at home?'

'I – yes, she is.' The words were brusque. The woman, effectively barring the way to the front door, did not move.

'I'd like to see her, please.' Rachel was gentle still, but her voice was firm.

'She isn't expecting you.' It was an accusation, sharp and questioning.

'No. I know. You haven't a telephone –'

'You didn't write.'

'I didn't have time to write.' Impatience began to edge Rachel's tone.

'Gwen?' The voice came from within the house. 'Gwen, who is it? Who are you talking to?' A figure came to the open door, shading her eyes against the sun. 'Who's there?'

Gwendoline Hertford shot a look of real dislike at Rachel,

unmistakable this time, before turning. 'It's Rachel, Mrs Patten.' Her voice had softened, her face became gentle, 'Your daughter.'

There was a moment's silence. Charlotte Patten stood like a statue, one hand lifted to the door jamb the other upon her breast. She was slender as ever and pretty still, though the fluffy fair hair had lost its colour and the pale and delicate skin showed tiny lines about the blue eyes. 'Rachel?' She spoke on a breath, as if shocked, or frightened.

'Yes, Mother. Rachel.' Determinedly Rachel pushed past the other woman and went to her mother, leaning to kiss her cheek. Charlotte made no move either to return the embrace or to withdraw from it.

'Well I –' She stepped back '– I suppose you had better come in.'

The interior of the cottage was dark and cool, as fastidiously maintained as the outside. The furniture was polished to the sheen of mirrors, the curtains were crisp and clean, no speck of dust marred any surface. A small fire burned in the grate. Over the mantelpiece hung a portrait, the head and shoulders of a man in uniform, a handsome man, laughing, the same man whose photograph adorned the piano and the sideboard. In the photograph on the piano he was in a wheelchair, sitting in the cottage garden with Charlotte on the grass beside him. Rachel knew him well. Uncle Peter. Her father's brother. The man for whom Charlotte Patten had left husband and daughter, dead now these many years.

'Well.' Charlotte took station in the window, the light behind her, her hands clasped before her. Her voice was too bright and did not mask the chill. 'This is a surprise! How are you?'

Rachel hesitated. The niceties, she supposed, had to be observed. 'I'm – well, thank you. And you?'

If Charlotte noticed the hesitation she did not show it. 'I'm quite splendid. Quite splendid. I had a little cold a week or so ago but dear Gwen nursed me through. She really is a treasure.' She wandered to the small piano, rearranged the photograph, ashtray and vase of flowers that stood upon it. Turned. Waited.

Rachel nibbled her lip. 'Mother –'

'You'll be wanting tea?' Gwen Hertford had appeared in the

doorway. She had taken her sunhat off and her sandy hair, crimped to waves close to her head, looked like a metal cap.

'Yes please, Gwen dear. And cake. The coconut cake you made yesterday. That would be nice.'

Rachel waited until the door closed behind the other woman. 'Mother –' she said again, and again stopped.

With every appearance of patience Charlotte raised her brows and waited. When Rachel did not continue she said quietly, 'Well? I don't suppose you've come all this way to enquire for my health and to take tea and cake?'

Rachel turned from her, stood for a long moment pulling off her gloves, finger by finger, then tossed them with her bag onto a nearby table. 'I'm in trouble.'

There was a very long silence.

'Why come to me?'

'I need money.' Rachel turned, suddenly urgent. 'Please, Mother. A hundred and twenty pounds. I need it quickly.'

Her mother's face was totally expressionless. 'Are you saying what I think you're saying?'

Rachel held the cool blue gaze for a moment, then dropped her eyes, ducking her head.

'How stupid. How utterly stupid!' The words were cold.

Temper blazed. Rachel gritted her teeth and held it, saying nothing.

Charlotte had turned back to the piano, was rearranging the flowers in the vase. 'Your –', she hesitated, '– father?'

'He doesn't know,' Rachel said, sharply. 'He mustn't know! You won't tell him?'

The other woman's laughter was short, and hard. 'When did I ever tell your father anything? When did he ever listen if I did? No, Rachel, I won't tell him.' The busy hands paused, she slanted a look across her shoulder. 'I still don't understand. Why come to me?'

Rachel flung up angry hands. 'Because you're my mother for Christ's sake! Because you once wanted what I want now! Because you surely owe me *something*? You surely must know – must remember – how I feel?'

Charlotte turned very slowly. Her face was rigid with dislike.

'The two cases could hardly be called the same, Rachel,' she said, coldly. 'I do assume that you were not –', she gathered her breath, pronounced the brutal word very clearly, '– raped?'

'No. No, of course not.'

Her mother shrugged, very slightly.

Rachel was shaking with anger and humiliation. 'I won't beg, Mother.'

'There would be no point. I won't give you the money anyway. Ah, Gwen, thank you. Put it on the table, please.'

Rachel turned away from the pale, accusing eyes. Folded her arms tightly across her breast, holding against temper, against terror. When she heard the door shut again she flung round to face her mother. 'I won't have it!' she spoke very low, through teeth clenched against screaming, 'I won't! I'll die first –'

Charlotte gave no sign that she had heard or understood the threat. Very calmly she sat, poured two cups of tea.

Rachel broke the long, difficult silence, deliberately goading, unable to stop herself. 'What was he like, Mother? My father – my real father – what was he like?'

The steady hands trembled just a little. 'Look in the mirror. That was what he was like.'

Rachel actually did lift her head to the mirror which hung in the alcove next to the fireplace. She looked for a long time at the reflection she knew so very well. 'He was handsome, then,' she said, very quietly.

'Yes.'

Some small edge to Charlotte's voice brought Rachel's eyes to her, consideringly. 'You knew him?'

'I'd – seen him.' Charlotte's face was very pale, very still. 'I hardly think –'

'You'd seen him –', Rachel followed her line of reasoning inexorably, '– and fancied him?'

'Rachel!'

'Did you? Did you – encourage him? This handsome gipsy lad?'

'He wasn't a gipsy. He was Irish.'

Rachel stared. 'What?'

Charlotte said nothing.

'What did you say?'

'I said he was Irish.'

'But – gipsy – you said gipsy. "Gipsy brat" you called me – I heard you –'

Charlotte shrugged. 'You looked a little gipsy, that's all. What the devil does it matter? I will not have you insinuating that I – what are you laughing at? Rachel! You're hysterical!' She half rose, sank back into her chair as Rachel, still laughing, sat opposite her and bowed her face into her hands, shoulders shaking. When she lifted her head at last her eyes were smudged with tears, but steady.

'Well, Mother dear, it so happens that I *am* expecting a gipsy brat. It may surprise you, but I know who the child's father is; a gipsy, not handsome, but infinitely fanciable.'

Charlotte turned her head, a faint flinch of disgust on her face.

Rachel leaned forward, face and voice venomously gentle. 'Yes. Infinitely fanciable.' She drew the words out. 'It's my father I take after, is it, Mother? My real father? Who raped you? So you say. Not you. Thank God, I don't take after you, do I? Hardly. You're a cold fish, Mother. A cold, cold fish. You ran away with a cripple because you couldn't stand a real man to touch you –'

Charlotte's hand lashed out, connected hard with Rachel's cheekbone. They stared at each other, in open, silent hostility. Then, moving stiffly and slowly Charlotte rose and without a word turned and left the room. Outside the door Gwen Hertford stood, openly listening. As Charlotte passed her the other woman put a thin, freckled hand to the soft and pretty face, in a gesture of possessive affection. Rachel averted her eyes. When she looked back the pale eyes within their fringe of ginger lashes were watching her with spiteful venom.

She stood, reached for her gloves and bag, turned as her mother re-entered the room.

'Little slut,' Charlotte said, very quietly as she tossed something onto the table cloth next to the untouched, cooling cups of tea. 'There. Take them. And never – you hear me, never – ever come here again.'

Very slowly Rachel picked up the tiny things that glinted and gleamed in the sunshine that fell through the window. Earrings. Small diamond studs. She lifted her head, looked at her mother.

Charlotte's lips curled. 'Yes. They're real. Ben gave them to me. They mean nothing. Take them. It's all that I owe you. All that I ever owed you. Now you have it. So go.'

Rachel tucked the studs into her handbag. She felt faintly sick, and tired to death. She straightened her back. Only once did she look back as she left the cottage. Automatically turning to shut the gate she saw her mother, Gwen Hertford's arm supportively about her, watching from the shadowed, open doorway. As she watched they turned with no gesture of farewell and disappeared into the house, Gwen Hertford reaching a hand to close the door firmly behind them, leaving Rachel standing alone in the lovely autumn sunshine.

Somewhere in the distance a train whistle echoed. Rachel turned her back upon the cottage and set off towards the station.

The underground train rattled and swayed noisily through the tunnel, slowed down, stopped, stood ticking impatiently in the sudden and unexpected silence. The mother and daughter who sat opposite Rachel conversed quietly.

Rachel lit another cigarette.

The train lurched, hummed, resumed its journey.

She tried to focus her eyes and her mind on the magazine upon her lap, tried to get further than the first sentence of the article she had been trying to concentrate upon for the past five minutes. 'Few outside the magic circle of collectors are even remotely aware that a number of women's names figure in the list of silversmiths who made London famous for her craftsmanship from early Tudor times –' She was cold. Her hands, her feet, the very organs inside her body were cold. She was shivering. She looked at her hands. They were perfectly steady. The shivering was inside, a trembling so deep and so terrible that it constricted her lungs, stifling her breath and making her heart flutter in panic. She was more afraid than she had ever been in her life before. She felt that anyone, even the most casual of observers, must see it; yet no-one stared, no-one indeed took any notice of her at all.

'Few outside the magic circle of collectors –'

It was not too late. She could get off the train now. No-one was forcing her to this. For a moment she imagined the coming ordeal; the neat, precise little man with whom she had made the arrangements had dispassionately and explicitly told her what to expect.

The trembling had reached her legs. She would never, surely, be able to stand – to step from the train – walk down those narrow streets, climb those stairs?

'Few outside the magic circle of collectors –'

She turned the page impatiently. A girl smiled vapidly at her over a coyly turned shoulder. 'The Loveliest Hair You've Ever Seen – Amami is Her Secret!' Who was she, this girl who smiled with such perfect and condescending confidence? Did she know what it was to be so afraid that despite starvation for several hours her bowels grumbled and ached with the fear? Was she a real person, this pretty paper girl with the shining hair?

The lights of a station flashed past the windows. The train slowed and halted, the doors hissed. Collectedly Rachel stood, dropped her cigarette, crushed it very precisely with a well-shod foot, gathered bag, gloves, magazine and stepped down onto the platform. People hurried past her, heads down against the underground wind. The escalator carried her inexorably to the surface.

It was a dark and cloudy afternoon, threatening rain. Almost without volition, determinedly without thought, she walked briskly across the road, past a shouting news vendor whose poster luridly proclaimed suicides on Wall Street. Rachel's feet carried her on, round a corner, across a narrow street, down an even narrower alley into a dirty cul-de-sac, its tall, run-down houses huddled like blank-faced beggars shuffled close together for warmth. There she stopped for one moment, hesitating. Half an hour. In half an hour it would be done. She would be on her way home; and then there would be no going back.

She tossed the magazine she still carried into a nearby dustbin, walked very quickly to the door of number eleven and rang the bell.

He was the same, the man who had given his name as Gardner

– small, neat, fussily precise. He had thinning hair and very red lips, and his voice was high and light. 'Up the stairs, dear. The room on the right. Get your things off. I'll be up in a moment.'

She said nothing. Walked past him. Climbed the stairs upon legs that ached with the effort she made to keep them from shaking. In fact every muscle in her body ached, rigid as iron.

The room was small, stifling hot and bare except for the paraffin heater that belched its nauseous stench into the already all but unbreathable air, a narrow trestle bed and a table upon which stood a bowl, a pair of rubber gloves and what looked like a long, bent knitting needle. Upon the back of the door hung a short nightshirt, much washed and faded. Her jaw rigid against the trembling that was now all but uncontrollable, Rachel undressed, piling her folded clothes upon the table since there was no other place to put them. The nightshirt was thin, the bed when she sat upon it hard. The rubber sheet upon it was revoltingly smooth and cold on her skin. She lay back. The pillow was flat and lumpy. A bare electric light bulb glared into her eyes, the flex looped across the ceiling. Hell could well be like this.

She heard his footsteps on the stairs. She sat up, her feet swinging above the floor, shoulders hunched. He bustled into the room, carrying an old kettle from which steam rose. 'Ready, dear? Good, oh good. Sooner done sooner mended they say.' He put the kettle on the table, stood, looking about him vaguely, as if searching for something. 'Just one little thing, dear –'

'Yes?' Rachel's lips were stiff.

'The – little matter of the – Ahem! –' He cleared his throat delicately, '– agreed fee?'

'Oh – yes, of course.' Rachel scrambled from the bed, fumbled in her handbag, nearly threw the bundle of notes at him. 'There.'

He stood and counted it.

In the silence the paraffin heater hissed and sputtered. Rachel thought she might suffocate.

'Right, then.' He stowed the money carefully in his pocket, splashed the hot water in the bowl. 'If you'd just lay back, dear, and open your legs – that's right. Oh, dear, you really must try to relax, you know. It's so much more difficult if you don't – come on, dear, let go –'

It was rape, and worse than rape. Every muscle, every fibre of her body revolted against the ungentle groping of his cold hands, the insertion of the brutal instrument, its rough violation of the softest core of her body.

He was impatient. 'Oh, come on, dear – if you fight it it'll be much the worse for you. I told you – relax –'

She was crying, crying through clenched teeth and closed throat. She was dying. Dying of pain and horror. She drew breath, at last, to scream.

'There.' He straightened. There was blood on his gloved hands. 'That should do the trick. Clean yourself up and get yourself dressed, dear. You haven't got much time.' He picked up a towel and tossed it to her. 'I'll see you downstairs when you're ready. But like I say – be quick as you can. We don't want anything happening before you get yourself home, do we?'

Numbly she swung her legs over the edge of the bed and sat up. Despite the heat of the room she was cold. Cold as death. The warm air brushed her skin like hot, intrusive fingers. There was blood on her thighs. Fighting revulsed nausea she stumbled to the table, dipped one end of the towel in the water and scrubbed at her legs. The bloody needle lay discarded upon the table. Tears still slid down her face, and she shook now as if she would never be able to stop. Weakly she struggled into her clothes, desperate to get out of the foul little room. On the landing she stood for a moment at the top of the steep stairs, collecting herself. At least the air was cooler, and less rank. At least she could breathe.

Very carefully she descended the dark stairway. He was waiting at the bottom, a small bottle in his hand. 'Right, dear. Home as fast as you can, then take this –'

'What is it?'

'Slippery elm. Helps with the contractions. Now – you remember what I told you? You know what to expect?'

'Yes.'

'Right. That's it then.' He still barred her way, small, neat, infinitely menacing. 'And, you do know, if anything goes wrong – mum's the word, eh? Don't want to get anyone into trouble, do we?'

'No. Of course not.'

He did not move. 'If anything – unfortunate – should happen and unhelpful people should count it my fault I should make very sure I did not suffer alone. I am, in all things, a companionable man, dear –' He peered into her face.

'I won't tell anyone.'

'That's a good girl.' He nodded, stepped back. 'Doesn't do to upset people, now does it? Like I said. Mum's the word.'

She pushed past him to the front door. The afternoon had darkened, and it had begun to rain. The world was grey, and drenched. Dirty water ran in the gutter. She leaned in the doorway for a moment. Exhausted and deathly chilled she could not face the walk to the station, the uncomfortable train journey. 'Wh – where can I get a taxi?'

She felt him behind her, felt his impatience to have her gone. 'Just walk up the alley there and round the corner. Charing Cross Road's at the end – you'll get one there –'

He shut the door behind her almost before she was through it.

Huddled into her coat, the throbbing pain between her legs almost unbearable she plodded into the rain.

The utter relief of arriving home almost swamped her fear of what now must, inevitably, happen. The fire in the living room had burned low. With slow, deliberate movements she built it up. Then, still huddled into her coat she went out onto the landing. Beside the bathroom that she shared with the upstairs flat was a cupboard containing a variety of little-used objects; mops, buckets, a couple of washboards and an old tin bath that had belonged to the old lady who had lived in Rachel's flat before her. Holding herself rigidly against pain and against too harsh an effort she dragged it through the door and into the living room. Then she went into the tiny kitchenette and set saucepans and the kettle to boil. Only then did she slip her coat from her shoulders, throwing it across an armchair where it slid into an untidy heap on the floor. She went into the bedroom, stepped from her clothes leaving them scattered where they lay, slipped into a thin wool dressing gown. She had grown almost used to the fits of trembling that swept her every so often, chattering her teeth.

In the kitchen the water was boiling. She emptied the various containers into the bath, set them, full, back upon the stove again.

Moving like an automaton she fetched towels, and a blanket that she hugged about her shoulders in a vain effort to get warm. A bottle of whisky stood half full upon the sideboard. With a quick movement she uncorked it and drank straight from the bottle. Then, still carrying the bottle she wandered about the flat looking for the handbag she had discarded, finding it at last on the floor beneath her crumpled coat. She took out the bottle of slippery elm, looked at it for a long moment, then threw her head back and drank it at a gulp. The bitterness made her retch for a moment. She stood, fighting the sickness. Then, slowly and methodically, as if some dispassionate stranger inhabited her body, she resumed her preparations.

Half an hour later she sat down in an armchair next to the fire, the whisky bottle beside her. In front of the fire was the small bath, half-filled with water. She watched the steam lift in wisps, drawn by the draught of the chimney. Despite the dressing gown and the blanket about her shoulders she shivered again, violently. The clock ticked. She waited.

It started slowly, whilst she was in the bath; a twinge of pain, another, and then the first quiet seeping of blood. She lay until the water cooled uncomfortably, then climbed painfully out, dried herself, shivering, struggled into a loose cotton nightshirt and lay, terrified, upon the bed. The pain continued for slow, frightening hours – days it might have been, a lifetime – until suddenly claws of unrelenting agony were rending her, clutching and twisting, wringing the life from her. There was blood everywhere. Not any of her preparations, not any of her forethought had prepared her for this. Outside, darkness fell. In the lull between contractions she managed to light one lamp. The fire died and the room became chill. Gritting her teeth she struggled to rebuild the fire. She was deadly cold.

It eased a little, the pain and the blood, and utterly exhausted, crying now, desolate and frightened, she dragged herself back to bed. When the onslaught started again she could not move; she bled where she lay. The nightmare went on, and on. She had utterly lost track of time. All but out of her mind with pain, shock and loss of blood she slid into unconsciousness. When she woke it was pitch dark and freezing cold. She had no idea how long she had lain so. Through the open door she could just see the last glowing embers of the fire and the faint glow of the lamp.

With a sudden, terrible clarity she realized that left to herself she would die.

She lay for long minutes considering it. Yet the clarity blurred; she could not concentrate, even upon such an awful thought as this. Words jumbled themselves in her brain 'Few outside the magic circle of collectors –' She must wash her hair. Whatever would Toby think if he saw her like this? Toby. Toby, bright-eyed, bright-haired, teasing; finding her crying, putting a brotherly arm about her. 'Who cares about mothers? Look at me, I never had one – hasn't done me any harm.' Toby, handsome in uniform, wearing his mud-stained khaki like a medal. 'Few outside the magic circle –' Stupid words. Go away. She must think. She *must* think –

Darkness rose like a sea about her, she sank for a moment then surfaced, a little dizzily. She could feel nothing, just a faint, throbbing pain that seemed to come from a great distance and did not greatly inconvenience her. Think about what?

Toby.

A number.

Clear and concise it echoed in her head. Three, nine, two.

With an enormous effort she focused her mind on the number. Three, nine, two. Toby's telephone number. Help. Toby would help. He'd know what to do.

Three, nine, two.

She reached for the telephone by the bed. It clattered back, uselessly. What exchange? What in God's name was the exchange?

She drifted again into the chill, pain-racked darkness that waited to close above her head like the cold waters of an ocean; woke to a renewal of the contractions and a fresh gush of blood, an agony that roused her, and in that split second of clear-headedness she remembered.

She reached for the telephone. It took an age before the operator answered. 'Bayswater three, nine, two.' Her voice was not steady, but it was clear enough. She curled about the receiver, drew the bedclothes around her. The ringing tone went on and on, distant, disembodied. No-one answered.

'I'm afraid no-one is replying.' The operator's voice, bored, disinterested.

'Please. Keep trying. I'm sure someone's there. It's – very important.'

The tone again, and then, at last, a voice, sleepy and anxious. 'Hello? Hello, who is it?'

Daphne.

Disappointment welled like sickness.

'Hello? Who is this?'

'Daphne. It's Rachel. Rachel Patten –'

'Rachel – whatever's wrong? It's three o'clock in the morning –'

'I'm sorry. I can't explain. Please – is Toby there?'

'No, he isn't.' A slight sharpness edged the words. 'I'm sorry. He's gone north for a couple of days. He won't be back until tomorrow.' She waited. Rachel said nothing. The knuckles of her cold hands were white as she gripped the phone. 'Rachel?' Daphne's voice was uncertain now, questioning. 'What's wrong?'

Tears of weakness and of terror were streaming down Rachel's cheeks. She could feel them, scalding hot on her cold skin. She could not speak.

'Rachel! Answer me! What's wrong?' The tinny voice echoed, uncomforting, unreal. Rachel very precisely replaced the receiver, rolled on to her side, knees drawn up, tears running into the pillow. The blood still seeped, hot and sticky, and the pain did not abate.

Daphne stood for some moments, telephone in hand. The hallway was chilly, the one landing light she had switched on as, shocked from sleep, she had run to the telephone threw an eerie light down the stairs. The big clock ticked quietly.

What for goodness sake was Rachel up to now?

'Is something wrong, Mum?' Parker, sleep-ruffled and unlovely, wrapped in a dressing gown that looked like a discarded horse blanket, stood by the foot of the stairs, rubbing her eyes.

'No, nothing. That is –' Daphne shook her head, her own brain still fuzzy with sleep and shock. She had been so certain, when she had woken to the shrilling of the bell that something dreadful had happened to Toby. The fear was still with her. Carefully and quietly she replaced the receiver.

Who knew with Rachel? Daphne had heard enough of the girl's exploits, observed enough with her own eyes, to know this could as well be nothing as something. She was probably at some party – tiddly, emotional and making mischief. On the other hand –

'Mum?' Parker, huddled against the cold, stepped a little nearer, indicating, a little nervously, the now quiet telephone. 'It must o' bin *something* at this hour o' the morning?'

'Yes, Parker. it must.' A furrow of worry drew Daphne's brows together. 'The problem is, what?' She tried to recall the sound of Rachel's voice, and flinched a little at the memory. If the words had said little, the manner of their speaking had been utter desperation.

Parker stood, confused but loyally determined to help. 'Who was it, Mum?'

'It was Miss Patten. A friend of Mr Toby's. She sounded – very upset. She put the phone down.'

'Where was she?'

Daphne shook her head. 'That's the problem. I don't know.'

'Tell you what –' In the democracy of emergency Parker's tone was comforting as she fell back on her own sure-fire answer to every problem. '– I'll make a nice cup o' tea.'

'Would you? That would be awfully nice.' Daphne was abstracted. Rachel's voice echoed, ragged with tension and with tears. And, even distorted by the telephone – fear?

Almost impatiently Daphne tutted to herself. Now she was exaggerating. The girl was in trouble somewhere and wanted Toby to bail her out. Toby wasn't here. Rachel had no doubt by now found some other willing hand to hold hers.

Or had she?

With sudden brisk movements Daphne went into the study, picked up the address book from the desk.

The telephone in Rachel's flat rang and rang.

'I'm sorry, Madam. No-one is replying.'

'Thank you.'

In the kitchen Parker, now thoroughly awake and obviously rather enjoying the drama of the moment had made the tea. Daphne smilingly accepted hers, sat and sipped it. The kitchen was cosy and warm, the banked-up stove glowing.

No-one is replying.

She came to her decision before the tea was half-drunk, but she said nothing until the cup was empty. In her opinion a hasty action was often the wrong one. A moment's thought never harmed anyone. That what she was about to do was probably both foolhardy and foolish did not make that any less a sound principle.

'More tea, Mum?'

'Yes, please, Parker. And then – I think I'm going to have to go out.'

'What?' Parker was startled into disrespect. 'Go out where?'

'Round to Miss Patten's flat. It isn't far. I can get a taxi from the all-night stand down by the station.'

Parker stood, righteous outrage clothing her in a surprising dignity. 'That you must not, Mum.'

Daphne shook her head. 'That I must, I'm afraid, Parker. As you said yourself – it must be something. If Rachel isn't there I'll have done no harm. If she is –' She let the sentence hang in the air.

'If she is –' Parker pulled tight the belt of her horse blanket

217

with a great sense of purpose, '– then you'll likely need some help. I'm not letting you go alone.'

'Don't be silly, Parker –'

'Silly I'm not, Mum. Though there's others can be surprisingly so. Let you go out at this time o' night – morning – in your condition and all alone? It'd never sit right with me conscience, Mum, believe me. If you think you got to go, I can't stop you. But I don't have to sit here supping tea and watch it.'

Daphne, more relieved than she would have cared to admit, smiled. 'Bless you, Parker. If you really don't mind then I'd be very pleased to have you. It's no doubt a wild goose chase – but I have to try. I find it hard to believe that anyone would call for help in such a way if the cause were not urgent.'

'Right.' Parker clattered the cups onto the draining board. 'I'll get some clothes on. And you make sure you wear your heavy coat, Mum.'

It was nearly four o'clock before, with the taxi waiting below, Daphne and Parker apprehensively climbed the ill-lit stairs to Rachel's landing.

The door was on the latch. Within a faint light glowed.

Daphne pushed open the door. 'Rachel?'

The silence hung, heavy. There was an odd and unpleasant smell upon the air. Draped silks and satins gleamed in the faint light of the single lamp. Mirrors winked emptily, reflecting the near-dead embers of the fire.

Daphne advanced into the sitting room. Parker hung back, a shadow by the door. A small bath half-full of water stood before the fire. Towels were heaped about. Stained towels. Very slowly Daphne bent to pick one up, held it to the light. 'Rachel?' her voice was suddenly sharp with panic. '*Rachel!* Where are you?' She turned, ran back into the hall, threw open the door to the kitchen. The tiny room was chaotically untidy, the top of the stove covered in receptacles of all kinds. 'Rachel?'

The silence was absolute. Daphne went back into the sitting room, pushed open the door of the bedroom. 'Rachel! Dear God, what's happened?' She flew to the bed, fell to her knees beside it. 'Rachel!'

Light flared as the practical Parker found the lamp and lit it. In the gentle glow Rachel's face was white as marble and as still. Blood was smeared everywhere. Daphne stared, appalled.

'Make up the fire, Mum. And get the kettle on.' Parker was stripping off her coat, rolling up her sleeves.

'But – Parker – she's – she's dead! What can we—'

'No, Mum. Not dead. Not yet. Not that she won't be if we don't get ourselves going. Don't worry. You leave her to me. But get that fire going and get some tea made. Strong. With lots of sugar. Get some clean towels, too, if you can find them. Or a sheet. Anything'll do. Come on, now, miss – let's get you woken up –'

Daphne fled to the kitchen, fumbled with water, gas taps, matches. She could hear Parker's brisk voice in the bedroom and then, blessed relief, Rachel's softly murmured reply. She flew to the door. 'Rachel – oh, thank God! – I thought you were dead. I'll send for the doctor – get you into hospital at once!'

'No!' Rachel's huge eyes glowed fiercely in a face pared to the bone. 'No! No doctors!'

'But Rachel –'

'No!' She turned her head on the pillow, exhausted by the effort. 'No doctors.' Her eyes found Parker's face. 'Tell her.'

Parker left her ministrations, came to Daphne, gently shooing her towards the door. 'Don't you worry, Mum. I've seen worse than this. Make the tea, get that bleedin' fire goin' an' find me some clean linen.' The painfully acquired accent of years had dropped away. Neither of them noticed it. 'An' let's 'ave no talk o' doctors, eh? Not yet, anyway. Needs must if the devil pushes, but best not. You know what I mean?'

Suddenly, and stunningly, Daphne did. 'Yes. I see. But – Parker – are you sure? She – supposing she dies? We can't let that happen. We can't!'

Parker, a totally different Parker than the awkward maid who shouted into the telephone and all but fell over whenever she bobbed a curtsey, smiled. 'You leave it to me, Mum. And – you be careful, you 'ear? We don't want more trouble, now do we? You got problems of your own.'

It took a surprising moment for that to sink in. In the past hour Daphne had given barely a thought to her own condition.

Parker was watching her shrewdly. 'You all right?'

'I'm fine.' She was.

There was approval in the maid's eyes. 'Right. Tea, then.'

Dawn was breaking, rosy and chill, before Rachel slept, peaceful at last but stirring often and muttering. Daphne sat beside her, drinking what seemed to be her hundredth cup of tea and watching the perfect, beautiful, empty face. Parker, seemingly inexhaustible, was busying herself about the wrecked sitting room. Daphne, checking first that Rachel slept, walked to the door. 'Parker?'

The angular figure stopped, lifted her head. 'Yes, Mum?'

'Thank you. Thank you so much. I don't know what to say. I never could have managed without you. I think that Miss Patten probably owes you her life.'

Briskly, Parker plumped a cushion. 'Oh, I wouldn't say that, Mum. Remarkable how a woman can recover from these things. You may not believe it, but more don't die than do.'

'How did you know so well what to do?' The question was unthinking, and only after it was spoken did Daphne realize the potential embarrassment involved in the answer. 'Oh, please – I didn't mean –'

Parker had stilled again, looked at her for a long moment, measuring her. Then, 'Me mother's a – kind of midwife,' she said, 'in Stepney.'

'I – see.'

'She –'elps, you know? Women who –' The pale, bulbous eyes flickered to Daphne and away, '– need 'elp, so to speak.'

'Yes.' Daphne stood awkwardly, watching, as the other woman efficiently brought order to chaos. 'And now? What should we do now?'

Parker straightened, rubbed her back, for the first time showing signs of strain and tiredness. ''Ard to tell. To be honest, I think there's damage. 'Appens sometimes. 'Specially if the girl's – you know –' She clenched her fists, pressed them hard together. '– not good at it,' she finished, a little lamely.

Daphne turned to look at the still figure upon the bed. 'Yes,' she said, simply. Then, 'And if there is? Damage?'

'Who knows? She'll have trouble for some time. She may need treatment, she may not. We'll 'ave to see. It's now's the problem. She shouldn't be left. She needs nursing.' Parker smiled, warmly, the smile of a friend. 'An' a good drop of raspberry tea.'

Almost Daphne laughed. 'Raspberry *tea*?'

'That's the ticket. And rest. And warmth. Comfort.'

'She must come home with us.'

Parker smiled, and nodded. 'That's the ticket,' she said, again.

Daphne walked back to the bedside, settled herself back into the chair. She had opened the curtains. Beyond the window the sky was wreathed in the pearl mist of dawn.

Rachel slept on.

Chapter Ten

In the few lucid moments Rachel experienced in the next twenty-four hours she was aware only of her own pain, her own terrible confusion. In those waking moments she willed herself back into the oblivion of unconsciousness. She could not – would not – stand the pain; worse, she could not face what she had done. For most of the time, delirious and dream-bound she tossed and turned, hair sweat-soaked, the glow of fever upon her skin. Again and again she saw that weasel face above her, experienced that monstrous violation of her body; again and again she struggled to escape. She was aware, sometimes, of soothing voices, restraining hands. But for most of the time she was alone, in darkness and in pain, in a nightmare world of distortion and terror. A world through which, suddenly, Gideon Best stalked, grown huge and black with anger, looking to destroy her as she had destroyed his child. She hid. She ran. She fled into darkness. But always he was there, behind her in the darkness, searching. Exhausted at last, she hung upon a thread of pain in the midnight void and waited.

He came.

He came mouthing words she could not understand. He came with huge hands stretched to capture her. To punish. 'No, Gideon, no! I'm sorry. I'm sorry!' He did not hear, cared neither for her terror nor for her remorse. Weakly she fought him, crying she begged for him to listen to what she was trying to tell him; yet she knew he would not, and the tears would not stop. Then, incredibly, he was holding her, firmly and tenderly in his arms as he might cradle an infant. She heard his voice, understood not a word of what he was saying yet recognized the soothing, gentle sound. She spoke his name, softly, very softly, and at last and for the first time he spoke hers. 'Rachel. Kushti rakli.

Rachel.' She clung like a terrified child, sobbing as if her heart would break. Woke to find herself cradled in strong arms. Woke to believe for one wild moment that Gideon had indeed come to find her, to forgive her. Almost she spoke his name; prayed she had not as she looked into the brilliant blue eyes of Toby Smith. The world rocked and settled. Cool air brushed her face. She was sore, deathly tired. Her cheeks were wet with tears. 'Toby?' Her voice seemed to come from a very long way away.

With enormous care Toby laid her back upon the pillows. 'Yes. How are you feeling?' His voice was quiet, very gentle.

She took some moments to gather her strength, to take stock. 'I'm – all right I think. Weak. And it hurts.' She lay exhausted for a second, summoned a pale shadow of a smile. 'Serves me right.'

Toby nodded, unsmiling. His eyes were very bright, the fair curls fell tangled across his forehead. 'Rachel –'

She shook her head upon the pillow. 'Don't. Not yet. Please.'

He watched her for a long moment, something close to pain in his eyes. 'You idiot. You bloody idiot,' he said, gentle still.

'Yes.' Weak tears slid down her face. She made an effort to smile again. 'Yes. So what's new?'

He took her cold hand in his; she could feel the warmth and strength of it, like new blood in her veins. His mouth was soft as he kissed her fingers. 'I'll tell Daphne you're awake.'

She closed her eyes, utterly exhausted. She submitted to their ministrations, Daphne's and the girl she called Parker, aware as she did so that this had become something of a routine with them. 'How long – have I been here?' She knew now where she was, remembered as a distant nightmare the harrowing taxi trip that had brought her to Bayswater.

Daphne sat beside her; a little awkwardly, her pregnancy was beginning to show. Rachel did not look at her. Daphne took her hand. 'Two days. Rachel, you've been very ill. Very ill indeed.'

Rachel closed her eyes.

'You're still losing blood.' Daphne's voice was very calm, the grip of her fingers firm. 'We've done everything we can. Parker knows a little of such things – but Rachel, my dear – you have to see a doctor –'

'No!'

The hand tightened on hers. 'Please listen. There's no danger, I promise you. Mr Preston – my own gynaecologist – he's a personal friend. He'll see you. And he'll say nothing. I promise.'

'No!'

'Here we are.' Brisk and efficient, Parker had appeared on the other side of the bed, slid an arm under Rachel's shoulders. 'Drink up.' She glanced in warning at her mistress, shaking her head a little.

Rachel gulped the warm, fragrant concoction.

Daphne stood up. 'Twelve hours,' she said, firmly. 'If there's no improvement by then – or if at any time there is deterioration – then I send for Mr Preston. This isn't worth losing your life for, Rachel!'

Bleakly Rachel lifted reddened eyes to the plain, determined face. 'Isn't it?'

'No. It isn't. And I won't hear such talk. Twelve hours.' Suddenly softening, Daphne leaned to her, smoothed the hair from her face. 'Try to get some sleep, my dear. We'll see how you are, and talk later.'

There was, in the end, no need to send for Mr Preston. Though her recovery was slow, thanks to Parker's not inconsiderable skills, it was steady. The pain ebbed, the steady bleeding abated. She slept, not dreamlessly but at least more comfortably. To her own dismay and exasperation she wept a great deal. The tears would come, suddenly and unexpectedly, from nowhere and for no apparent reason. Physically she healed; yet there were other wounds, no less dangerous, no less painful, that refused to mend; and for the moment at least her will was not strong enough to overcome them. The nightmares haunted her still.

Five days after Daphne and Parker had rescued her she was able to sit in a chair by the window. Her room was a pleasant one, the floral wallpaper russet, cream and gold, heavy rust-coloured velvet curtains draped beside the big sash window. A fire burned in the hearth against the autumn chill. Wrapped in a less than stylish but very cosy woollen dressing gown of Daphne's she sat in a deep and comfortable armchair enjoying the last of the mellow afternoon sunshine, a jigsaw puzzle taking satisfying shape on a tray on the table before her. When the door opened she glanced up, and smiled. 'Toby. Come in.'

'I'm not disturbing you?'

She shook her head. 'Not at all.'

He entered the room, closing the door behind him, walked to the fire and stood with his back to it, hands clasped behind him. 'How are you feeling?'

'Very much better thank you. I'll be right as rain in no time.'

'Good. That's good.' Toby shifted a little restlessly, ran a hand through his hair in a characteristic gesture.

Rachel watched him, a small frown on her face. She knew Toby well enough to know when he had something on his mind. This, then, was the interview she had been dreading; the sinner, spared, must be brought to book for her transgression, such iniquity must not be allowed to pass unremarked. She glanced down at the jigsaw. It was made of wood, the colours subtle, the picture – a huge vase of autumn flowers – deceptively complicated. Very steadily she picked up a piece, tested it next to another. 'I've been meaning to thank you,' she said. 'You and Daphne. What I did was stupid. To say nothing of criminal. I couldn't have blamed Daphne if she had just dumped me at the nearest hospital and left me to talk my own way out.' She glanced up.

He shook his head, almost abstractedly. 'Don't be ridiculous. Daphne did the only thing possible. There's no need for thanks. Just thank the Lord it all turned out right in the end. You're sure you're feeling better?'

She blinked. 'Yes. I'm sure. I'll be up and about in a day or so.' She glanced down at the jigsaw again. The hand that held the spare piece was thin and very white, the fingers claw-like. She snapped the piece neatly into place, waiting.

Toby had left the fire and come to stand behind her, looking over her shoulder. He leaned forward, one hand resting on her shoulder, picked up a piece, tried it, turned it and set it in place, the heart of a great crimson overblown rose. With a small stirring of surprise Rachel realized that his touch, casually bestowed, had been as casually accepted. Until recently such intimacy would have wrenched her heart to a perilous and probably provocative response. Now she was able to turn her head, look at him, unshaken. Still restless he turned away, moved to the window, stood looking into the fading light. 'Rachel?'

'Mm?' She picked up another piece of jigsaw. The rose completed, the picture was becoming suddenly clearer. She leaned forward.

'What is the man Gideon Best to you?' His voice was very quiet.

She froze.

He turned.

Very, very carefully she put the piece down, clasped her hands in front of her. She did not look at him.

Her face told him. 'Christ, Rachel!' he said, very low.

She lifted her chin.

The silence was long, and fraught. When at last she broke it she still could not bring herself to look at him. 'Is it any of your business?'

'No.' The word was bleak.

'Well, then.' Apparently composed she bent back to the jigsaw.

'But – you could have anyone! Anyone! What's wrong with you that you let a – a brute like that touch you? Jesus, it makes me ill to think of it.' The words were violent.

Her swift, small movement knocked the board, scattering some of the pieces. 'Leave it, Toby.'

'Leave it? Just like that?' He spun on her. 'I've known you since you were born. We've been like brother and sister. God Almighty, Rachel, I know we fight like cat and dog, but damn it I care about you! I always have. You must know that! And to think that bastard did this to you – left you to face it alone –!'

'Toby!'

'I heard you! I heard what you said! You thought I was him! You –' He stopped. Swallowed hard, controlling himself.

'What?'

'Nothing.'

'Toby? What did I say?'

He knew her too well, knew what it would do to her to know

how abjectly she had begged. 'It doesn't bloody well matter what you said! What matters is that that animal had you, and left you to face the consequences, and he's getting away with it!'

Carefully and none too steadily she stood. 'That's enough.'

'The hell it is –'

'Enough!' She clutched at the back of the chair for support, but would not take her eyes from his. 'Have you mentioned this to anyone else?'

'Of course not.'

'Promise you won't. Swear it.'

'There's no need.'

'There is need. Swear it.'

The blaze in the blue eyes died. 'Very well. I swear.'

'Did anyone else hear what I said?'

'No.'

The strength drained from her. She sat down, suddenly, her face pale. He took a step forward. 'Are you all right?'

'Yes. I – could do with a cup of tea –'

He walked to the fireplace, pulled the tasselled bell cord.

'Toby.'

He turned.

She held out a hand. He came quietly to her and took it. 'Thank you for being concerned about me. But please – forget it now? I've learned a lesson. A tough one, but it's no-one else's fault. Let's leave it at that.'

His hand was firm about hers. 'It was Gideon Best's child?'

'Yes.'

His eyebrows lifted a little in unspoken question.

A small, acid smile flickered. 'Your faith is touching. But there's no doubt.'

'He didn't –' His face darkened again. '– force you?'

For a moment the temptation was there. Who would know? Who would believe Gideon's word against hers? And how sweet to reap the sympathy that such a lie would sow. Then 'No,' she said.

He dropped her hand. His expression did not change. He was watching her intently. 'Why didn't you take precautions?' he asked, bluntly.

How often had she asked that question of herself? 'I don't know.'

'I find that hard to believe.'

'I find it hard to believe myself.'

He contemplated her for a long, hard moment, weighing, measuring, drawing his own conclusions. The door opened. 'You rang, sir?'

'Yes, Parker. Miss Patten would like tea, please.'

'Yes, sir. For two?'

'No, Parker. For three.' Daphne appeared behind her, smiling. She walked into the room, her gait already taking on the ponderous care of pregnancy. 'Why, Rachel, how very well you've done! I can't do jigsaws for toffee! I don't think that one's ever actually been finished.' She settled herself on the arm of the chair, smiling from one to the other. 'There, isn't this nice? Draw the curtains, Toby, would you? Let's make it nice and cosy –'

Hugo Fellafield looked gloomily into his beer.

Where the hell was she?

In the weeks since that last disastrous encounter he had tried to forget her. He had. He'd even tried seeing that pretty, empty-headed Sybyl Bainbridge that Charles and his father were so anxious for him to impress. Though why, he thought savagely, he should do anything to please his blasted parsimonious family was beyond him. But nothing he did could get Rachel Patten out of his mind. Neither pride nor sense could stand against this almost demented infatuation. For the past week or more he had been trying to telephone her. Once he had even gone round to the flat. To no avail. The telephone rang interminably. The flat had been very obviously shut up and empty. Now, for three nights, he'd been reduced to this; touring those spots he knew she frequented, hoping to find her, desperate for a glimpse of her, hoping against hope that that awful scene in the flat had been the product of one of those capriciously cruel moods that he knew she suffered and so often, later, regretted. But there had been no sign of her.

So where was she?

He leaned his chin on his bunched fist. Off with some man,

obviously. A man, no doubt, with money. A man who could buy her the things she coveted, take her to the places she wanted to go. A man whose father didn't pay him a pittance for working his guts out on the pretext that he was gaining experience. Gaining experience! His brow furrowed with an anger that had been seething for a week. He already knew more than his father and Charles put together about the Madeira trade. He was doing well, he knew it. Producers and shippers trusted him, trusted his knowledge and his judgement. It was to him they turned, not to Spencer Fellafield, when they wanted something done. His father's and his brother's political ambitions were grounded in the profits of Paget and Fellafield; and he it was who now ran the company. And for what thanks, let alone decent remuneration? None. Sir James knew; had indeed congratulated him, thanked him for taking on the day to day running of the company's affairs so readily and efficiently. But when he had asked his father for more money, for the wherewithal to set himself up in his own small establishment in London you'd have thought he'd asked for the crown jewels! 'When you're ready to settle down, boy – ready to marry a girl of good background and breeding and settle to family life – come back to me then. Believe me I'd be only too pleased to discuss the matter with you in such circumstances. But in the meantime if you think I'm going to finance your man-about-town ambitions and pay for the pink gins and green goddesses of a succession of silly flappers, you have another thing coming. You have a perfectly good home here in Cheyne Walk. You have gainful employment and a comfortable life. Do you think, Hugo, that money grows on trees?'

Bloody cheek. The old man treated him like a half-witted child. And he held on to the family purse strings like a miser. Unless, of course, some opportunity arose to advance the likelihood of Charles' adoption as a Tory Parliamentary candidate. The pennies rattled quickly enough then!

Hugo drank his beer, the sting of self-pity almost bringing maudlin tears. If it weren't for the quiet support of his mother he'd be in the poorhouse, that's what! And now, to top it all, Rachel had gone off with some rich fancypants who no doubt had houses in Belgravia and Cannes, safes full of diamonds, trunks full of furs – Oh, damn it! He was aware that he was not thinking either as clearly or as logically as he might be. He looked about owlishly. The bar was crowded, and very noisy. A girl with a face that was faintly familiar caught his eye and waved. Grinning inanely he waved back. She made a quick gesture with her hand, inviting him to join the group she was with, then turned to talk to someone else. Hugo considered. Why not? He had nothing better to do. As he pushed his chair back a man walking past him sidestepped quickly, almost colliding with it.

Hugo stood hastily. 'Oh, I say, I'm most awfully sorry.'

'That's all right, old man. No harm done –' The man was tall and slender, very fair. Soft straight hair fell across a wide forehead. He was dressed impeccably, the evening dress suit cut to perfection, soft pearl gleaming upon cuff and shirt front. About to turn away he stopped, a small frown creasing the handsome brow. 'I say – it's Fellafield, isn't it? Hugo Fellafield?'

'I – yes, it is –' For a moment Hugo was utterly disconcerted. Then his slightly fuddled brain caught up with itself. 'Maurice Playle,' he said, with genuine pleasure. 'You were up at Cambridge with Charles. A year or so ahead of me.'

'That's right. Well, fancy meeting you here. How's old Charles? How's the family?'

'Well, thank you.'

Playle put his head on one side, thoughtfully. 'Let me think – Madeira, isn't it, your business? Your mother lives there – charming woman – Charles and I spent a very happy vacation there in 'twenty-three. Your Pa's something hush-hush in the Foreign Office as I remember? And Charles – he's still a rampant reactionary intent on a safe seat in Surrey?'

Hugo laughed. 'You have a very good memory. Yes, that's right. Especially the bit about Charles.'

Playle laughed, easily, linked a friendly arm through Hugo's. 'You all alone? Me too, as it happens.' He cocked an elegant blond eyebrow. 'My date has stood me up. I think her husband must have come home early. Come and have a drink. We've a lot to talk about.' He laughed again, an attractive sound, quiet and genuinely amused.

Hugo smiled back and allowed himself to be guided firmly towards the bar.

The first pheasant shoot of the season at Breckon Hall was held at the beginning of October. After a couple of fine weeks the weather was showing signs of deterioration. Gusting north westerly winds rattled the treetops and the sky was leaden. On the evening before the first day's shooting Toby sat in the library, his feet on the fender, a glass at his elbow. Dispersed about the room were several groups of men, their talk and laughter superimposed against the sound of the rising wind outside. Snatches of conversation came to his ears.

'Damn bad business if you ask me. Europe won't escape, you mark my words. What affects Wall Street affects the rest of the world. Bound to.'

'– and blowed if it didn't turn out to be old Buster Benton. You remember Buster – big fellow, Master of Hounds at Branscombe –'

'This young Bradman might be the best the Aussies can produce but he'll never outclass the likes of Hobbs and Sutcliffe. Were you at the Oval when they knocked 'em for six this year?' Toby stirred, comfortably, reached for his glass.

'A refill, sir?' Parks, the Pagets' butler stood at his elbow, smiling.

'Yes, please, Parks. Thank you.'

'Everything all right, young Toby?' Sir James, resplendent in old-fashioned frock coat, waistcoat and wing collared shirt that must surely, Toby thought, have seen its first service before the war, beamed down at him expansively. 'Ready for the off?'

Toby stood. 'I certainly am, sir. Looking forward to it.'

'Should be a good day, if it doesn't rain too hard tonight. Damn birds won't fly well with their feathers soaked. Wind'll be no problem. Best has the drives well planned to take advantage of it, you can be sure of that. What a pity your charmin' wife couldn't be with us. Fee's very disappointed.'

'Yes, sir. So was Daphne. However, doctor's orders, I'm afraid. Mr Preston thought it best that she doesn't overdo things just as the moment.' Not strictly true, in fact; Daphne continued in excellent health, though the doctor certainly had recommended that she take things quietly; her decision not to come to Breckon had had rather more to do with nursing their still poorly guest than coddling herself.

'Quite, quite. Difficult time, eh? Lookin' for a boy, I'd say, what?'

'We really don't mind, sir. As long as the child's fit and healthy.' Again, not quite true. Toby wanted a son. He wanted one, he had discovered to his own surprise, very badly indeed.

'Of course.' Sir James raised his voice. 'Right, gentlemen, if you're ready? Shall we join the ladies? The dinner gong should be sounding any moment –'

Toby had willingly fallen in with Fiona's request that he sit next to Philippa at dinner. 'Toby, she's so very quiet – Eddie's really worried. It seems there's even some doubt that she'll take up her place at the college next year. Sally's death seems to have knocked the stuffing out of her entirely. We had a terrible time even getting her to come down here for these few days. Yesterday she took the boys to a circus – a local fair they visit every year – Jeremy said she cried all the way through it. Just sat there and cried. As if she didn't realize she was doing it, he said. Poor lamb. We're trying to get her to come to Madeira with James and me in February, when we go to visit Hugo's mother. Do see if you can persuade her? The rest – the change – it'll do her so much good, I'm sure. God knows, Sally's death was a terrible shock to all of us; but Philippa has her life in front of her. She really mustn't be allowed to let her grief overwhelm her like this.'

He glanced now, sideways, at the pale profile. Philippa was pushing her food around her plate listlessly, her wine glass stood untouched. 'Flip?'

She turned. Her brown eyes, usually so friendly and bright, were dark-ringed in a face that had lost flesh and colour.

'How are you?'

'Oh – all right –' She looked back at her plate, mashed a piece of potato with her fork, pushed it into a heap. 'I – can't get used to it somehow. You know?'

'Yes. I know.'

Around them the hum of conversation rose and fell. Inevitably the disastrous financial collapse on the New York Stock Exchange was causing most comment. Everyone had a theory, a story, a point to make. Many people thought the worst was past; a few pessimists felt that it was yet to come. Most agreed that the crash would affect not only the United States but Europe and the rest of the world as well. Toby listened with half an ear.

'I really can't believe she's dead.' The small, lost voice brought him back to Philippa. Her head was down. She was, he realized with a pang of sympathy, very close to tears again.

He laid down his knife, covered her small hand with his. 'Flip, listen to me.' He hesitated, uncharacteristically lost for words. Philippa sniffed. She was wearing a pretty pale blue evening blouse with a plain, long straight skirt. A very few months ago, he knew, she would have been delighting in her first really grown-up outfit. Now, he guessed, she might as well have been wearing the hated school uniform for all the pleasure it gave her. 'Flip, this really won't do, you know.' He squeezed her fingers. She lifted her eyes to his. And with a shock, for the first time, in the thin face, the wide, set mouth he saw her mother. 'Sally Smith's daughter,' he said, very quietly, very carefully, 'surely isn't going to let the first real blow that life deals her defeat her?'

Philippa sniffed again, looked down at her plate.

Toby picked up his wine glass, sipped it, held it before him, watching the candle light flicker in the ruby depths of the liquid. 'You've had it pretty easy until now, Flip.' He ignored her quick, half-protesting movement, did not look at her. 'You've been fed, clothed, cared for. You've had a comfortable home, a good education. You've had security, and love. You've never had to fight for anything, you've never had to face this rotten world alone. Sally did that for you.' He drank again, put the glass very carefully down, long fingers still wrapped about the fragile stem.

Philippa was watching him now, a small frown on her face.

'She did it for me, too. A long time ago. And under very

different circumstances. We've had our ups and downs since but I'd never deny her that. Sally was a fighter, and a tough one. She came up through a tough school. She wouldn't want to think she'd bred—' He stopped.

Philippa's chin was up. 'A coward? Is that what you were going to say?'

He shook his head, smiling suddenly. 'No, of course not. You're no coward, Flip. We all know that. You've simply never had to face up to tragedy before. And it's hard. It's always hard. But you mustn't – you mustn't! – let it get the better of you. Grieve for Sally – of course you must. But you know as well as I do that she'd be the first to say,' he paused, slanted a small, bright glance at her, 'come on, Flip, enough's enough. Off your behind and do something!' The accent was exact. Philippa winced, then laughed. 'She'd also be the last one to want you to be unhappy. You know it,' he added, gently.

The brown eyes did not waver. 'I do know. But I can't seem to help it.'

'You have to. You have to believe that the pain will ease. It may be hard to believe at the moment, but you –' he hesitated, '– won't ever exactly get used to it, but you will learn to accept what's happened. You have to. You have a life of your own to live. The sooner you grit your teeth and get on with it the better. You must see that? It's certainly what Sally would have wanted you to do.'

For a long time she said nothing. Someone across the table laughed, high-pitched and strident, and she flinched a little. 'Yes. I know you're right,' she said at last. 'It's just – Toby, she was my mother – the only person of my very own in the whole world. She was always there, always waiting for me. I loved her so much. We were so very close. I – can't seem to let her go. What will I do without her?' The tears spilled now, and ran quite openly down her thin face. She was too miserable even to be aware of the curious glances that were thrown towards them. Fiona, worried, was watching; she pushed her chair back, half stood, as if to come to them. Toby shook his head reassuringly, turned back to Philippa. The conversation had died a little, now buzzed again, somewhat over-loud.

Philippa absent-mindedly mopped at her eyes with her napkin.

Toby, gently, removed the napkin and substituted his own handkerchief.

'Thanks.' She blew her nose, unself-consciously. 'I'm terribly sorry. I keep doing this. I know I have to stop.'

'Yes, you do.' His voice was firm. 'Now, listen to me – I want you to promise me something. Several things, in fact.'

She lowered the handkerchief, looked at him seriously.

'First promise me that if you need help – if you find yourself really in trouble – the kind of trouble you'd have taken to your tough nut mother you'll come to me.'

She smiled a small, watery smile, hesitated only for a moment. 'I promise.'

'And second, promise me that if you ever want to talk about Sally – about the things she said, the things she did, the things you miss – you'll come to me for that, too.'

She nibbled her lip for a moment.

'I need it too, sometimes, Flip,' he said, with an honesty that surprised himself. 'No-one really knew her the way we did. Not even Eddie, or Fiona.'

Philippa nodded. Smiled again, stronger this time. 'Any more promises?'

'Yes. You'll go to Madeira with Fee and Sir James next spring. And you'll take up your place in the training college in September and become the best damned teacher ever. Nothing would please Sally better than that.'

She took a very long breath, pushed her plate away from her. 'Yes. You're right of course. I do have to pull myself together. All right. I'll go away with Fee. I'll go to college.' She managed another small, lost grin. 'I just hope I can stop crying long enough.'

He reached a long arm about her shoulders and hugged her. 'You will. It'll take time, but you will. Now – one more promise?'

'I don't think I can manage any more.'

'You can this one. I want you to promise to eat the apple tart. Fee will be most put out if you don't, and one shouldn't upset one's hostess, you know. It's the first rule of good behaviour as a guest.'

It was a poor attempt at humour, but she made the effort and laughed a little. 'I'll try.'

Toby applied himself to his own food, mouth twitching suddenly to a small, dryly self-deprecating smile. Rachel, and now Flip. Much more of this and he could apply for a position as a fully qualified nursemaid.

The guns gathered next morning at nine in gusting wind and beneath lowering skies outside the big barn. The dogs sniffed around the yard excitedly, tails wagging, eyes eager. The small, numbered, mother of pearl tabs were drawn to establish the first order. A horde of young lads, beaters and 'stops' for a shilling a day, horsed about, pushing and shoving, waiting for the order that would take them out into the coverts. Sir James, in his element, battered hat firmly pulled down against the wind, equally well-worn jacket, breeches and gaiters already muddy, for he had been out and about since six that morning, conferred with Gideon Best – who had been out for longer – his labradors beside him, heads cocked, watching his every move.

'Jubilee Stand it is, then. North side. The numbers are out? Good man.' He glanced a measuring look at the sky. 'Doesn't look too promising. Better arrange the drives to bring us back to the house for lunch. Right. Off we go then.'

They tramped out across the fields, heads down against the wind in which a few stinging drops of rain flew, dogs casting and scenting the ground as they ran. Toby found himself in company with a sharp-faced young enthusiast he had met the night before whose conversational subjects then, as now, consisted entirely of shooting and fishing. 'Jubilee, eh? Jolly good. Best stand on the place. One of the best in Norfolk, I'd say. Might as well start with the best, what? And this wind should make for good sport.' He pulled out a silver flask from his pocket, offered it to Toby who declined with a smile and a shaken head, then toasted him and took a sip. 'Here's to a good bag, what?'

They arrived at the stand, and Toby took his position by the hazel twig that held the number five. 'Best position on this stand, sir.' The young manservant Davies, who had offered to load for him loaded and checked the gun and handed it to him. 'Piece of luck drawing five. 'Specially if we go on to Berkeley next, as we probably will if we're goin' back to the house for lunch.'

'Oh?' Toby, eyes narrowed, was watching the tall, dark figure who stood, spaniel as always at his heels, the beaters in a group behind him, talking to Sir James.

Cheerfully Davies set about loading the second gun. 'Five here, you'll be on seven at Berkeley. Another good 'un.'

'Splendid,' Toby said, absently.

Gideon had turned and was striding away across the field towards the edge of the woodland, the beaters, sticks in hand following. Toby watched the distinctive figure, apparently indifferent to the battering wind as it strode over the uneven ground and disappeared into the woods. For a moment he allowed himself to remember that telltale hesitation in Rachel's voice, and his blood seethed. A few moments later there came a shrill whistle. Sir James raised the small silver horn he carried to his lips. A single, melodic note rang out and in the distance, clattering their sticks, the beaters began their advance.

It was a good morning's sport. The birds, helped by the wind, flew high, fast and well. The racks in the game wagon filled. As they made their way back across the fields towards the house – Breckon's stands being well enough spaced around the estate to make transport unnecessary – the talk turned to other shoots, other drives.

'You did jolly well, sir.' Davies trudged beside Toby, carrying the guns. 'You got a dead eye, I'll say that.'

Toby laughed, a little grimly. 'I learned in a hard school.'

The cheery youngster nodded, sagely. 'The war, you mean.'

'That's right.'

'My Dad can't stand it.' Davies side-stepped a rabbit hole, fell back into step.

Toby glanced enquiry. 'Oh?'

The lad jerked his head, confidentially. 'The guns. The shootin'. It's the sound, you see. He were in Flanders. Three year. Afore the war he were an underkeeper. Loved it. Now – can't get near nor by when they're shootin'.'

'Ah.'

'Never bin the same since. Shakes, you know?'

'Yes. I know.'

The boy cast a small, admiring look. 'Didn't do you no harm?'

Toby smiled. 'No. I suppose not.'

They had reached the house. 'I'll see you later, then?' Davies lifted a nonchalant hand to his cap in half-salute. The democracy of the sport, needless to say, did not extend to the breaking of bread. Toby watched the boy join the other keepers and beaters and turn towards the barn, where bread, cheese and ale awaited them.

'Toby, old chap –'

He turned. Charles Fellafield, square, heavy-jowelled face pink with the exertion of plodding through the still steadily-rising wind, laid a weighty hand upon his shoulder. 'Just the man I'm looking for.'

'Oh?' Toby smiled at Hugo, who, shoulders hunched, hands in pockets, walked on the other side of his brother. Hugo gave him the shadow of a grin in acknowledgement, retreated into the brown study in which, it seemed to Toby, he had been enveloped for the whole of the last twenty-four hours.

'Got a proposition. Looking for investors. Damn exciting project, and right up your street, I'd have thought. Come on – tell you about it over lunch. Oh, for Christ's sake, Hugo! Why don't you look where you're going?'

Hugo, who had stumbled into his brother's stolid form, mumbled apology.

'Right, chaps – lunch is laid in the main hall – no need to disrobe and all that. Next best thing to the open air, what?' Sir James ushered them into the wide, marble floored hall where a long table was laid with immaculate linen, shining silver, gleaming crystal. An immense rib of beef stood on a side table, waiting to be carved. A huge fire leapt and danced about the logs in the fireplace.

'Madeira, sir?' Parks was there, the picture of neat and dapper cleanliness beside the muddy tweeds and corduroys. 'Sercial or Bual?'

Toby took a glass of warming Bual, sipped it appreciatively. 'This is good.'

'Good year,' Hugo said, automatically. '1910, I believe. Not a lot of it about.'

'Toby.' Charles took a ponderous stand, rocking on his heels, glass in hand. 'Been looking for a chance to talk to you. How do you feel about making a fortune?'

Toby lifted his glass, eyed the tawny red liquid appreciatively. 'Pretty positively, I'd say.'

'Right. Opportunity of a lifetime. Housing. Not your common or garden two-up, two-downers that are going up all over the place, but *real* housing. Big and beautiful in a lovely setting. A market just waiting to be opened up. We – that is a business acquaintance and I – we've got the site, we've got the plans. We're looking for investment. Looking for capital. It's a guaranteed winner –'

Hugo wandered away. Charles had been beating this same drum for the past month, in the ear of anyone who would listen. Hugo wasn't interested. He wasn't interested in Charles' schemes, or in his appalling politics; he wasn't interested in this ridiculous, hearty gathering, he wasn't interested in blasting a few poor innocent birds out of the sky. He wasn't interested in anything but the whereabouts of Rachel Patten. If he could find her, now, if he could show her he was not the insignificant and penurious boy she obviously thought him, then all would be well. The small favour Maurice Playle had asked had been easily, ludicrously easily, executed. And he had money in the bank to show for it. Rachel, surely, would look at him with different eyes if he could squire her around London in style? But – where the hell *was* she?

He stood at the great leaded window, glared out into the stormy afternoon. He'd find her. He'd find her if it damned well killed him.

Behind him a melodic gong rang, singing on the air. 'Gentlemen – luncheon is served.'

*

The afternoon's drives went as well as the morning's, though as the day wore on the rising gale caused problems. At last, one planned drive from the end of the day, Sir James decided that it was time to call a halt. The rain had started in earnest now, beating down with punishing force, and birds driven once, their plumage heavy with water, would not fly well if driven again. The day had gone well, and there was always tomorrow. Baths and dry clothes beckoned. The party started back.

Toby had not done as well in the afternoon as he had in the morning; and he well knew why. The Madeira had flowed easily at lunch, and Charles Fellafield, for once in his life, had had something of interest to say. Once back out in the field Davies, grinning, had offered him a flask. 'Gid's best,' he'd said, laughing cheekily at his own pun. 'Pinched 'un while his back was turned.'

The whisky had been remarkably good. Toby wondered how the hell a gamekeeper had been able to afford good malt. Time and again during the afternoon he had found his eyes riveted to where the tall, saturnine figure of Gideon Best stood, loading now for Sir James, by his master's side. On occasion their eyes met and each time Toby's hackles rose. He could not rid himself of the image of Rachel's face, thin, agonized, flushed with fever and pain, the sound of her voice – oh, above all, the sound of her voice – pleading like an abandoned child. And then, the instant's hesitation before she had denied that the man had forced her.

In the huge barn a tot of Madeira was waiting for all; a tradition of the estate. Boots were stamped, the rain shaken from clothing. The beaters and stops received their payment and left, with the underkeepers. Gideon stood in the corner deep in conversation with Sir James, presumably planning the drives for the following day. Toby tossed back a glass of full warm Madeira, his eyes on the dark, closed face.

'Another, sir?'

'Thank you.'

Gideon turned and without a glance at any of the guests strode out of the tall doors.

Without conscious thought Toby stepped forward. 'Best!' he called, sharply.

If the gipsy heard he made no sign. He strode on, out into the buffeting wind and rain, Kili at his heels.

Toby put down his glass and started after him.

'Toby, old man – just one more thing –' Charles, pompous as ever, planted himself squarely in front of him. 'You do understand that – in the matters we were discussing earlier – time is, as they say, of the essence?'

'In a moment, Charles, in a moment. There's someone I want to talk to –'

'Of course, of course. I only wanted to make sure that –'

Toby slid round him. Gideon had gone. Toby half-ran to the open door of the barn. The rain clouds had darkened the afternoon to an early dusk. In the distance a broad-shouldered, shadowy but unmistakable figure flickered and was gone beneath the grove of trees that edged the lake.

Again almost without conscious volition Toby followed. The wind had risen now to real violence. The heavy tree canopies, still in leaf, bowed and tossed, a restless, noisy sea of foliage. Rain drove in gusts across the open spaces. Toby made for the spot where he had last seen the man. Once there the light was still strong enough to see the ride that led through the woodlands. Toby followed it.

He caught up with Gideon almost at the door of his hut. 'Best!' His voice rose against the wind.

Gideon turned. He had opened the door. The brim of his hat streaming rain, Toby came up to him. 'I want a word.' He made to step through the doorway into the hut.

A long arm shot out, barring the way, braced against the doorjamb. 'My vardo,' Gideon said, evenly. 'My place. Only those invited enter.'

They stood for a moment, eye to eye, the wind shrieking about them. 'Very well.' With huge effort Toby reined in his temper. 'I'll say what I have to say here. Rachel Patten. If you ever lay a filthy hand on her again I'll have your gipsy hide. You hear? Think yourself lucky not to have paid dearer this time. For Rachel's sake I'll keep it quiet. But by God, if you so much as look at her again I'll have you flogged off this estate and out of the county. You understand?' The bile of fury in his throat he turned to go.

The hand that caught his arm was like a vice. Willy-nilly he found himself flung around to face fierce eyes. Kili, at their feet, growled low in her throat. 'What did you say?'

'You heard me. Stay away from Rachel Patten. You cur!'

Gideon released him, violently, pushing him away so that he stumbled to keep his footing. As he righted himself the other man took a step forward. 'Who told you?' Though quiet the words were quite clear above the wild thrashing of the trees about them. *'Who told you?'*

'What does it matter? I know. I know what you did, you bastard. And I know what Rachel's suffered because of it.'

'She told you?' Gideon's face was a mixture of anger and incredulity.

Toby's rage got the better of him entirely. 'She told me, yes. She told me while she bled like a stuck pig! You and that butcher between you nearly did for her!'

'What are you talking about?'

'The sodding abortion! That's what I'm talking about! Don't play the innocent with me! Are you so used to such things? Didn't you even care enough to bother to discover what happened?'

Gideon rocked back on his heels, his face, wet with rain, stark in the half-light.

Toby hit him, with all the force he could muster, open handed. As if dazed, Gideon accepted the blow, barely flinching. A thin trickle of blood ran from his lip and was blurred by rain. 'Coward!' Toby shrieked against the wind, and made to strike him again.

This time Gideon moved, blocking the blow, backing defensively, shaking his head. Incensed, Toby drove at him, fists flying. In a moment they were on the wet ground, rolling in mud, beating at each other with insensate rage, Kili barking and snapping around them. From the start Toby, once the element of surprise had deserted him, was overwhelmed by the other man's heavier frame and toughened muscles. Pinioned, he struggled, kicking, using his knees. Gideon grunted and rolled away. Toby threw himself after him, his hands in the mop of hair, banging the black head on the ground. Gideon twisted, bucked him off, backhanded him away. Panting they both scrambled to their feet, crouching to attack.

'Enough!'

The roar was outraged.

In the silence the wind howled like a horde of gleeful demons in the branches above their heads.

'What the hell is going on here?' Sir James, attended by a stocky underkeeper whose eyes bulged from his head, stood, feet straddled, hands on hips, face furious. 'Best! Good God, man, what do you think you're doing? And Toby!'

In silence both men straightened. Gideon wiped the blood from his mouth with the back of a dirty hand. Toby shook the wet hair from his eyes.

'Well? Do you have anything to say for yourselves?'

There was a short, tense silence. Then 'No, sir,' Toby said.

Gideon stood like a statue carved in ancient wood.

'Best. I came to rearrange the drives for tomorrow. In the circumstances it won't be necessary, I think. Burrows here can take over.' Sir James' voice was controlled, almost expressionless.

'Yes, sir.'

'As for you, Toby – if there is an explanation for this disgraceful behaviour I'd be pleased to hear it – here or in private.' He left the words hanging on the noisy air.

Toby shook his head. 'I'm sorry, Sir James. It's not a matter I'm prepared to discuss.'

'A matter nevertheless that I trust is settled?' The old Baronet's voice was icy.

'Yes, sir.'

'Then I suggest that you return to the house with me. The less said about this affair the better, I think. Burrows. You understand?'

Burrows, still gaping from Gideon to Toby and back again, stammered, 'Y-yes, Sir James.'

'Best. I'll see you tomorrow, at eight, in the Estate Office.'

Gideon said nothing.

Sir James, his usually easy-tempered face flushed with anger, turned on his heel. Toby held Gideon's eyes for a long, furious moment, then turned to follow.

Kili pushed her head into Gideon's legs.

A long time after they had left Gideon pushed his way into the hut, grabbed a battered canvas bag from the hook behind the door and began to pack.

Philippa it was who deduced where he might have gone. Inevitably word of what had happened – or some version of what had happened – had got out. 'But, Toby – why?' she had stormed when it had become apparent that Gideon had disappeared. 'How *could* you? You've lost him his job – his livelihood –'

'He'd have lost a damn sight more than that if I'd had my way.' Toby, himself in no good odour with his peers over the incident, was grim.

'But *why*? What's he ever done to you?'

'Flip, just take my word for it. Best deserved everything that he got and more. I can't tell you any more than that.'

'Why not? Gideon was my friend. I don't believe he'd do anything so very dreadful! Why won't you tell me?'

'Because the reason isn't mine to tell. Leave it, Flip. Let the matter lie now. Just take my word for it, justice has been done.'

That afternoon, whilst the guns were out and the ladies played whist in the library Philippa borrowed a kitchen maid's bicycle and headed off to the village three miles away where she had taken Jeremy and Jonathon Paget a few days earlier. In a field outside the village the small, shabby circus tent was being taken down, the roundabouts and sideshows dismantled and loaded into a battered lorry. Philippa leaned the bicycle against the hedge. The wind had dropped, drizzle clouded the air. She climbed onto the gate, studied the activity in the field. No-one took the slightest notice of her.

By a covered truck a fire burned and a woman stirred a huge pot of stew. Children dashed about, shrieking and tumbling. The men strained at ropes and wires, fought with the billowing canvas.

Then she saw the dog.

'Kili! Here, Kili!'

The little spaniel ran to her, tail wagging. Philippa dropped to her knees, hugging the animal, ruffling her long silky fur that was dewed with rain. 'Where is he, Kili? Where's Gideon?'

She found him on the far side of the field, helping to dismantle a brightly painted set of boat swings. He straightened, frowning, as he saw her. His hair glistened with rain and his shirt was soaked and clinging to his back. 'What are you doing here?'

'I came to look for you. I guessed you might have come here. Gideon – please – come back with me. Come home. I don't know what happened – Toby won't tell me – but it can't have been as bad as all that! It'll blow over in time –' She stopped. Gideon, grim faced, was shaking his head. 'It will! I know it will.'

Gideon put down the huge spanner he had been holding, turned and walked away from the hubbub, Kili at his heels. Philippa followed, still talking. 'Please, Gideon – Sir James is in just as much of a paddy with Toby as he is with you – he'll get over it.'

Gideon turned, took her gently by the shoulders. 'No, child. It's over. Finished. I'll not come back.'

'But why not?'

'Because nothing can be the same now. A trust is broken. I know it. Sir James knows it. He'd not have me back unless I could give him a good reason for scrapping with one of his guests. And I can't give him a reason. Neither will I beg, not to him, not to anyone. I'll not stay around to beat for a living. Like I said – it's finished.'

Philippa's shoulders dropped beneath his hands. 'You won't even try?'

'No.' He let go of her, stepped back.

'Gideon? What was it all about? Whatever were you and Toby fighting about?'

Gideon shook his black head.

Defeated she pushed her hand into her blazer pocket and pulled out a grubby piece of paper. 'I've written my address down.' She held it out to him. He reached a slow hand and took it. 'Promise me you'll write. Promise,' she added again, firmly, as he said nothing. 'You swore we were friends. Friends don't lose touch with each other when there's trouble. Promise.'

'Can't say I'm much of a hand at letter writing.'

'It doesn't have to be much of a letter.' Philippa was not to be so easily put off. 'Promise.'

He grinned suddenly. 'All right.'

'Say it.'

'I promise.'

'On your honour?'

The smile turned a little grimmer. 'On my honour.'

She nodded, then took an impulsive step forward and flung her arms about him. 'Oh, Gideon, I'm going to miss you so much! Can't you stay? For me?'

He put her from him, firmly, shaking his head. 'No, my rakli, not even for you. I'm dromengro now – a man of the road.' He shrugged. 'It's not the first time.'

She pushed her bedraggled hair from her wet forehead, tried to smile. 'What's Romany for "good luck"?'

'Kushto bok,' he said, unsmiling.

She nodded ruefully. 'Well, kushto bok, Gideon Best.'

'Kushto bok, Philippa.' He turned to leave her.

'Gideon!'

He looked back.

'You will write? Let me know where you are? You promise? Really promise?'

He smiled a little at her urgency. Nodded. 'I promise. Really promise.'

She watched him rejoin the group around the swings, bend to the task without glancing back at her.

'Kushto bok, Gideon Best,' she said again, very quietly, then thrust her hands into her pockets and walked back through the fine, drifting rain to the gate. She wheeled the bicycle around, made to mount it, glanced once more to where Gideon worked. As if sensing her eyes on him he turned his head, then lifted his hand in a last salute.

She waved, climbed onto the cycle, pedalled determinedly off, not looking back.

It was a full month later before Rachel was well enough to return home. She still bled sometimes, irregularly, still suffered occasional pain, but the physical damage seemed to be mending. She had however lost a lot of weight and was constantly tired. She made, at first, no attempt to pick up the threads of her old life; it was easy enough to avoid old acquaintances, to lie brightly on the telephone about other engagements, other interests. No-one was surprised at her sudden reappearance; no-one questioned her. She lived a life of impulse – this was not the first time she had disappeared for weeks on end. So as the days shortened and Christmas approached she kept the world at arm's length and let herself drift upon a dark tide of depression and listlessness that she seemed incapable of fighting, eating too little, drinking too much, troubled sleep her only refuge.

She returned to the flat one day in early December darkness, a carrier bag of shopping in her arms. The stairs and landing were shadowed but not so dark that she could not see where she was going. Not bothering to turn on the light she plodded tiredly up the stairs, leaned against the door fishing in her pocket for the key. Within the flat the telephone rang. Daphne, she guessed, with her well-meaning daily enquiry about her health. She did not hurry to open the door. The ringing stopped.

She sensed the presence behind her just as the key slid into the lock. Drawing a sharp breath she turned. In the shadows a darker shadow loomed, moved towards her. In utter silence she stood, terrified, as the very image of all her nightmares materialized before her.

'Gideon.' The word was barely a breath. She could not see his face, but the gleam of the deep set eyes, the outline of his head and of his broad shoulders were unmistakable. Weakly she shrank from him, shaking her head.

In silence he reached past her, turned the key in the lock, pushed open the door.

In the time it took her to obey his brusque gesture, precede him into the flat, turn on the lights, stir the small fire back to life she regained some fragile control of herself. She turned. Still he had not spoken. 'How did you find me?' she asked.

The light revealed him to be shaggy-haired and unshaven, his rough clothes shabby and none too clean; but a real and solid figure at least, no figment of a night-terror this. 'Philippa,' he said. His eyes had not left hers. 'She counts herself my friend still. I'm travelling with DeVine's Circus. When she found we were wintering on the Heath she came to see me. It wasn't hard to lead her to speak of you.'

'She gave you my address?'

He shrugged. 'Yes. She doesn't know it, but yes, she did.'

The fire flared and crackled in the silence.

Rachel slipped her coat from her shoulders, tossed it on to a chair, then turned to face him again with something of the old defiant arrogance in the lift of her head and the direct gaze of her eyes. 'What do you want?'

He waited for a long moment, then he stepped close to her, the unfathomable black eyes glinting in the leaping firelight. 'To hear from your lips what I heard from another's. To discover the truth.'

She moved back from him a little, tried to keep her voice light and steady. He couldn't know. He couldn't! 'Truth about what?'

'The child. My child, he said.'

'Who? Who said?' Her lips were stiff with shock, her body suddenly numb with it, yet her voice remained quiet, calm as still water.

'My child,' he repeated, very softly, as if he had not heard the question, the two quiet words somehow more infinitely menacing than any uttered threat.

'There is no child,' she said, steadily, still hoping.

He let bleak and unbelieving silence deepen and lengthen between them before reaching and taking her wrists in his hands, drawing her with fearsome strength but no violence close towards him. She did not resist. So close did he stand that she had to throw her head back to look at him. 'But was there,' he asked, quietly, 'was there a child?'

It came as a surprise to her that in that moment she could not lie. 'Yes,' she said. 'Yes, there was.'

'And you – destroyed it?'

Her voice all but died in her throat at that. 'Yes,' she whispered after a moment.

He stared at her. The grip of his hands tightened painfully upon her wrists, as if he would snap the slender bones. She flinched.

He flung her from him and turned away.

She stood for a long moment, rubbing her sore wrists. 'How – how did you find out?'

'Does it matter?'

'I suppose not. But – hardly anyone knows.' She rubbed her forehead tiredly. She felt dizzy, and exhausted with shock. 'Daphne – Toby –' She stopped. 'Surely – not Toby?'

He nodded, grimly. 'He thought to take it out of my gipsy hide.' The words were vicious.

'Oh, God.' Rachel's shoulders slumped. 'Gideon – I didn't tell him – not on purpose – I was delirious. I said something – he guessed – I never thought he'd –' She stopped.

Gideon shrugged, dismissing the subject. He had turned and was studying her face again, a small frown drawing his brows together and narrowing his eyes. 'Why did you do it?' he asked, abruptly. 'In God's name why did you do it, girl?'

Suddenly she was shaking, with anger and with shock. 'What else could I do? What would you *expect* me to do?' she snapped harshly, flinging the words at him like sharp edged stones.

His face changed. Real anger, clamped until now with an iron control, flickered dangerously close to the surface. 'You? I'd expect you to do nothing but exactly what you did,' he said, with cold and bitter emphasis.

That cut deep and hurtfully, as he had intended. 'How dare you? How *dare* you!' She advanced towards him, trembling with a rage so strong that it entirely vanquished fear. 'I was alone – afraid – I didn't know what to do – what should I have done? *Tell me!*' Tears welled and ran down her face, unnoticed, her breath caught in her throat in choking sobs. She lifted a hand to strike him. 'Tell, me, damn you!'

He caught the blow easily, grasping her wrists, holding her with no effort as she struggled, fingers clawed, to reach him.

'What you could have done – is told me,' he said. '*You could have come to me!*'

She stopped struggling, gazed at him with wide, wet eyes. 'What good would that have done?'

He did not reply. Holding her eyes with his he put her from him, carefully, as if afraid of the possibilities of his own strength, and stepped back. They regarded each other in silence for a long, thoughtful moment.

Rachel shook her head in disbelief. 'You – you don't mean what I think you mean? You – and me? And – the child?' Brutal, hysterical laughter was rising in her throat. She turned from him, her hands to her mouth, holding it back. She threw her head back, eyes tight closed against tears. 'Oh, wonderful! I can just see it. Me and a gipsy brat in a caravan! Home sweet home! "Eat your rabbit stew, my darling, Daddy's gone a-tinkering, he won't be long –"' The words broke on a wild sob. She bowed her head into her hands, shoulders shaking. 'What a stupid – ridiculous – thing to suggest!' She could not stop crying. Desperately she wanted to turn, throw herself into his arms, have him hold her, just for a moment, warm and strong and certain. She clenched herself against movement, fought back the hysterical tears. Slowly she quietened. At last, into the silence she said quietly, 'Gideon, don't you think I *know* what I've done? Don't you think I hate myself for it?' She turned. The room was empty, the door standing open. 'Gideon? Gideon!' There was no sound in the flat, nor on the stairs outside. She ran to the window.

In the dark street below the tall figure strode, head down, collar turned up, hands in pockets. Walking very fast he passed beneath the street lamp that glinted on wet black hair and wide shoulders, then he turned the corner and was gone.

Rachel leaned her hot forehead to the window and closed her eyes.

PART THREE

1930

Chapter Eleven

Hugo Fellafield hunched over his arms that were folded upon the ship's rail, head ducked against the wind. Far beneath him the heavy, swelling waters of the Bay of Biscay were black, foam-tinged, lit by the reflected glimmer of the lights that decked the *Lady Bronwen* as she steamed steadily through the storm towards Lisbon and – hopefully – calmer seas. Above the noise of wind and water he could hear the sound of dance music from the salon behind him as those braver souls amongst the passengers – or perhaps simply those with stronger sea legs – determinedly enjoyed their second night at sea. The more fragile amongst the company had in twenty-four hours not yet emerged from their cabins. Light splashed across the deck. A young man, a girl clinging to his arm, staggered onto the bucking deck, slipping and sliding, clinging to the rail. The girl shrieked excitedly as the wind buffeted them. 'I say! What fun!' Hugo turned away.

How the devil had he got himself into this mess?

Maurice Playle's light, elegantly accented voice echoed mockingly in his ears. 'Mess? My dear fellow – there's no mess! Nor will there be so long as you continue to do as you're told.' The words had been accompanied by an inimitably charming smile. 'Just one or two more little jobs, that's all. And my dear old chap you can't deny that our masters pay you well –'

That, of course, had been how it had started. Bloody money. Or rather the shortage of it. But no – he shifted his stance, leaning backwards against the rail, turning his collar up against the wind – to be fair to himself there had been more to it than that. There had been Playle's persuasive tongue, the heady talk of a fairer society, a new golden age of equality, brotherhood and justice. The feeling, during those first few friendly meetings that here was a man of intelligent and far-reaching ideals, a man of influence what's more, a well-known and respected journalist whose witty attacks upon bureaucratic authority and upon the threats posed by European Fascism were read with admiration by many of the most influential thinkers in the land; a man who was part of the new thinking. There had been too, of course, the flattering attention paid to his own half-thought-out, woolly-minded views.

He grimaced to himself, skin crawling. What a fool he must have sounded!

Yet those views had been, were still for that matter, sincere, for what they were worth. For all his easy-going nature he had always hated his father's cynical politics, had grown with others to detest and fear the creeping stain of Fascism that was spreading across Europe. He could not stand to hear his brother Charles' often expressed contempt for the working classes and their attempts to claim their part of the rewards of a society they had worked harder than most to build. He, Hugo, might not be a brilliant thinker but always he had held against the inequalities of a political system that favoured the rich at the expense of the poor; always he had believed that there must surely be a fairer way. No, it had not just been the money. But then neither could he fool himself that his actions had been prompted entirely by idealism. In fact, in truth, he thought with bitter self-contempt it had to be admitted that the strength and excellence of Playle's whisky and the frequency and generosity with which it was offered may well have had as much to do with his agreeing to the man's soft-voiced suggestions in the first place as anything else. And then – once started – God! If he could just go back those few months – he'd never –

'Hello. Bit fresh, isn't it?'

He jumped. Turned to the figure who had appeared at his elbow. Philippa Van Damme smiled companionably.

'It'll get better after Lisbon,' he said, automatically, his mind still elsewhere.

'Oh, it's all right. I don't mind. In fact I'm rather enjoying it. Aunt Fee isn't feeling too well, though.' Her voice was unfeelingly cheerful.

'I'm sorry.'

Philippa grinned. 'She says it's nothing a dose of terra firma won't cure.'

He nodded, absently.

Philippa did not notice his abstraction. 'When are we due in Lisbon, do you know?'

He looked into the darkness. 'It's a head wind. It'll hold us up a bit I should think. Tuesday night – perhaps Wednesday morning –'

'I'm looking forward to it. I've never been to Lisbon.' To her own surprise Philippa was loving every moment of this trip. The shock of her mother's death and the depression that had followed was receding with each day. She was sad still, and missed her mother desperately, but she was young, healthy, intelligent and the lure of the world about her was irresistible. As Toby had pointed out Sally herself would have been the first to tell her to get out there and enjoy it. As Toby had promised, too, the harsh edge of grief had dulled. She was alive, and life was exciting. The healing had begun.

'It's a lovely city,' Hugo said.

'You've been often, I imagine?'

He turned to face her, leaning on his elbow. 'Yes. Quite often. The cruise ships usually call there.'

'And Madeira – you must be looking forward to reaching there? Aunt Fee called it your second home.'

His expression, that had been oddly set and grim – an expression that sat strangely upon his open, boyish face – softened visibly. 'Yes. It is.'

Philippa leaned against the rail, cuddled into her warm wrap, hugging herself against the wind. 'Tell me about it.' The clear brown eyes were friendly and trusting as a child's.

He thought for a moment. 'It's a mountain that rises from a blue sea. A flowery mountain.' He amended, suddenly inspired by the intense interest in her face. 'I've heard it said that it's part of the lost land of Atlantis. The climate's subtropical – it's never cold, though it's never too warm either. It rains, but not too often. Funchal's quite busy but the island itself is incredibly quiet and peaceful, and the pace of life is very slow. I know I keep saying it, but the whole place really is spectacularly beautiful. At this time of the year the mimosa trees will be out – the perfume is amazing. The levadas will be full of running water –'

'What are levadas?'

'Narrow waterways – irrigation channels, like tiny canals. There are miles and miles of them on the island, used to bring water to the vines, each with a path running alongside. You can walk for ever – through the mountains, in the valleys, along the cliffs.' Watching her enthralled face he warmed to her, and to his theme. As always, his heart lightened as the ship steamed away from England and towards his island home. He had a month's respite. Maurice Playle and his sinister activities could not follow him to Madeira. In a month – perhaps longer if he could wangle it – almost anything could happen. Playle's 'masters' as he called them might change their minds. Playle himself might get run over by a bus. Or, less bloodthirstily, he might find a victim who would be of more use to him. Hugo's natural optimism began to reassert itself. Perhaps, after all, things were not so very desperate. Aware of wilful self-deception he smiled into Philippa's eager young face. 'Mother's house is on the mountainside overlooking Funchal – it's the most splendid position; truly must be one of the most spectacular views in the world. We can toboggan down into the town –'

'Toboggan?'

He laughed at her open astonishment. 'That's right. You can toboggan down the cobbled streets in big basket-like sledges. Two men control the sledges with ropes. It's great fun.' He grinned, remembering. 'Providing you hang on good and tight!'

'It sounds it!' Philippa pulled a wary face, only half convinced.

'I'll take you to see them making the wine. And we can go for picnics in the mountains, if you'd like. You can get all over the island in a bullock cart. You'll never see better views, I promise you –'

She nodded, suddenly a little shy. 'But please – you really mustn't think I'm expecting you to squire me around all the time. I promise I shan't impose. You have work to do, I know.'

He shook his head. 'It will be my pleasure to show you the island.' He looked down into the warm and friendly eyes and his depression lifted further. 'Showing it to other people – to people who like it, and I'm certain you will – is like seeing it for the first time myself. There's always something new to discover. There's tennis too, of course, and swimming if you like it. And there'll be parties and dances – Mother always lays on plenty of social life when I come out.'

Philippa glimmered a smile. 'Trying to get you married off to an Island girl?'

He laughed easily. 'Probably.' He turned back to the windy darkness and fell to silence for a moment. The last time he had visited Madeira his obsession with Rachel Patten had been at its height; now even the painful memory of it was fading. Rachel had stubbornly refused to see him; refused even to speak to him on the telephone. When at last they had met accidentally at a nightclub in London he had been shocked at the change in her; always slim now she was thin, always active she had seemed to him now to burn with an almost destructive energy. Surrounded, as always, by an entourage of young men she had greeted him in friendly enough fashion, invited him to join the party then ignored him all night. It had been, perhaps, exactly the medicine he had needed; he had watched her, watched the frantic, somehow senseless activity, the empty laughter and – astonishingly – had felt sorry for her; all other emotion had fled. Half way through the evening she had simply disappeared; others of the party had shrugged, uncaring – Rachel was always doing things like that – why worry? The following morning he had telephoned to check that she was all right; and this time, briefly, she had spoken to him. 'Find a nice girl, Hugo and settle down. Forget me. I'm no good – not for you, not for anyone.' Her quiet voice had been firm. In the background he had heard another; a man's voice, murmuring something.

'You've got someone with you?' Hugo had asked.

'Of course,' she had said, and put the phone down.

He had not attempted to contact her again.

Beside him Philippa shivered a little. He put a brotherly hand under her elbow. 'You're cold. Come on inside. If you can stand my two left feet we could try a dance –'

•

Lisbon was everything Philippa had hoped it would be, a small picturesque jewel of a city set about its wide river in a jumble of narrow, ancient streets. Much smaller than London, its streets and markets teemed with life, and everywhere was colour, in the ornate, brightly tiled exteriors of the buildings, in the parks and the gardens, in the fruits and vegetables set out upon the stalls, in the gaily decorated pottery that was typical of the country and its capital. In the day she spent with Fiona exploring the city the sky was pale and clear and the sun shone, pleasantly warm; London's thundering traffic and chill fog seemed very far away. In the late afternoon they went back to the ship to change, then ventured to the casinos of the city for an evening of dining, dancing and a little genteel gambling – an activity that Philippa found, to her own mild disappointment, entirely lacking in appeal. She had quite fancied cutting a dash at the tables; the reality she found extraordinarily boring not to say somewhat silly.

The ship left at daybreak the next day, Philippa on the deck to watch the lights of Lisbon recede into the grey mists of dawn, despite having had only three hours' sleep.

'You liked Lisbon?' Hugo, tousle-haired and still in evening clothes, appeared by her side, smiling sleepily, not quite steady on his feet.

'Very much.'

He waved a hand, like a magician about to produce a rabbit from a hat. 'Next stop Funchal.'

She laughed a little. 'Have you been to bed at all?'

He considered that, gravely, for a moment. 'No. I haven't.' His straight fair hair flopped over his forehead, his wide-set hazel eyes blinked slightly bemusedly. 'Not since—' He puzzled for a moment, gave up, shrugged, grinned engagingly.

Philippa slipped an affectionate arm through his. 'Come and get some breakfast,' she said, 'then I'll beat you hollow at deck quoits. That'll teach you to stay up all night in the fleshpots of Lisbon—'

Their arrival at Funchal could not have been staged better. The *Lady Bronwen* steamed into the beautiful sweep of bay just as the sun rose, and anchored some little way out, in the deeper water. Mist wreathed the small islands beyond the bay, the sun glinted on white walls and red tiled roofs within a riot of tropical greenery upon the mountainside. The perfume of the island – mimosa, pine, a thousand other subtle, flowery scents – drifted across the water. Philippa was entranced. Hugo, standing beside her at the rail, was despite himself almost equally excited. 'Look – there's the house. See it? Up above the trees there – you can just see the roofs –'

'Yes! Yes, I see it.'

'And there's Reid's – over there at the far end of the bay, see? And the fortress –'

Boats were being lowered, excitable exchanges taking place between the people clambering into them.

'Mother's bound to have sent someone to meet us,' Hugo said. 'Come on –', he caught her hand, '– let's get ourselves ashore!'

And in his eager excitement utterly failed to notice the grip of her small hand on his, or the soft lift of colour in her face.

Fiona Paget, however, standing quietly beside them, noticed both. And smiled.

They sat together, the following day, upon a wrought iron bench in the gardens of the Quinta do Sol, looking down onto Funchal, the bay and the *Lady Bronwen* still riding there at anchor.

'She looks like a toy,' Philippa said. 'Like those little ducks that sail on mirrors in toy farmyards! And, oh Hugo! Look at the mimosa trees! I've never seen anything so lovely!' The trees billowed upon the hillside above them, golden against a clear blue sky, shimmering in sunshine.

Hugo smiled. He was dressed in flannels and open-necked shirt. The sun had already brought a slight flush to his fair complexion. He sat, relaxed and entirely at home, his arm along the back of the bench behind her. Philippa thought him – not for the first time during this magical trip – quite the nicest looking young man she had ever come across, and wondered a little that she had never noticed it before. The oddly confusing thought brought a mortifying warmth to her cheeks; she turned, ostentatiously focusing with great interest on the blue sweep of the bay, as if something had caught her attention.

She really must stop this, before she made a complete idiot of herself and embarrassed both of them.

She had lectured herself long and soundly last night, safe and comfortable, if a little disorientated, in a bed that did not move with the lift and swell of water. Hugo was an exceptionally nice young man, and he had been kind to her. That was all. The last thing he would want would be her running after him like a lovesick puppy. The flush deepened in her cheeks at the mere thought. She must not take advantage of his good-natured and certainly casual interest. She must not – she must not! – make a fool of herself, mistake friendship and possibly sympathy for a deeper interest. But – this was the first time she had ever felt the stirrings of physical attraction for a young man; it was hard, given her open nature, not to show it.

'Those lilies really are quite beautiful, aren't they?' Her voice sounded odd to her ears; forced, a note too high. She glanced at him. He was looking at the masses of lilies that she had indicated, that grew in profusion upon a nearby bank. 'It seems so strange to see them growing like that, just wild –' She could still hear that silly, brittle note in her voice. She swallowed hard.

'You should be here when the flame trees are out,' he said, easily, into a silence that to Philippa had seemed for a moment deafening. 'That's a really spectacular display.'

She said nothing, fell again to studying the view with apparent absorption. Again she found herself talking, unable, it seemed, to stop. 'It's so very odd – it's early spring, most of the trees aren't even in leaf, and yet it's as warm as a summer's day at home! And just look at all the lovely flowers! Tell me about the island – when was it discovered? Why is it called Madeira? Have people always lived here?'

He shook his head, laughing at the sudden spate of questions. 'Apparently not. When it was first discovered it was deserted. It was discovered by a Portuguese explorer named Zarco – well, his real name was Joao Goncalves, he was nicknamed "O Zarco" because he had a magnificent squint. He was one of the first men to dare to sail out of sight of land. He named the island Ilha da Madeira – "island of timber" – because at that time it was so thickly wooded. It's said that to clear the timber the earliest settlers set fire to the forests and they burned for seven years. That's supposed to be the basis of the fertile earth in which the vines grow. Mind you, there's a story that says that the Island was first discovered in the middle of the fourteenth century by a pair of runaway English lovers –' He hesitated, 'I say, are you sure I'm not boring you? I do go on a bit about the Island, I know.'

'No, no.' Her small face was eager. She would happily have sat and listened to him reciting the alphabet if he had so wished. And on a more practical level at least while he talked it prevented her from gabbling. 'Please – do tell me –'

Margaret Fellafield was a competent woman, cool, collected and enormously likeable. She was tall and slim, the bones of her strong face sharply defined. She dressed with a uniquely haphazard elegance; none of her clothes, Fiona was convinced, could be less than ten years old, and all she was equally sure had been worn at sometime to pursue Margaret's one overwhelming passion, gardening. Yet on her narrow, wide-shouldered frame a faded silk blouse and a grass-stained skirt by some alchemy of character and stance could look as stylish as any top flight of fashion. The two women sat together now upon the wide terrace of the Quinta do Sol, watching as the two young people strolled towards them across the gently sloping lawns. Around the house the eight hundred acres of garden that were the pride of Margaret Fellafield's life spread, colourful, lovingly tended, a tribute to the verdant and fertile island she had made her home. The forty acres of flower garden, terraced, fountained, their walks shaded by rose arbours and bougainvillaea were her especial love. Beyond them less formal wooded parkland spread across the clifftops above Funchal.

Philippa's laughter rang clearly in the sunlit air. A bright nasturtium flower tucked behind her ear matched the one that Hugo wore in his lapel. They ran up the terrace steps together, smiling. 'Hello, Aunt Fee. Mrs Fellafield. What a marvellous day. And what a wonderful, wonderful garden!' Philippa turned to Margaret, her young face aglow with admiration and enthusiasm. 'Hugo tried to describe it to me on the boat on the way out – but he didn't do it justice, and I see now why! No-one could!

I've never seen anything so beautiful. It must take just hours of work and planning to keep it so lovely! And all the trees – it looks as if you've got one of just about every tree in the world!'

Margaret smiled, openly pleased. 'Very nearly, my dear, very nearly. The delight of it is that here almost anything will grow.'

Philippa sat beside her, chin on hand, face absorbed. 'Did you start entirely from scratch? I mean – there's so *much* of it. Was it a garden when you came?'

'A small one, yes, neither very well stocked nor greatly cared for, though a lot of the woods, laurel groves and parkland was already well established –'

Fiona leaned back and sipped her tea, watching and listening, well content. The small campaign she had taken it upon herself to wage was going very satisfactorily. Hugo, so uncharacteristically strained and melancholy at the start of the voyage, looked relaxed and happy; Philippa too was almost her old self again. That these two young people seemed eminently suited to one another had occurred to her quite some time before. Despite the age difference – Hugo at twenty-seven was ten years older than Philippa – and the contrast in their backgrounds, Fiona's loosely-made and cheerfully manipulative plans had not yet included how to overcome what would certainly be the fiercest of opposition from Hugo's pompous father and brother. There was something about the pair of them, an artless and uncomplicated attraction, that seemed to her to make them a perfect match for each other. She had watched on the voyage out Philippa's shy awakening; now she noted with approval that Hugo was watching the girl as she talked with a warm gleam of affection in his eyes. Philippa herself had plumped innocently and unerringly for the subject closest to Margaret's heart; an ally there, thought the happily plotting Fiona, would be invaluable. She drew a long breath, leaned back in her chair, her eyes upon the golden horizon where sea and sky merged almost into one. Was she, perhaps, growing old? Young men now did seem so very, so very tiresomely, young; since Toby there had been an empty dalliance or two, but none to hold her attention or affection, and oddly she had not missed it at all. Her long mouth turned down in the smallest of smiles. One interest faded she would have to practise another; she would become an interfering old woman. Perhaps indeed – her eyes flicked from Hugo to Philippa and back – she already had? The smile widened.

The conversation had moved on from gardening. 'I want to see every inch of this lovely place,' Philippa was announcing, purposefully. 'Just every single inch. I don't want to miss anything.'

'Right.' Hugo jumped up, caught her hand. 'We'd better start now, or we could be here for the rest of our mortal lives! Your carriage awaits, madam – though I hope you aren't expecting too much. A bullock cart isn't exactly a Rolls-Royce, you understand.' He grinned widely, pulled her, laughing, towards the house. 'We're well provisioned, well watered, and we're off.' He waved cheerfully to his mother and Fiona. 'Don't worry about us. If we aren't back in three weeks, send out a search party. Come on, Flip, you'd better grab a sunhat if you don't want to come back looking like a stewed beetroot –'

Margaret laughed softly as the two disappeared through the open french doors. 'He's such a fool sometimes.' Her tone was indulgent.

Fiona flicked a small, sly glance at her. 'They get on very well those two,' she said, casually. 'Don't you think?'

There was amusement in the other woman's eyes as she returned the look. There was a long moment of perfectly understanding silence. 'They certainly appear to.'

Fiona stretched a little, lazily, rearranged her long legs, shook her short red hair back from her face. 'Her mother was a good friend of mine,' she said, with apparently guileless irrelevance.

Margaret smiled composedly and picked up her cup, eyeing Fiona over its rim, her dark eyes still alight with good humoured if very slightly wary laughter.

Fiona cast another oblique green glance from beneath half-closed lids. 'Her father's family are Belgian. Bruges, actually. He was killed in the defence of Brussels in '14.' She was speaking apparently idly, her eyes sharp beneath the lazily drooping lids. 'Her stepfather, Eddie Browne is a Labour MP. Not exactly what Spencer would describe as a pedigree, I realize. But the child is worth her weight in gold.' She waited. Heard the chink of cup upon saucer. Was aware of the other woman's calm, smiling gaze upon her.

'What Spencer feels,' Margaret Fellafield said after a moment's thoughtful silence, 'about pedigrees or about anything else always seems a little –' She paused not hesitating but weighing her words carefully, ' – irrelevant at this remove. I'm perfectly certain that both he and Charles,' she made no attempt to disguise the distaste that edged her voice at mention of her husband and older son, 'have other things to concern them than your young friend's antecedents.'

'And fortune, or lack of it?' Fiona queried, suddenly blunt, her unwonted discretion thrown to the Madeiran breeze.

Margaret nodded, equably. 'Just so.' She turned suddenly sober dark eyes directly onto Fiona. 'Am I right in believing that Hugo has but recently extricated himself from – a somewhat different kind of affair?'

Fiona hesitated for only a moment. 'Yes,' she said, candidly.

The other woman played idly with her teaspoon, tinkling it in her saucer. 'A most unsuitable young woman from all acccounts.'

Fiona eyed her sharply and with surprise. Smiled. 'You have a good intelligence network.'

Humour flickered again in the astute face. 'I need it.'

Fiona waited, half hoping for further elaboration, but received none.

'Hugo's a nice lad,' Margaret said at last, looking out over her garden towards the sparkling sea. 'A bit of an idiot I must admit, and not too long on strength or commonsense. But – nice. There isn't an ounce of harm or ill will in him. I wouldn't want to see him hurt.'

'Flip couldn't hurt a fly,' Fiona said.

'I had noticed.'

Again there fell a long, thoughtful silence.

'Well.' Margaret laid her hands flat upon the table in readiness to rise. 'You suggested a game of tennis, I seem to remember? Still feel like it?'

'Certainly.' Fiona was up and ready, all indolence falling away.

Tall as she was the other woman's eyes were on a level with hers.

'So – let's see what develops, shall we?' Margaret Fellafield said, gently. 'With no fear –', the astute, friendly eyes glimmered again, '– and no favour?'

Fiona grinned. Nodded, well satisfied. 'Fair enough.'

They linked arms companionably and strolled into the house.

Margaret's down to earth words about her favourite son came back to Fiona later as she luxuriated in a bath in a wonderfully old-fashioned bathroom after a hard three-set game that she had won by the skin of her teeth. Not long on strength, or commonsense – well, Sal, she said in her mind, if there are two qualities your girl's inherited in abundance, there they are. I'm doing my best. The rest is up to Philippa – she grinned a little at her fancy, seeing Sally's tough, smiling face in her mind – and to you. Have a word with Someone, will you?

Philippa sat cross-legged, lap full of flowers, gazing rapt across the mist-wreathed mountain peaks to the shimmering diamond glitter of the distant sea. Beside her Hugo lay stretched out, hat tilted over his eyes.

'Hugo, however can you *sleep* with all this around you?' A herd of goats cropped the short grass nearby, bells melodious in the still silence.

She saw the hat twitch a little to his smile. 'It'll still be there tomorrow.'

'Philistine!'

'No,' he said, undisturbed and with a touch of smugness, 'just a native. I know what's out there. I don't have to sit there gawping like a tourist –'

'Pig.' She threw a handful of flowers at him. They settled incongruously on his hat, dangling drunkenly from the brim. She giggled. Sipped her Madeira. Nearby the bullocks grazed, still harnessed to the colourful cart. The driver was sound asleep in the shade of an outcrop of rock. She studied the long slender shape of the young man beside her as he lay relaxed and dozing. 'You're snoring,' she said, and laughed again.

'Gentleman's privilege,' he said, lazily.

In the quiet a scented breath of mountain breeze rippled across the flowered grass.

'I wonder –' she said, softly, and stopped.

He came up on one elbow, pushed his hat onto the back of his head, watched her, smiling. 'What?'

'You said that some people thought this was part of the lost land of Atlantis.'

'The Portuguese certainly thought so.'

'I wonder if it was.' Her voice was dreamy. 'I wonder if – out there –' She gestured to the distant, glittering spaces of the ocean. '– there are drowned cities, bell towers and cathedrals, crystal palaces –'

'Shouldn't think so,' he said.

She wrinkled her nose and poked her tongue out. 'Is there no romance in your pragmatic soul?'

It was almost as if the innocent words were a trigger; there was a sudden, small strange silence. Their eyes were locked, their tongues still. Faint colour rose in Hugo's face. Philippa sat very still, barely breathing. For a long second she was certain – absolutely certain – that he was going to lean forward and kiss her. Then he sat up abruptly, crooking his knees, linking his hands about them, looking out into the sparkling day. 'It's a pretty thought,' he conceded, a little gruffly, 'your crystal palaces and things. But unlikely, I'd say. Have another piece of cake.'

They munched the sweet honey cake, the rich Madeira wine a perfect accompaniment, in silence. Above them a huge bird of prey wheeled in the clear air and disappeared into the peaks.

The quiet enveloped them, a cocoon of perilous intimacy.

'Time to go,' Hugo said, abruptly.

They scrambled to their feet, Philippa making much of the opportunity to brush the crumbs and pieces of grass from her full skirt, Hugo dumping the basket into the bullock cart. The huge, patient animals lifted their heads and gazed at him, went back to their grazing. 'Ola, Jorge,' Hugo said, good-naturedly. 'Time to go.'

The driver stirred, yawned, grinned. Very white teeth gleamed in the darkness of his face.

Hugo held out his hand to Philippa to assist her into the cart, then leapt in beside her. She was quite painfully aware of his closeness, of the way their bodies brushed as the cart bucked and swayed its way down the narrow mountain tracks. For the duration of the journey they said little, smiling when their eyes met, stopping every now and again to appreciate another spectacular view. When the roofs of the Quinta do Sol appeared beneath them Hugo said, 'You'll meet the gang tonight. They're good fun. I'm sure you'll like them.'

Philippa said nothing. All through this long and lovely day she had been trying not to think of the party tonight. There were quite a few English families on the island, all of them connected in one way or another with the wine trade and all of them connected, by birth or by marriage, with one another. Tonight she was to be introduced to some of them. She was not, to put it mildly, looking forward to the ordeal.

Hugo noticed her silence. He waited a moment, and when she neither spoke nor looked at him, stretched out a hand, took her chin gently in his fingers and turned her face to him, lifting his eyebrows in quizzical question.

'I'm – not much of a party person,' she admitted, smiling ruefully. 'I get nervous and talk too much. Especially when I don't know anybody.'

'You know me.'

There it was again, that almost involuntary spark that lit the air between them and invested their most mundane of words with meanings and depths that surely neither had intended. She thought that he would drop his hand from her face, but he did not. He laid the palm of his hand very gently along the line of her jaw, a quiet caress that made her heart thump like a frightened rabbit's. 'You know me,' he said again.

'Yes.'

The cart lurched as it turned in through the huge wrought iron gates and lumbered down the drive that was edged with camellias. Outside the door Philippa scrambled out before Hugo could proffer any help. 'Thank you,' she said. 'Thank you for a lovely, lovely day.'

'It's been my pleasure.'

'I'd better go. We've only got a couple of hours before everyone arrives.'

The cart wheels turned, clashing on the gravel. Jorge lifted his whip to the brim of his hat, flashed them a swift grin and urged the animals on. Alone they stood upon the shaded porch. Philippa turned to go.

'Flip?'

She stopped, turned back eagerly.

Hugo looked confused. 'I – nothing. I'll see you tonight. Just – don't worry –' He smiled a little. 'No-one's going to eat you. They really are a nice bunch.'

She nodded. 'I'm sure.'

They stood so for a couple of oddly uncertain moments, watching each other. Then Philippa with a small almost embarrassed smile turned and fled into the cool depths of the house, taking the shallow stairs of the sweeping staircase two at a time, leaving Hugo alone in the deep shadows of the porch, watching after her.

It was with nerves barely controlled that she came down that same wide staircase some two hours later into the cool, marble-floored hall. She stood for a moment, listening. From the terrace beyond the graceful drawing room came the sound of talk and laughter, the clink of glasses. A maid hurried past, black and white uniform crisp and pretty. She smiled shyly at Philippa. 'They're in the garden, miss. Through there.'

'Yes. Thank you.' Philippa moved slowly into the drawing room, a well-proportioned room with high ornamental ceilings and half a dozen tall windows all of which were opened to the balmy evening air.

'Philippa, my dear – come and join us –' Margaret came to her side, tucked her arm firmly into hers. 'I'd like you to meet the Sandersons – Maria and George, and this is their daughter Christina. And the Reece-Jones; this is Barbara, and Mervin. Mervin, be a dear and pour Philippa a drink, would you? And this handsome young devil is Brian Stewart – he and Hugo grew up together, what a pair of monkeys they were – and this is the Bowen tribe, really there are so many of them I think they should introduce themselves. This, everyone, is Philippa Van Damme – a young friend from England.'

Philippa acknowledged introductions, smiled, shook hands, took in not a single name. She took the drink that was offered – inevitably in this gathering the dry, light wine from the island known as Sercial, that was drunk as an aperitif – and glanced around looking for Hugo. When she found him she rather wished she had not. He was standing a little way along the terrace, leaning relaxedly against the balustrade talking to a tiny red-headed girl whose pretty face sparkled with laughter as she tilted her head to look at him. He had not noticed Philippa.

'How was the trip?'

She turned. The tall dark boy – Brian Something, she thought – had joined her, smiling.

'Oh – very nice. A bit stormy to start with –'

'Biscay. Yes, it often is.' He waved a hand, taking in their surroundings. 'What do you think?'

'Of the island? Oh – it's perfectly beautiful.' Philippa kept her eyes on his face; was as aware as if she had been staring straight at them of Hugo's and the red-headed girl's laughter, the intimate way the girl leaned to him as they laughed. 'I'm – I'm sorry?'

He grinned. 'I asked if it was your first visit. Hardly scintillating conversation I grant you.'

She had to laugh. 'Sorry – it's all the noise – I didn't hear.' As she spoke a tall fair girl swept across the room, gave Brian a firm kiss, held out a hand to Philippa. 'Hello, I'm Patsy Bowen.'

Philippa shook the hand. Turned her back determinedly on Hugo and his partner. 'Philippa Van Damme. Nearly everyone calls me Flip, I'm afraid. How do you do?'

It seemed an age before Hugo came in search of her; and when he did she tried furiously not to resent the fact that he had the tiny red-head in tow. 'Flip – I want you to meet Sandra Bowen. Sandy, of course – Patsy's cousin. We've known each other since, cripes, since we were about three, I suppose. Little beast used to torment the life out of me.' He grinned broadly.

Sandy held out a small, freckled hand. She was, Philippa

forced herself to admit, quite extraordinarily – the word that actually came to mind was distressingly – pretty. Her wide eyes, dark lashed despite her fiery hair, were a lovely blue-green, her smile was warm and open. 'How nice to see a fresh face. I've been saying to Hugo – we must get something organized for you – A trip perhaps – picnics – we can't let him keep you all to himself –'

Philippa smiled noncommittally.

'We could get a bunch of us together and go up to the crater – stay overnight at the farm. It'd be great fun, it's ages since we've been up there –'

There was a general murmur of approval.

'And the peak – we must take you up to the peak. It's a bit strenuous, but oh, just marvellous when you get there –'

Someone in the crowd that had grown around them groaned melodramatically. 'Come off it, Sandy. We aren't all mountain goats you know.'

The red head tossed, laughingly. Sandy leaned to Philippa confidingly. 'Take no notice of Brian. Those looks are deceptive. Beneath that manly exterior beats a heart of pure goat's cheese –'

Philippa smiled politely into the laughter that greeted the friendly jibe. Despite the smiles, despite the overtures of friendship she felt totally and utterly out of place – alone. These young people had grown up together, had known each other all of their lives. And it showed. They were bound in a small, secure and utterly private world that she felt might as well have had the barbed wire of no-man's land edging it for all the chance she might have of entering it. Already, though she had lost tally of who was related to whom, she had realized that she stood within an easy freemasonry of brothers, sisters, cousins, in-laws. They communicated in half-sentences, their references and their laughter were, with no cruelty but with punishing self-confidence, beyond the understanding of an outsider, however apparently welcome.

And Hugo was one of them.

She stood for a moment, at the centre of the crowd but totally apart, hearing nothing. She looked down into the drink that she clutched tightly in her hand, wondering how to extricate herself. The peace and quiet of her bedroom upstairs – would anybody miss her?

'Come along everyone – dinner inside. It really isn't warm enough to eat out yet –'

She tramped with the rest of them into the long panelled dining room, that was lined with paintings of the island, some of which she recognized with a pang that was close to homesickness were very like those that hung along the gallery landing of Breckon Hall. It was not until she saw Sir James standing, head thrown back, studying one of them, Fiona beside him, one hand upon his arm, her green eyes sympathetic upon his face, that she remembered they had been executed by his dead son. Oddly, the thought was something of an antidote to the rising tide of self-pity that she had until then been making no attempt to resist.

'You're here, Flip –' She heard Sally's voice inside her head as clearly as if she had been standing next to her. '– make the bloody best of it. Chin up. You're as good as any of 'em. Better than most.'

She wished she could believe it.

She had been seated between Hugo and Brian. Sandy sat opposite, between two young men who bickered amiably above her head and treated her with an easy affection that stirred guilty jealousy in Philippa. She had never until now resented being an only child, had taken for granted whilst Sally was alive that no relationship could be as good as that she had shared with her mother. She had had school friends. She had had Toby, and Rachel, though they were both much older. She had never known this affectionate, easy give and take of contemporaries. Above all, and worryingly, she found she resented the number of times that those mischievous green-blue eyes lifted to Hugo's, the number of times he took the girl's part in the sometimes sharp-tongued bantering around their end of the table. For the most part she, Philippa, could contribute nothing. She answered when spoken to, laughed in appropriate places, watched and listened. Plans were laid for the trip to the crater; Brian it was who explained to her the story of the village of Curral das Freiras

– the 'nun's shelter' – a tiny settlement founded in the sixteenth century by nuns fleeing through the all but impassable mountain passes from a pirate raid on Funchal. The rich volcanic soil upon the apparently impossibly steep mountainsides had been terraced and cultivated. The enclosed valley boasted a wonderful climate. Sandy's uncle – the girl Patsy's father – owned an almost disused farmhouse just outside the village, that the youngsters had used before on such expeditions.

'How will we get there?'

Brian laughed. 'Sandy's last crazy idea was for us all to ride donkeys. But don't worry – Patsy's brother will take us in the farm truck. Not the most comfortable of transport but a damned sight better than walking. Or donkeys!'

'And the peak?' Sandy asked, eagerly, from across the table. 'Who's game for the peak walk? The cissies needn't actually brave the mountain you know, but it's such a good day out. What do you say? Next week? Wednesday – would that suit?'

Philippa caught Fiona's encouraging eye, smiled brightly back. 'Yes, yes of course,' she said in answer to Hugo's question. 'I'd love to come.'

And regretted the silly rashness of the words the very moment they were spoken.

The following day Hugo was in Funchal almost all day on business. Philippa spent the day wandering in the garden, exploring every colourful nook and cranny, delighting in the sights and smells; the billowing mimosa, the clumps of creamy lilies, the carpets of bright spring flowers that spread beneath the trees. After lunch she played tennis with Fiona, and then took herself off to the bench in the clearing on the clifftop that she had shared with Hugo a couple of days before. She sat for a very long time breathing in the sweet-smelling air in the still, sea-girt silence. When finally she walked back towards the pretty, rambling house with its painted shutters and tall, fluted chimneys she had achieved at least some measure of peace. Foolish and romantic – and aided, to be sure, by the sea voyage and the wonders of this garden island – she had mistaken her feelings for Hugo. It was not something to be surprised at, she had done nothing of which to be ashamed. But now commonsense must prevail. Nothing, after all, had happened. Nothing at all. She had allowed her imagination to run away with her. She would be friendly, and sensible, and in three weeks and two days she would board the ship to go back to England and the teaching college with a whole heart and a clear conscience.

Her resolve lasted all of forty minutes; until the time when, lazing on the terrace in a deck chair, a book open but unread upon her lap she looked up to see a tall, angular form loping across the lawn towards her, tie loosened, jacket hooked upon one finger over his shoulder, straight straw hair flopping over his forehead.

The wave of emotion that engulfed her at the sight of him was terrifying.

He galloped up the shallow steps, flung himself into a near-by chair, reached for the jug of orange juice. 'Gosh, that's good.'

'How did it go?' She was astounded at the coolness of her voice.

'Fine. I can come out to play again now for a couple of days. I say – there was something I meant to mention –'

'Yes?'

'This expedition that Sandy was plotting last night – to the peak. Do you have a good head for heights?'

Philippa hesitated.

'Only – well the path is a bit –' he hesitated, grinned, '– I think vertiginous is the word. I wouldn't like you to try it if you aren't happy about it.'

Philippa opened her mouth, grateful to have had put into words something she had suspected – and dreaded – since the conversation the evening before.

Hugo reached for the jug again. 'Sandy never takes into account the fact that not everyone has an iron nerve. She dances up that blessed path as if she's walking along Oxford Street. There'll be quite a few can't face it.'

Philippa picked up her book, shut it with a grim snap, swung her feet to the floor. 'I'll be all right.' She smiled brightly.

Hugo stretched. 'Well, just don't feel badly if you don't want to tackle it.'

'I'm sure I'll manage.'

Hugo knocked back his orange juice in one thirsty gulp. 'Come on – time for a couple of sets before dinner –'

Chapter Twelve

Daphne Smith, apparently unruffled by an argument that had at times verged upon the violent, folded her hands in her lap, looked at her husband, and shook her head. 'No, Toby. I'm sorry, but no. I trust neither the man nor the scheme. I won't risk Underscars for a speculative gamble of such a –' she hesitated, '– questionable nature.'

Beside her, Amos Tobias Smith mewed a little in his silk-draped cradle, tiny fists twitching convulsively before he settled again to sleep.

For once neither of his parents were to be distracted by him.

'Daphne, for God's sake, you don't know what you're talking about!' Toby was far beyond tact or good manners; both had been tried and both had failed against Daphne's steel-stubborn determination. He had not believed she would ever truly defy him so; to face this firm, unshakeable and to him unreasonable obstinacy infuriated him beyond measure. 'The whole thing is perfectly reputable. It's a risk, yes – you'll never make any appreciable profit if you aren't ready to speculate –'

'There must be many people in America who believed that until a very short while ago.' Daphne was dry.

He ignored her. 'Charles and this fellow Greenham are absolutely sure that they can –'

This time it was she who interrupted him, her normally pleasant voice rising a little. 'Toby, it's no good! You can argue till you're blue in the face. I've backed you against Father before, many times, you know it; but not in this. I've never liked Charles Fellafield; I neither like nor do I trust Mr Greenham –'

'On what grounds, might I ask?' Toby was tight-lipped and flushed with temper.

She fell to silence.

Toby turned and strode to the fireplace, stood drumming impatient fingers upon it. 'Feminine intuition one can only assume?' It was perilously close to a sneer.

Daphne's head came up. 'Call it that if you like. I'm simply utterly certain that the man is not to be trusted –'

Toby swung around, almost exploding with anger. 'You have absolutely no grounds for believing any such thing!'

Daphne's lips folded over her prominent teeth to a long, stubborn line. She said nothing.

Toby advanced on her, leaned upon the arm of her chair, his face a few inches from hers, blue eyes blazing virulently. 'You'd take your father's part against me? What's the matter – are you afraid to upset the old man? Are you afraid he'll stop his infantile doting on the child? Are you going to give in to every –'

'Toby, stop it!' She pulled away from him, turned her head from him in a gesture of real distress.

In the silence his breathing was heavy. He straightened, walked back to the fireplace, obviously and openly struggling to control his temper.

After a long, difficult moment Daphne spoke, and her voice was creditably and perfectly controlled. 'Toby, listen to me. You know very well how unfair that is. I've voted with you and against Father often enough when I've believed in what you want to do. It's just that I know – I feel – that this is wrong. Despite the Depression the shops are doing well – obviously not as well or as fast as we had all hoped, but under the present economic circumstances that's hardly surprising. In spite of everything the business is building. To take money out of it to invest in this hare-brained scheme would in my opinion be irresponsible, not to say lunatic. I can't change my mind simply because you want me to. I'd do most things to please you, you know that. But this is far too important. Call it feminine intuition if you will; call it what you like – I don't like the man and I don't trust him. So far as I can make it out his whole plan rests on obtaining planning permission for these houses using what can only be described as dubious means. As for Charles Fellafield, in my opinion the man's a fool, and a greedy one at that –'

Toby spun to face her. 'Are you insinuating – ?'

'I'm insinuating nothing!' she snapped. In the cot the baby stirred again, as if in protest at the lifted voices. 'Toby, have you any idea how hard my father has worked all of his life to build Underscars? Things are hazardous enough at the moment – I won't risk a penny of Underscars money on this crack-brained scheme, no matter what the promise of profit. You'll just have to accept that. There's no point in putting the plan forward because it will be defeated. For heaven's sake, my dear,' she put out a tentative, appealing hand, 'don't we have enough?'

'No,' Toby said, tightly. 'We don't have enough. We have a good business, that's growing slowly. Too slowly. If we made a killing through Greenham's scheme we could put the proceeds back into Underscars and—'

'No.' The word was utterly and absolutely final.

He straightened, balancing on the balls of his feet, fingers linked lightly in front of him. She watched him. Toby Smith was no longer an engagingly good-looking boy; his face had squared and strengthened, his body was lean and strong. Maturity and fatherhood suited him. He was more attractive now than he had ever been; and she knew beyond doubt that she was not the only one to find him so. His interests and activities outside their marriage she had until now calmly ignored, suppressing all feelings of hurt or jealousy. He was always faultlessly discreet, he rarely showed her anything but kindness and consideration, she had long since schooled herself to accept that given the circumstances of the marriage that must be enough. Between them she had felt they were building a structure more firmly based than any mere love affair, and the arrival of little Amos had apparently confirmed that. Toby quite openly adored the child; shared parenthood had brought them closer than they had ever been, coming as it had so soon after that other shared conspiracy of looking after Rachel. Everything had been, quietly and steadily, going so well.

Until now.

The one thing that Toby Smith detested above all others was to be opposed. And now, unemotionally and with unshakable purpose she had to oppose him. She could not help but remember that Sally Smith had once done the same.

The silence this time had lasted for a very long time. The baby moved again, fighting his way from the enveloping lacy shawl, his blue eyes suddenly open and alert upon the world. She leaned above him, offering her finger, feeling her husband's cold gaze upon her like a chill wind. The small face screwed up, wrinkled as a walnut, the tiny mouth opened in a tinny cry of hunger. She reached into the crib and drew him to her, settling him upon her lap, fingers busy with the buttons of her blouse. Here was evidence of yet more obstinacy; she had totally refused for the child to be handed to a nanny with a bottle. Amos Tobias Smith would be fed by his mother and no other. She had quite enjoyed scandalizing the household, to say nothing of the wider society of friends and acquaintances in pursuance of that particular end. And Toby had backed her up. He had taken quite often to coming to sit with them whilst Amos greedily suckled and his mother held him close, marvelling. After the first few disconcerting visits she had overcome her initial almost crippling shyness and come to enjoy his presence. Others there might be in her husband's life, but surely only she could share this particular experience with him? Now, with the atmosphere sharp with acrimony and resentment, her clumsy self-consciousness returned in full and she turned a little from Toby as she bared her breast to his son.

The soft mouth groped for, found and fastened upon the nipple. After the first needle-sharp pain, waves of warmth washed through her body. Mesmerized and languid she watched the tiny face. She almost jumped when Toby spoke.

'So. That's your last word?'

She sighed. Nodded. 'Yes.'

'I shall invest my own money with Greenham.'

'Of course. That's your decision entirely.' They both knew that the only sum of any consequence that Toby possessed was tied up in his Underscar shares. To invest that money he would have to sell some or all of the shares. Since he, like the rest of the family, was bound to offer them first to Amos Underscar and thus give up any influence upon the company, it was a course he was highly unlikely to take however tempting the thought might be of quick and easy money. Daphne kept her head bowed to the baby.

Toby perched on the armchair opposite, elbows on knees, watching his son's rosy face. His expression was still grim.

'Toby?' Still she did not look at him; sensed rather than saw his questioning glance. 'I'm sorry. I really am. But I think you're wrong, and you must see there's too much at stake?'

He shrugged. His expression did not soften. In the quiet, the baby snuffled against the smooth breast. Toby extended a long finger, touched very gently the soft and downy head.

Daphne glanced at him. 'There was something else I wanted to talk to you about.'

'Oh?' He did not give an inch. Neither warmth nor interest flickered in his face.

'Rachel.' Daphne ploughed on. Anything – anything! – to change the subject and ease the tension, to wipe that distant, brooding expression from his face. 'I'm really worried about her. She's acting awfully strangely. She disappears for days at a time – God only knows where – and then when she comes back she locks herself in that flat and won't answer the telephone. She's as thin as a rail. She looks terrible and I'm sure she isn't eating properly –'

Toby stood up, his eyes still on small Amos' milky face. 'I can't see what I can do about it.'

'Talk to her. She'll listen to you.'

At the door he turned, smiling with no humour. 'Rachel? She's never listened to anyone in her whole life. It's unlikely she'll start now.'

'Won't you try? She really does seem to have gone wild since –' she stumbled a little over the words, '– since that dreadful business. She isn't strong. I'm so afraid she'll damage herself further. Will you at least talk to her?'

He lifted one shoulder. 'I'll try.'

'Thank you.' She felt as if she were walking on eggs.

He turned to leave, hesitated, turned back. 'Don't wait up for me this evening. I'll be late. I may stay at the club.'

She opened her mouth, shut it again, nodded. 'Very well.'

The door closed behind him, very quietly.

Daphne steadily watched the baby's precious face; yet in spite of her efforts the soft lines of it blurred and ran as, in silence, the tears came.

Rachel, ignoring the covert and none too friendly glances she knew were being cast her way, leaned to the greasy window and rubbed the running condensation from it. Outside the morning sky was dark still, the outline of the surrounding buildings dense against the gloom. On the stained and grubby oilcloth-covered table before her an untouched cup of tea steamed, thick and strong as treacle.

She felt filthy.

Her thin-faced reflection looked sombrely back at her from the window. The smooth and luminous beauty she had for so long taken so much for granted had gone; the hollow cheeks and heavy, shadowed eyes belonged, she found herself thinking disgustedly, in one of her father's fever wards.

In God's name, what was she doing to herself? And why was she doing it?

Memories of the night flickered – distorted images, nightmare images.

The raucous and cheery conversation about her was formless and noisy as an ocean battering rocks. Within her head was stillness and silence, unhappy emptiness.

'This seat taken, duck? Hello?' A pause; bright eyes glinted a smile. 'Anyone at home? This seat taken?'

'Sorry?' She jerked from her reverie. A small man of indeterminate age, neat and dapper, not unhandsome in his neckerchief and cloth cap stood grinning down at her good-humouredly, his gleaming teeth too regular and straight by far for nature. His skin was dark, his eyes a gimlet blue. His straight black hair was slicked greasily to his neat skull. 'Er – no. No, it isn't.'

He slid neatly and compactly into the chair, tea and a huge plate of sausages and mash awash with gravy precariously balanced in his hand. His smile was friendly, the bright and piercing eyes openly curious as he took in the fur coat, the glimpse of silk beneath it, the jangling bangles and the long, elegant earrings.

Rachel avoided the interested gaze, looked gloomily down into the stewed and unappetizing tea in its stained cup. Leaving the docked merchantman in whose cabin she had abandoned a case of empty bottles and three young officers in various degrees of stupor and in various and extreme stages of undress she had, disregarding danger, walked blindly the narrow and dirty dockland streets until she had quite unexpectedly emerged into the small hours' Sunday bustle of Petticoat Lane Market. Aching with cold and sick with excess and self-revulsion she had, like a maltreated animal, taken refuge in the first warm corner she could find. The café was full of market traders – men and women, though the distinction was hard to make given the ragbag of trousers, sacking aprons and worn jackets and flat caps that was the almost universal uniform – tough, roughly friendly, but none too taken with intruders. She did not care. What could they do to her that had not already been done? She sank her head into her hands.

'You all right, duck?' The voice had real solicitude in it. She lifted her head tiredly. The shrewd, bright eyes of her table companion were fixed upon her, the weather-beaten face concerned.

'Yes,' she said, 'I'm fine.'

He grinned and the white and too-even teeth flashed again. 'Can't say yer look it. Bin on the razzle?'

She smiled, faintly and bitterly, and said nothing.

'Drink yer tea up. It'll make yer feel better.'

She sipped her tea. It was strong and hot and very sweet. The little man tackled his sausages. Rachel, stomach churning, turned her head away.

'On yer own?' he asked.

'Yes.' She glanced back at him, surprised an astute and understanding gleam in his eyes that arrested her movement. 'Yes,' she said again with faintly bitter emphasis.

'Ain't we all?' The words were tinged with sympathetic humour. He laid down his fork, wiped his hand on the sleeve of his grubby jacket and extended it across the table. 'Jimmy Bennet. Known to one an' all as Curly.'

Rachel took the hand. It was calloused and warm and surprisingly strong. 'Rachel Patten.'

'An' tell me, Rachel Patten –' he resumed his enthusiastic attack on his sausage and mash, '– what brings you to Barney's Café at this time of a Sunday morning, all alone? You ain't got a stall down the Lane, that's fer sure.'

She laughed a little, drawn to the man and his open and interested friendliness despite herself. 'No, I haven't.' She propped her elbows on the table, the teacup warming her cupped hands, watching him. 'I –' She fell to silence, shrugged.

He stopped eating for a moment and those bright blue eyes focused intently upon her face, studying her. Then, 'Try some of this,' he said amiably, indicating the plate in front of him. 'Yer look as if a square meal'd do yer no harm at all.'

She shook her head.

'No better sausage an' mash than Barney's, I can tell you.'

'I'm sure.' She sipped her tea.

'Ran out on yer, did 'e?' he asked matter-of-factly after a moment's silence.

'What? Oh.' She shook her head. 'No.'

'So.' He demolished another mouthful. 'You ran out on 'im.'

Her mouth twitched to a small, self-mocking smile. 'You could say that.'

He cocked his head, watching her. 'Yer don't look too 'appy about it?'

She put down her cup, folded her arms upon the table. She was warmer now, and as she relaxed a little tiredness was rising. 'As a matter of fact, Curly Bennet,' she said, wearily, 'I can't say that I can think of a single thing I am happy about.'

The expression on the dark skinned face altered subtly, the bright eyes were suddenly a noticeable degree or so cooler. 'Oh?' He scooped up the last of the potato, dripping with gravy. 'Well, that's a shame, ain't it?' His tone was faintly and caustically mocking. His eyes, very deliberately, examined her; she suddenly became acutely aware of the lavish fur coat, the gold that gleamed in her ears and at her wrists. 'There's a couple o'million

282

unemployed,' he said, amiably, ''d probably have somethin' ter say about that.' He waited, watching her. She said nothing. 'Poor little rich girl,' he said, quietly, 'come slumming?'

She flushed a little. 'No.'

He raised his brows.

'I—' Sudden and mortifying tears flooded her eyes. She clamped her mouth shut and turned her head sharply away.

After a moment his hand came across the table to cover hers, clenched to a fist. 'Sorry, duck. Didn't mean to upset yer. Honest I didn't. Come on now –' Clumsily remorseful, trying not to imagine how many good things the cost of that coat would provide for a wife and a family, he patted her hand '– cheer up. Grizzlin' inter yer tea won't 'elp. Worse things 'appen at sea as me old mum always used ter say.'

She smiled unsteadily. The tears overflowed and trickled down her cheeks. She sniffed. Shook her head. 'It couldn't be any worse.' A perilous and familiar mixture of self-disgust and self-pity was threatening to overwhelm her.

''Old on. Don't go away.' Jimmy Bennet slipped from his chair and left her. She wiped her eyes with the heels of her hands , uncaring of the interested glances being cast by those sitting near her. A moment later, with her self-control at least partially restored, the little man came back with two fresh cups of tea. 'There we are. Nothin' like a nice cuppa ter make yer feel better. Now,' he sat down, 'drink up. Then tell Uncle Curly all about it, why don't yer? Yer never know – it might 'elp.'

She sat for what seemed a long time, sipping her scalding tea. The temptation to unburden herself to this down to earth and oddly emphatic stranger was enormous. He came from another world. He knew nothing of her. She guessed that he would neither judge nor pontificate; and the urge to talk, that she had for so long stubbornly resisted, was all but overwhelming. 'I – lost a child,' she said. 'A – miscarriage.' She saw the bright, intent eyes flicker to her bare ring finger. His expression did not change. 'I can't seem to forget about it, that's all. It's stupid.' She shook her head. 'I sometimes dream that—' She stopped speaking, nibbled her lip. He sat very still, watching her. She looked directly into the bright, sympathetic eyes. 'I've been behaving very badly lately,' she said, steadily, the relief of confession inexpressible, 'very badly indeed. I know it, but I can't seem to stop myself. Last night –', she shrugged, flinching a little, '– well, never mind. You wouldn't want to know the gory details.' With long, thin, scarlet-tipped fingers she played with the tin teaspoon for a moment. 'I disgust myself,' she said at last, quietly. 'I'm good for nothing.'

He leaned back easily. 'I wouldn't say that, duck. Everyone's good for something.'

She shook her head.

He came forward again, leaning on his elbows. 'It wasn't your fault yer lost the kid, love.'

She looked at him long and steadily; cast the die. 'It was.'

'Ah.' He nodded, unsurprised.

'Now do you see?' For some strange reason it had become important to her that this unknown, friendly soul should understand, should offer the commiseration she had steadfastly refused from others.

'No.' He raised a surprisingly long, dirty finger as she opened her mouth to protest. 'Just a minute, duck. Let me get it straight. Yer feel badly about what yer did – though there must 'ave bin what seemed good reasons fer doin' it – Gawd knows we see enough of it around 'ere –' Someone called a greeting from the doorway, and he grinned absently and raised a hand in greeting, hardly taking his eyes off Rachel's face. 'Mornin', 'Arry. An' now you're drivin' yerself into the ground – fer what? Ter try ter forget what 'appened? Ter punish yerself?'

'I don't know.'

'Either way it's pretty daft.'

She said nothing.

'Look at yer –' The good-natured face lit with a sudden and disarming smile. 'Yer the best lookin' woman I've seen in a long wet week. Yer got style an' yer got money –'

She grimaced, laughing with him. 'Not much.'

'More than most, love, more than most. An' I'll bet my last farthin' you've not done a hand's turn in yer life?'

It was said easily and totally inoffensively, but nevertheless she flushed.

'Don't get me wrong – it's none o' my business. It just strikes me you'd 'ave a sight less time to worry about yerself if you 'ad ter earn a livin' the way most folk do.'

'I told you –' Defiantly the habitual sardonic smile flickered. '– I'm good for nothing.'

'An' *I* told *you* everyone's good for somethin'.'

'Tell me what?'

'Well fer a start,' he said with that neat and enterprising promptness she was to come to realize was a part of the market breed, 'yer could give me an 'and on the barrer.'

'What?'

He grinned engagingly into her startled face. 'I said yer could give me an 'and. In the market. This mornin'. Cloth's my trade. The old stall could do with a bit o' class –'

She laughed incredulously. Shook her head.

He regarded her for a moment, head on one side, eyes narrowed, sucking his lip, openly pondering. Then he shook his head briskly. 'Nah. You're right. Yer couldn't manage it. Ferget I spoke.'

'Hold on a minute –'

'Curly, you old bugger – 'ow's it goin'?'

Jimmy turned and struck hands with a burly, grey haired man who had stopped at the table.

''Ow's young Nellie – up an' about agen yet?'

Jimmy shook his head. 'Poor little blighter's laid up fer at least another couple o' weeks.'

'Missin' 'er, I'll bet?'

'That I am.'

'Who's Nellie?' Rachel asked when the man had gone.

'Me eldest daughter.' His face was guileless. 'She 'elps me up the market.'

'What's happened to her?'

'Broke a leg a few weeks back.'

'So you really are short-handed?'

'Tha'ss right. The missus 'elps out when she can, but with the two youngest not at school yet she doesn't get a lot of time –'

Rachel was intrigued. 'How many children have you got?'

285

He grinned. 'Eleven.'

'Good Lord.'

He shook his head. ''E didn't 'ave a lot ter do with it.' He pushed his chair back. 'Well, I'd better be pushin' along.'

'Wait.' Impulsively she stood too. The little man beside her came only to her shoulder. He cocked his head to look up at her. 'Look, Curly –' She grinned suddenly at the entirely inappropriate name. 'I could give you a hand if you wanted. For today at least.' At the intriguing prospect of a new experience her tiredness and her misery had evaporated like fog before sunshine.

He shook his head firmly. 'I told yer, duck. It's too tough for the likes of you. You'd never stand it.' His bright glance was sly.

'Let me try. I'll show you.'

He pulled at his lower lip doubtfully.

'Please. Let me have a go.'

A beatific smile lit the dark face. 'Well – if yer really want to –'

'I do.'

'Rightyo, then. Why not?' he asked, magnanimously, for all the world as if he were doing her the most gracious of favours. Sympathy and a natural kindness of heart had prompted Curly Bennet to the side of a lonely and unhappy-looking young woman; there was no law he knew of against profiting from a genuinely benevolent impulse. 'Can yer count?'

'Just about.'

'Can yer use a yard stick?'

'I can learn. What are we selling?'

'Cloth, love. An' trimmin's. Dress lengths, skirt lengths, curtains – tassels, buttons, bindin's, sequins – you name it Curly Bennet sells it. You comin'?'

'Hold on a minute.'

'What's that?'

'What are you paying?'

'Tanner an hour,' he said, smartly.

'A shilling.'

286

He grinned. 'A bob an hour, Duchess? Yer tryin' ter break me or somethin'? Ninepence. That's me last word.'

'Done.'

He stuck out a rough hand. 'Shake on it, Duchess. An' get that tea down yer – yer workin' fer Curly Bennet now, an' there's a stall to set up –'

In a lazy and happy week at the Quinta do Sol Philippa had managed to push to the back of her mind her rash promise to accompany Hugo and his friends up the mountain to the Pica do Arieiro and its companion, the Pico Rivo, the highest point of the island and accessible only by foot. By the time a dozen or so young people in high spirits congregated at the house for the trip it was, of course, far too late to confess to Hugo – or to anyone – her fear of heights. With the others she clambered aboard the battered vehicle that stood in the gravelled yard. Patsy's brother Michael and the farm truck had been pressed into service for this expedition as well as the planned trip to the crater village a few days later. They rattled and wheezed up the narrow, dusty mountain roads in high spirits, picnics tucked into baskets beneath the roughly constructed bench seats. They set off early, the plan being to start the walk from the lower peak to the higher at about ten in the morning. By Hugo's reckoning those that made it would be back at Pico do Arieiro by two o'clock, in time for lunch. Those who decided not to join the expedition to the other peak would wait for them by the truck. Of the party, two cheerfully and with no embarrassment absolutely refused to attempt the walk. 'The second rung of a stepladder's too high for me,' Brian Stewart said, undisturbedly. 'I'm staying put. And if I know Christina, she'll stay with me.'

Christina, a plump, dark girl with the eyes of her Portuguese ancestry, giggled. 'I'll say. You won't get me up on that path. I'm just along for the ride.'

Two or three others expressed reservations, agreeing that they would see how they felt when they reached the starting point of the expedition.

Philippa, her stomach churning a little – due, she assured

herself with sturdy lack of sense, to the fact that she had not felt like eating the breakfast that Teresinha the cook had smilingly provided for them all – said nothing.

When they reached the peak and stood looking out over as bleak and mountainous a landscape as she had ever seen her worst fears were realized. Here was none of the lush, soft green of a garden; here was the mountain, the rock on which the island was founded and built. Mist wreathed beneath them, filling the gorges and valleys, drifting, breaking, revealing here and there views of towering magnificence and dizzying height. The track from peak to peak, such as it was, climbed like the trail of a snail along the ridges of the mountains, in many places no more than two or three feet wide. In some places even from this distance it was clear that the drop on one or in some cases both sides of the narrow crumbling path was sheer. From the vantage point where they stood it was possible to follow much of its length with the eye, winding through and around the jagged volcanic peaks, cutting up and down sheer and dangerous scree slopes, appearing and disappearing in the mists. The air was cold. As they tumbled from the truck, woollen pullovers were dragged over tousled heads, light shoes discarded for heavy walking boots and woollen socks. A girl whose name Philippa did not know shook her head. 'Nope. I've done it once. I don't think I'll bother again. I'm with Brian and Christina. See you later.'

'Me too.' The young man who was with her looked immeasurably relieved. 'The view from here looks good enough to me.'

As if to illustrate his words the sun drifted from behind the mist and the rugged landscape was lit to a glory of light and colour. Inevitably in the distance the ocean glimmered seductively, the brilliant horizon merging sea and sky.

'You sure you're all right?' Hugo was beside Philippa. 'Please don't come if you don't want to.' He looked a little anxious. 'One tends to forget just what a tough walk it is. It really is quite steep in parts.'

'I'll turn back if I can't manage it,' Philippa said, steadily.

'Come on, you lot!' Sandy, bright hair hidden beneath an emerald green woollen hat that clashed magnificently with her shabby purple jumper, looked every inch the mountaineer. 'If we don't get started we'll never get back!'

In the event seven of them set off, waving with cheery confidence to those settled comfortably about the truck with books and packs of cards in the strengthening sunshine. They strung out along the path, each walking at his or her own pace, Sandy's bright green hat in front.

It started easily enough. The first part of the path, quite wide and well-walked, led down a steep and slippery slope of scree not too hard to negotiate, and then up and around solid rock, the drops not too steep and far enough from the path not to be worrying. Hugo stuck close by Philippa, waiting for her when she fell behind, offering a helping hand when the going got harder. Obviously he knew the path well, obviously it held no terrors for him. He must have been up here many times before. With Sandy, who led the group onwards with the confidence and speed of a mountain goat?

Philippa gritted her teeth. 'Hugo – I'm all right, honestly. I don't want to hold you up. You go on.'

He shook his head, but as they reached a wider flatter ridge his stride lengthened a little and it was with a feeling of relief that she saw him walking ahead with another member of the party. Her own terrors were easier faced alone.

She stood for a moment, looking about her and catching her breath. The views were truly magnificent; it was like standing on top of the world. The sun shone now from a clear, sparkling sky whilst far beneath them the mists swirled and billowed above the valleys. For a moment the thumping of her heart eased and she relaxed. Ahead Hugo and his companion had scrambled up a small stand of rocks and were standing silhouetted on the skyline, waiting for her.

She scrambled up to join them. And froze.

On the other side the path that had been wide and flat as a country lane suddenly became a ribbon; a shining, slippery ribbon that curled itself about the rocks and then laid itself, narrow and unprotected across a ridge no more than a few feet wide with sheer drops on either side. Sandy and a young man in a bright yellow pullover were already across and scrambling up and around the rock face on the other side. Two figures were on the fragile-looking bridge, feeling their way carefully across.

Philippa's stomach turned to water.

Hugo was talking. ' – the most spectacular views from the other side there. I once came up in winter, when the peaks were covered in snow. Flip – you sure you're OK?'

Philippa nodded. Her teeth were gritted together so hard that her jaw hurt. The two on the ridge had reached the other side and stood, arms extended, pointing out landmarks. No-one seemed in the least put out by the vast spaces beneath them. She would not give in. She would not.

Hugo's companion slid down the last few feet onto the path and stepped out across the rock bridge. Hugo followed him, turned to hold out a hand to Philippa. She snatched her own away. 'No!' she said, through stiff lips. 'No! Truly, Hugo, I'm all right. I don't need any help.' How could she explain the terror of having him touch her – the horror of seeing him slip, of dragging her with him as he fell? The thought, the image, made her feel physically sick and brought a trembling to the muscles of her legs that she thought must surely prevent her from taking another step. In that moment she knew what an utter fool she was being; she was a danger to herself, a danger to the others. She should go back.

With her eyes fixed on the back of Hugo's head she stepped onto the path.

It was the worst thing she had ever endured. It was as if the maw of a beast yawned magnetically beneath her, beckoning, encouraging her to fall. For what seemed an endless space of time, trembling in every limb, she followed Hugo's steadily moving figure, sidling behind him, hardly daring to breathe, aware of every moving stone, every glassy piece of rock beneath the painfully curled soles of her feet; whilst one oddly calm and detached part of her brain noted how sharp was the line of Hugo's jaw, how slender his neck, how endearingly silly he looked in his red woollen hat, his straight fair hair sticking out like a scarecrow's mop. The relief when she reached the other side was so great that the trembling, far from easing, increased to the point where she knew she must at least for moment stop moving. Apparently easily she leaned against a rock as if studying the spectacular view, pressing herself against the blessed, unmoving strength of the mountain, keeping her eyes fixed upon the horizon, ignoring the vertiginous drop to the valley beneath her.

The path wound again through rocks. She saw the flicker of the red hat ahead of her, and then she was alone. She stood for some moments, breathing deeply, making a physical, punishing effort to still the trembling that seemed to pulse from some chill pit at the very centre of her body through the muscles of her limbs and the marrow of her bones. At last she pushed herself shakily away from the rock; at least this next bit didn't look too bad; that, inevitably, she would have to cross the fearful bridge behind her to get back was a thought she simply had to suppress. She had done it once; she could do it again.

She moved forward, scrambling up in the direction that Hugo had taken. And within moments knew she could not go on.

The path had rounded a corner. Ahead it cut directly across a precipice – not for any great distance, only perhaps fifteen or twenty feet – but here the rock beneath sloped sharply inwards so that the path hung terrifyingly suspended above empty space whilst above it the overhanging rock reared menacingly. She stopped, every last stubborn grain of courage draining from her. She could not – she absolutely could not – step out above that terrifying void. Tears stung her eyes. Hugo was already very nearly on the other side, balanced precariously, bent almost double beneath the dripping overhang. Philippa opened her mouth to call to him, shut it again, unable to make a single sound, watched him disappear once more into the rocks on the other side. Dizzily she turned away, eyes and fists clenched tight, stomach rolling. Around her, majestic and indifferent, the mountains reared their savage peaks. The chasms dropped, bottomless, intimidating pits of empty space. Panic rose. Teeth clamped into her lower lip she found herself scrambling blindly back the way she had come. On the shaly path she slipped and fell, bruising her knee and scraping her elbow painfully. Tears of pain and of sheer terror ran down her cheeks. By the time she reached the rock bridge she was sobbing like a frightened child.

All she could think of was getting back to safety. Pride, jealousy – Hugo himself – were forgotten. The primitive urge to flee from danger had taken over.

She stood shaking, clinging to the rock looking out across the awful bridge. What she realized now, that had not been apparent before, was that the narrow path with its perilous drops was also sloping. It lifted away from her across its slender and dangerous causeway, rising in its length perhaps twenty or thirty feet to the solid safety of the mountainside. There was no way in the world that her shaking legs would carry her across it.

Philippa clenched her teeth, controlled her tears, dropped onto all fours and began to crawl.

She never forgot that fearful, lonely journey on scraped and burning hands and knees, driven by muscles so clenched with terror that by the time she was half way across they throbbed with pain; sometimes she relived it in nightmares. She supposed, afterwards, that it could only have taken a matter of minutes; at the time it seemed she had spent long hours dragging herself inch by inch across those brilliant, fearsome, sunlit spaces.

Safe on the other side she all but collapsed, crouched behind a rock away from the precipice, her head buried in her arms. At last, still shaking a little and deadly tired, she pulled herself to her feet and set off back to the truck. With the terror of the past minutes behind her now a small thorn of worry embedded itself in her mind; she should have called to Hugo, told him she was going back. But confused as the memory of that moment of sheer panic was, it was still strong enough to remember its paralysing effect. She could no more have called, spoken logically, than flown in the air. Hugo would guess, surely, that she had turned back?

She found herself back at the truck in a ridiculously short space of time. Out of breath from the final steep and slippery scramble she emerged from the rocks to be greeted with grins of encouragement and sympathy. 'Been there and back?' Brian asked, innocently.

She was beyond offence or pretence. She shook her head ruefully. 'Not now, not ever. I'd as soon try to get up Everest.

And I can't say that's ever been one of my ambitions.' She was amazed that her voice sounded perfectly normal, perfectly sane. With relief she threw herself down beside Brian and Christina, accepted a bottle of orange juice that Brian passed to her with a grin.

'We're playing rummy,' Christina said. 'Care to join us? Stakes aren't too high.'

Philippa was suddenly exhausted. She shook her head. The sun was high, and very hot, though at this altitude a cool wind blew. 'No thanks. I think I'll find a sheltered spot and have a snooze after all the excitement.' She stood, waved to the others, who had lit a small fire and were brewing tea, walked around the battered truck to a sheltered hollow in the rocks. Settled alone, stretched out on her back, her hands behind her head and the sunshine warm and benign upon her face and her aching body she looked up to where a kite wheeled high in the spaces of the sky and thought that nothing in all of her life had ever felt so secure or so comfortable. Within moments she slept.

She woke to the sound of voices, one undeniably and furiously angry, the other calming and conciliatory.

'Bloody idiot kid – I'll murder her!' It took a shocked moment for Philippa to identify the voice as Hugo's. 'Of all the half-witted, irresponsible, *stupid* things to do! I thought – we thought – she was bloody dead! Where the hell is she, anyway?'

'Ssh. Hugo – calm down. She's asleep.'

'*Asleep?*' Hugo's outraged voice rose unsteadily. 'She's *asleep* while we risk life and limb clambering all over these sodding mountains looking for her? What does she think this is, some kind of bloody kid's game?'

'She couldn't make it. She was frightened I think.'

'Then why didn't she *say* so?' Philippa flinched from the violence of the words. 'For God's sake, what's the matter with the child? She didn't have to come – nobody forced her. You and the others stayed behind – she could *see* it wasn't going to be a stroll through bloody Hyde Park!' Hugo was becoming all but incoherent. Philippa lay frozen. 'Christ, I could wring her skinny neck! I thought – I was afraid— God! can you imagine going back and telling Lady Fee that her protégé was dead at the foot of a Madeiran cliff?'

'Hugo! Shut up, do! She's here and she's safe. Leave her for now. Let her sleep. And do calm down! Here – come and have a drink –'

They moved away.

Philippa sat up, curling her knees to her chest, resting her forehead on them, arms about her head to shut out the suddenly harsh and blinding glare of the sun. She sat like so for a very long time, miserably hunched, as every dream she had nurtured over the past few days crumbled about her. Idiot kid. Stupid child. Lady Fee's unwanted, irresponsible protégé – in all of her seventeen years she had never felt such humiliation. It took the most enormous effort of will she had ever exerted finally to stand, brush the dust from her jumper and trousers and scramble from the rocks to face the prematurely returned walkers.

Hugo at least was calm. 'Where the hell did you get to?'

Philippa, aware of surreptitious glances and interested ears lifted her head. 'I'm sorry. I tried to call to you. I – couldn't.' She swallowed. 'I apologize if I've caused you trouble.'

His grim expression did not soften. 'Trouble? You nearly gave me a bloody heart attack.'

'Leave off, Hugo, do,' someone said, easily. 'All's well that ends well. Come on, Flip, give a hand, will you? The hampers need unpacking.'

It had been, Philippa told herself that night, safe at last in bed, quite the most unhappy day of her life. Nothing had been able to arouse her from her misery, and Hugo had not even tried. They had all but ignored each other for the rest of the day. Philippa, after her first flush of remorse, could not forget the words she had overheard, nor the implications of them. She was obviously a nuisance. A child to be entertained. Worse – an irresponsible child, a burden. An 'idiot kid'. Well, she'd show Mister Hugo Fellafield, that she would! She'd show him that she didn't give a fig for his opinions. She didn't need him. Brian Stewart had been extra nice to her all that afternoon – had come to sit beside her at the picnic, saved a place next to him in the truck as they had set off home, eating fresh picked bananas and singing a beguiling variety of popular songs. She didn't need horrible Hugo Fellafield. Oh, no.

Determinedly she ground her fists into her eyes, wiping away the tears, turned restlessly in the bed, buried her head under the pillow, searching for sleep.

Chapter Thirteen

Over the next couple of days Philippa hardly saw Hugo, except at meal times, and was thankful for it. She kept to her room for most of the next day with a not altogether feigned headache. Hugo had not mentioned the incident at the Peak, either to her or to anyone else so far as she could tell and for that, at least, she was grudgingly thankful. She lay in her darkened room listening to the sounds of a normal, happy day outside and tried, unsuccessfully, not to brood over her humiliation and unhappiness. Over dinner that evening she discovered that Sandy Bowen had called during the day to organize a tennis tournament for the following week.

Philippa picked at her food and remembered that as she had lain alone she had heard Hugo's voice and a girl's laughter in the garden.

The following day Hugo had to go into Funchal with Sir James to the family's wine lodge to do business with a prospective customer. Philippa spent the day quietly, wandering the garden, gazing out across the sparkling bay, avoiding company.

At dinner that evening Fiona eyed Philippa shrewdly as the girl played with her food, speaking when spoken to, smiling politely. 'Hugo –' Fiona said, as they left the table and walked to the drawing room for coffee, '– have you taken Philippa down on the sledge from Monte yet?'

'I – no,' Hugo said, making much of handing vegetables around the table, 'No, I haven't. Though I must, of course. Flip can't come to Madeira without riding the sledges.'

Margaret smiled at him gently. 'You could take her tomorrow. And perhaps stroll up to Reid's for tea?' She left the question hanging delicately on the air.

'No,' Philippa said, far too loudly, then, embarrassed. 'That is

'– I haven't been feeling all that well over the past couple of days, to be honest. Perhaps we'd better leave it, for now at least.'

Hugo looked pained, as he might, Philippa thought, at the antics of a recalcitrant child. 'As you wish.' His voice was cool.

Margaret frowned, concerned. 'Are you unwell, my dear?'

Philippa flushed. 'No. Just –' she shrugged self-deprecatingly, '– well, tired I suppose. I had a bit of a headache yesterday and it's left me feeling a little off colour, that's all.'

'Well,' Fiona said briskly, watching her with sharp eyes, 'best get some rest then, don't you think? You want to be in good order for the trip to the crater.'

Philippa looked at her, helplessly. The last thing in the whole world she wanted to do was to be trapped into a two day trip with Hugo and his island friends. What might have seemed a dream a couple of days before had now distorted to nightmare.

Fiona smiled, blandly. 'A couple of days' rest and you'll be as right as ninepence. You'll enjoy Curral das Freiras – it's like going back several centuries. And the farm, if not exactly the Ritz, is marvellously situated. We visited it a year or so ago. Hugo – James – I'm always confused by the connection between the English wine families on the island – tell me, do Paget and Fellafield buy from the Bowens?'

The talk moved to the wine business. Philippa walked to the window and stood looking out onto the starlit night. She had to resign herself to it; she couldn't, without being both childish and rude, get out of going on this wretched trip. It had, after all, been more or less arranged – by the pretty, energetic and no doubt well-meaning Sandy – to show her the crater village.

'Philippa?'

She jumped at the voice in her ear. Hugo stood unsmiling beside her. She could not as she looked at him prevent the rise of blood to her cheeks. Anger stirred. At least he might have the sense to leave her alone. 'Yes?'

'Something wrong?'

She shook her head, turned back to the window. 'I told you. I'm a bit tired, that's all.'

'You're sure you want to come on Friday? It isn't too late to call it off if you want.'

She shook her head again.

He was watching her narrowly.

She moved a little from him, irritated. Turned. 'Don't worry. I won't do anything stupid this time, if that's what's worrying you.' She could have bitten her tongue out the moment the words were spoken. Her tone, she knew, had been unforgivably rude.

Hugo's wide, easy-going mouth tightened. Without a word he left her.

Eyes stinging, Philippa turned blindly back to the window.

Fiona and Margaret caught each other's eye; Fiona pulled the faintest, exasperated face and lifted her eyebrows in question. Margaret equally discreetly shook her head, raising her eyes to the ceiling in amused incomprehension.

Philippa's back remained stubbornly turned.

There were six young people apart from Hugo and Philippa in the party that set off up the mountain road in the Bowens' farm truck early on Friday morning, packed into the open-backed truck that bumped and bounced slowly over the rough track. It was cloudy in Funchal when they left, and a fine drizzle drifted in the air. The spectacular views over the city that Philippa had been promised did not materialize. Yet within twenty minutes or so, as they gained altitude they pulled out above the clouds into clear, warm sunlight.

'Often happens,' Brian told Philippa as she exclaimed with pleasure at the sudden change. 'If the clouds hang about the coast quite often it's glorious up here. It can work the other way as well, of course.'

As a crow might fly the village they were heading for was less than ten miles distant; but in country such as this such comparisons could not be made. The track wound steeply into the mountains behind Funchal, first through plantations of bananas then on up through mist-hung eucalyptus and laurel woodlands that skirted the Socorridos ravine. At a speed not much beyond walking pace Patsy's brother Michael, a rangy and competent lad who quite evidently was not driving this route for the first time, edged the battered truck upwards around hairpin bends that could not always be taken in one sweep. It was a bone-shaking journey, but at every twist and turn the reward was a spectacular view. When at last they emerged at the pass of Eira do Serrado the truck ground to a halt and they clambered stiffly out to survey the panorama beneath them. Philippa found herself looking down into a deep, enclosed valley ringed by volcanic peaks. Far below the red tiled roofs of a small village glowed warmly in the sunshine and fertile green terraces of cultivated land climbed high up the mountainsides. The running waters of the *levadas* that criss-crossed the countryside glinted silver.

'It isn't really a crater.' Hugo had come to stand beside her. 'Though you have to admit it looks like one. That's the village. The farm is –' he searched the distant countryside, eyes crinkled against the light, '– over there.' He pointed. 'A mile or so outside the village. It's fairly primitive. I hope you won't mind? It's a bit like camping out.'

'I shan't mind.' She was still awkward with him.

'Come on everyone – into the truck. We're doing well. At this rate we'll be there for lunch –'

They pulled into the yard of the farm at about midday. Gasping relief – the journey down into the valley had been no more comfortable than the trip up the mountain – they jumped down, stretching cramped muscles. Two huge, handsome, beaming women, as alike as two peas in a pod, stood waiting to welcome them. Both were dressed exactly alike in long black skirts and shabby jumpers, identical bright scarves about their ample shoulders. 'Rosa! Maria!' Both Michael and Patsy leapt forward and hugged them. 'As alike as ever!' Michael grinned. 'I still can't tell one from the other!'

'I'm the fat one, Master Michael,' said one, and both shook with laughter at a joke that was obviously well worn.

The farmhouse was small, and as Hugo had warned, primitive. There were three fair sized rooms and a tiny lean-to kitchen – most of the cooking Patsy explained was done outside on an open fire. Water was carried from a nearby *levada*, and there was no bathroom, an ill-smelling tin shack some considerable distance from the house being the only toilet. 'Sorry about that,'

Patsy said, cheerfully, her favourite phrase Philippa was coming to realize, that always brought a groan from her listeners. 'Right, come on you chaps, lunch on the verandah in ten minutes. Then we'll go for a walk. Girls in the room on the right, lads in the one on the left. Rosa and Maria and their husbands are in the one in the middle, so no hanky-panky!' She grinned engagingly. 'Not indoors, anyway. Sorry about that!'

Amidst laughter they disposed themselves about the rooms. They had brought camp beds and sleeping bags with them. Patsy insisted the girls draw lots for the single battered bed that stood in the room they were to sleep in and when Philippa drew the long straw let out a shout of laughter. 'That, my poor Flip, is the world's most uncomfortable bed! Sorry about that!'

For lunch they ate bread and sausage and drank good Madeira. Sitting on a rickety cane chair listening to the silly light-hearted backchat around her, Philippa's gloom suddenly began to lift a little. She glanced across at Hugo. He caught her eye upon him and grinned. Her own eyes dropped, and she did not smile back, but it was as if a small bright ray of sunshine had flickered into a darkened room. She glanced up again. Hugo was still watching her. This time she smiled.

'Come on, everyone. Boots on.' Patsy scrambled to her feet. 'Let's get out into this lovely air – no-one's expected to walk all the way back to Funchal – though you could if you wanted to – but at least let's get to see something of the valley.'

It was, Philippa had to admit as she sat on the wooden steps tying the long laces of walking boots borrowed from Margaret Fellafield, the most spectacular setting one could wish for. Around the crater-like valley almost perpendicular walls of rock rose to towering peaks. Yet in this hidden and protected paradise the neatly terraced volcanic soil was fertile, the countryside green and lush. Winter was scarcely over, the trees of the orchards had yet to bud into leaf, yet the air was warm, and walls and hedgerows and the banks of the *levadas* were festooned with flowers.

They walked up into the village, that nestled beneath the shelter of the protective cliff walls, past small farms irregularly dotted about the countryside, an easy walk on relatively level ground. Philippa found herself remembering the Pico, and her stomach squirmed.

'How's it going?' Hugo was beside her.

'Fine.' She smiled suddenly. 'Lovely,' she amended. 'I'm so glad I came. It's beautiful.'

He nodded, pleased. They were walking a little behind the others. Now or never. Before she could waver Philippa said, firmly, 'Hugo?'

'Mm?' He was looking upwards, to the bowl of the sky that appeared to rest upon the peaks around them.

'The other day? You know – on the mountain? I'm sorry. Sorry I worried you so. I know I should have called you, told you I was going back, but I couldn't – I was –' she swallowed, '– I was terrified. Really terrified. I couldn't think of anything but getting away from there –'

The bright, wide eyes rested on her. 'It's all right. Don't worry about it.'

'But –'

He interrupted. 'Flip – it's all right! The best thing is simply to forget it –'

'I can't.' She walked on. Gravel and earth crunched beneath her feet, the sun was warm. 'I heard,' she found herself blurting, 'I heard what you said – about me being an idiot kid – and – and about wringing my skinny neck.' She stopped, appalled that her tongue should run away with her so. She had never intended to tell him.

He had stopped walking. Was staring at her, a tide of fierce colour rising in his fair skin. 'Oh, Lord!' he said at last. 'You *heard*? How on earth – Flip –' He rubbed a hand over his straight fair hair, making it flop haphazardly over his face. 'Flip, you mustn't take any notice – I lost my temper, that's all. It was sheer relief really – I'd been so *worried*. I'd thought – I'd thought – God, I was beside myself – I was just letting off steam, that's all –' For a long moment they faced each other. Whose laughter came first neither could ever afterwards remember. In a few seconds they were breathless with it, holding on to one another.

'Why "skinny"?' Philippa gurgled, 'Why were you going to wring my *skinny* neck?'

The question brought on another paroxysm.

'I say –' Mild and smiling Patsy strolled back from where the rest of the group were watching, grinning. 'Is this a private joke or can we all have a laugh?'

They sobered, slowly. Hugo took Philippa's hand in a gesture that could only be construed as possessive. 'Private,' he said, 'strictly private.'

Patsy grinned. 'OK then. Sorry about that. Just came back to say relief's at hand, we're nearly there. Make for the little bar at the end of the street.' She raised a hand and strode back to the others.

Slowly, still laughing each time one caught the other's eye, Hugo and Philippa followed.

He kissed her that evening. With the firelight glowing behind them and the murmur of voices and laughter in their ears he gathered her very gently to him and as gently kissed her, as she had hoped – had known – he would. The tender night, black and starlit, shadowed by mountain peak, enclosed them. They had walked some distance from the others, stood within a little grove of trees; small night sounds surrounded them. Philippa snuggled closer, lifted her face to his again, and again his mouth brushed hers. His arms tightened; she could feel his restraint in the tension of muscle and bone. With age-old and instinctive craft she lifted her arms, tracing the structure, the planes and hollows of his face with her fingertips, her body arched tightly to his, her breasts, aroused and almost painfully sensitive, brushing against his chest.

'Jesus, Flip –' He broke away, turned from her.

'What?' She was taken aback. Her body throbbed in a most alarming manner. 'What's the matter?'

'I'm afraid –' he stopped, started again. 'Flip, I don't want to – do anything to hurt you –'

'Why should you?'

He turned back to face her, stood for a long moment in silence. Then he came to her, took her very gently in his arms again. 'Flip, you're seventeen years old – only seventeen.'

'What's that got to do with it?' Her voice was edged with real exasperation.

'It's got everything to do with it. I'm twenty-seven –'

'And a man of the world?' She relaxed, giggling a little, raised her head again, kissed the line of his jaw. 'That seems to me to be an advantage rather than a disadvantage!'

'You don't understand.'

'Oh yes,' she was suddenly very serious, 'I understand. Very well indeed. I understand that I love you.'

In the silence that followed the words, embarrassed, she ducked her head. 'I'm sorry. I suppose I shouldn't have said that.'

His arms were about her again, tightening painfully. Hugo kissed her again, very long and very thoroughly. The sound of voices rose and fell behind them. Cicadas chirped noisily. 'What you need,' Hugo said into her hair, 'is someone around to keep you out of trouble. Frightening everyone to death on mountains – telling strange young men you love them – what will you get up to next?'

She stayed snuggled very close to him. 'Someone a little older, would you say? Someone with more experience of this wide and dangerous world?'

'Definitely.' He kissed her nose. 'Indubitably. But – Flip –' he stopped suddenly serious again.

She put a finger to his lips. 'Don't. Don't say anything, not now. I said I love you; I know I do. You don't have to believe me. You don't have to love me back. I understand. Love isn't like that. At least –', she added, painfully honest, '– sometimes I suppose it isn't. I promise I won't ever expect you to love me just because I love you.' Brave words. She flinched from them, and with an effort lightened her voice. 'But that doesn't mean I can just stop loving you, does it?' she laughed, very shakily. 'Just don't come this old soldier about my being too young. Juliet was only fifteen, remember?'

'I remember,' he said soberly, kissing her nose.

There was a moment's silence.

'And look what happened to *her*.' They chanted the words together amidst sudden peals of laughter.

'Hey, you two, grub's up,' Patsy called from the fireside.

'If you can tear yourselves away from the view, that is,' another voice put in, slyly.

Hugo, ignoring the laughter, turned Philippa's face to him in the dim light of the stars. 'Flip –' his voice was suddenly deadly serious, '– listen to me. Don't give your heart too easily. Least of all to me. Wait –' he cut short her protest sharply. 'You don't know me. The time – the place –' He waved a hand, taking in the warm night, the crackle of flame, the sound of laughter. 'Just be careful. That's all.'

For one moment the sombre tone of his voice made her skin prickle in an odd and uncomfortable way. Then she lifted her chin. 'No,' she said, simply. 'I shan't be. Faint heart never won anything at all; and you've done it, now. I'm not letting you get away that easily, so there.' The words sounded jauntier than she felt by far. 'Let's go and eat. I'm starving.'

Hugo stood for a moment longer, watching her as she ran to the fire. The echoes of Maurice Playle's voice, that haunted him always no matter how he tried to still them, were with him again – light, insistent and suddenly even more menacing than before. No effort could dim them.

He walked, smiling, to Philippa's side, kissed her lightly, to friendly applause, and accepted the sausage she laughingly proffered.

The rest of that trip to the Bowens' farm and the days that followed were a time of intense happiness for Philippa. She had meant what she said; she was utterly and fearlessly certain that what she felt for Hugo Fellafield was love. And for the moment at least that was enough. It was enough to be with him, to catch his eye across the room, to hold his hand as they strolled the garden and cliff top, visit vineyards and wine lodges, to laugh with him, squabble amiably about silly and insignificant things, exchange secret kisses and caresses. This was today, and she would not look to tomorrow. Determinedly she put aside the misgivings of that strange disturbing moment when he had come close to warning her against her feelings for him. She was well aware that he had not at any time told her that he loved her; told herself stubbornly that it would be all the more significant when he did.

The days flew by. They took a sledge from Monte down the narrow cobbled streets, shrieking with laughter as the ungainly vehicle slithered at breakneck speed down the steeply sloping hillside, skilfully controlled and guided by two young men in colourful costume. They took tea and Madeira honey cake at Reid's amidst the gentle clink of fine china and silver service, every voice to be heard as English as if they were sitting in the dining room of the Savoy in London. He showed her in painstaking detail how the wines of Madeira were made. The unique method, born in such unlikely circumstances, fascinated her. Gravely she watched and listened – such things were not taken lightly on Madeira – and her reward was his smile. There were picnics and parties and a dance held by the Bowens; and at all of these it was clear that subtly the attitude of their companions had changed; in the eyes of this enclosed little world Hugo and Philippa had become a couple. To Philippa's relief the older members of the party at the Quinta do Sol seemed as ready to accept it as anyone. Margaret treated her with fondness, scolded Hugo affectionately if he kept her out too late, herself suggested many of the excursions and diversions they most enjoyed.

But still Hugo had not told her he loved her, and as the days slipped by and the date for their return to England drew inexorably nearer some small part of her began to doubt if he ever would. In the daytime when they were together she was as happy as she had ever been in her life; but sometimes as she lay awake in the dark hours of morning the cold and miserable voice of reason made itself heard no matter how hard she tried to ignore it. Had Hugo done this before? Was that what he had tried to warn her about? Was she simply a diversion, an island romance, to be discarded and forgotten when they returned to the real world? Was that why Hugo's mother seemed so very content to see them together? Did she know from experience that such things always came to nothing when put to the test? Was she, Philippa – awful thought! – making a fool of herself? Fiercely she told herself that even if it were so she did not care.

She loved Hugo, that was enough. She could not, would not demand that he love her in return. She had promised him that, and she would keep her promise.

Towards the end of their stay the weather broke. Cool winds and drifting rain brought the temperature down and kept them indoors. They played whist and gin rummy in the pleasant library, played the old wind-up gramophone and danced. In the afternoon the clouds cleared a little and the rain stopped, so they wrapped themselves up and walked the gardens that were as lovely in the misty light and drenched with gentle rain as they had ever been in the sunshine. 'What's that?' Philippa pointed to a roof that nestled amongst tall trees. 'I've never noticed it before. It looks like quite a big building?'

'It's the old farmhouse. The house that was on the site when my great grandfather first bought it. The family lived in it for a while when the big house was being built.'

'What's it used for now?'

'It's empty as far as I know.'

'Is it very old?'

'Yes, I suppose it must be. Do you want to take a look?'

They followed an overgrown path through laurel groves and woodland to a clearing where stood a long, low building with rose red walls and a tiled roof. Climbing plants rioted about its walls. The windows were small, the door four-square and solid. It was in a severe state of disrepair.

'It's lovely,' Philippa said, simply.

Hugo glanced at her in some surprise. 'You think so?'

'Well, don't you? Look at that wonderful colour – it's as if someone painted it a hundred years ago and then just left it to the sunshine and the rain.'

'They probably did,' Hugo said.

'And the situation – it's like Hansel and Gretel! Oh, what a pity no-one lives here! Can we see inside?'

'Of course.' Hugo turned the handle of the front door. It swung open with an argumentative creak. The air was chill and the house smelled of disuse and neglect; yet it was dry, and the floorboards and flaking walls were solid. Odd pieces of roughly made furniture stood about the place, long abandoned. A battered wooden crucifix hung at a wild angle upon one of the walls. The rooms were low-ceilinged but well proportioned, rambling about a central hallway in which a long disused fireplace was black with ancient soot. Philippa ran from room to room, exclaiming with pleasure. 'The view from this window is absolutely marvellous! And – oh, Hugo, look at this window seat! The walls must be *feet* thick! And what a huge fireplace! You'd just *pray* for a day like today with a fireplace like that! Just imagine a log fire, a jumble of lovely old armchairs and settees – and books, look, all along that wall, a huge bookcase. And rugs on the floor. The boards are as solid as rock; I bet they'd look lovely polished. Can we go upstairs?'

The upper storey was simple, a long row of fair-sized rooms off a wide corridor set with more small windows. At the end of the corridor was a narrow set of stairs. 'Let's go and see the attics –' Philippa was already half-way up the stairs. Grinning, Hugo followed her. The attics, a string of small rooms running from one into the other, were dusty and almost completely bare; the views from the dormer windows that nestled amongst the ancient tiles of the roof were stunning. 'Hugo, do come and look – the sun's coming out – it's perfectly lovely!'

Hugo came up behind her, slid his arms about her waist, rested his chin gently upon the top of her head. 'What a marvellous, marvellous house!' she said, dreamily. 'Don't you think?'

'Yes.' His voice was very quiet. 'Yes, it is. Funny. I've known it since I was a child, and I've never noticed how nice it was before.'

'But how can you—?' She twisted, laughing in his arms and then stopped, eyes suddenly wide.

There was a very long moment's silence. Then he bent his head and kissed her. Dust drifted about them, the motes glistening like gold in the faint sunshine. It was very still and quiet. She felt his hands upon her body, made no attempt to stop their exploration. Her own slid beneath his jumper, felt the warmth of him through the cotton shirt he wore beneath. The sound of their breathing was loud in the silence. Slowly, very slowly he droppped to one knee, drawing her with him, giving her every chance to break away if she wished. She did not wish. She let

307

him lay her gently upon the dusty floor, closed her eyes as he began to unbutton her blouse. 'I won't hurt you,' he said, his voice very nearly steady. 'I promise I won't hurt you. Oh, Flippy, darling, I love you so –'

Her eyes flew open.

'– love you and love you. God, you just can't know – I swear I've never felt like this about anyone before. But I'm so afraid that –' Voice and hands stilled.

'What? What are you afraid of?' Her voice was hushed in the quiet. 'Hugo, please? What are you afraid of?'

He shook his head helplessly. She reached her arms to him and he laid his face against the small, bared breasts. She shivered as his lips touched her. They lay for a long time, bodies pressed close. 'Hugo?' Philippa whispered at last. 'What is it? What's the matter?'

He lay still for a moment longer. Now. Now was the moment. Tell her. Tell her now. Tell her that you're nothing but trouble. A traitor. A coward to boot. Not worth her loving.

He shook his head. 'Nothing.'

'Are you sure?'

He kissed her breast very gently, ran his lips across the nipple. 'I'm sure.'

'You said—' She stopped.

'I said I love you. I do. I've never been so certain of anything.' His quiet voice was quite firm.

She twisted beneath him, clinging to him, kissing him fiercely. For a moment he reacted as wildly, turning on top of her, crushing her with his weight, thrusting his body upon hers. Then as suddenly he rolled away from her, came up in the one movement to a sitting position, ran his hands through his hair, for a moment holding his head in his hands, as if physically willing himself to stillness.

She lay unmoving, watching him, wide-eyed.

'No,' he said, his voice very quiet but quite firm. 'Not here. Not now. Not yet. I want you to be very sure indeed before that.'

She hesitated for only a second. 'I am sure.'

He turned at that, half-smiling, shaking his head a little. 'Oh, Flip –' He shook his head again, at a loss for words.

'Don't you – want me?' Her voice was steady but her eyes were very uncertain.

He leaned to her, gathered her to him, kissed her hair, her eyes and, lightly, her mouth. 'Oh, of course I do! More than anything! But not here. Not like this. I won't risk it. I won't risk hurting you.'

She snuggled against him, reassured. 'How, then?' she asked.

He cradled her head, laid his cheek upon her hair. 'Who knows – perhaps one day we'll come back here. We'll have food and wine, a huge fire and a wonderful, comfortable bed. Then ask me if I want you.'

She twined her arms about his neck, pulled his face down to hers, kissed him softly. 'I'm not sure I can wait till then.'

'Much more of this,' he put her firmly from him, 'and you won't have to! What price all my gallant efforts then?' He put her from him, started – remarkably competently she realized – to button her blouse.

She watched him, her eyes luminous in the soft light. 'Hugo?'

'Mm?'

'Are you always so – gallant?' She could not hold his surprised glance, dropped her own eyes for a moment then lifted them again, wide and questioning, brown and shining as fresh-peeled chestnuts.

He considered her seriously, decided upon honesty. 'No.'

'That's what I thought.' In smothered silence she tucked her blouse back into her skirt, smoothed her hair. Lifted her head, a hint of challenge in the movement. 'Then why?'

He jumped to his feet, held out his hand, pulled her up after him with a single strong movement that carried her back into his arms for another kiss. 'Because, my Philippa,' he said at last as she drew a little away from him, 'I love you. And I want more for you – for us – than this.'

She regarded him in silence for a long time. Then, almost shyly, she took his hands. 'You mean – there is an "us", then?' she asked, all of the happiness, all of the uncertainties of the past days clear in her voice.

He nodded more than a little ruefully. 'Oh yes. That battle's been fought and well and truly lost. There's an "us" all right.'

He pulled her to him. She leaned against him, eyes closed, the most contented of smiles upon her young face.

Hugo laid his cheek against her smooth hair, a faint, sombre line drawn upon his forehead.

They walked back to the house through wet grass and woodland, Philippa for one totally unaware of drenched feet and damp clothes. As they reached the edge of the clearing she looked back at the old house. 'We will come back?' she asked, a little anxiously.

He slid an arm about her waist. 'Most certainly we shall.' He hesitated only for a moment. 'For our honeymoon,' he added, firmly.

She tilted her head to look at him. Grinned, suddenly and brilliantly. 'Aren't you taking something rather for granted, Mr Fellafield?'

He pretended to look puzzled. 'No. I don't think so.'

'Beast!' She pulled away from him, reached up to ruffle his damp hair. 'What about all this down on one knee stuff? Don't I get a proposal before I get a honeymoon?'

'When I'm good and ready, and not before.'

'Cheek!' She caught his hand, danced beside him like a happy child.

He stopped suddenly, his face serious. 'Flip?'

'Mmm?' She had her head tilted back, watching the cloudy skies above the tree tops. It had begun to rain again, gently.

'Listen to me. Please listen. It's not going to be easy, you know. There could be – problems,' he hesitated before the word.

She stilled. Sighed. 'Your father,' she said, flatly.

He shrugged, avoiding her eyes. 'Partly, yes. And then there's your stepfather. He might not be too pleased. You're so very young.'

'And you're so *very* old,' she teased, but he was not to be sidetracked.

'I'm not much of a catch.'

She laughed, delightedly. 'Good. Then no-one will mind that I've caught you and we won't have any trouble.'

'*Flip!*'

She turned, her hand still in his, her eyes shining upon his face. 'It's no good, Hugo, you won't frighten me. You can't. I know it won't be simple. I don't care. I want you. You say you want me. So there it is. If the worst comes to the worst we can wait until I'm twenty-one and then no-one can stop us anyway. If they cut us off without a penny –' She danced a few steps from him, laughing, ' – then I'll go and work in Woolworths. And scrub floors at night. You could be a ticket collector. We'll manage.'

Her gaiety, the love in her eyes, was all but irresistible. He could not help but laugh with her. 'Love conquers all.'

'It certainly does,' she agreed, cheerfully.

'Just one thing.'

'What's that?'

'I don't think I fancy being a ticket collector.'

She considered that. 'Oh? That's a pity. I thought you'd look a corker in the uniform. How about a bus conductor?'

'If you're dead set on a uniform I could always join the Guards?'

She snorted in a very unladylike way. 'Oh, no you don't! Then all the girls would fall for you, and where would that leave me?'

Laughing still, hand in hand they strolled across the wet lawn towards the house.

'Well.' Fiona turned from the library window, dusting her hands as at a job well done. 'It looked a little rocky for a moment, but all seems to be well now.'

Margaret smiled very slightly, but her eyes were serious. 'Let's hope it stays that way.'

Fiona cocked a red brow. 'You doubt it?'

Margaret's mouth turned down in a wry half smile. 'I've grown very fond of Philippa in these past few weeks,' she said, reaching for the bell-pull. 'Young she may be but she seems to have a kind of courage and a capacity for love that any mother would be happy to see offered to her son. I only hope that Spencer sees it.' Her voice was very low. Fiona turned, watching her with sharp eyes.

Margaret joined her at the window, watched the laughing youngsters as they ran through the rain to the door. 'Hugo was never a great one for standing up to his father,' she said, quietly.

Chapter Fourteen

'You'll never *guess* what Rachel's doing!' A hectic few weeks after their arrival back in England, on a long-plotted and much-anticipated visit to London, Philippa danced across the grass beside Hugo, their linked hands swinging.

Hugo, for whom the mention of Rachel's name could still be disconcerting, glanced at her. 'No?'

Philippa crowed with laughter. 'She's working on a market stall in Petticoat Lane! Did you ever hear anything like it!'

Hugo stopped walking, stared at her. 'She's *what*?'

'Working on a stall in Petticoat Lane. She goes every Sunday. She's made friends with a funny little man she calls Curly – he's an absolute scream. She's been doing it for a couple of months or so now.'

'*Rachel?* Working on a *market stall*?'

'That's right. She's loving it. I saw her yesterday. Sounds as if she's all but taken the thing over – got all her fancy theatre friends coming to the Lane for materials. Curly says she'll make his fortune for him.' She giggled. 'He needs it if you ask me – he's got eleven children. *Eleven!*' She reached up to kiss his cheek. 'How many are we going to have? I'm not sure I could manage eleven!'

'Well, of all the—' Hugo was shaking his head in amazement.

'Two? Three? No, not three, let's make it evens. Four. What do you think?'

'What?'

'Children, silly. How many shall we have? Is four enough?'

He threw an arm about her shoulders and hugged her to him. 'Four will be plenty.'

'Two boys and two girls. And all looking like you.'

'I don't think you can order them.' He grinned down at her,

'We'll probably have four horrible little boys who all look like their Uncle Charles.'

She pulled a gracelessly childish face. 'Perish the thought!'

In the distance the waters of the Serpentine glimmered in the sunshine of late spring, though a biting wind blew across the spaces of the park, ruffling the grass and tossing the treetops. A bench stood empty beneath the spreading branches of a majestic elm newly come into leaf. With no words they made for it, and Philippa, snuggled beneath Hugo's arm, sheltering from the wind, lifted her face for his kiss. He kissed her long and gently. When at last he lifted his head she sighed a happy sigh and burrowed tighter into his comforting warmth. There was a long, quiet moment.

'Flip?'

'Hm?'

'We have to talk.'

'No we don't.'

'Yes. We do.'

She said nothing.

'You spoke to Eddie again?'

She remained silent for a moment longer before, reluctantly, she answered him. 'Yes.'

'No change?'

She shook her head against his chest. 'Nope.' The word was defiantly jaunty. 'It doesn't make any difference. He can't stop us.'

'For the moment he can.'

She straightened, pulling away from his arm and looking solemnly into his face. 'I hope you understand – he isn't being horrible about it. Not like your father is. He's just worried, that's all. He feels responsible. He still thinks of me as a child. You have to admit it's difficult.'

'I suppose so.'

'He could be much worse about it – he could try to stop me seeing you, but he hasn't. He likes you. He said so. He just thinks I'm too young to know what I'm doing.'

Hugo's smile was not as light-hearted as he had intended. 'And are you?'

'No.' There was nothing but certainty in the word. She lifted a hand and touched his lips with her finger. 'What about your father?'

He shook his head, grimly. 'We had another terrible set-to a couple of days ago. Now he simply refuses to discuss it. He's of the firm opinion that you're a gold-digging young hussy who's no better than she should be. Mother's letter impressed him not at all.' He sighed. 'And Charles is no better. God, they drive me up the wall between them! As a matter of fact I'm thinking of leaving Cheyne Walk.'

Her face lit up. 'What a marvellous idea!'

He glanced at her, surprised.

'Somewhere to go, silly – somewhere for us to meet! I'm tired of Lyons Corner House and park benches! If you had a room somewhere –' she stopped, colour suddenly blooming in her face, '– we could – spend some time together.'

He kissed her, wagged a firm finger in her face. 'And that, young lady, is *exactly* what your stepfather fears!'

She shrugged. 'Don't you start, for heaven's sake! Oh, Hugo –' She leaned dreamily against him, cheek against the roughness of his jacket. 'In September I'll be down here at college – just think of it! I'll be able to meet you whenever we want.'

'As long as you're back by eight.'

She giggled. 'Oh, I don't suppose it'll be that bad. Anyway, at least we'll be close. Hugo, I do so love you.' She turned her face fiercely into his chest, her voice muffled. 'You won't let them stop us, will you? Promise me you won't?'

He laid his face against her hair. 'I promise.'

'I'm sure we can convince Eddie. It will just take a little time, that's all. And perhaps once we're married your father will come round?'

'I don't much care if he doesn't.' The usually easy-going line of his mouth was harsh.

'Don't say that, darling. He's your father –'

'He's a bigot and a prig.'

'Hugo!'

Hugo shook his head. 'You don't know him, Flip. Mother does. That's why she stays in Madeira.'

'Madeira.' Philippa repeated the word happily and quietly: a talisman against all ill.

'She got away from him; so can I.' Doggedly he refused to be sidetracked. 'I'm leaving Cheyne Walk. I'll tell him tonight.' The plan, that he hoped would solve more problems than one, had been in his mind for months. Why had he allowed his father and Charles to bully him out of it yet again? He could expect no help; he would ask for none. He had his salary, and many, many people were living on less. In common with most luxury trades the Madeira market was beginning to suffer from the depression that was deepening every day. But Paget and Fellafield had survived before and they would again. And of one thing he was confident – no matter how his father might disapprove of his actions the old man would not now dismiss him from the company. The firm had old and faithful servants who knew the day to day running as they knew their own families, but when deals were struck and wine was shipped it was a Fellafield with whom the customers wanted to negotiate. And the Fellafield they had grown used to asking for over the past year or so was Hugo. The promise had been made; in a few years a directorship, a seat on the Board. Hugo intended by then to have made the company his own, and his father's and brother's preoccupation with politics and power made the goal more attainable than it might have been. Charles had been promised adoption as a candidate for the Conservative and Unionist Party in the next election. With any luck that and the housing scheme he was so certain would make his fortune would keep him thoroughly occupied and out of Hugo's affairs. His other problems he would deal with himself; he had Philippa now, and he intended to keep her. Safely, and with no fear of harm. He would leave Cheyne Walk, he would break with Maurice Playle. He would wait for Philippa – the four years to her twenty-first birthday if necessary – and they would marry. He experienced, as he so often did when he was with her an enormous surge of protective strength. Sitting here in the sunlit chill of an April day, Philippa snuggled against him, her face bright and trusting as she watched him, anything and everything seemed possible. 'I'll tell him tonight,' he said again.

Inevitably, it was not that easy.

To begin with all went well; Charles was out attending a political meeting and Spencer Fellafield, in expansive mood, suggested that he and his younger son should eat comfortably in the Snug, a small and pleasant room on the first floor of the tall town house, book-lined and comfortable. Hugo, having delivered Philippa safely back to the small and somewhat shabby hotel she and Eddie stayed in when he was attending the House, had arrived home in quiet and determined mood. He was a full-grown adult. He need ask for nothing. His father must be told, firmly and civilly, of his plans.

They ate an excellent meal. Spencer Fellafield's cook, like everything else in his life, had been chosen with an eye to excellence and efficiency. The conversation was light and impersonal – the likely revolution in travel promised by the new breed of airship, notably the Graf Zeppelin and the R101, the coming attempt by Amy Johnson to fly alone from Britain to Australia, the brilliant batting of Don Bradman, the unlikelihood of a Channel tunnel ever being sanctioned let alone built. Hugo, who had started the meal tense as a wound spring began to relax. His father was in good spirits, important and highly secret negotiations he was involved in were going well. He seemed receptive, ready to listen. He himself spoke entertainingly in his own especial caustic manner of friends, colleagues and politicians with whom he had been recently in contact.

'Rumour has it that our own pet aristocratic Socialist is about to resign from the Cabinet –' He poured two brimming glasses of Bual, passed one to Hugo.

Hugo looked up, startled. 'Mosley? Really? Why?'

'Reform, it seems, is not coming fast enough for the precious boy. He intends to start his own Party.'

There was a small silence. Hugo knew Oswald Mosley well, the man had dined many times in Cheyne Walk in his days as a Conservative MP. He and Spencer Fellafield were united in their admiration of Hitler and Mussolini. 'A Fascist Party?' Hugo asked now, distaste edging his voice. 'Here?'

'Yes. A Fascist Party, certainly.' Spencer Fellafield eyed his son narrowly. 'You object?'

'Of course I bloody do! Sorry, Father.' The apology had been occasioned by the merest raising of an eyebrow, and Hugo obscurely resented it the moment it was spoken. He went on with far more truculence than he had intended. 'Mosley's a worm, Father, and you must know it. And as for his precious Fascists – do you want an army of sanctimonious anti-semitic boy scouts marching around telling us all what to do or think? And – please! – spare me the homily about Mussolini and the Italian trains. There are more important things in life!'

There was a moment of frigidly pained silence. 'Hugo, your simplistic not to say childlike observance of things and ideas is sometimes entertaining. But not always.'

A deep flush rose in Hugo's face. He sipped his drink.

His father held his glass up to the light, looking with appreciation into the ruby depths of the wine. 'The Fascists aren't anti-semitic.' He took a sip. 'At least – no more than the rest of us are.'

'Speak for yourself.'

His father's eyes flickered like a steel blade. 'I always do.'

Hugo downed his drink in one, ignoring his father's frown. 'How can you say they aren't anti-semitic? The man Hitler is a raving lunatic. He hates the Jews.'

'So do many people. It doesn't mean they'll ever have the power to enshrine such hatred in the constitution of a political party. Adolf Hitler, so far as I understand it, advocates merely a – cleansing of the national character.'

Hugo made a sharp, derisive noise.

'He is also in my opinion and the opinion of many others our best defence against the canker of Communism, which as you know I oppose utterly, and against Liberal Socialism which as you also must be aware I detest even more heartily. Europe – the world – must not be allowed to slip into chaos again. If Hitler can stabilize Germany as Mussolini has stabilized Italy it can only be regarded as a good thing.'

'No matter what the cost?'

'Exactly.'

Hugo crossed to the decanter and poured himself another drink. 'It's an abominable creed.'

The silence behind him was telling. He turned. Spencer Fellafield was regarding him in true astonishment. 'Your words, Hugo? Or – someone else's? Who, I wonder, has been instructing you in the subtleties of world politics?'

Hugo cleared his throat. 'No-one.' Somewhere in his brain a small flutter of panic had begun. How the devil had he got into this? 'Father – actually – I wanted to talk to you about something else –'

'Oh?' The single syllable was cool.

'I—' He fidgeted with the heavy cut glass decanter stopper, moving it from hand to hand. 'I intend to leave home.'

Silence. Spencer Fellafield sipped his Madeira, looked at it again, appreciatively. 'Indeed?'

'I'm a grown man, Father. I need my own place.'

'I can see no reason why.'

Very carefully Hugo replaced the stopper. 'I need my freedom.'

'Oh? Freedom to do what?' The words were deceptively, dangerously pleasant. 'What can you do in a "place of your own",' he laid ironic stress upon the words, 'that you cannot do here?'

'I –' Hugo battled with the embarrassing stammer that any confrontation with his father could bring on, '– I don't know. I only—'

'Would I be right in concluding,' his father cut across the words, 'that this sudden decision has more than a little to do with the – young lady –' he made an insult of the words, 'to whom you have – become attached?'

'No. It has nothing to do with Philippa.' Beneath the sardonic, level, disbelieving gaze of the other man he felt colour rise in his face again. 'Father, please – it isn't so unusual, is it? I'm twenty-seven. It's time I left.'

'Charles feels no such compulsion.'

'Charles wouldn't.' They were the words of a sulky child. Spencer Fellafield, with a pained glance, ignored them.

'I've told you before; when you choose to settle down with a suitable wife I shall be only too pleased to endow you.'

'I don't *want* you to give me anything!' The words were violent. 'I just want to go! I'm perfectly capable of looking after myself! I've got a job – which is more than a lot of people can say – I earn my own living. I'm entitled to spend my own money as I please. Father, I didn't want an argument – but I'm not asking you. I'm telling you. I'm leaving. I'd rather go with your blessing, but either way I'll go. It's – best for everybody.'

There was a very long silence. Spencer Fellafield finished his drink unhurriedly, his eyes steady upon his son, put the glass back upon the table. 'I see. And where, might I ask, do you intend to live?'

'I don't know. I'll rent a place.'

'Alone?'

'Yes, Father, alone!' Hugo curbed with difficulty the sudden fierce rise of temper. 'I told you – Philippa has nothing to do with this. If you'd only meet her, you'd see –'

'No.' The word was steely.

Hugo stood dumb with frustration.

His father stood, a full head taller than his slighter son, the aristocratic cast of his face disdainful. 'Very well, Hugo. Go if you wish, though I may say you'll get not a penny's worth of help from me. And what's more –', he raised his hand, palm out as Hugo started heatedly to reply, '– what's more I want this clearly understood; if you at any time carry through this idiotic plan of yours to marry this nobody, this fortune-hunting miss, I warn you you will regret it for the rest of your days. I will – in the words of melodrama – cut you off without a penny. Without a farthing. And valuable as I concede you are to the firm it will be the end of your career with Paget and Fellafield. Think about it. Go off – have your fun with her. Then come back to me and we'll find someone sensible and suitable and as pretty as you could wish. Someone I am happy to welcome into my home as my daughter-in-law and the mother of my grandchildren. Until that day – and believe me, Hugo, it will come – I don't think we have much more to say to one another, do you?'

Hugo was shaking. The man who stood cold-eyed before him had dominated him all of his life; the anger of years boiled within him and, humiliatingly, robbed him of words.

In the silence the discreet tap on the door sounded loud. 'Come.'

A manservant put his head round the door. 'A phone call, sir. For Mr Hugo.'

'I'm coming,' Hugo said. 'Ask them to wait just a moment, would you?'

'Yes, sir.' The man withdrew.

Ostentatiously relaxed Spencer Fellafield settled himself back in his chair and reached for the newspaper that lay on the table.

'I'll go,' Hugo said, very quietly, unable to keep his voice from trembling. 'And I won't come back. Do what you like, Father, you won't separate me from Philippa.'

'We'll see.' His father did not bother even to look at him.

Hugo left the room, closing the door very quietly after him. He ran down the stairs very fast, snatched at the telephone. 'Yes?'

A quiet and pleasant voice spoke at the other end of the line.

Hugo stiffened, automatically turned, hunching his shoulders against the space of the wide hall and staircase, though there was no-one to hear. 'I told you not to call me here!'

The voice spoke again.

'I can't. Playle – I can't, I tell you! I—'

The other man interrupted him.

Hugo stood for a long time in silence, listening. Then, 'All right,' he said, his voice low, 'all right. I'll do it. But this is the end, you hear? I'm not—'

The telephone clicked and went dead.

Hugo stood for a long while with the receiver in his hand, the knuckles white, tendons raised with the strength of the grip. When, very carefully, he replaced it he had to make a conscious effort to release it. He stood for a moment longer looking down at it; his head bowed, the muscles of his face knotted with tension. Then, turning, he trod heavily upstairs to his room.

Rachel had taken to working the market as a duck might take to water – right from that first day she had felt it to be, strangely, almost a homecoming. She enjoyed everything about it, the good and the bad. She loved the camaraderie, the fierce loyalty that welded the market folk together, she loved the bustle, the laughter, the usually good-natured, often witty and always entertaining backchat. She enjoyed the challenge of a reluctant customer, the decking of the stall to catch the eye and the imagination, the coaxing of an extra half-crown from a punter who came looking for kitchen curtains and went away with a dress length she had had no intention of buying. She was amazed at how quickly after an initial, cool appraisal the market people came to accept her. In her exotic clothes, her baubles and bangles, and with her clear cut West End accent – that no-one seemed likely to tire of good-naturedly deriding – she was a feather in Curly Bennet's cap, as he undoubtedly had been the first to see. Within weeks they had struck up the firmest of friendships; he delighted and amused to see how quickly his protégé took to the street life of the Lane, she quick to respond to the warm, down to earth and undemanding friendship he and others like him offered.

'Yer got coster blood in yer, gel,' Curly was fond of saying. 'Somewhere along the line, you mark my words. Coster blood. Yer a born trader.'

That this could very possibly be true was something that Rachel kept firmly to herself. Not even to Curly would she give away that much of her background.

Word had very soon got around the London clubs and drinking holes that on a Sunday morning come rain or shine Rachel Patten was to be found shouting the odds in Petticoat Lane. Friends and acquaintances came to chat, no doubt to snigger, though she cared not a fig for that, and often stayed to buy; especially after Rachel had persuaded Curly to let her go to the warehouse with him. To her amazement she found that materials, slightly flawed to be sure and a little less than perfect, that might be had in the London stores for a price to make even the most extravagant flinch were here virtually being given away. With the enthusiasm of the converted she persuaded Curly to look at something other than the serge, the gingham, the good serviceable wool that were his normal stock in trade. To show good faith she even invested a few pounds of her own in the more exotic stock; within weeks Curly's stall was blooming with the greens and golds, the blues and the purples that Rachel herself so loved, draped and decked with sequins and tassels, a delight to the eye and an irresistible draw to every girl within a square mile with money in her pocket and a lad to impress.

'Looks like a bloody knockin' shop, you arsk me,' said Harry, Curly's neighbour, more than once, his grin caustic.

'Bloody Turkish Bazaar more like it,' Curly acknowledged happily. 'Bloody marvellous, ain't it?'

It was not just the local girls who were drawn to Rachel's materials, and, as time went on, to her helpful comments and suggestions for their use. The theatre people, hard-up as ever, who had so often slept on her floor, cadged her money and drunk her whisky were eager customers too. What if a length of silk were a little blemished? Cut and draped so it would never show. What if a pattern were a little irregular, a dye not quite perfect? Cleverly incorporated into a garment – and Rachel was a near genius at that they all agreed – who would ever know? The word spread; down the Lane on Sunday morning and you can look like Greta Garbo by Friday, if you can supply the long raincoat and the accent.

Rachel herself was Curly's own best advertisement. The gipsy colours and exotic accoutrements that had always suited her so much now became a positive advantage. When her supple, slender-waisted figure was draped in the alluring colours of a peacock's tail feathers every female who laid eyes on her believed – or hoped – she could look the same. The perfect oval face, the brilliant eyes beneath exotic scarves and head-dresses contrived from worthless off-cuts, ears decked with long, swinging earrings, tempted them all, from schoolgirls to ample matrons, to emulate her. In the way of the market a nickname was coined for her, half-scornful, half-admiring, wholly friendly.

'Got a magic lamp there, 'ave yer, Duchess? Care ter give it a rub fer me?'

She had, at first, some trouble with the market Casanovas to whom the unexpected arrival of an apparent innocent at first appeared like an answer to a fellow's prayer. She quickly and with some force disabused them. The unholy alliance of Curly, huge Harry and her own unabashed and intemperately rough tongue soon discouraged any thought of pursuit, let alone conquest. On the contrary amongst that particular segment of the market population she acquired a reputation not altogether flattering, which she did nothing to discourage.

She was soon working other markets with Curly, almost all in or around the East End – Stepney, Upton Park, even as far afield as Romford. Curly was delighted at his unexpected luck. He took her home to meet the family, eleven children aged two to nearly seventeen, living in five rooms in Stepney; five good rooms at that, she recognized, remembering the folk to whom her father had ministered in the past. Curly earned good money on the markets and while he was more than fond of his pint he did not stint his family. They ate well and were healthy; the youngest noisy and agile, the elder ones lively and quarrelsome. Rachel, much as she liked Curly, was not sorry to leave. Betsy, Curly's wife, a wisp of a woman with lank blonde hair and tired eyes had said not more than two words directly to her, the whole of the flustered two hours being taken up with the serving of tea, garbled apologies for the ill behaviour of one or other of the offspring, loud arguments with the three older girls or the rousting out of one of the tribe of cats that curled in every warm corner and upon every flat surface in the room.

Curly, walking Rachel to the Underground station shrugged, cheerful and apologetic. 'No place like 'ome.'

Rachel slanted a quick grin down at him. 'Never a truer word spoken in your case,' she said, 'I'm exhausted! I'd rather do a twelve hour stint down the Lane than face that alone for an hour!'

'They liked you.'

Her glance this time was flatly dubious. 'They did?'

'Oh, yeah,' he shrugged nonchalantly, bright blue gaze mischievous. 'You can't get a word out of them if they don't.'

Rachel rolled her eyes. 'Remind me to do something very dislikable next time I come.'

Curly grunted with laughter, drew on the Woodbine he held between stained fingertips.

'Curly?' Rachel hesitated for a moment. 'You're sure that Betsy doesn't mind? My working with you, that is? And Nellie

323

– didn't you say she helped you sometimes? She doesn't think I've pushed her out?'

''Course not, duck. Betsy's never liked the market – nor Nellie neither come to that. 'Smatter of fact they both think you're up the pole.' He grinned up at her. 'Nellie's got a job of 'er own, down the trouser factory – it don't break her 'eart not to 'ave ter get up at three o'clock on Sunday mornin' I can tell yer!'

'Well, as long as you're sure.'

'Sure I'm sure.' He cocked a bright, inquisitive glance at her. 'An' you? You still enjoyin' it?'

'I certainly am.'

He laughed, shaking his head in mock amazement. 'Who'd 'a thought it? It was a lucky day fer Curly Bennet when you walked into Barney's Café, I'll tell you that.'

Rachel slipped an affectionate arm through his. 'Nowhere near as lucky as it was for me, Curly lad. Nowhere near.'

'So – how long will you keep this up do you think?' Daphne's pleasant voice was amused. She poured a cup of tea, passed it to Rachel.

Rachel shrugged. 'As long as I feel like it. Honestly, Daphne – I love it! I really enjoy it. I'd no idea anything could be such fun. And what's more, I'm good at it!'

'What does your father think?'

'He doesn't mind – why should he? I think he's pleased I've found something relatively constructive to do.' Pensively she stirred her tea. 'I wasn't going through a terribly constructive phase at the time, if you remember.'

Daphne smiled a little, said nothing.

'Rock bottom,' Rachel said, very quietly.

Impulsively Daphne leaned forward and laid a hand over hers. 'Don't think about it. It's over. You're enjoying life. You look wonderful. Look forward, not back.'

Rachel nodded, but her eyes were still sombre.

'Rachel? You are all right?'

'Yes, of course.' The words were just a little too emphatic.

'But?' Daphne prompted gently.

Rachel put her cup down, stood, wandered restlessly to the

window, stood looking into the soft early summer rain. 'But – sometimes I wonder –'

'What?'

'Sometimes I wonder if I'll ever really feel anything ever again.' The words were lightly spoken but the line of her shoulders was tense.

'Oh, Rachel, of course you will!' Daphne hurried to her, slipped an arm about her waist. A very real friendship had grown up between these two in those terrible weeks of Rachel's illness. Opposites in almost every way, yet each liked and trusted the other and an odd bond had grown between them.

Rachel shook her head. 'Sometimes I wonder if I want to. Perhaps it's better this way.'

'No.'

Rachel's glance was both sympathetic and sardonic. 'Are you sure?' She was, perhaps, the only one, and with good reason, to have realized the depth of Daphne's feelings for her handsome, difficult husband.

Daphne held her eyes, her colour a little high. 'Oh yes,' she said, 'I'm sure.'

Rachel shrugged, strolled back to the table, picked up her teacup. 'Well I'm not. Nothing but trouble and grief, these men. I'm better off on my own.'

'For now.' Daphne smiled, and suddenly Rachel grinned back.

'For now,' she agreed. 'Now, where's this famous son of yours? He doesn't sleep all afternoon, does he? His Aunty Rachel's brought him a present.'

'I'll get Parker to fetch him down.' Daphne tugged at the bell pull, spoke over her shoulder. 'Have you seen Philippa lately?'

Rachel nibbled a biscuit. 'Mm. Just the other day as a matter of fact. What a transformation! She's grown up overnight.'

'Ah, Parker, ask Nanny to bring the baby down, would you?' Daphne turned back to Rachel. 'It's amazing what love can do.' The words were not entirely joking. 'Do you think they'll get round Hugo's father?'

'No, I don't. Spencer Fellafield's one of the most arrogant and snobbish men I know. If Hugo and Philippa do marry it'll be without any blessing of his. He'll do everything he can to stop them.'

'And Philippa's stepfather?'

'Eddie, very sensibly, has simply suggested that they wait until Flip is older. He has nothing against Hugo. On the contrary. But he feels that Flip is too young. Flip understands – though given her head I think she'd marry the lad tomorrow.'

'It's better that they wait.' Daphne turned, smiling, as a young girl in nurse's uniform entered the room carrying Amos. She held out her arms for the baby. Rachel watched, a shadow in her eyes, before picking up her handbag, rummaging through it and bringing out a little silver rattle. Daphne accepted it, smiling, rattled it above the baby's small face. 'Thank you, how lovely! See, Amos, what Aunty Rachel's brought you –'

The child blinked solemnly.

'Would you like to hold him?' Daphne asked.

Rachel drew back, shook her head swiftly, hair flying. 'No fear! I'm not good at these things. I'd be sure to drop him.'

Daphne settled in the chair opposite, tucking the child into the crook of her arm. 'And you? What do you think? About Philippa and Hugo Fellafield?'

'Hugo's an extremely nice young man. A bit daft, but aren't they all?'

'You – knew him quite well at one time, didn't you?' There was a gleam of feminine curiosity in Daphne's eye that brought laughter to them both.

'You could say that,' Rachel agreed, ruefully. 'He had a crush of the worst order, that I suppose I didn't do enough to discourage. But there – it didn't do him any harm in the long run. Philippa's much better for him. I'm glad he's had the sense to fall for her. If anyone can instil the guts in him to stand up against Fellafield père, it's our Flip.' She grinned maliciously. 'Spencer Fellafield is certainly having a bit of trouble with his sons at the moment. It couldn't happen to a nicer bloke.'

'Sons? You mean Charles?' Daphne was surprised. 'Whatever can Charles have done to upset his father?'

'Got himself involved in some speculative building scheme that's blown up in his face, or so I gather. Very unsavoury business apparently – bribery and corruption, and now the fellow he was in partnership with – Grenfell or Greenway or some such name – has absconded with the funds, leaving Charles with a rather large hole in his wallet and egg all over his face.'

Daphne was sitting very still, the hand that held the rattle, that she had been gently shaking to divert the baby, suddenly motionless.

'It's all being hushed up, of course,' Rachel continued, un-noticing. 'Spencer's made quite sure it won't get into the news-papers, nor is anyone being prosecuted or anything honest like that. But word is he's furious with Charles.'

'Yes. I expect he would be.' Daphne's voice was very quiet. 'How did you come to hear about it?'

'Oh, I still see some of the old crowd occasionallly. Bertie Chadworth lost a packet too. He told me, though it's all very hush hush as I said.'

'Of course.' Daphne shifted the baby to a more comfortable position on her lap. 'Well, young man, time for tea, I think.' She began to unbutton her blouse.

Rachel stood abruptly. 'I'll be off then.'

'But Rachel –' Daphne stopped. Rachel's eyes, fixed upon the child, were full of pain. 'Of course. If you must. But, oh Rachel, do come again soon. I really love to see you.'

'I will.' Rachel reached a hand to stroke the child's head, all but snatched it back again.

'And I'm so pleased that you're enjoying life again.'

'Oh, you can always trust me to do that,' Rachel said, lightly. At the door she turned. 'Bye for now.'

Daphne smiled, nodded. The door closed. Daphne sat for a very long time, quiet and still, staring into space. The baby grizzled a little. Slowly and still pensive she began to unbutton her blouse.

Toby was late home that evening. She was waiting for him in the drawing room.

'Still up?' he asked, coolly. For the past weeks the atmosphere between them had noticeably lacked warmth.

'As you see, yes.' He had been away from home more often

than he had been there; and on those nights that he had slept in the house he had not once come to her bed.

He crossed to the sideboard where stood a decanter and glasses. Daphne watched him pour himself a small measure, reach into his pocket for his cigarette case, light a cigarette, draw on it slowly. 'Rachel was here today,' she said.

'Oh? How is she? Still playing costermongers?'

'She's fine. Better than she's been for a long time. And yes, she is still working in the market. She appears to love it.'

'There never was any accounting for our Rachel.'

Silence fell. Toby reached for the neatly folded newspaper that lay upon a small table.

'She told me—' Daphne stopped.

His eyes did not leave the paper, barely curious. 'What?'

'She told me about Greenham absconding with the money. She said – some sort of scandal was being hushed up – '

He put the paper down, turned to face her. His face might have been carved of marble, so still and so cold was it. 'I see.'

'It's true then? This was the deal that you were involved in?'

'Yes.'

'Why didn't you tell me?'

'Why do you think?'

She shook her head.

He picked up the paper again, his hands, almost imperceptibly, a little less than steady. 'It has nothing to do with you.'

'What?' She stood, hands clasped tightly before her. 'Toby – how can you say that? You're my husband – Amos' father – '

'Don't worry. There'll be no scandal. And it wasn't Underscars money I lost.'

'That's not what I'm saying – '

'Oh? Then just what are you saying? "I told you so"? "Perhaps next time you'll listen to me"?'

'No! Toby – you're being terribly unfair. I wanted to ask – to ask – if you needed any help. Money, perhaps. Toby – if you're in trouble I want to—'

'No.' Neither voice nor face gave an inch. 'I don't need help. And I don't need money. The deal has collapsed. I won't bore you with the unsavoury details. Yes, I've lost the money I put into it. Charles Fellafield and a couple of others have lost more. There's an end to it.' He tossed the drink back in a single neat movement, stubbed out his cigarette, stood up. 'Now, if you don't mind I have a busy day ahead. I'd like to go to bed.'

'Toby –'

He turned. 'Daphne – I really have no intention of discussing this with you. You made your choice. I accepted it. If you want me to say it, I'll say it; you were right and I was wrong. Let's leave it at that.' He walked towards the door, stopped. She saw the effort it took him to ask, quietly, 'Will you tell your father?'

'No. Of course not.'

'Thank you for that at least.'

'I mean it. I only mentioned it because I wanted to help.'

'I told you. I don't need help.'

Nor anything else. Defeated, as he left the room she dropped into a deep armchair, sighing, pushing her fingers into tired eyes. She understood. All too well she understood. Toby Smith had come from nothing. One thing and one thing only he had that was his; his pride. Anyone instrumental in or even witnessing the denting of that pride was in for a bad time.

But how, as a wife, could she not be witness to it? And how could she show him it did not matter?

And how, more importantly, could she show him that to oppose him occasionally was not to betray him?

The quiet of the still room sang in her ears. She ached for him; ached for his hurt and for the feel of his body upon hers.

She sat for a long time, watching the fire. When she finally left the room and climbed the stairs to her empty bedroom its glow had fallen to ashes.

'Morning, Charlie.'

'Mornin', Duchess. Lovely day.'

'It certainly is.' Rachel dumped an armful of material onto the stall, began to sort the rainbow colours. Summer had settled in at last; the air even this early in the morning though fresh already promised warmth. All around the market stalls were being set out in expectation of a good day's trading; there was nothing like sunshine to bring the customers out, and once they were out they could be persuaded to spend. Rachel clambered onto a box to drape the sides of the stall with bright floral silk.

'Mornin', Duchess.'

'Morning, Bert. How's the wife?'

'On the mend, thanks.'

'And business?'

'Boomin', Duchess, boomin'.' The man grinned. 'The missus said to say thanks for the piece you sent 'er by the way. Fair beside 'erself she was.'

Rachel glanced over her shoulder, smiling. 'I'm glad she liked it. It certainly was a –' She stopped, head suddenly lifted, eyes narrowed across the heads of the growing crowd. '– a very pretty colour,' she finished, abstractedly.

'What's up?' Bert, a big, red-faced man with shoulders like an ox turned to follow the direction of her gaze.

'I – nothing.' Rachel's eyes were still searching the crowd. 'I thought I saw – someone I know. That's all.'

He chuckled. 'Be 'ard not to by now I'd 'a thought.'

'Yes.' Her smile was brief and preoccupied.

Bert ambled off. Rachel turned, stood foursquare on the box, steadying herself with a hand on the frame of the stall. Very slowly and very carefully she quartered the street with her eyes, searching each profile, each shadow.

Gideon Best was not there.

She had been mistaken.

And yet – in that moment when she had glanced across the street – she would have wagered her life that it was his dark and sombre eyes that had met hers, his still face she had seen, shaded beneath a slouch hat, watching her.

'Mornin', gel. Fancy a cuppa?' Huge Flora, who kept the haberdashery stall across from Curly's stood beneath her, arms folded across her massive bosom. 'Got time before the rush starts I reckon. Got a few bits an' pieces ter show yer.'

Rachel glanced at Curly, who grinned and jerked his head. 'Off yer go. Place won't fall ter pieces if yer gone 'alf an 'our.'

On and off all day she looked for him. On and off all day the thought of him invaded her consciousness no matter how she fought against it. An unwary moment and there he was. Fragments of memory, like the razor-edged shards of a broken mirror embedded themselves painfully in her mind and heart, both of which had been blessedly numb for so long. Why did she look for him? Was it in fear or in hope? She did not know. Their lives had touched, disastrously for them both; commonsense dictated that since any further contact could bring nothing but trouble Gideon Best was a man to avoid. Then why, suddenly, did she remember every line of his face, the mobility of his long mouth, the picture he had made in his borrowed whites standing defiantly alone at the wicket that first day at the cricket match? To her horror she felt the first true stirrings of physical desire since the agony of the abortion as she remembered that night, when he had stood like a statue in the rain, watching her, naked, as she emerged from the water into the storm –

God above, she must stop this! She had achieved at least some measure of peace. It would be madness to throw away that hard-won stability for the sake of a half-glimpse of a face that probably was not even Gideon's. The market was full of gipsies. The cast and colouring of face, the angular, wide-shouldered build she had seen before and had noted, almost unconsciously, the resemblance.

No. Gideon Best would never come looking for Rachel Patten.

The enraging complication was that in honesty she could not decide whether that knowledge was a welcome relief or a bitter pill she must swallow as best as she could. And the more she thought about it the more unsure she became.

So: the answer she told herself tartly was simply not to think about it.

Yet, still, she found herself looking for him.

The following Sunday he came again. And this time there could be no possible mistake.

It was mid-morning. The crowds were at their densest and most noisy. The weather was sultry. Rachel and Curly had had a good morning. Bolts of cloth were spread in rare disorder across the stall.

'Golly!' Rachel made a great show of wiping perspiration from her brow. 'We could have sold at least another bolt of the red silk. The crêpe de Chine's nearly finished too. And the flowered stuff's going well. Curly – I was wondering – I don't want to tread on Flora's toes, but mightn't it be a good idea to—' Her words were cut as if by the blade of a knife.

Curly, busy with a huge roll of blue serge glanced up, irritated. 'What?'

Rachel was standing like a statue, her eyes fixed on some point beyond the milling crowds that Curly with his smaller stature could not see. 'Duchess? What's the matter?'

'Nothing. Curly –' Distractedly Rachel ran a hand through her hair. '– give me a minute, would you? There's – someone I want to talk to.' Before he could respond she was gone, slipping around the stall and into the crowds, pushing and shoving with the best of them.

'Duchess? Bloody 'ell – where the devil?' Curly pushed his flat cap to the back of his head, shrugged. 'Can I 'elp yer, ducks?'

Rachel pushed her way through the crowds to where she had seen Gideon. This time there had been no possibility of mistake; she knew it. He was somewhere here. But when she reached the corner of Middlesex Street, where she was sure he had been standing, there was no sign of him. She stopped, standing on tiptoe, raking the jostling crowds with her eyes.

And then, turning, she saw him, striding fast away from her, crossing the wide thoroughfare of Aldgate High Street, dodging a clattering tram, turning south towards the river.

Rachel glanced around. Not far from her stood a market urchin with a mop of sandy hair, a rash of freckles over his pale, dirty face, and a pair of astute blue eyes. He caught her eye on him, and had his hand out ready as he moved towards her.

'Do you know Jimmy Bennet? They call him Curly.'

''Course I do.'

'Run and tell him Rachel won't be back today, would you?' She searched in her pocket, tossed him a sixpence, her eyes on Gideon's rapidly disappearing figure. 'Tell him not to worry. I'll see him Tuesday.'

'Right, Missis.' The boy turned and disappeared into the crowd like a rabbit into a warren.

Rachel, blessing the impulse that had dressed her in wide-legged sailor trousers and flat shoes that morning, turned and unashamedly ran after Gideon.

The tall figure had reached and was turning the corner of the Minories.

'Gideon!' Her voice was lost in the sound of a rattling omnibus. 'Gideon, wait!'

If he heard her he made no sign. She ran to the corner. The familiar, easy, long-legged stride had already carried him perhaps a hundred yards from her. 'Gideon!' Breathlessly she dashed after him. She would not lose him now. She would not! 'Gideon, stop!'

This time she was quite certain that he heard her; there was a noticeable hesitation in his step before he strode on.

'*Gideon!*' Exasperated she shrieked it.

Very reluctantly his pace slowed. He stopped. Turned. His face was shadowed by the slouch hat. His collarless white shirt was clean and over it he wore a worn but still colourful waistcoat. His neckerchief was a splash of scarlet. As she approached him she too slowed her pace, trying to regain her breath after her inelegant dash. As she came up to him he neither smiled nor greeted her.

Taking her cue she did not herself bother with the niceties of the occasion. 'Gideon – what are you doing? Why are you here? Were you – were you looking for me? Who told you? Why did you – ?' She let the question tail into mid-air; she knew the words 'run away' would not please him, but she could think of no others.

He held his silence for a moment longer. 'Philippa came to see me,' he said. 'She always comes when we're on the Heath. She told me.'

'So – you did come to find me?'

He shrugged.

'Then – why did you run away?' This time the words were out before she could think to stop them.

He glowered.

'Gideon?'

He turned and began to walk slowly. She fell into step beside

333

him, watching the closed dark profile. 'I didn't think you'd want to speak to me,' he said at last.

'Then why did you come?' She was suddenly infinitely, gently patient, as she might have been with a wary wild animal that came step by step towards her open hand.

He shrugged again, squinted into the far distance.

'Gideon? Please? Won't you tell me?'

'I wanted to see that what Philippa said was right. That you were –' he hesitated for a telling moment, '– better.'

She fell silent for more than a few paces. Ahead of them the bulk of the Tower of London loomed. 'I'm better,' she said, quietly.

They emerged onto Tower Hill. The great fortress, wrapped in a dignified Sunday quiet unbroken by gawping queues of visitors and their noisy offspring, stood deceptively peaceful in the hazy sunshine, belying the centuries of cruelty and violence. They crossed the road to the greensward, stood looking at the ancient building with its crenellated battlements and grim, grey towers. Beyond it the river glittered. A tug hooted with busy impatience. Rachel and Gideon stood a little apart, hands in pockets, as if absorbed in the small craft's bustling progress upriver. Neither spoke for a long time.

Then 'Gideon –' she began and turned, to find that he had in that same moment taken breath to speak.

'You first,' she said.

'I didn't say anything.'

'You were going to.'

'Was I?'

They had begun to walk again, slowly. Gideon, his hands still rammed firmly into his pockets was watching the pavement as if he expected that it might imminently open up and swallow him.

'Why?' she asked.

'Why what?'

'Why did you want to know if I was better?'

'I don't know. I just had to.'

'You misunderstood me,' she said.

He waited.

'That last time. At the flat. You misunderstood me.'

He shook his head.

Brutally clearly her words that day came suddenly back to her. '– me and a gipsy brat in a caravan –' She winced a little. 'I didn't mean it,' she said. 'Gideon – I wasn't myself. I tried to tell you ; but you'd gone –'

They walked on through the quiet streets, the river glinting between the buildings on their left. The wharves and docks were silent, the usually busy waters peaceful.

'Philippa says you've been through a bad time?' He broke the long silence at last; his voice, still Norfolk-tinged, was quiet.

'Yes.'

'I'm sorry for that.'

'It wasn't your fault. Well –' She slanted a sudden gleam of rueful laughter up at him. '– I can't deny you had something to do with it.'

He smiled back, a very little, but his face was grim.

'It was pretty awful.' Her eyes now were fixed ahead, distant, and there was no laughter in them. 'It wasn't just the pain, though that was pretty bad, nor the length of time it took me to recover – I was quite ill I think for quite a long time –' The sentences, softly spoken, were disjointed. 'It was – the emptiness. The sadness. Nothing I could do would make it go away –' The pent words, for so long obstinately unspoken, welled within her. She wanted to talk. She wanted to tell him. She wanted – desperately she wanted, though she could not tell why – his understanding.

She paused, biting her lip.

'Go on,' he said.

She went on. She went on for some time. He listened in silence – that, indeed, was all she asked of him – but it was not the silence of condemnation or disinterest. When she faltered he prompted her, and as she spoke, as the ugly words came like pus from a wound, the pain, that had still nagged, was truly eased at last. 'I kept having this dream, night after night after night, that I had a baby – a –' She swallowed, painfully. '– a boy, always a boy – I'd hear him cry – and then I couldn't find him – God, it was awful – and so real! I'd wake up, time after time, crying –' Never had she told anyone of those dreams. Telling it now was like a burden lifted. And as for what had followed, she did not spare herself. The degradation of those months that were now like some distant, awful, self-destructive fantasy she catalogued coolly. The excesses. The self-disgust. They walked on, pacing together, unaware of any other soul about them – Lower Thames Street, Upper Thames Street, and finally out onto the Victoria Embankment with its majestic stretch of river, its magnificent buildings, the spires of Westminster in the distance.

And still she talked.

'– and then I met Curly, bless him. I really was about as far down as I could have been. I didn't give a damn what might happen to me. I thought – I remember thinking –' She drew a long, careful breath '– that I'd be far better off dead. And then – there he was. Asking me to help him was a cheeky joke I think really – he didn't dream I'd take him up on it. But there we are – I did and I'm glad I did. I really do enjoy the life. I love the market. I like making money – and we are making money – I like the freedom and I like the people. I like – well, I just like having something to *do*, something to think about, I suppose.' She smiled faintly. 'A lot of people have been trying to tell me that for a long time, I know. Including you, if I remember rightly.' They were leaning on the parapet of the Embankment, watching the river. A wheeling gull called above their heads, pigeons pecked busily at their feet. A pleasure steamer tooted cheerfully, heading for Westminster Pier. 'Curly says I've got coster blood running in my veins.' She leaned forward on her elbows, watching the wash of the little ship lap against the stone. 'He could be closer to the mark than he thinks.'

'Your father?' He was watching her intently.

She raised her eyes to his. It seemed like an age since that day in the sunlit woods that she had told him the story of her birth. 'Who knows?'

'Do you care?'

Her eyes held his. She shook her head. 'No. Not any more.'

The line of his mouth softened. Another steamer tooted. She

held out a hand. He took it. 'Have you ever been to Kew?' she asked.

They caught the boat with seconds to spare, running, hands still linked, laughing breathlessly. The wind on the river was chill, but he did not offer an arm to protect her. They sat side by side, for the most part in silence, watching the history of London slide past them as the steamer headed upriver. At the gardens they paid their penny and strolled the paths and lawns, admired and commented upon the splendid collection of trees and plants, visited the greenhouses with their exotic palms, wandered back along the riverside like any couple out to enjoy a day in the London sunshine. Indeed they made a striking pair, and it amused Rachel to see how many glances they attracted. They talked of everything and of nothing; of Philippa's romance with Hugo, of Gideon's life with DeVine's Circus – a life to which he declared himself, with a few laconic words and an expression that forbade all argument, to be perfectly suited – of Rachel's unexpected successes in the market. She made him grin with her demonstration of her sales patter, he convulsed her with a dry description of life on the move with two bears, a motheaten tiger, a lion so old he'd lost his teeth and wanted to do nothing but sleep and a raft of fairground equipment that had seen service since the accession of the late lamented Queen Victoria. They avoided, as if by mutual agreement, all mention of Toby or any further mention of their scant shared past. The conversation was light, and general. Gideon had not commented earlier upon Rachel's soul-searching; not did he now attempt to reopen the subject, a fact for which Rachel was profoundly grateful. It had all been said, and at some cost. Perhaps, now, it could be forgotten.

Perhaps.

They caught the bus back into London. The air was still heavily warm, the sky a blaze of too-vivid colour, the under-bellies of purple clouds lurid with the reflection of a setting sun the colour of blood. Distant thunder rumbled, lost in the noise of traffic and the clip of steel-tipped heels upon the pavements of the city. A few large drops of rain fell in a desultory fashion, wide-spaced, splashing the warm paving stones and drying almost immediately.

'Gideon?'

'Yes?'

They were walking along a dingy residential street in the direction of Rachel's flat. Rachel's tentative suggestion that the best bus for Hampstead Heath could probably be caught at a stop in the opposite direction had been ignored.

'Why *did* you come to the market?'

'I told you. To find you. To make sure you were all right.'

'But why?' she asked, doggedly.

'I'm not sure.' The words held no subtlety; they were honest, and painfully so. Dusk had fallen, the red sun lost behind the skyline, thunder still rumbling but distantly. Gone to the countryside, Rachel found herself thinking, where its sound still held some majesty, some menace.

Suddenly the carefully constructed gaiety of the afternoon had fled; and the silence between them was not easy.

'Well. Here we are.' Her voice was spuriously light. She hesitated, torn between the desperate need for him to leave and an equally strong and wholly disturbing desire to keep him with her. 'Would you like a drink?' What else, she asked herself, prevaricating, could she say?

'Yes.' His answer was unhesitating. He preceded her up the stairs, a swift-moving shadow sure-footed in the gloom.

She stood for a moment, still, at the foot of the stairs, taking a deep steadying breath. One drink. A little light conversation. Then he would leave.

Inside the flat she made great ado of turning on all the lamps, adjusting curtains, throwing open windows, twitching cushions. She turned on the electric gramophone, guided the needle onto the wax. Music blared, ragtime, the lively, syncopated beat too loud, too artificial.

'What would you like?'

'Whisky.' He had to raise his voice above the music.

Her eyes flicked to his, a gleam of humour lighting them. 'Old malt?'

The dark mask of his face lit. He nodded.

She poured the drinks, brought one to him where he stood, too big, too masculine for the silk-draped feminine room. The tinny piano played a final flourish and stopped abruptly, leaving an untenable silence. She hurried to the machine, turned the disc over. Again it blared, brash and intrusive.

Collectedly he tossed back his drink, carefully placed the glass upon the crowded mantelshelf, walked to the gramophone and lifted the needle arm.

The silence was deafening.

Deftly he replaced the arm upon its cradle. Turned.

In the shadowed silence she asked again, tiredly, as at loss for an answer as she suspected he was himself. 'Gideon? Why are you here?'

In the quiet someone hurried down the street outside. Rain hissed. 'I told you. I'm not sure.'

'For Christ's sake!' The words were suddenly, uncontrollably violent, and carried reminders of a Rachel who had by no means been vanquished. 'If you don't know, who does?'

The air hung heavy and warm between them. Thunder still scowled in the far distance, the rain fell, but did not cool the air.

'You want me to go,' he said.

She turned from him, shoulders hunched, said nothing.

'Rachel? You want me to go?'

'Yes!' she shouted. 'No! I don't know. Bloody Hell! What a great pair we are!'

He came to her, and held her. He laid his lean cheek against her tears. He lifted her, and cradled her, and then he loved her, fiercely and with skill unselfishly used. She cried out, once, lay within his arms for a little while then rolled onto her stomach, her face buried in her arms.

'You asked me why I came,' he said at last into the quiet.

'To do that?' Her voice was muffled.

'Partly, I suppose. But – something else, too. I had to come. I couldn't do anything else.'

She lifted a tearstained face. 'And?'

'Rakli, there are two roads here. One is mine and one is yours. I can't travel your road for you.'

She sat up, naked, her back to him, clenched against him. 'Do you care?'

He took a very long time to answer. She would not look at him. 'Rachel Patten,' he said, 'the choice, if there is one, is not mine but yours.'

'I can't,' she said, and shook her head. 'I *can't*!'

The air beyond the window moved distantly with thunder, dying. The rain had stopped. A cool breath moved the curtains.

She sniffed. 'I'm afraid,' she said, her voice quite calm.

She almost felt his shrug. 'We're all afraid. It's a fool who feels no fear.'

Her mouth turned down in bitter self-mockery. 'In my case I'd say it was a fool who does.'

'No.' Surprisingly gently he caught a heavy, shining handful of hair, turned her face to him. 'No,' he said again. His kiss was long and surprisingly gentle. Final. 'It's good that you feel fear. You're no fool, Rachel. Don't think it.' He swung away from her, reached for his clothes. The air was fresher, and smelled of rain. Rachel shivered a little, reached for her wrap. 'I was right from the start,' Gideon said from the shadows. 'Your road is not my road. Always they've been too far apart. I shall not come again. I'm sorry for what's happened. Sorry you've been so hurt. You're right to avoid further harm.'

She did not hear him going, was not aware of the exact instant that he left. She sat for a long time, hunched upon the side of the bed, unmoving. 'I'm afraid,' she had said; but she had not explained her fears. Just as well. What kind of female fool was afraid of warmth, afraid of affection, afraid of the giving and taking of love?

I shall not come again.

He had meant it, she knew. There was no art in the man.

Good. That would make things a whole lot simpler.

Stiffly she stood, wandered to the window, shut it against the lifting breeze.

I shall not come again.

Stony-faced she went into the tiny kitchen, switched on the light, reached for the kettle.

Chapter Fifteen

Amos Underscar was tired. Bone tired. And not entirely settled in his mind.

More and more he was having to leave the day to day running of the company in Toby's hands; that this had always been the final intention did not ease the sting of having it forced upon him. The small, nagging pain in his side prevented him from concentrating; and always he fought a desire to sleep. Two days ago he had actually nodded off during a meeting with Berenger. The man had been overly concerned; had treated him as if he were a dotard.

He sat now in front of the fire that even in the warmth of summer did not seem to him to take the chill from the room, eyes closed, thinking. Rumours had reached him. Rumours that, if true, needed careful consideration. Rumours that linked Toby Smith's name with some unsavoury property deal; a deal that had cost its investors money.

His head sank lower on his breast. Baby laughter sounded. He smiled. The boy was a wonder. Amos could see him as if he were here, perched upon his lap, solid and warm; the wide, bright eyes, the down of hair, the smile that lit the little face when he saw his grandpa –

He jerked awake. Dammit, he'd done it again! No wonder Berenger had fussed about him like an old woman! He shifted in his chair. Where was the blasted girl who was supposed to keep the fire in? The place was like an icebox!

Grumbling aloud, he struggled from the chair, jerked the bell pull ill-temperedly.

'Yes, sir?'

'Make up the fire, Mary. It's like the Arctic in here! What d'you think I am, a blasted penguin?'

Mary wrinkled a small well-made nose behind his back. The room was fuggy as a bear's den in her opinion; a bit of air would do it no harm, never mind more coal. Noisily she did as she was bid.

'And Mary — see this note is delivered to Brittain, Lee and Robinson, in Bradshaw Street, will you? At once, if you please.'

'Yes, sir.' The girl stood and waited as he scrawled untidily, blotted the paper, folded it and put it in an envelope. 'Tell Mr Lee that it's important, girl. I want to see him. Here, tomorrow morning, first thing.'

'Yes, sir.'

As the door closed behind her Amos took his stand almost in the hearth, back to the fire, rubbing his thin buttocks. The small episode had woken him up. He'd speak to Frank Lee, see what he would advise. That was best. And meanwhile he'd perhaps take the time to pop over to Bayswater, see Daphne and that little rascal of a grandson. An Underscar through and through that one, and it showed already. Blood will out. Amos nodded, sagely. That little devil will never lose money on a deal; his Grandpa would wager lives on that.

Amos stood with remarkable patience in the hall allowing Mary to cluck and tut him into his heavy overcoat and muffler, his thoughts elsewhere.

And as for young Toby — well — it would do no harm to take precautions. What might be changed now could, after all, just as easily be changed back later if he were proved wrong. Better safe than sorry, that was Amos Underscar's motto. Better safe than sorry.

Well pleased with himself the old man nipped jauntily down the steps and into the street.

'Mr Underscar — you've forgotten your hat! Mr Underscar — wait —!' Exasperated Mary stood back, hands on hips, shaking her head. Daft old creature. Deaf as a post he was, and twice as silly sometimes.

Amos, hatless, hailed a taxicab and made for Bayswater and his grandson.

*

Two days later he went down with a cold.

'Really, Father, I told you the other day about coming over to us without a hat!' Daphne's scolding was meaningless. Affectionately and efficiently she tucked the bedclothes around her scowling parent.

'Do shut up, child,' he growled. 'There's nowt wrong with me but a snuffle. That silly chit never should have sent for you –'

'Mary was only doing her best, now don't be such a bear! She was worried about you. And she didn't "send" for me as you put it, she telephoned to tell me that you were off-colour. It was my decision to come.'

'Without bringing the bairn I see.' He was determined not to be mollified.

'Of course without bringing him. We don't want both Amoses down with snuffles, do we?' She grinned at him, in affectionate exasperation.

He shrugged thin shoulders beneath the heavy striped cotton nightshirt, but there was a hint of an answering smile in his faded eyes.

Daphne plumped the pillows, smoothed his thin, disordered hair. Odd; until now she had not realized how frail he had become these past months. The robust frame had withered, though the spirit that fired it was the same. 'You really should take more care of yourself.' She tidied the bedside table, held out a hand. 'Let me have your water bottles. I'll refill them.'

'Don't fuss, woman. They're all right as they are.'

She laughed a little, shrugged. 'As you like.'

He cocked his head, watching her. 'How's that husband of yours?'

Taken aback by the sudden and direct question she made a great show of shaking and smoothing the quilted eiderdown. 'He's fine. Working hard, I think.'

'And playing hard, too?' The old eyes were suddenly disconcertingly shrewd, and openly eschewed finesse.

She straightened, hands on hips, surveyed him for a moment during which he had the grace to attempt a half-shrug and a craftily pathetic smile. 'I expect so,' she said, calmly.

'I heard—' He stopped.

She eyed him with patient politeness, apparently incurious.

His mouth shut like a trap. 'Nothing.'

'And so I should think,' she said, mildly. 'Now – what would you like for tea?'

'Not sure I can eat any.' He was grumpy at her refusal to rise to his bait.

She smiled, sweetly. 'And I'm quite certain that you can,' she said, firmly. 'How about muffins? Toast? Tea cakes? I happen to know that Cook has made your favourite walnut cake. You can surely manage a piece of that?'

He pulled a face, unimpressed.

'Honestly, Father, you are the giddy limit!' She was suddenly and genuinely laughing. 'Why they all care so for you is beyond me! I'm surprised they don't just leave you to stew in your own juice!'

He straightened, as best he could, with dignity. 'That's because I'm a fair and reasonable employer. Always have been.'

She chuckled. 'Nonsense! It's because they're fond of you, you old reprobate! As we all are!' She bent over and kissed him firmly upon the cheek, ignoring his token resistance to such typically female lack of restraint. 'So. Tea cakes, I think. They've always been your favourites. I'll go and organize it. Are you comfortable?'

''Course I am.'

'Right.' Her hand lingered for a moment on his shoulder. 'Shan't be long. Ring the bell if you need me.' She pushed a small brass bell across the bedside table, and turned to leave.

'Pet?'

The small, affectionate diminutive, not heard since childhood pulled her up short.

'Things are all right with you?'

She came back to the bed, perched upon it, took his hand in hers. 'Of course they are, Father. Of course. Whatever you may have heard, whatever's worrying you, just forget it. If I were unhappy or in trouble, who would I run to?' For a second, or perhaps for a fraction of a second, that nostalgic childhood pet name echoing in her ears, she almost believed it, and her tone was warm enough to reassure him. She patted his hand and stood. 'Back in five minutes.'

He watched her to the door. Why did he remember, so suddenly and so clearly, a plain, too skinny little girl with eager eyes and a softly pretty voice; a child sensitive, eager to please, yet obstinate as the devil when it came to a fight? Why, suddenly and urgently, did he regret – something – what –? He was tired. Very tired. Blasted cold. She'd been a good kid. Bright. Very bright. Took after him, he supposed.

He closed his eyes.

Daphne returned with laden tray less than ten minutes later. She pushed open the door with her shoulder, backed into the room. 'There. Just look at this. This'll put hair on your chest if nothing—' She stopped.

The clock ticked. The fire crackled in the hearth.

Daphne walked very steadily into the room, laid the tray upon a table by the window. Turned. 'Father?'

Her voice dropped into silence like a stone into still water.

She approached the bed. The quiet was oppressive. No breath stirred the silence. His hands, brown and knotted with age, lay peaceful upon the silken quilt.

'Father!'

She did not have to touch him, did not need the lax, cooling skin to tell her that death had taken him. She sat on the bed beside him, hands clasped in her lap, looking at the face she had known all of her life. Only now did she see how it had changed. Until that moment it had always been the same; the face of love, the face of security, the same through the endless years. Always there. And now, in the space between one breath and another, gone.

Much later, as the light paled at the window she stood and walked to the bell pull, waited, contained and calm until the door opened and Mary peered into the gloom. 'Yes, Miss? Oh! Lordy, Miss –!'

'Yes. I'm sorry, Mary. Would you telephone to Doctor Lister? I think we should notify him.'

'Y – yes, Miss. Oh dear, Miss – o-oh –' Pinafore to face,

ribbons flying, Mary fled, to spread the dire news and to set in motion the last rites that the living owed to the dead.

Daphne walked to the window. She had said her farewells. She leaned now into the faded and musty velvet curtains that had draped this window ever since she remembered it and closed her eyes.

Toby, she should telephone Toby and tell him.

Memories still clamoured, more real than this strange empty moment in which she stood, the past streaming by her like a river.

She would tell Toby later, when he came home. No purpose would be served in searching for him now. She would tell him face to face. There was comfort in that.

Stark honesty, her constant foe, confronted her.

Only then would she know whether he truly grieved.

The pale-faced, angular man in the dusty morning coat and high winged collar of a generation before laid the document from which he had been reading neatly and squarely upon the desk in front of her. 'That completes the reading of the bequests,' he said, quietly. 'I think it's all perfectly clear?'

Daphne, in some state of shock, did not dare look at her husband.

'May I ask a question?' Toby's voice was deadly calm.

'Of course.'

'When did Amos – Mr Underscar – change the original will?'

The man flickered a pained look over the half-moons of his reading glasses. 'Mr Smith, I—'

'When?' The word snapped across the room like the crack of a whip.

Frank Lee shrugged. 'Just two days before his death.'

'I see. And did he give any reason for the changes?'

The man hesitated, tellingly. Then. 'Yes,' he said. 'But I must tell you that the conversation was confidential.'

'I see,' Toby said again.

Daphne sat perfectly still, head bowed, staring sightlessly at her locked fingers in their black lace gloves against the heavier black of her skirt. The reading of her father's will, that she had expected to be painful but uneventful had brought a shock for which neither of them had been prepared. Most of the bequests had been as expected; the Islington house and most of its contents to Daphne, some moneys and stocks and a few mementoes to the Yorkshire aunts, a fairly large sum in trust for young Amos. It was the disposal of his forty-five per cent holding in Underscars, that it had always been understood would go to Toby, that had been the bolt from the blue. Nineteen per cent of the shares had been bequeathed to Toby; the other twenty-six per cent Amos had left to his daughter, leaving Daphne in control of fifty-one per cent of Underscars stock.

She glanced at her husband. Two high spots of colour burned in his cheeks. His mouth was tight.

Her heart sank.

'Well.' In some faint and obvious relief that the awkward moment was over Frank Lee placed his long, thin hands flat upon the table before him in a gesture of finality: 'I trust all is clear? May I, Mrs Smith, offer my own condolences at your father's death? He was an old and admired friend, we shall miss him.'

Daphne murmured her thanks, aware only of the husband's body, tense as a spring, beside her.

'If there is any way in which I can be of further assistance I do trust you will contact me without hesitation?' The man stood, came around the desk, hand outstretched.

She took it. 'Thank you.' Toby, too, shook the outstretched hand, waited, coldly polite, for her to precede him out of the room.

In the dark, tiled corridor outside she turned. 'Toby –'

'Not here, Daphne.' Firmly he took her arm and steered her towards the door. 'Not now. Explanations – and you surely have some explaining to do – can wait until we're home.'

She pulled away from him. 'Me? Explanations? What do you mean?' She was genuinely taken aback.

He lifted a hand, calling a taxi. The square black vehicle manoeuvred a tight turn and drew up beside them. Toby all but wrenched the door off its hinges as he opened it for her.

'Toby –'

'Get in,' he said.

She got in, sat very still and straight in the corner, as far from him as she could manage. As the full import of his words dawned upon her an unusual lift of pure and all but uncontrollable fury set her stomach churning unpleasantly. She gritted her teeth against words, against the desire to shout, very loudly, into his pale and angry face.

They confronted each other in the privacy of the drawing room, he taking his stance by the empty fireplace, she standing apparently calm and controlled as the maid served tea upon a silver tray and, curtseying briefly, withdrew.

'So,' Toby said quietly into the silence. 'Underscars is yours after all. What an extraordinary change of mind your father must have undergone.'

She had had the length of the journey to battle her anger, to force good sense to oust hurt. She took a long breath. 'Ours, Toby. Ours. Underscars is ours, as it has always been. What difference does it make in whose name an odd two per cent of shares is registered?'

He made a small, harshly derisive sound.

Trembling slightly in her efforts to remain cool, to think clearly, not to give way to the towering rage that built within her she talked steadily on. 'If you suspect that I in any way influenced my father to do this let me tell you now that you're utterly wrong. We never discussed it. Nor did I at any time mention the Greenham affair – or any other affair come to that.' Her voice was suddenly waspish, the pinprick of malice irresistible. She regretted it almost the moment it was spoken, though wild horses would not have dragged it from her. 'I can only say again that I simply don't see that it makes any difference –'

'Difference?' He exploded into movement, flinging himself forward to face her, raging. 'Don't talk such bloody tommy rot! And don't play the silly innocent with me, Daphne. It won't wash. I'll tell you the difference it makes; deny it if you will. Everyone knew the company was to come to me. Everyone. How do you think they'll see this? The most empty-headed shop girl, the youngest snot-nosed errand boy will know what's happened! What kind of respect can a man expect to command if he can at any time be overruled by his wife? How many times will Berenger come sneaking to you behind my back, trying to get my orders countermanded?'

'I wouldn't *do* that!'

'Wouldn't you? Think carefully, Daphne.' His voice was bitter. 'Wouldn't you?'

She folded her arms tightly across her chest, gripping her upper arms, fighting to contain her own hurt and anger. 'I say again, the company is ours. I wouldn't dream of interfering with your day to day running of it. You know it. Major decisions we've always shared anyway –'

'It wasn't what I was promised.'

'I know.'

'Then why? Why did your father go back on his word?'

She shook her head despairingly. 'Toby, I don't *know*! Perhaps someone did tell him about the Greenham business –'

'Oh, somebody told him all right,' Toby said, very quietly.

There was a long, suddenly cold silence. 'And you still think it was me?' Daphne was astounded at the chill calm of her own voice. He looked at her, coolly, his handsome face closed. 'I find it very difficult under the circumstances to believe that it wasn't.'

'Under *what* circumstances? Are you truly suggesting that you think that I deliberately went to father – knowing he was ill – that I *persuaded* him to do this –' High colour was rising in Daphne's cheeks.

Toby, in the bitterness of his disappointment, was beyond the dictates of commonsense, let alone the ability to admit he might be wrong. Deliberately he allowed silence to answer for him.

'You're despicable,' Daphne said.

'Possibly.'

Barbed and bitter acrimony prickled in the air between them. Toby turned away.

'I didn't influence Father, Toby,' Daphne said, very quietly. 'I swear it.'

At the door he stopped, looking back at her. 'Well someone sure as hell did,' he said, 'and I know who's come out the loser.'

Temper finally snapped. 'Loser? You can speak of losers? What have you lost, Toby Smith? Promised control of a company that was only ever yours through me anyway! And I? I've lost a father, Toby! A father! Do you care about that?' Tears of rage and grief blotched her plain face. 'Have you given a single thought to that?'

The door closed, infinitely controlled and quiet, behind him.

After a long moment Daphne walked to the table where stood the tea tray. She poured milk into the cup, gripping the handle of the jug with strength enough to break it, then picked up the teapot. The spout clattered violently upon the cup, tipped it spilling tea over the starched white cloth. She slammed the pot down. 'Damn it! Oh, *damn* it!' Wretchedly she dropped into a chair, buried her face in her hands, her shoulders shaking.

The spreading stain reached the edge of the table and tea dripped, steadily and unchecked, upon the patterned carpet.

It was not a rift that was going to be easily healed. The words hastily spoken on both sides had been too harsh, the disappointment for Toby too keen. The atmosphere in the house was intolerable.

Daphne, usually the peacemaker, was in this case as firmly entrenched as was Toby. She was also, she had slowly to acknowledge, the more unhappy. Strife was not in her nature; the words that had been spoken, the awful and unexpected hostility of the quarrel haunted her. In the week that followed she spent long hours at the Islington house, ostensibly putting her father's affairs in order, going through the harrowing task of itemizing furniture and personal effects, supervising their disposal as gifts, putting some into store, bringing other pieces to Bayswater; in fact as often as not wandering unhappily from room to room going over and over in her head the things that had been said and, even more often and less constructively, the things that had not. Toby she saw hardly at all, and their exchanges when unavoidable were brief, cool and invariably impersonal.

It was whilst tackling the attics of the Islington house that the ridiculously simple and at the same time totally unacceptable answer to the problem occurred to her. Sleeves rolled to her elbows and face shining with perspiration in the enclosed, dim lit space of the narrow roof she had come across some of her own childhood toys and a small crib, presumably hers also, that had been lovingly tucked away in this far corner of the house – for what? To await the coming of another child? A child who had never materialized? She turned the battered doll she held in her hands. Another child.

Dust danced in the faint beam of light that fell from the tiny, dirty skylight.

Another child.

She was not young. With every year – every month – that passed the chance of conceiving and successfully bearing another child receded.

With every night that Toby spent at his club – or wherever it was that he actually spent his nights – with every night he slept in the bedroom that had once been designated as the guest room but now by common consent was termed his, the chance receded further.

Tiredly she pushed the lank hair from her hot face, leaving a smear of grime on her cheek.

There was such a thing as a bargain.

'No,' she said, aloud. And then again, '*no!*' She scrambled to her feet, tossed the doll into a corner. 'Damn and blast it. No.'

'Hello?' The voice, crisp and familiar, came from below. 'Daphne? Are you up there?'

'Yes. I'm here.'

Rachel's perfectly groomed head appeared at floor level. She peered through the rickety banisters. 'Good God,' she said, mildly, 'looks like a set for *Fanny by Gaslight*. Didn't your Pa ever throw anything away?'

'Very little.' Daphne laughed, ruefully. 'Whatever are you doing here?'

'There's a fine greeting.' Rachel perched on the top step, to the detriment of a pair of expensive-looking cream slacks. 'I called at Bayswater. They said you were here. So I came over to see what you were doing.'

'And if you could help,' Daphne supplied, shrewdly.

Rachel grinned, shrugged. 'Whoever heard of me helping any-one? But I don't mind watching while you work.'

Daphne laughed, brushing the dirt from her hands. 'I think

this has defeated me for the day. How about a cup of tea?'

'Sounds good to me.' Rachel left the top step with some alacrity and ran lightly down the narrow steps.

'We'll have to make it ourselves, I'm afraid. The house is closed up. There's no-one here.'

'I'm sure we'll manage.' Rachel led the way down the oddly echoing staircase. The rooms on either side stood, empty or nearly so, cleared of warmth and of memories. Rachel lingered on the main landing. 'Funny feel a house has about it when no-one's living in it.'

'Yes.' The word was short.

Rachel glanced at her, said nothing, ran on, light-footed, downstairs.

Settled around the kitchen table with a pot of tea between them she asked, suddenly and flatly, 'Are you all right?'

Taken by surprise, Daphne, she knew, let too much show in her face for a moment before she said, very firmly. 'All right? Of course I am. Why shouldn't I be?'

Rachel tapped her nose with a long, scarlet-tipped finger. 'Old market trader, me. Touch of the Gypsy Rose Lees. Crystal balls and all that.' An amused twitch of the brows and a slight change of emphasis and voice turned the last sentence into something close to vulgarity.

'Rachel!' Daphne giggled into her tea, almost choking.

'I saw Toby,' Rachel said.

'Ah.' Daphne's laughter died. She picked up her cup, sipped the scalding tea. 'And what did he have to say for himself?'

Rachel was lighting a cigarette. She narrowed her eyes against the drifting smoke, shook the match out. 'Not very much. But enough for me to put two and two together and make a not very healthy five. You forget how well I know him.'

'Better than I do.' The words were sombre.

'Quite probably,' Rachel said, with blunt candour. 'I've known him all my life, remember. And I've never been married to him.' She shrugged, only half-humorously. 'Marriage doesn't seem to me to be the best institution in which to get to know someone.'

'What an odd thing to say.'

Rachel shook her head.

They sat for a long time in silence.

Rachel fingered her cigarette, eyeing it absently. 'Funny,' she said at last. 'I used to hate you. Did you know that? Really hate you. If anyone had told me I'd side with you against Toby I'd have laughed in their face.'

Daphne was staring at her, shocked. '*Hate* me? – Me? But why?'

Rachel shrugged. 'Because I wanted Toby for myself. I was wild about him – infatuated – for years. When I heard he was going to marry you I'd have cheerfully torn your throat out.'

Daphne sat silent, watching her, a faint frown upon her brow.

'Funny,' Rachel said again, and made a swift, graceful movement with her hand. 'Now you see it, now you don't; one minute here and the next minute gone. I guess that's the nature of infatuation. I've seen it in others. Now I've experienced it myself.' She grinned faintly. 'It's rather encouraging, actually.'

Daphne, as unused to such unsolicited confidences as was Rachel to bestowing them was still watching her, the faintest hint of wariness in her face. 'So – you don't want Toby now?'

'Good Lord, no. You could say I grew out of him rather suddenly. Last year.' Rachel drew on her cigarette, watched the smoke. 'I grew out of a lot of things last year.'

'Rachel –'

Rachel ignored the interruption. 'Fee knew. She put her finger on it as always; the one man I couldn't have.' She rested her chin on her hand, tapped ash into a saucer. 'Not untypical,' she said, wryly. 'But now? No. I don't want Toby. I don't want anyone, actually. At least—' She hesitated, seemed about to say something, shrugged, shook her head. 'It's a mug's game. So I bequeathed him to you, so to speak. Which is why I'm not about to see it all fall apart without doing a bit of healthy interfering. It's those damned shares, isn't it?'

'Yes.'

'Why did your father change his mind, do you know?'

'No. We never spoke of it, honestly we didn't. I can only assume that he heard some rumour – that someone told him about the Greenham fiasco. Toby thinks it was me.'

'And it wasn't?'

353

'Of course it wasn't!'

Rachel held up placating hands.

'Sorry.' Daphne picked miserably at the scrubbed kitchen table with a chipped fingernail.

'Do you care?'

'What?'

'Do you care? About the shares – about which one of you actually controls the company?'

Their eyes met in a glance of perfect and for Daphne uncomfortable understanding. Similar thoughts had been running in her own mind up there in the attic. 'No,' she said. 'I don't. Not as much as I should. But I care about what he said. About what he thinks I did.'

'What he says he thinks you did,' Rachel corrected, softly.

Daphne shook a stubborn head.

'There's a way,' Rachel said, quietly. 'You must have thought of it? It depends of course on just how much you want hostilities to end.'

Daphne lifted her head, pale eyes direct. 'Give him the shares.'

'Yes. It's the only thing that will satisfy him.'

'I know. But no. Absolutely not.'

'Of course not.' Rachel grinned lopsidedly. 'Fine Fairy Godmother I am.' She lifted her teacup. 'Any more tea in that pot?'

Daphne poured tea with a not quite steady hand.

Rachel took a cup, sipped it thoughtfully. 'He won't apologize,' she said, 'if that's what you're waiting for.'

'If he apologized from now until Christmas it would make no difference,' Daphne said stiffly. 'And anyway, there's no question of it. Why should he apologize for something he believes to be true?'

Rachel raised her eyes to the ceiling. 'Oh dear, oh dear,' she said softly. 'The joys of the marriage bed.'

Daphne glanced sharply at her, caught the gleam of mischief in her eye. And blushed, very deeply.

Rachel ducked her head to hide her smile and stirred her tea.

'*I want to be happy, but I can't be happy, da da da da da da da –*'
Philippa danced a few light steps to the window, stood looking

out over the roofs of Pimlico. 'Why don't we go over to the market to see Rachel?' she called. She ran a finger along the windowsill and giggled. 'Honestly, Hugo – just look at this windowsill! It's *filthy*!' She turned and wandered back into the tiny kitchen where Hugo was sitting in the only chair hunched over a scratched and battered table that was covered by the dismantled insides of a small clockwork train. Coming up behind him she slid her arms around his neck, laid her cheek against his straight, soft hair. 'You need someone to look after you, my lad. That's what you need. Shall we?'

'What?' Hugo did not look up.

'Go over to Petticoat Lane,' Philippa repeated, patiently, 'to say hello to Rachel.'

'I'd rather not.'

A small spasm of irritation crossed Philippa's face, but she kept her voice light. 'The park then? Shall we go to the park? It's such a lovely day – a real Indian Summer – it can't last much longer –'

'No.'

Philippa straightened, biting her lip. 'Then – what would you like to do?'

He shook his hair out of his eyes. 'Do we always have to be doing something?'

'No. Of course not.'

The silence was not an easy one. Philippa stood, arms folded, lips folded determinedly against speech, eyes suddenly suspiciously moist.

Hugo, concentrating altogether too ferociously on fitting a tiny flywheel, ostentatiously did not look at her.

She turned, wandered back into the sitting room her face set grimly, all her attempt at good humour defeated. She flung herself into an overstuffed armchair with horsehair sprouting from its arms, picked up a newspaper that had been thrown on the floor, tucked her legs beneath her and stared at the blurring print with unseeing eyes.

'Flip – I'm sorry. Please don't get upset again.' Hugo had appeared in the doorway. His collarless shirt was open at the neck, his pullover had a ragged hole worn in the elbow. His hair flopped over his eyes. Impatiently he tossed it back. His face was thin, the bones too sharp, and his wide, easy-going mouth was drawn, as it seemed so often to be drawn lately, to a tense unsmiling line.

'I'm not upset.' She did not lift her head.

'We can go out if you want.'

'I don't care.'

'Oh, for goodness sake!'

She shrugged. Turned a page.

'Please don't sulk.'

'Sulk? Me? I like that!' She threw the paper from her, scattering it across the floor of the small room. 'Hugo, you've been as miserable as sin for weeks – you don't want to do anything – you don't want to go anywhere – you don't want to see me –' Treacherous tears were very close again. She swallowed violently, cutting off her impassioned words.

'Oh, don't be daft. Of course I want to see you –'

'Then why don't you show it? Hugo – what's the *matter* with you?'

'Nothing. Nothing's the matter with me.'

'*You keep on saying that!*' She leapt from the chair, caught his arm as he turned from her. 'Hugo, for God's sake, what's happening?'

He wrenched his arm away. 'Philippa, please! Don't start this again! I can't stand this constant nagging –'

'What?' She fell back a step, her face paled, then took on the high colour of pure, miserable temper. 'Nagging? Is that what you think I'm doing? You go around with a face like a wet week, I can't get a word out of you, everything I say is wrong, everything I do you criticize –'

'Flip!'

She was shouting now and beyond any effort at control. 'Why don't you just admit it – why don't you just tell me you don't love me any more – that you don't want to see me any more –' Blindly she was groping for the jacket she had flung over the back of the chair earlier.

'Flip, stop it! Please! Of course I still love you – of course I want to see you – I've told you, I've had some problems at work –'

'But what has that to do with *me*?' She turned back to him, face tearstained, hands spread helplessly. 'Hugo, why do you take it out on me?'

'I don't.'

'You do!'

'I don't –'

'*You do!*'

'Oh, for heaven's sake, don't be so—' He stopped.

She was suddenly, dangerously, still. 'Childish?' she supplied, very quietly. 'Was that what you were going to say?'

He did not reply.

'I see.' She shrugged into her jacket, grabbed her handbag from the table. Her colour was very high.

'Flip – don't go off like this.'

She turned to face him, her chin in the air. 'A nagging child, Hugo? You surely don't want a nagging child about the place to interfere with your –' She cast a scornful glance through the kitchen door to the dismembered train. '– adult occupations?'

'Flip!'

The door slammed behind her with enough violence to bring the old building down to its foundations. He ran to the window. She was already out of the front door, running blindly down the steps, across the road, away from him. He threw open the window, leaned out. 'Philippa! *Flip!*'

She neither stopped nor turned.

'Oh, shit!' He slammed the window down, stood leaning, palms flat on the wide windowsill, head hanging, eyes clenched shut.

Philippa walked very fast. Her teeth were clamped painfully into her lip, tears ran almost unnoticed down her face. She had to face it. He didn't love her any more. It was perfectly obvious; equally obvious that he didn't have the heart – or perhaps the nerve? – to tell her so. Well, in that case, she would have to act for both of them. The conviction had been growing for many miserable weeks. Now she was sure. The world had been right after all. A holiday romance; sunshine and flowers, and absolutely no substance.

She turned into the gates of a small park. Sat very suddenly on a bench. The young couple who already occupied it looked at her curiously. She ignored them.

She would not go back. And he, she was certain, would not contact her. In these past few weeks it had been she who had made the effort, she who had contacted him by telephone at the office, or by silly, lovingly written notes, who had turned up unexpectedly at the flat with muffins, or a bottle of wine, she who had asked, anxiously, at each parting, 'When shall I see you again?'

No more.

She was openly crying now. She groped in her handbag for her handkerchief.

'I say – are you all right?' The girl on the bench was looking at her in a mixture of embarrassment and sympathy.

Philippa sniffed. 'Yes. I'm fine.' She stood, walked away straightbacked and entirely without direction.

She did not get back to the hostel until early in the evening. She had walked her feet to blisters, her nose was blocked and sore, her eyes red-rimmed, but she was calm at least. The pain had not eased. The breaking of a young heart is an agony not easily sustained and never forgotten.

'That you, Philippa?' A small dark girl bounced out of the next room as Philippa struggled with her key in the lock. Philippa did not turn, made great play of opening the door. 'There was a message – well, not exactly a message – he wouldn't leave one – it was your young man, Biddy said –'

'What? When?' Philippa flung to face her.

'Earlier this after— Oh, good Lord, whatever's wrong?'

'We – we had a quarrel –'

'Ah. That'll be it. He telephoned. Fortunately the old cat downstairs wasn't in – I'm sure she doesn't pass on messages, you know, so Biddy took it.'

'What did he say?'

'Nothing.'

'What do you mean, nothing?'

The girl shrugged good-temperedly. 'Just that. He said who he was and asked for you. Biddy said you hadn't come back yet, asked if he wanted to leave a message. He said no.' She grinned cheekily, winked. 'Too personal, eh? Hold on – where are you going?'

'Pimlico.'

'But Flip, love – it's nearly seven. You'll have to put your skates on to be there and back by nine. She'll lock you out.'

'Let her.' Philippa was running for the stairs. 'Oh, damn!' She skidded to a halt, dashed back to her door, fiddled with the key. 'Money. Money, money, money. And a clean handkerchief. Oh, yoiks! just look at me –' She had caught sight of her disordered reflection in the small mirror above the fireplace. She leaned to it, grimacing, ran her fingers through her hair. 'What a fright!' She grabbed a money box from the mantelpiece, shook it fiercely. A couple of shillings and a sixpence slipped from the hole and fell upon the floor.

'Aha,' the dark girl at the doorway, watching the activity with much amusement, said, 'so that's where you keep the loot, eh? I must remember that.'

Philippa was scrambling about on the floor collecting the coins. 'Much good it'll do you. What you can find in this dump you can have.' She tossed the key to the other girl as she dashed back through the door. 'Be a pet, would you and lock up after me –' and she was gone, clattering down the stairs, hair and coat flying.

The bus crawled through the almost empty streets at a snail's pace. Philippa sat and stared out of the window, willing the stupid vehicle to speed up. At every stop people clambered on and off, slowly, slowly. There seemed to be a passenger waiting with arm outstretched at every request stop, the bell tinged monotonously, once for stop, twice to go, once for stop, twice for go. She thought, truly that the sound of it might drive her insane.

The bus conductress, ticket machine settled upon her ample stomach, was full of good nature; helping people on and off, chatting with anyone who caught her fancy. 'That's right, dear, mind the step – steady now – plenty of time –'

She reached the stop at last. Nearly eight o'clock. He wouldn't, surely, have gone out? Oh, please God, don't let him have gone out. She ran, coat flying, from the stop around the familiar corner, her eyes going automatically to the window of the flat, the converted second floor of a small and shabby house about halfway down the street.

There was no light.

Perforce she slowed down to a fast walk, her heart beating painfully in her chest. It wasn't dark yet. He wouldn't necessarily have turned the light on.

She ran up the steps to the front door, pushed it open, went on up the narrow, dark staircase. The key Hugo had given her when he had first moved into the little apartment was already in her hand. The tiny landing was unlit. She groped for the switch. In the light of the dim bare bulb shadows danced.

She pushed the key into the lock, opened the door.

'Hugo? Hugo, it's me –'

There was neither light nor sound. The room was cold; there was an odd, strong smell that she could not for the moment identify.

'Hugo?' Heart sinking she walked into the untidy room. It was just as she had left it; the newspaper scattered still across the floor, the big old chair askew. Automatically she straightened it as she passed it on the way to the kitchen door. 'Hugo?' she called again, but with little hope. 'It's Flip –'

The door to the tiny kitchenette stood open. She swung around the door jamb, glanced in. And froze.

Hugo lay slumped across the table, his fair head lying amongst the scattered pieces of engine. One glance took in the whisky bottle that lay empty upon its side, the small white cardboard cartons that were scattered across the table, the glass, tipped over and spilled beside him.

'Hugo!' She flew to him, grabbed him by the shoulders, shook him furiously.

He was a dead weight. His arm flopped from the table, swung obscenely like that of a discarded doll.

360

'Hugo! Wake up!' She was shaking with terror. She grabbed one of the empty cartons. Aspirin. Packets of them – all empty. 'Oh, God!' Her stomach heaved. With a sheer effort of will she controlled it. She touched his forehead. It was still warm. Leaned to his mouth, her hair brushing his. He was breathing, shallowly and harshly, but he was breathing. His eyelids fluttered.

'Hugo, wake up! You've got to wake up!' Instinctively she tried to drag him upright, again his weight defeated her. 'Please! Hugo!'

He moaned, turned his head.

Almost hysterical with relief and terror she shook him again, tried to drag his all but lifeless arm over her shoulder in order to pull him upright.

His eyes closed again.

'Hugo no! Listen to me! Open your eyes! Hugo – please –' Her breath sobbed wildly in her throat.

He groaned again, moved convulsively.

'A doctor!' she said. 'I must get a doctor – Hugo – I'm going to get help –'

His hand lifted, tried to catch hers, fell back uselessly. His eyes rolled.

She caught the hand. 'I won't be long. I promise.'

'No – doc—' he said.

'What?'

He made a superhuman effort. 'No – doctor –' The last syllable was a gasp.

'Hugo – you'll die!'

He rolled his head frantically. One of the train parts caught his cheek, bringing blood.

She dropped to her knees beside him. 'Hugo – I have to have help – I don't know what to do! I can't let you die – I won't! Please, Hugo, please! Stay awake. The phone box is almost outside the door. I'll be two minutes. Hugo – stay awake!' She caught his shoulders, heaved him upright for a moment. He swayed, slipped, fell from the chair. Let his head sink to the floor, eyes closed.

Philippa glanced around. On the worm-eaten wooden draining

board stood a dirty cup and saucer. She flew to the sink, filled the cup with cold water and dashed it into his face.

He gasped, and coughed. Again his eyes opened.

She did it again, and again. '*Wake* UP!'

He moved feebly.

'That's right. Keep moving. Don't go to sleep. You hear me? *Don't go to sleep!*' She was rummaging in her handbag. 'Oh, God, I must have some coppers somewhere – ah –' Clutching a handful of pennies she flew to the door, clattered down the stairs and out onto the darkening street. The telephone box was blessedly empty.

Within seconds she had inserted her tuppence and was asking in a voice that shook uncontrollably for the only person her frantic brain could think of to whom, since her mother's death, she could turn for help.

Chapter Sixteen

Toby's arrival was heralded by a screech of brakes at the corner of the street and a sharply slamming door. Moments later he erupted through the open doorway, shrugging off coat, silk scarf and dinner jacket as he came, pulling at the intricate bow of his black tie. 'Flip?'

'Here.' Philippa rose from where she had been crouching beside Hugo, holding him, shaking him, talking to him. Her face was anguished. 'Oh – Toby –'

'Out of the way.' In two strides Toby was across the room and with one quick and easy movement had hoisted Hugo first onto his feet and then over his own shoulder, arms dangling. 'What's he taken?' He strode through into the tiny kitchen, banging the door open with his shoulder.

'Aspirin. And whisky. A whole bottle of it, I think.'

'Bloody idiot. Come on, lad, on your feet, snap out of it.' He swung Hugo roughly onto his feet, supporting him with one strong arm, bent him over the sink. 'This as they say is going to hurt you a lot more than it does me. And serves you bloody right.' He forced Hugo's mouth open, unceremoniously thrust his fingers into it.

'Toby! What are you doing?'

'Making him sick. Put the kettle on. Salt. Got any salt?'

'In the cupboard.' She was shaking, but much calmer.

'Salt water, strong and warm. Quickly.'

With trembling hands she lit the gas ring, put the battered kettle on it, reached for the salt. Behind her Hugo retched violently and coughed. She flinched.

'That's the lad. And again. Come on.'

Hugo moaned, struggled feebly to escape the brutal ministrations of his would-be saviour.

'Toby, you're hurting him!'

Toby cast a single, grim look over his shoulder. She turned back to the kettle.

Hugo retched again.

'Hurry up, Flip.'

'I'm coming. It's here.' She heaped salt into a mug, poured water onto it. The smell made her feel sicker than she already did.

'Right.' Toby turned Hugo, propped him up against the sink, held the mug to his mouth. 'Down the hatch, Hugo old man. Come on. Drink up.'

Hugo's head rolled, his eyes shut.

'Oh no you don't.' Toby buried his hand in the straw-coloured hair and pulled his head up. 'No sleeping. Get this down you.'

Philippa could not watch.

'Coffee, Flip,' Toby said, briskly, still wrestling with the now ineffectually struggling Hugo. 'Strong as you can make it.'

She put the kettle back on the hob, dropped to her knees, searching in the cupboard of the dresser. 'I can't find the – ah, here it is –'

Behind her, at last, Hugo was being miserably and comprehensively sick.

'Attaboy.' Toby's voice was crisp and cool, entirely devoid of any emotion. The tiny kitchen smelled like a midden. 'Get the window open, Flip. And the front one. Get some air through here. We've got to keep him awake.'

Hugo was sick again. He hung over the sink, kept upright by the strength of Toby's arm, shivering and moaning, muttering disjointed, nonsensical phrases. Toby heaved him upright, propping him efficiently with one hand whilst he reached for the mug with the other. 'Last drop. Get it down you.'

Hugo shook his head. He looked ghastly, his face bleached skeletal white, his eyes unfocused. 'No,' he mumbled. 'Can't. No.'

'Go and open the front window, Flip.' It was an order, quietly delivered, but an order nevertheless. Philippa did as she was bid, and as she struggled with the awkward sash window she heard a sharp sound, that could only have been a blow, a gasp of pain and then Toby's voice, soothing and mercilessly determined. 'That's better, old lad – that's the way. One more time. Good lad.' Hugo spluttered desperately and there was another bout of noisy retching. For an unstable moment Philippa stood, eyes clenched shut, hands over her ears. She stood so, trembling, breathing deeply the cool air from the window, fighting her own nausea for perhaps a minute. When she dropped her hands and lifted her head the lacerating sounds from the kitchen had ceased.

She ran to the door. Hugo was slumped in the chair, his head on the table. Beside him Toby stood, methodically removing gold cufflinks from his ruined dress shirt and turning the sleeves up to his elbows. 'Coffee,' Toby said, brusquely. 'And put some more on. We're all going to need it.' He straightened for a moment, shaking his wide shoulders, readying himself. 'Come on, old man.' He bent to Hugo, slipped an arm under his. 'Let's take a stroll, eh? Oh, no you don't –'

Hugo's eyelids had drooped over his unfocused eyes and his head had rolled onto his chest.

None too gently Toby caught him again by his dishevelled hair and, lightly but stingingly, slapped his face. 'Wake up. Hugo – wake up! You mustn't sleep. You hear me? Stay awake. Or by Christ I'll really belt you one. You hear me?'

'Toby!' Philippa put out a hand in protest.

'Shut up, Philippa. Make the coffee.' Toby heaved the protesting Hugo to his feet, slipped a supporting arm about his shoulders. 'Wake up, Hugo. Walk with me. One. Two. That's the way –' Hugo took a couple of stumbling steps, staggered, almost fell. Toby heaved him upright. 'OK. I've got you. Now – again. Left, right, left, right.' He marched the other man across the untidy living room, turned. Hugo's feet dragged on the threadbare carpet. 'Stand up straight, lad. Head up. Come *on*! Left, right – that's the boy –' Toby's voice drove him on, sharp and incessant, bullying and cajoling in turn. 'What the hell do you think you're up to, you daft bugger? That's better – that's right – keep going – no, Hugo – walk! Keep walking! You mustn't give in – you mustn't sleep. Flip, where the hell is that coffee?'

'It's here.' Philippa could not control the shaking of her hands and the poisonous-looking black concoction spilled onto the carpet. 'It was too hot to drink. I put some cold water in it.'

'Good girl. Here, Hugo, get this down you.' Toby dumped Hugo in the armchair, where he sat back with a sigh of relief, head lolling. Toby laughed a little, grimly and with no humour, hauled him upright, set the mug to his lips. 'No sleeping. Drink,' he said, implacably.

Philippa hovered, anxiety for the moment ousting terror. 'Toby – I – that is – are you sure that this is right?'

The smile flickered again. Toby did not take his eyes from Hugo's face. 'It's right.'

'But – how do you know? Are you sure you aren't doing more harm than good? Shouldn't we get a doctor?'

'Of course we should.' Still watching Hugo, Toby handed her the empty mug. 'If you want the papers in on the act and the lad possibly prosecuted.'

'That's better than having him die.'

This time his head turned. He eyed her with commendable patience. 'Flip – do you think this is the first time I've done this?'

She blinked.

'Attempted suicide wasn't unknown in the trenches; it was simply unmentionable. If your best mate tried it it was up to you to save him; no-one else would. No, Flip, this isn't the first time. Nor even the second.' He stood again, heaved Hugo unsteadily to his feet. 'I just bloody well hope it's the last. Put some more coffee on, would you, that's a good girl?'

'Will he be all right?'

'He'll be all right.' The words were uncompromising. 'He won't be comfortable, and he'll have a hell of a hangover, but he'll be all right. As long as we don't let him sleep.' He threw a quick, genuine smile at her before settling Hugo once more against him. 'I hope you weren't planning on going anywhere tonight?'

It was long, exhausting hours before Hugo showed signs of normality. Hours of walking, talking, pleading, exhorting, shaking and another bout of sickness. Philippa felt like a rag; only

366

the most resolute effort of will kept her from falling to the floor and letting sleep overwhelm her. God only knew what poor Hugo felt like.

Toby was alert, bright-eyed, watchful. He appeared to feel neither strain nor exhaustion.

'What's it all about, do you know?' he asked her a couple of hours after full darkness had fallen, as they walked the room supporting the slumped Hugo like a sleepwalker between them, his arms about their shoulders, but nevertheless showing signs that the worst of the crisis might be over.

'I –' The tears that had been close for so long brimmed over. 'I don't know – he's been acting so oddly lately. We – well, we had a row. This afternoon. Toby – I walked out on him. I didn't realize – I never thought –'

Toby shook his head. 'You think he tried to kill himself because of that? I doubt it, young Flip. There has to be more to it than that.'

She sniffed miserably. 'It can't have helped, though, can it? Whatever else is wrong – and there is something, I'm certain of it – but, oh Toby, if he dies it'll be my fault! Mine! And I do love him so much! How can it have happened? I don't understand!'

'I told you,' Toby was brusque. 'He isn't going to die. Take the blame for that if you like. If you hadn't come back he might well have done. Tell me – was there a note?'

'No. Not that I've found. Toby – what can there possibly be that would drive him to this?'

'I've no idea.' Toby shifted Hugo's all but dead weight, shook him until his head lifted and the closed eyes flickered. 'But you're going to tell us, lad,' his voice was firm, 'aren't you?'

Dawn and a songbird outside the window ended at last the longest night Philippa had ever endured. Surely no less exhausted than Hugo himself she rubbed her knuckles into painful, red-rimmed eyes, stretched her aching back. Behind her she could hear Toby's voice, easily, almost callously cheerful. 'Drink it, Hugo. All of it. You've got to keep drinking.'

Hugo mumbled something.

'Drink,' Toby said, then lifted his voice cheerfully. 'You sure you don't want something to eat, Flip?'

'No, thank you.'

The smell of scrambled eggs and toast made Philippa's stomach churn. Toby had stood, whistling, cooking them, as if he had had twelve good and solid hours' sleep. Sitting opposite a fragile and gaunt-looking Hugo, he tucked in now with gusto. His eyes were very sharp. 'Philippa? If you won't eat at least come and have a cup of tea. We don't want you keeling over next.'

Philippa left the window, accepted a hot strong cup of tea; extraordinarily comforting, extraordinarily strengthening. She looked up. Hugo was watching her with fiercely pained, deeply-shadowed eyes.

'I'm sorry,' he said.

She shook her head tiredly. 'Was it my fault?'

'No. Please, Philippa – no. Believe me.'

'Then what?' she asked, her voice almost shockingly calm.

Toby sat quite still, watching and listening, his face alert. His fair hair curled crisply and neatly. There was no trace of tiredness about him; the tilt of his head, the blue gleam of his eyes betrayed nothing but lucid interest.

Hugo looked down into his cooling tea.

'Drink it, Hugo,' Toby said, pleasantly.

Obediently Hugo drank.

'You didn't really want to die, did you?' Philippa asked of her own teacup, her eyes refusing to lift to Hugo's.

'I –'

'Leave it,' Toby said, crisply and firmly. 'Wait. We'll talk in a minute. Hugo – have another cup of tea. You'll be able to sleep soon. But not yet. Not till we're certain you'll wake up.'

'I met a man called Maurice Playle,' Hugo said. 'In a bar. Well – to be honest I suppose I've realized since that he met me, if you see what I mean.'

Silence. Philippa, face screwed to tired concentration, sat opposite him, leaning forward, her eyes so intense upon his face that it was doubtful that her ears were functioning at all. Toby stood by the still open window, his back to the room.

'Playle,' he said, quietly. 'That fag?' And he turned.

'Of course –' Hugo said, tiredly, '– you know him.'

'Knew him,' Toby corrected. 'We were up at Cambridge together.'

'Yes. And with Charles.' Hugo's voice held a trace of rue. 'He mentioned that.'

'Who is this Maurice Playle?' Philippa asked.

'A journalist,' Toby said. 'Very clever. Very intellectual. Fashionably Bolshevik.' His eyes, piercingly bright, were on Hugo.

'More than fashionably,' Hugo said.

There was a small, significant silence. Philippa frowned, looking from one to the other. 'Ah.' Toby came further into the room. 'So. You met Playle. Or he met you. Then what?'

Hugo looked terrible. His face, already thin, was pared to the bone, his eyes burned as if with a fever.

'Toby – does it matter?' Philippa asked. 'Can't it wait?'

'No,' said Toby.

And 'No,' Hugo said, tiredly. 'No, it can't.' He was talking to Toby, face lifted, hands clasped in his lap; as if, Philippa thought suddenly, he were in a confessional. 'We had a drink together. Several drinks,' he corrected himself, painfully. 'We talked. I was – well, not very happy at the time.'

'Go on,' Toby said, quietly.

'We met again. He invited me to his home. To meet a few friends, he said.' His eyes flickered towards Toby, whose fair head had moved sharply. Colour slowly mounted in his face. 'No. It wasn't like that. You're right – Playle is –' he hesitated, painfully, glanced towards Philippa.

'A queer,' Toby said, brutally matter of fact.

'Yes. But – we did only talk. Oh – if I had been interested –' Again his glance flicked painfully towards Philippa. '– then I suspect he might have made some kind of play. But – when he realized I –' The words were becoming more and more disjointed. '– wasn't that way inclined – well, he seemed happy simply to talk.'

'How very dangerous,' Toby said, quietly.

'Why?' Philippa asked.

Both men ignored her.

Toby stood over Hugo, towered above him, looking down. 'So. You went home with the delightful Maurice.' He pronounced the name in the French fashion. 'Then what?'

Hugo took a long breath. 'I told you. We talked. And drank. A lot.' His mouth twisted a little, wryly.

'You talked politics?'

'Yes.'

'Alone?'

'Sometimes. But quite often in company. Select company, Playle called it.'

'And?'

'At first – well it all seemed quite all right. I enjoyed it. When Playle puts himself out he can be a very charming chap. And his friends are – interesting –' Hugo hesitated, searching for words. 'They're committed people, they've really thought about things. It makes a change.'

Toby nodded. Smiled, not altogether pleasantly.

'I was living with my father,' Hugo said.

'Yes.'

'And I hate what he is. What he does. What he stands for.'

Toby cut across Philippa's exclamation. 'So?'

'Playle suggested –' Hugo fell silent.

Toby turned away, walked to the window. 'What did he suggest, Hugo?' For the first time an edge of tiredness sounded in his voice.

'That I – keep him informed,' the words were coming more and more painfully, 'of some of the things that my father was involved with.'

'You mean – politically?'

'Yes.'

'For his articles?'

'So I believed at first.' Hugo's voice was very low.

Philippa had stopped even trying to take part in the conversation. She watched, one to the other, silently and with breath bated.

The silence lengthened. Toby did nothing to ease it.

Hugo rubbed his forehead tiredly. 'I went along with it. To be honest – well, it was quite exciting. I felt I was doing something. Part of the group, you know? And—' He stopped. Painful colour rose in his face.

'Playle paid you,' Toby suggested, flatly.

'Toby!' Philippa exclaimed, angrily.

'Yes.'

Philippa bit her lip, shook her head sharply.

'And – once you were hooked – he asked for more?'

'Yes.'

'And then?'

Philippa was watching Hugo again, eyes wide, chewing her thumbnail.

'And then he started pushing for more. And more. Copies of documents. Photographs. I began to realize –' Hugo ducked his head, looked down at his linked hands.

'What?' In the face of his obvious distress Toby did not give an inch.

'I faced him with it. Asked him. He told me. The information wasn't for articles. It was being sent to – to Moscow –'

Philippa made a very small sound, instantly stifled.

'He laughed. Called me naïve. Told me they had me now, and they wouldn't let go. With Father's position and Charles in Parliament, possibly eventually in Government –' Hugo bowed his head, covered his eyes.

Philippa was beside him in an instant, arms about him, his head cradled against her. Her face was fierce as she looked at Toby.

Toby turned, walked back to the window, stood balanced, looking out into the blooming light. Then, suddenly and decisively, he turned. 'Right. Let's go back to the beginning. Anything and everything you remember –'

'Toby, for God's sake! Can't you leave him alone?'

'No. If we're to get him out of this we have to do something, and very fast.'

'There's nothing to be done,' Hugo said, dully. 'We can't stop Playle without implicating me – and to a certain extent Father.

Mud sticks. His son a spy? He'd be ruined. I may not care for him or for his politics – but how could I do that to him? Now you see why I—' He stopped.

'Back to the beginning,' Toby repeated, quietly. 'Where? When? These people you spoke of that were there – Anything, Hugo – think! Anything that might help.'

'I don't *know* anything!'

'Try!' The word was crisp. 'Names if possible.'

Hugo took a deep breath, extricated himself from Philippa's defensive embrace but kept her hand gripped painfully in his. 'Most of the time we met in Playle's flat.'

'Which is where?'

'Bloomsbury. Southampton Row.'

'Right. So – these other people you met – who were they? You remember names?'

'One or two. A couple called Prestwick – I can't remember their first names – they run some kind of left-wing press. Pamphlets and things, the odd intellectual novel. A poet called Steven Minster – he was there quite a lot.'

'Yes. Anyone else? Come on, Hugo – think, dammit! Anyone at all?'

Hugo shook his head. 'Mostly just what you would expect. Left-wing intellectuals, all idealism and passionate debate. Writers. Artists. Political activists. Revolutionaries they liked to call themselves. Oh, but yes, just once, the second or third time – there was someone different, someone who surprised me – but I only saw him the once –'

'Who was he? And why did he surprise you?'

Hugo's brow furrowed. 'He just wasn't like the rest. He was very quiet. And very out of place. But I remember that Playle – well, I suppose deferred to him. I think perhaps they were – rather more than good friends. The thing was that he spent rather a long time talking to me. This was before I'd started to help Playle – I – was a little drunk I think – I don't remember that much of the conversation, but I do remember thinking that he wasn't the kind one would usually meet at Playle's – but then I never saw him again, so I don't suppose it meant anything.'

'His name?'

'I didn't know it then. I found out later – but I didn't take that much notice, it didn't seem to be important. The only thing I do remember was that it was an odd sort of name. Silly really, but –'

'What?'

Hugo shrugged a little self-consciously. 'It was something to do with dancing,' he offered. 'Don't ask me why I remember that, but I do. It must have amused me or something.'

'Polka?' Philippa asked. 'Waltz?'

'de Coverly.' Toby had moved back to the window. His voice was quietly thoughtful, but positive. 'Simon de Coverly.'

Hugo's head snapped back in surprise. 'Yes! That's it! Simon de Coverly! I don't think his name was actually mentioned that time when I met him at Playle's flat – but I saw his picture in the newspaper not long after; he's some kind of financier, isn't he? Something big in the City? That's why I thought it so odd to have met him at Playle's.'

'Yes.' Toby's voice was very thoughtful. An abstracted line divided his brows.

'You know him?' Philippa asked. 'And does it help?'

'Knew him,' Toby corrected again.

'At Cambridge?' Philippa guessed.

'That's right.'

'Does it mean anything?'

'I have absolutely no idea.' Toby tapped his teeth with a fingernail. 'Hugo – you say that this was before you started to spy on your father for Playle?'

'Yes.'

'And you can't remember anything else? Anything significant?'

'No.'

Philippa scrambled to her feet. 'Toby? What are we going to do?'

Toby turned. His sudden smile was seraphic. 'You're going to do nothing at all, little one. After you've satisfied yourself that this young man has nothing worse than a well-deserved hangover, get back to your hostel – if they'll have you –'

'Sarah and Bunty will have lied for me,' she said with perfect confidence.

'And you, Hugo, stay here. Don't go out – don't go to work – don't go anywhere. Lock the door and like Br'er Rabbit lie low an' say nothin'. Acquire a bad bout of influenza. Measles. Bubonic plague.' His smile was caustic. 'Looking at you one might even believe it. Just lie low. Give me a couple of days.'

'To do what?'

He shrugged. There was a glint in his eyes that lit his sharp-planed face all at once to youthfulness. A glint that looked to Philippa, with sudden misgiving, suspiciously like the reckless enjoyment with which the young Toby Smith had embarked on many a mischievous project that had more often than not landed both herself and Rachel in hotter water than was comfortable. 'Toby – what are you going to do?'

He had rolled down his sleeves, picked up his jacket, was shrugging it neatly upon his shoulders, tucking tie and cufflinks into his pocket. He settled it to his satisfaction, slung the white silk scarf about his neck, reached for his coat, ran a hand through his mass of hair. 'A little hunting,' he said. 'It may or may not be successful. Don't bank on it. Whatever happens, Hugo old son, get things in perspective. The worst that can happen is that you have to 'fess up, then what?'

Hugo shook a doleful head. 'Don't!'

Toby stood very still for a moment, watching him. 'It might come to it, lad. I want a promise.'

'You have it,' Hugo said, simply, painful colour rising in his face.

Philippa stepped to his side, slipped her hand into his.

'I'm sorry,' Hugo said. 'I don't know what came over me. It was unforgivably stupid.'

Toby scooped his keys from the table. 'Yes. It was. Now – remember what I said. Keep your head down for a couple of days. I'll be in touch.'

The door closed behind him.

With no words Philippa and Hugo turned each to the other. Philippa buried her head against his chest. 'Oh, Hugo!'

'I'm sorry,' he said. 'I'm sorry. I'm sorry!'

In the dawn quiet they heard Toby's car start up and move away.

They stood for a long time without moving.

Philippa took his hand. 'Come on.' She led him across the room, pushed open the door that led into the bedroom. 'Get out of those horrible clothes and get into bed. I'll tidy the kitchen and make us another cup of tea.'

Within minutes she was back. She poured them both tea, climbed up onto the bed beside him. He sighed, settled comfortably back against the pillows. Some colour had returned to his thin face.

'We have to talk,' Philippa said. 'And not about this idiotic situation you've got yourself into. Wait to see what Toby can do. We'll face it later. It's us we have to talk about.'

'I wouldn't blame you if there was no "us" to talk about.'

She looked at him levelly. 'Is that what you want?'

'Of course not.'

'That's all right then. What we have to do is work out the quickest and simplest way to make them let us get married. As I said this morning – yesterday morning – God, was that all it was? It seems like a month ago – you need someone to look after you.'

He turned his head on the pillow, watching her. 'There's nothing I want more.'

'Right. It's Eddie that's the main problem. You're over age. No-one can actually stop you.'

'They can make it damned difficult.'

'Do you care?'

'No.'

She grinned, her first unrestrained smile for almost twenty-four hours. 'Me neither. So – we have to convince Eddie.'

'How do we do that?'

'I get pregnant.'

There was a long, astonished silence.

'I said I get pregnant,' she said again, a little too loudly, not looking at him.

'I heard you.'

She stole a glance at him. 'And?'

He was watching her, eyes half-closed, warmth and laughter suddenly in his drawn face. 'I hope you don't mean right this minute?'

'Nope.' She snuggled close to him. 'Later will do. Tomorrow. The next day. I'm in no rush.'

He took her chin gently in his hand, turned her face to him. 'Flip – you know what you're saying?'

'Yes.'

'What about teaching?'

'I can teach just as well in Madeira as I can here. I'll just have to learn Portuguese.'

He blinked. 'Madeira,' he said.

'That's right. That's where we're going to live.'

'You've got it all worked out.'

'Yes.'

He closed his eyes for a moment, she felt his body relax beneath the bedclothes. 'Wouldn't that be nice.'

'I mean it. I'm not playing. There's no reason why we can't. Your mother will help –'

'Flip, you're forgetting –'

'I'm forgetting nothing. I'm planning. Whatever happens – even the worst – sooner or later we'll marry. Hugo, I'll wait. For ever if I have to.' There was nothing histrionic about the simple words. 'Though I'd rather not,' she added, practically. 'And meanwhile, there's nothing wrong with making plans. Hugo, just think – we can live in the little farmhouse. It's there, just waiting for us. Made for us. All we have to do is to get through this horrible—' She stopped, listening to his slow, regular breathing. 'Hugo?'

Silence. She turned her head a little. He was sound asleep.

Panic stirred. 'Hugo? Hugo!'

His eyes opened. 'Sorry?'

She let out her pent breath. 'Nothing. Sorry. Go back to sleep.'

He sighed, moved closer to her, closed his eyes.

Just minutes later, her head resting in the hollow of his shoulder, Philippa too was fast asleep.

*

She got back to the hostel early that evening. Jessica, the dark haired girl from the room next door, bounced onto the landing like a jack-in-the-box at her approach. '*Flip!* Where *have* you been?' Her eyes were alight with avid and friendly curiosity. 'Bunty and I have lied our *heads* off for you – I don't know if anyone believed us – what on earth happened?'

Philippa took her key from the other girl's fingers, flipped it into the air, caught it neatly. 'I stayed with Hugo,' she said, nonchalantly.

'*What!*' The other girl was gratifyingly scandalized. 'Philippa – you *didn't.*'

'I most certainly did.' Philippa opened the door, turned to smile happily into the other girl's disbelievingly astounded face. 'Times are changing, Jessie, didn't you know?'

Jessie rolled her eyes. 'Not that much they aren't. Not here anyway. You'd better be careful. If anyone finds out you'll be out before your feet can touch the floor. Oh, by the way –' On the point of turning away she stopped. '– you had a visitor.'

'Oh?'

'Absolute stunner. Tall, dark, lovely eyes.' Jessica pulled a graphic face. 'The kind of figure I'd give my eye teeth for. Said her name was Rachel something.'

'Rachel? What did she want?'

'Dunno. Wants you to ring her. She put the number through the door. In case you'd forgotten it, she said.'

'Right.' Philippa made to shut the door.

'Flip?'

'Yes?'

Jessica's eyes were big. 'Did you – did you – you know?' She made a small, embarrassed, awkward gesture.

Philippa smiled serenely, and she hoped enigmatically, and shut the door.

Toby parked the car in the street outside the house and climbed the steps to the front door. Before he could get his key out it opened to reveal a tall, gap-toothed servant girl carrying a coal scuttle. She bobbed a curtsey of sorts, grinning impudently. 'Mornin', sir. Saw you comin', through the window.' Her small sharp eyes, black as the coal she carried, took in the disarray of his evening suit, the shadows beneath his eyes, and the smile widened a little before she assumed a more suitably demure demeanour.

Toby smiled a little. 'Good morning, Violet. Thank you.'

'Thank you, sir.' She dropped another apology for a curtsey and turned to walk heavily up the stairs, her back expressive.

Toby closed the door quietly behind him, divested himself of coat and scarf. From the drawing room upstairs Violet noisily cleared the fire. The rest of the house was still.

With care, he climbed the stairs. As he passed the open door of the drawing room the maid lifted her head and grinned again, knowingly.

On the next landing the door of Daphne's bedroom stood closed, as did the one leading to the night nursery. He walked past, very quietly, had reached the bottom of the flight to the next floor and his own bedroom when a sound behind him made him turn.

Daphne stood framed by the door. She was in nightgown and dressing robe, but her hair was neatly combed and her face did not have the look of being fresh from sleep. 'Toby?'

Toby let out his held breath. 'As you see. I'm sorry. Did I wake you?'

'No. I was waiting for you. I wanted to talk to you.' There was nothing in voice or demeanour beyond pleasant normality. She made no comment on his appearance. They might have been meeting for tea at four in the afternoon.

He watched her warily.

'Could you spare me a moment? I won't keep you long, I promise.'

'Now?'

'If you wouldn't mind.'

He gestured. 'Daphne – I can't say that this is the best of times –'

'I'd have been as happy to speak to you last night,' she said, and raised her pale, unprepossessing eyes directly to his, 'but I had no chance. Parker said you took a telephone call and left earlier than you had intended.' She paused, to let that sink in.

This time, by the merest flicker of her eyes she indicated the dishevelment of his dress. 'Please. It will only take a moment, I promise.'

He let his hand drop from the banisters. 'Very well. If you insist.' He moved towards her.

'Wait.' She put a finger to her lips, stepped to the night nursery door. Very gently she pushed it open, crooked a finger at him to follow.

The baby lay, rosy and beautiful, his head turned to one side, his small hands, loosely fisted, thrown wide upon the pillow. Infinitely tenderly Daphne pulled the bedclothes up about the small chin. Toby stood as if suddenly struck to stone at the foot of the cot, watching.

The linking door to the Nanny's room stood open. The girl stirred, and settled.

For a long time they stood watching the sleeping child. Then without looking at Toby, Daphne turned and led the way out of the room.

He followed in silence, shutting the door carefully behind him.

Unspeaking she walked into her own bedroom, waited for him to follow, shut the door.

Toby stood in watchful silence.

Daphne did not glance at him. The bed was neat, and barely rumpled, the clothes thrown back where she had slipped from it when she had heard his arrival. On the bedside table a book lay, open. Beside it, propped against the bedside lamp, stood an envelope. Daphne picked it up, turned, walked back to him and held it out without a word.

Puzzled, he took it. Held it, watching her.

'Open it,' she said.

Neatly he slit the envelope with his thumbnail, extracted the document within.

In the long silence that followed, distantly in the house, Violet's coal scuttle clanged, and a sleepy voice remonstrated.

Toby lifted bright, cautious eyes.

Daphne, regarding him steadily, waited.

'I – don't think I understand.'

379

'Oh? I thought it clear enough. And Mr Lee assures me that it's all quite legal and proper.'

'Why?'

For one small perhaps unworthily triumphant moment she thought she had never seen him so much at a loss. She smiled. 'Oh, Toby – if I tried to explain that to you I'd have to explain it to myself. And I'm not certain that I can,' she said, very lightly.

Brow ferociously furrowed he turned away, walked a few paces, turned back again, the envelope tapping a rhythm upon his thumb. 'This – gives me control of Underscars.'

'Yes. That's what you want, isn't it?'

'You know it is.'

She shrugged. 'Well then.'

'Why?' he asked again.

'I told you. I'm not sure myself.' She saw the flicker of uncertainty in his narrowed eyes. 'There's no catch, I promise you. I trust you. This, I suppose, is just to prove it.' She had momentarily forgotten, until the words were spoken, the unconventional circumstances of this meeting. Oddly, it was she who blushed.

He appeared to notice neither her confusion nor the somewhat awkward choice of words. He fingered the envelope. Lifted his head. 'Thank you,' he said.

She smiled.

As he turned he caught sight of himself in the mirror. For a long moment he stood quite still. A dishevelled figure confronted him, tieless, dress shirt crumpled and stained, cuffs turned untidily back over the sleeves of his jacket. His hair, never the tidiest thing about him was tangled as a thorn bush; his eyes betrayed, despite himself, a total lack of sleep.

Suddenly and softly he laughed. Turned. His face was an urchin's, exploding with gleeful mirth. 'You *trust* me? Look at me – I look like a very long weekend in Dublin!' The laughter bubbled uncontrollably, infectiously, the situation a joke to be shared.

She nibbled her lip, trying not to laugh back, not to appear to condone whatever escapade might have been the cause of such disarray. 'Is that where you've been? I didn't like to ask.' A spark of near-happiness lit her eyes. They had not laughed together in months.

He sobered as suddenly as he had laughed. 'I'm sorry,' he said. He made a small, almost childish gesture; a shrug, half defiant, half conciliatory. 'I can't tell you where I've been. Nor why I look like something the cat might have dragged in –'

'It isn't in character,' she said, lightly.

They stood for an awkward moment, the laughter once lost impossible to regain.

He walked to the door, turned again, lifting the envelope. 'Thank you again.' The words, totally inadequate, hung in the air between them and dispersed, like smoke.

She nodded, smiling a little, did not speak.

For a long time after the door had closed behind him she stood quite still, looking into some far distance. Then she left the room, walked quietly to the night nursery, stood for a very long time looking down at the baby.

'Oh! Mrs Smith! It's you!' The words were accusing. Amos' young Nanny stood, aggrieved and sleep-dishevelled by the open door. 'I declare – you gave me quite a turn!'

'I'm sorry.' Daphne's pleasant voice was very contained. 'I thought I heard him stir. I just came to check.'

'I'm sure I would have heard if he had –'

'Yes, of course.' Daphne was soothing. 'And – see – he's perfectly all right.'

'So he is, the little darling.' Nanny advanced, bent over the cot, adoration in every line of her young face. 'Why, isn't he just the sweetest bairn there ever was? Quite the loveliest baby – and so good –' She straightened. She was alone. She tutted, irritated, cast one more loving look at the sleeping child and with relief repaired back to her own warm bed.

In the room next door Daphne, her face pensive, climbed back into bed and lay, propped amongst frilled pillows, weighing, measuring, hoping. She had not thought herself a gambler. But there, the die was cast.

She put a hand to her mouth, to cover a small smile.

Judging by her enjoyment of the hazard it might be wise to stay away from the racecourse.

In the moment before sleep overwhelmed her she found herself remembering Toby, dishevelled, oddly alert, nerves sharp, blue eyes over-bright. Wherever he had been tonight, she found herself thinking suddenly, her instinct was sure, that he had not been with a woman.

An odd unease stirred, and was suppressed. The game was in play. Wait and see.

In the room above, Toby undressed thoughtfully, pulled on a dressing gown, stood for a long time studying the document with which Daphne had presented him. Then, with a shrug he propped it on the mantelpiece, went to the wardrobe, pulled from its depths a battered suitcase that had once been virtually his only possession. He carried it to the bed, dumped its contents unceremoniously onto the counterpane. An assortment of objects that might have graced a stall at Hampstead's Summer Fair cascaded onto the bed; a few battered books, a gold-trimmed fountain pen, letters, an almost unrecognizable toy bear, a small Belgian lace handkerchief, and a packet of photographs. He picked up the photographs, stuffed the other bits and pieces back into the case, went to the window. There he stood, shuffling through the small, faded prints, holding them to the light. At last he extracted perhaps half a dozen, put the rest back into the packet and tossed the case back into the wardrobe. He studied the snapshots; a group of young men in cricket blazers and flannels smiled confidently into the camera. One tall, elegantly slim, fair-haired, his arm about the shoulders of a short and stocky young man with a fierce face. Toby narrowed his eyes, stood looking at the photograph for a long time, searching memory, before walking to the mantelpiece and propping the picture against the clock.

Then, without bothering to draw the curtains and with the sun creeping brightly into the room he tossed the dressing gown onto the floor, climbed into bed and fell immediately to sleep.

*

Rachel Patten penned the letter very carefully and very clearly. She could afford no more mistakes. No more confusion. She used simple, basic words for no other reason but that the situation in which she found herself could not be more simple nor more basic. She exercised neither artifice nor pride. She could only hope that he would understand, after all the misunderstandings that had gone before.

With the letter written, however, the uncertain address, ascertained at last from a distrait Philippa, printed clearly upon the envelope and a stamp affixed she suffered a sudden failure of nerve and the thing sat upon her mantelpiece, mute and challenging, for a full twenty-four hours.

Until, with a resolution born as much from defiance as hope she took it down and, whistling into the autumn wind, dropped it into the post box on her way to the market.

Chapter Seventeen

The man at the bar had been drinking, alone and steadily all evening.

Maurice Playle, from his accustomed quiet corner, had been watching him, pensively and unobtrusively, for some time. It had been a pleasant evening; friends, acquaintances and contacts had come and gone, the conversation had as always been both entertaining and stimulating. Playle picked up his glass, turned it in long, fastidiously manicured fingers, his eyes now quite openly on the figure at the bar.

The man leaned with casual grace, one foot hooked upon the rail. His fair-skinned face still held the colour of summer, against which his eyes were startling, the colour of sapphires. The bright cap of his hair, corn fair and curly, a little longer than was the fashion, tumbled with some art upon his forehead. He was quite the most handsome thing Maurice Playle had seen for months. And more; if he were not much mistaken, this was an old acquaintance he had good reason to remember.

Toby Smith. Cambridge. Sportsman, war hero, one of the Golden Boys. Much sought after. Hard to get.

But not, it seemed intriguingly possible, tonight? Playle, poised and attentive, rested his chin on his hand and watched the pretty pantomime at the bar with amused and interested eyes.

Toby was talking to the barman: the man grinned, polished the bar, laughed aloud. Toby's own smile was beguiling.

Playle stood. Tall, very slim, impeccably dressed, not a hair of his silver-fair head out of place he sauntered between the tables towards the bar.

'Smith, isn't it? Toby Smith?'

Toby turned, took a fraction of a second too long to focus his eyes. 'That's right.' He smiled, pleasantly, faintly and politely enquiring.

Playle extended a narrow, well-tended hand. 'Playle. Maurice Playle. We were –'

'Why, of course!' With every appearance of sudden recollection Toby straightened, took the hand, shook it warmly. 'Playle! Delighted, old chap! You've made quite a name for yourself since last we met!'

Playle, smiling, made a small, self-deprecating gesture.

'I read your column often. It's good stuff.'

'Thank you.' Playle eased himself onto the stool next to Toby. 'Will you join me in a drink?'

Toby's over-bright eyes rested on the other man's narrow, handsome face for a long moment. 'Yes,' he said.

'A celebration, I think? Champagne?'

Again a small, smiling pause. 'Why not?'

Playle ordered the champagne, watched as the barman opened the bottle and poured the sparkling liquid into two tall glasses.

Toby studied him with a disarming openness. The fine, spun silver hair was thick and straight and expensively cut. The evening suit fitted the spare figure almost too perfectly. When Playle turned, smiling, to offer Toby his glass, the pale, intelligent eyes were clear as water, disconcertingly intent. He lifted his glass. 'To – old friends.'

Toby's own eyes gleamed suddenly with a graceless amusement he made no attempt to hide. 'Old friends,' he agreed.

'So –' Playle put down his glass, rested his elbows on the bar. 'What news? The world has been treating you well, I trust?'

They talked their way through the bottle. Maurice Playle, when he put himself out to be so was easy company, sharp-witted, mischievously entertaining. Through the stream of small talk and anecdotes Toby allowed himself to be gently catechized, fell readily into the small traps the other man devised, waited for the invitation that he knew, sooner or later, would be extended.

The conversation slipped from the present to the past; they talked of Cambridge, of mutual acquaintances, of the happy irresponsibilities of youth.

'What splendid days they were, eh?' Playle refilled Toby's glass, eyed him reflectively.

Toby grinned.

'We never got to know each other as well as we might have.' Playle sipped his champagne, glanced at Toby across the top of his glass. 'Did we?'

Toby's smile widened.

'A pity, I always thought.'

Toby leaned on his elbows over his glass, head bent, face still lit with that brilliant smile. He lifted his head. 'Our interests were different,' he said, gently.

Playle glanced sharply at him.

'Politics,' Toby said, innocently, 'never interested me. Still don't.'

Playle watched him for a moment, face intent. 'They fascinate me.'

'Yes. I remember.'

'And you?'

Toby slanted a bright glance across his shoulder. 'Me?'

'What fascinates you?' Playle's clear eyes were narrowed suddenly, and very sharp.

Toby kept his own gaze wide and steady, an open acknowledgement of the undercurrent that swirled darkly between them. Then he shrugged. 'Making money,' he said.

'Which you're doing fairly successfully?'

'Fairly.'

There was a moment's silence. 'I was wondering –' Delicately the man stopped.

'Yes?'

Playle flicked the bottle with his long fingernail. 'Terrible stuff, this. And at an extortionate price. It happens –' He paused again. ' – it happens that I have a couple of bottles of the real McCoy at home. Vintage stuff. Only to be drunk with the discerning.' He folded long fingers quietly before him and waited.

Toby sat for a long second, studying his image in the gleaming mirror behind the bar. Then, 'Why not?' he asked, brightly, and straightened, none too steadily. He laughed a little.

The other man slipped a quick, supportive hand under his arm.

Toby bestowed upon him another brilliant smile and gently extricated himself from the helpful hand.

They travelled by taxi, largely in silence. Playle's apartment in Bloomsbury was on the top floor of a tall and elegant town house. A quietly efficient lift, all shining mahogany and brass, deposited them on a small carpeted landing. Playle led the way to one of the two doors, slipped a key into the lock, pushed the door open and stood back for Toby to precede him into a charmingly spacious and well-proportioned room.

Toby sauntered ahead of him, hands in pockets, looking about him in open curiosity. 'Ver-ry nice.'

'Thank you. Here, let me take your coat –'

Toby shrugged, tossed coat and scarf onto the back of a chair. 'That'll do.'

As Playle slipped his own coat off and went off to hang it up, Toby wandered about the room inspecting the pictures and the objets d'art. 'You have a fine collection.'

'Odds and sods I've picked up over the years.' Playle came back into the room, smoothing his hair with the palms of his hands, crossed to where a door stood open to a tiny, well-fitted kitchen. 'Be a chum and fetch the glasses, would you? They're in the cabinet by the window.'

Toby found the glasses, followed Playle into the fastidiously tidy kitchenette, leaned by the door watching as with the neat elegance that characterized all his movements he opened a bottle of champagne. 'Do you ever see anything of the old Cambridge crowd?'

'What?' Playle shook his head. 'Oh, no. Lost touch years ago.'

'Really?' Toby set the glasses gently upon the small table. 'I thought – I seem to remember that you were pretty thick with one or two of them?'

Playle lifted a shoulder. 'One grows out of these attachments,' he said.

'Yes, I suppose one does.' Casually inquisitive Toby opened a cupboard, peered into its neat and tidy depths. 'What was the name of that fellow you used to go around with? Small, dark, rather fearsome as I remember it. Terribly intense. French name. De Courcy?' He cocked his head to one side, thinking, snapped his fingers. 'No. De Coverly, wasn't it?' He turned, smiling guilelessly.

Playle shook his head, poured the wine with a steady hand. 'We weren't that close. Lost touch ages ago. We haven't run across one another in years. Shall we?' He waved a hand, picked up the tray that held the glasses and bottle.

Toby went back into the handsome sitting room. Playle set the tray down on a table beside a deep, leather upholstered settee. Toby wandered past and settled himself, smiling amiably, in an armchair at right angles to it.

Playle smiled back, openly amused, openly enjoying himself. 'Music?'

'Why not?'

'Bach? Mozart?'

Toby spread his hands. 'Whichever you like. Do you mind if I smoke?'

'Not at all.' Playle was on the other side of the room. The wonderfully, almost mathematically melodic notes of Bach's Violin Concerto in E filled the room. Playle fussed a little with the controls, adjusting the volume.

Toby watched smoke drift to the ceiling, and waited.

Playle picked up a glass, handed it to Toby. 'You like Bach?'

'Very much.'

'So. Perhaps our tastes aren't so very far apart after all?'

'Perhaps not.'

Playle lifted his glass. 'Cheers.'

'*Zah vahsheh zdahrovyeh*,' Toby said, gently and very pleasantly but with no smile, and returned the salute before sipping his drink.

Only the most attentive watcher might have observed the other man's flicker of reaction. Within a fraction of a second the small shock of stillness had been shaken off, and the glint of unwary surprise in his eyes was gone. Smoothly he lifted his glass and drank. 'I don't know that one.'

Toby smiled.

'It's – Russian, perhaps?' Playle prompted.

'It's Russian,' Toby agreed, equably.

The music lifted, passionate and beautiful. They sat for a long while in silence, listening.

'I seem to remember,' Playle said at last, very softly, 'embarking – or attempting to embark – on an evening something like this once before? A summer's night by the river. After a cricket match. And a young man – a rather beautiful young man as a matter of fact – with mischief in mind.'

Toby stubbed out his cigarette, lifted wide and candid eyes to the other man's intent gaze, and held it for a long moment before, suddenly, throwing his head back and laughing delightedly.

Playle pounced, leaning forward. 'You do remember, then?'

'Of course I do.'

'And – tonight – you did know who I was?'

'Of course I did.'

'That night. The night we both remember. You led me to believe –' Playle did not continue.

Toby's eyes were alight, gleaming with something close to malice. 'That – to quote our earlier conversation – our interests were not so very different?' he suggested.

'Quite.' Playle, still smiling, eyes narrowed, shook his head, tutting, 'Unkind.'

'So I was.'

'And deliberately so I always suspected.'

'Probably,' Toby said, lightly. 'I find I sometimes am.'

Playle stood. 'But you do remember?'

'Yes.'

'And – you are here.'

'So I am.'

Playle had moved towards him, stood tall and slender above him. Toby had not moved. Playle dropped to one knee beside him, laid a long hand upon his arm. 'Why? To be unkind again?' There was a glitter of excitement about him, Toby could feel that the hand upon his arm trembled a little.

He let the moment linger between them. Then, 'Yes,' he said, in a tone suddenly perfectly clear and conversational, and moving sharply his hand snapped about the other man's narrow, long-boned wrist, the grip obviously deliberately painful. 'I'm afraid so. More than you'd possibly believe, Maurice, my dear.'

Playle cried out once, the fair head jerking back, then he crouched awkwardly, absolutely still, watching Toby uncertainly, only the beginnings of alarm showing in eyes that were shadowed with a kind of elated apprehension, and with pain. This was a game he'd played with others, and enjoyed. He waited.

Toby exerted cruel pressure, bending the fragile wrist backwards. Playle gasped, eyes widening.

The music built to a last crescendo, and stopped.

'A word in your ear, Maurice,' Toby said, quietly into the silence. 'You've been bothering a young friend of mine. I want you to stop.' He released the other man's wrist so suddenly that he sprawled from him.

Playle, very slowly, nursing his bruised wrist, got to his feet.

Toby, too, stood.

'What the devil are you talking about?' Playle's face was very still, utterly without expression. Only his stance, the ragged unevenness of his breathing, betrayed the sudden depths of his fear.

'No games, Playle. You know what I'm talking about. Hugo Fellafield. Lay off him.' Toby's voice had lost all trace of softness. His eyes were bright and clear, and hard as stone.

'Fellafield? I don't know any Fellafield. I tell you I haven't the first idea what you're talking about –'

Toby hit him, hard, open-handed. Playle staggered, fell onto the sofa, his hand to his bleeding mouth. 'What the hell's the matter with you? Have you gone raving mad?'

'I told you –' Toby stood above him, preventing him from rising. 'No games. Hugo's told me. About your – little arrangement.'

Playle did not move. Blood bloomed brightly upon his lip. He sat up, reached into his breast pocket for a handkerchief, dabbed at his mouth, wincing.

'Hugo tried to commit suicide,' Toby said, very quietly.

That brought the other man's head up sharply.

'Tried, I said,' Toby repeated, his voice grim.

'The damned fool.'

'For trying? Or for failing?' Toby leaned forward, took the other man by his shirt front and hauled him to his feet. Playle flinched. Toby let him go.

'I'm very much a coward, as I suspect you have probably guessed,' Playle said after a moment, his voice low. 'But if you think you can intimidate me by physical violence into—'

'No.' Toby's voice cut sharply across his words. 'No,' he said again, 'I rather had something else in mind.'

'Oh?' Playle watched him, warily.

'The biter bit, so to speak. A little reciprocal blackmail. An intriguing opportunity to use your masters' own favourite weapon against them. Against you. I wonder – how do you think they would take to the knowledge that you were picking up strange young men in bars? Not entirely kindly, I would assume. Not the best way to stay out of trouble, Maurice my dear. There are laws about such things, are there not? As you and those that control you know all too well. You've used the filthy trick often enough yourself.' He shook his head, smiling, clicking his tongue. 'Naughty, naughty, Maurice.'

'They wouldn't believe you.'

'Ah, but I think they might. The barman – remember? – knew well what was going on. I made sure of that. Oh, and I also took the number of the taxi. We make quite a striking pair, wouldn't you say? I'm sure the driver's memory wouldn't take much jogging? Except that I don't for a moment believe that it would come to that, do you? Because the man who matters almost certainly would believe it. The man you insist that you haven't met for years. The man who was your – shall we say constant companion – at Cambridge. The man Hugo met here in this apartment less than a year ago. Simon de Coverly. He'll believe me, I think. He knows you well. Very well. But he won't be pleased, Maurice, will he?'

Playle had lost colour. The battle he fought to retain his composure was quite obvious. 'I told you,' he said doggedly, 'I haven't seen de Coverly for years.'

'You lied then. You're lying now,' Toby said, agreeably.

'Now, look here, Smith –' the attempt at bluster lacked conviction entirely.

'No, you look, Playle. You've been rumbled. You thought to blackmail Hugo –'

'I still can.' Waspish now, all pretence suddenly dropped. 'Nothing's changed.'

'Oh yes, something's changed. First, you have me to face – what I know, what I can guess, what you know I'm perfectly prepared to do about it. Second, Hugo's ready to stand up to you. He's been through hell, but he's survived it, and he'll face anything the authorities might throw at him rather than carry on dancing to your filthy tune. He's discovered his backbone, Playle. How's yours? He's got friends. Have you?'

Playle stared at him, tongue worrying at the bloody gash on his lip.

'I'm willing to bet you're a very small fish indeed in a very large pool. You've cocked it up, Maurice. Your masters are not going to be pleased with you.' Toby, watching him still, backed to the door, picking his discarded coat and scarf up on the way, stood with his hand on the doorknob behind him. Playle's eyes followed him, murderous with rage.

Toby smiled, venomously sympathetic. 'If I were you I'd get out while I can.'

'You've no proof,' Playle said. 'They won't believe you.'

'Oh, I think they will, Maurice.' Toby opened the door. 'I think they will. Especially de Coverly. Who knows you and your – interests – so very well. It's a dangerous game you're involved in – people tend not to bother with proof. Suspicion is enough. You've blown it, Maurice. Go while the going's good. They aren't known for their patience and kind hearts, your masters.'

He shut the door behind him, ran swiftly down the stairs. On the pavement outside the building he stopped, shrugging into his coat and looked up.

Maurice Playle stood at the window, a still, dark figure lined in light, looking down.

Toby favoured him with a cheery salute and strode away. He'd done his best. Whether the gamble he'd taken would pay off remained to be seen. Maurice Playle, as he remembered him, could not be described as the most stout-hearted of men. Perhaps he'd been persuaded into panic, perhaps not. Toby turned a corner, stopped by a postbox, took a letter from his pocket. A turn of the screw would not come amiss. If he had truly guessed wrongly then he knew it had to be accepted that the whole miserable affair might come out and Hugo would suffer. But if his instinct served him well, then this affair made Maurice Playle a liability to his paymasters and something would be done about him.

With only the barest second's hesitation he dropped the letter into the box. If Simon de Coverly were not what Toby suspected him to be he would, like any innocent man, make the contents of Toby's letter known to the authorities. If he were, his actions would be quite different.

And Hugo, hopefully, would be safe.

'Hugo, I'm sorry – I *know* it's hard! But I still think you have to tell him –' Philippa's voice was stubborn. 'We have to start afresh. We can't live with this hanging over us. We can't!'

'But – to tell Father?' Hugo shook his head in a combination of disbelief and desperation. 'Flip, you don't know what you're saying!'

'I know exactly what I'm saying. And I know it won't be easy –'

'Easy!' Hugo threw up exasperated hands, shook his head. 'Bloody hell – why don't you suggest I cut off my right hand with a carving knife while you're at it? That'd be a doddle compared— Oh, who the hell is that?' He broke off at the quick, rhythmic rap on the door.

Philippa opened the door.

Toby leaned on the door jamb, grinning. In his hand he held a paper that he brandished with a dramatic flourish. He had a bottle tucked under his arm. 'Is this a private fight or can anyone join in?'

Philippa grimaced and threw open the door.

Hugo ran a hand sheepishly through his hair. 'Hello, Toby.'

'Sounds like a touch of stir fever?' Toby eyed them both shrewdly.

'Could be.'

'Well –' Toby tossed the newspaper onto the table. 'Looks as if that'll be put right now. Seen this?'

Philippa glanced at the headline and the graphic picture that took up most of the front page. 'The crash? Yes – awful, isn't it? All those poor people! It'll surely be the end of airships? Who'll travel on them after this?'

'Not the crash. This.' Toby's finger rested on a small item pushed by the other more immediately sensational news to the foot of the page.

Philippa leaned over, reading. 'Maurice Playle – well-known journalist and political commentator – disappeared two days ago – astonishing defection – Toby! Playle's in *Moscow*?'

'It seems like it.'

'But – how? Why?'

Toby lifted over-innocent brows. 'What makes you think that I should know?'

Hugo had snatched the paper and was racing through the account. 'It doesn't say anything about –'

'Espionage is the word you're looking for, I think,' Toby suggested. 'No. It doesn't. Why should it? The inference is simply that as a well-known Leftie he's crossed to the camp where his views are welcome and his ideals are being put into action. Good riddance many will say. The Soviets are claiming a moral victory – intelligent, sensitive man can't stand the brutalities of Western capitalism and all that. Good luck to them. I'm sure they'll all be very happy together. Now – to more important things –' He put the bottle of champagne he was holding onto the table. 'If someone would be kind enough to supply the odd glass we could celebrate.'

'But – Toby – how did it happen? What did you *do*?'

'Did he jump or was he pushed?' Toby rolled his eyes and grinned like a child. 'Does it matter? He's gone. Glasses, Philippa!'

The news was only slowly sinking in. Suddenly Philippa let out a muffled shriek and flung her arms about Hugo. 'Hugo! Darling! You're *safe*!'

Hugo hugged her back, shaking his head bemusedly. 'I – suppose I am?' He looked at Toby.

Toby nodded.

Sobering, Philippa stepped back. 'But you still have to tell your father. More than ever now.' Her voice was utterly determined, utterly certain.

'What?' Toby glanced at her sharply.

'It's what we were arguing about when you came in. Toby – I think – I'm sure! – that Hugo should tell his father what's happened. He'll never have any peace if he doesn't, and neither will I.'

'Doing the honourable thing? Confession being good for the soul?' Toby's tone tended, a little doubtfully, towards amusement.

'Yes. A bit of both of those things if you like.' Philippa was stubborn. 'But more than that. We want a fresh start. We want to go to Madeira. We want to put the whole thing behind us. He'll never do that if he doesn't tell his father what he did. I know it. It'll hang over us like that beastly Sword of what's-its-name –'

'Damocles,' Toby supplied, interestedly.

'– for the rest of our lives.'

'Supposing the charming Spencer turns him in?'

'He wouldn't.' Philippa's confidence slipped a little. She eyed Hugo doubtfully. 'Would he?'

Hugo shrugged gloomily. 'Who knows? Look Flip – I know what you're saying but now, is there any need? If it's finished?'

'How can it ever be finished if you don't put it straight with your father? Supposing, God forbid, something comes out, sometime in the future? It could, you know it could. And your father – he'd be completely vulnerable. Can you imagine what it could do to him? Hugo – he has to know. For his own protection, if for nothing else. You have to tell him.' She turned to the silent, listening Toby. 'Toby? What do you think?'

'That it's absolutely nothing to do with me,' Toby said, very promptly. 'It's not something that I'd care to advise you about. If I were Hugo –' He lifted a shoulder. '– I daresay I'd cut and run. But – yes, I can see the point you're making. The decision is Hugo's. Just one thing.' He cocked his fair head, his gaze level. 'Keep my name out of it all, yes?'

Hugo's head snapped up. 'Of course!'

'Then it's something you must work out between you.' Toby looked from one to the other. 'Madeira,' he said. 'So. You've made plans.'

'Cooped up here we haven't had much chance to do anything else for the past few days,' Philippa said, then blushed poppy red at the spark of questioning amusement that had appeared in Toby's face. 'Toby, don't be beastly!'

'And Eddie? Have you found some magic way to overcome his opposition to your marriage? Or is there a good old-fashioned trip to Gretna Green on the agenda first?'

Philippa's colour deepened. There was a moment's awkward silence.

'Sorry I spoke.' Toby was laughing.

Philippa shook her head. 'I may as well tell you. I had planned to – to get, you know, pregnant –'

'*What?*'

'But then I decided – well I couldn't be underhand with Eddie. I know he means things for the best. So I told him. What I intended to do, that is.' She glanced, a little defensively, at Hugo. 'And *that* wasn't particularly easy, I can tell you!'

'I imagine not!' Toby was laughing harder. 'And how did he react?'

'He was mad as murder to start with and yelled a lot. But then all of a sudden he laughed. Said I was exactly like my mother and that he might as well try to stop a steamroller with his bare hands as try to change my mind. He said since he didn't have any spare ivory towers around to lock me in he'd better give in gracefully. Toby, what are you *laughing* at?'

'Nothing. So.' Toby looked from one to the other. 'You're getting married?'

Philippa nodded, her face suddenly lit to a radiant smile.

'Congratulations!' Toby tapped the bottle. 'Yet another cause for celebration. Where the devil are those glasses? A man could die of thirst around here!'

'Philippa and Hugo are getting married.'

Daphne pushed away her plate, with its untouched toast and marmalade and smiled a smile of unaffected pleasure. 'They are? Oh, Toby, I'm so pleased for them. I know she's young, but they seem so very right for each other.'

Toby straightened the newspaper he had been reading, laid it neatly upon the table. Daphne, who had been even for her remarkably quiet throughout the meal watched him as he folded his napkin and prepared to rise.

'Toby?'

He paused, looking at her. Her colour was high, her face set in recognizably determined lines. There was a small, awkward silence as he sat, politely waiting.

'I am, as my father was far too fond of pointing out, someone to whom plain speaking is the only kind that comes naturally. I'm afraid –' She smiled – the smile over-bright – as her voice was over-crisp. ' – you must have noticed, that the clever feminine subtleties are entirely beyond me.' She flicked a glance at him and her colour, already unusually warm, deepened, staining her cheekbones. She drew a breath, injected a more normal touch of abrasive humour into her voice. 'To attempt straightforwardly to seduce you hardly seems practical under the circumstances. To say nothing of such a course being pretty well certainly doomed to failure.'

He said nothing. Astonishment, pure and simple, held his tongue.

'I want another child,' she said after a moment, and with scrupulous calm. 'And soon. I'm not getting any younger –'

'Who is?' His voice was bemused.

A small flash of temper sharpened her voice. 'Toby, please! Do you think this is some kind of joke?'

'Not for a moment. On the contrary.' Toby waited. Quiet fell. Daphne was biting her lip.

'I thought –' Toby said at last, very gently.

'What? What did you think?' Daphne blinked rapidly several times, folded and refolded her napkin.

He considered delicacy; rejected it in favour of blunt honesty. 'I truly thought you were happier without me in your bed. You – we – have Amos –'

She lifted her head. Colour stained her cheeks again. 'No,' she said.

He studied her.

She took breath, not looking at him. 'My father undoubtedly would have suggested that I should have bargained while I could.'

The thought, it could not be denied, had occurred to him. 'I'm sure he would. Why didn't you?'

'Don't think it didn't cross my mind. I was quite surprised to discover that I couldn't. There are things that can't be bought. At least – ' Her glance flickered to him and away. ' – I hope there are. I want you – ' She struggled with her pride, and vanquished it. She continued very steadily, ' – I want you on your own terms, not on mine. I'm not sure why. For better or for worse we are married, and are likely to be so, please God, for a very long time. It seems that the least we can do is to share bed as well as board. If of course that is your wish also. If it is not, I may as well know now.'

After a very long moment of silence she heard him push his chair back and rise, sensed his movements as he came around the table to her. As she lifted her head he bent to kiss her, as he always did, scrupulously, at every leavetaking, lightly and coolly on the cheek. His hand rested upon her shoulder.

'I have a meeting this afternoon,' he said, 'I'm not sure how long it will take. Berenger's digging his obstinate heels in again, and I think we well may be in for yet another battle. I really must get rid of that man one of these days. I'll have to stay till I've got it sorted – then I have to meet the builder about the new Croydon store.' He straightened.

She watched him in silence to the door.

With his hand on the knob he turned. 'So – perhaps you might ask Cook to delay dinner a bit? Shall we say eight o'clock? I'll certainly be back by then.'

'Of course. I'll tell her,' she said, calmly.

As he left she picked up her teacup, surveyed her absurdly shaking hand, and put it down again rather quickly.

The door opened.

'Ah, Parker. Yes, you may clear the table. Oh, and Parker – ask Cook to come up and see me, would you? I'd like to talk to her about –' She hesitated a moment, a small smile suddenly lighting her face. '– the menu for dinner tonight.'

Hugo faced the storm with as much fortitude as he could muster. The vicious tongue-lashing, more savage than any physical beating he had endured from his father, went on. Into the heavy silence that fell at last he said, for the hundredth time, hearing and understanding also for the hundredth time the total inadequacy of the words. 'I'm sorry.'

His father eyed him with contempt.

'I'm truly sorry.'

'I would prefer to hear that you're ashamed.'

'That too.' Hugo tried to keep his eyes upon his father's cold face and could not.

'You have betrayed me, your country, your family and your honour.'

'Yes. I know.'

'I trust you understand also that you have forfeited any right to your place in this family? That I can no longer consider you to be my son?'

It was no more than he'd expected, than he'd steeled himself to face; but he was astounded at how deeply the harsh, savagely quiet words cut. The hurt was all but unbearable. He said nothing. The past hour had been the worst he'd ever lived through. His father had heard out his stammering, sometimes all but incoherent confession in growing disbelief and outrage. He'd then questioned, concisely and coldly. Then had come judgement and just retribution. Hugo felt bruised to the core.

'What – what are you going to do?' he ventured now.

His father's thin, fine-boned face was as bitter as his tone. 'The only thing I can do under the circumstances. Compromise myself as you have already compromised us all. I shall of course have to confide in Lord Beresford –'

Hugo was shocked. 'But –'

'– who will, I am sure, agree with me that this sorry matter under the circumstances need be taken no further. The thing is done. No good purpose will be served by making this disgraceful affair public. Indeed a great deal of real damage might be incurred. If you have told the truth –'

'I have, I promise.'

The look his father cast him was scathing and brought violent colour to his face. 'If as I say you have told the truth then little if any information of any value has been passed to our enemies. Though God alone knows what mischief you might have wreaked had it gone on. For myself,' his face was closed and chill, a muscle throbbed in the hollow of his cheek, 'I have no desire ever to see or to speak to you again. I ask you to respect that.' He turned away, but not before, for one shocking moment, Hugo saw the flinch of grief and pain in the clenched jaw and the suddenly drawn brows.

'Father!'

'Get out, Hugo.'

'Father, please!'

The icily turned back did not budge an inch. Hugo gathered himself, spoke through the agonized tightening of his throat. 'Philippa and I are to be married. We're going to Madeira. I shall tell Mother what's happened – I trust you have no objection to that?'

'None.'

'And – Paget and Fellafield? Am I to be allowed to continue in employment with the firm?'

There was a long silence. 'What else would you do?' Spencer Fellafield was austerely patient.

Hugo shook his head. 'I don't know. I have to earn a living. Perhaps some other shipper?'

His father turned. 'Are you entirely stupid, Hugo? What kind of talk would that cause? We're trying to avoid gossiping tongues, not encourage them. In any case, untrustworthy as you are, how could I possibly allow you loose on others, to betray as you have betrayed me?'

Hugo closed his eyes for a moment and his already tensed shoulders hunched.

'No. You will remain with Paget and Fellafield and you may be certain I shall ensure that your every move is watched and monitored. You're a disgrace to your name, Hugo. Now go. And be very sure; never will I look upon you as my son again. Go, I say.'

Hugo made no attempt to argue, neither did he bid the bitter man before him farewell.

In the street outside the October wind had risen and was whipping the leaves from the trees, blowing them in dusty whirlpools about his feet. Teeth gritted and eyes burning he turned the collar of his coat up against the blustery chill and set out, walking fast, to where Philippa awaited him.

She soothed him as best as she could, held him when the violent tears came at last, her own eyes brimming.

'God, I've made such a bloody mess of things!'

Her arms tightened about him.

'Everything he said was true.'

'No!'

He was sobbing now, the agonized sobs of a man taught never to cry.

'Hugo, please, listen. It's done. It's over. You've punished yourself enough. You have to think of the future. Our future.' She talked on, holding the tense, tear-racked body to her own, stroking his hair, his wet face, rocking him like a distressed child. 'Don't think of it, darling. Don't think of it. It's all going to be all right, I promise you. Remember Madeira. Think of the sunshine. The flowers. You and I together, for good. Children, Hugo. Lots of them.'

The daylight faded, and night washed into the room. Philippa drew the patched counterpane about them.

And at last, exhausted, tearstained, but with some measure of tranquillity, they slept.

Chapter Eighteen

He did not come. As, Rachel told herself in those rare moments when she allowed the thought of him to cross her mind, she had known he would not. As the days and then the weeks slipped by she stopped looking for him. It was in any case, she assured herself, most certainly best this way. The letter to Gideon had, in honesty, never been one of her most sensible ideas.

On a cold afternoon in mid-November she visited her father, for the first time in a very long while. His delight at seeing her caused pangs of guilt that she disguised, as ever, beneath laughter.

'I'm a working girl now, Pa. No time for socializing. I've been up since four this morning. You'll have to pardon me if I nod off over my tea!'

She did not look as if she were about to nod off. Her always slender body had toughened to litheness, colour glowed in her cheeks. A flawed and brittle shell had broken and from within it had emerged at last the real and positive personality that was Rachel Patten; animated, opinionated, exasperating, inimitable. Ben bestowed upon this difficult daughter of his a bearhug of bonecracking proportions, and for a moment she clung to him, very tightly.

He put her from him, scrutinized her face with serious and questioning eyes. 'You're all right?'

The reason for the distance she had put between them over more than a year he would not ask. It was enough that she was here.

'I'm fine.'

'And this grand new career you've embarked upon –' A smile lit his square, craggy face. '– you're still enjoying it?'

402

Rachel plumped into an armchair, poured the tea, helped herself to a gigantic slice of cake. 'Enjoying it? I'm loving it! Every minute. Whoever would have believed it? It was a pretty lucky day for me, the day I met Curly Bennet, bless him.'

'Lucky for him too, I should think.'

She shrugged, dismissing that. 'I just love the markets. Funny, isn't it? She laughed. 'Duchess they call me – did you know that? Gosh, this cake's good. Curly and I are going into partnership.' She gleamed a small, bright glance above her teacup.

Ben, always to be relied upon to take a broad hint, reached for his tea. 'And you're – inviting investment?'

'No,' she said, cheerfully. 'I'm begging for it. Not much. A few hundred. Perhaps a thousand if you were willing. All straight and above board and all that of course. I'll pay you back, I promise. We thought we might take another pitch. And the theatre business is going really well – I've done a bit of designing – amateur companies, cabaret acts, that sort of thing. We're making quite a name for ourselves. Who knows – this week East Ham Town Hall, next week Her Majesty's Theatre? Well, I suppose that's expecting a bit much but it really is going well. We thought if we could take a small permanent premises, preferably somewhere near the Lane –'

He watched her as she talked, animated and flamboyant, her hands as much in use as her tongue. Strange how much he loved her, this girl who was not his, and yet more his than any other's. Nothing, not the circumstances of her birth nor the cold-hearted defection of her mother, nor the child's own sometimes perplexingly perverse character could mitigate that love by a fraction. She was, almost, the loveliest thing that had ever happened to him. He smiled, watching her.

'Have I got a smut on my nose?'

He shook his head.

'What are you laughing at then?'

'You.'

She grinned. 'Fair enough. Can I have another piece of that cake?'

'Have the lot if you want to.'

'Don't tempt me. I'll finish up the Fat Lady of Petticoat

Lane.' She chuckled, licking her fingers. 'There's a fair bit of competition for that title, mind. By the way – have you heard about Hugo and Philippa? It seems all the dragons are slain. They're getting married and are off to Madeira to live. Not bad, eh?'

'So I heard.' Ben waited until she lifted her eyes to his before he added, gently, 'Philippa comes to see me every now and again.'

She pulled a face. 'Come on, Pa, it's no good trying to make me feel guilty about that – Philippa goes to see everybody.' Her lips quirked in a self-derisory smile. 'She always was a tiresome kid.' But her eyes slid from his. She paused for a moment, her teacup half way to her lips, her face thoughtful. 'I don't suppose Flip – ' she hesitated, ' – explained it all by any chance?'

'Explain? What is there to explain?'

Rachel shook her head. 'Oh, don't be dim, Pa. It does all seem a little strange, don't you think? One minute everyone's against their marrying, and then suddenly – bang! – the knot is tied and they're on the way to their enchanted island. I'm intrigued, that's all.'

'Nosey,' her father said.

'That too. Ah, well. I don't suppose we'll ever know. And not that it matters anyway. Just as long as they live happily ever after.'

'Do you think they will?'

'Who knows?' Her voice suddenly was not as light as it might have been, not as light, he thought, as she would have wished it. 'Does anyone, ever, do you think?'

He shook his head, infected despite himself by the subtle change of her mood. 'I'm hardly the one to answer that, am I?'

She smiled, too brightly. 'I think it's all a sham,' she said, lightly. 'I think that Hugo beats Philippa up in secret and she's only marrying him for his money. All that lovey-dovey, Romeo and Juliet stuff's strictly for show. And I will have just one more piece of cake, please – '

As she left she kissed him, holding his face tightly between her hands. 'You do know I didn't only come about the money, don't you?'

He grinned, playing her at her own game. 'Do I? How?'

'Because you're clever. Because you know me. Because I love you.'

'The last one will do.'

She kissed him again. 'I'll come back, soon. I'm sorry. I went through a bad time. You couldn't have helped. You do understand?'

'No. But it doesn't matter.'

She ran down the steps into the darkness of the cold afternoon, lifted a hand to him, saw the flash of his rare smile as he waved back.

Hurrying towards the tube station she made several good and determined resolutions, and felt better.

It was almost full darkness by the time she arrived home, an over-full paper carrier bag of groceries in her arms, her hat askew in the wind. She pushed open the downstairs door with her back, thankful to be out of the wintry weather, pulled off the slipping hat, shook her hair from her eyes, turned all in the same movement to hurry upstairs, and stopped. Stopped more truly than she ever had in her life before; her movement, her breath, her heart.

Gideon did not stir. He sat above her on the dark stairs, beside him a scruffy bundle and a small shadow, liver and white, that pressed to his side, tongue lolling, bright eyes uncertain on this newcomer, this possible threat.

'Holy Moses,' Rachel said, very faintly, and leaned against the wall, lapsing again to speechlessness.

His face was a shadow within darkness, she could not fathom it. His boots were shabby and mudcaked, his corduroy trousers patched. He wore a mismatched jacket over a shirt and the same bright waistcoat she remembered from before. A flat cap was pushed to the back of his head. His neckerchief he had taken off. It dangled, a brilliant splash of scarlet in the shadows, in one long brown hand that rested upon his knee. The other hand reached to his waistcoat pocket, brought out a torn and filthy, much crumpled envelope. He held it up.

She stood, still clutching the bag, head tilted to him as he sat above her, eyes riveted to the smudged and grubby paper.

'Did you mean this?' he asked.

In the silence the wind buffeted at the door behind her. Someone in the upstairs flat called, and a voice answered.

'Yes,' she said. 'I did. Every word. Do, that is. Do mean it. Why did you wait so long? I'd given up. I thought you weren't coming.' She discovered to her surprise that she was shivering, perhaps with cold.

'So did I.' After that neither of them spoke for what seemed to Rachel a quite ridiculously long time.

Then, 'And you?' she asked. 'You're here. Do you mean it? I said in the letter not to come unless you –' Her voice trailed off.

He tucked the letter back into his pocket, stood up, swung the bundle easily over his shoulder, came down the stairs, lifted the bag from her arms. The dog, her attention diverted from Rachel, sat watching his every move.

Stiffly Rachel squeezed past him in the narrow hallway and climbed the stairs. She rummaged in her bag for her key, opened the door, turned on the light.

He walked behind her into the room, clicked his fingers to the dog to follow.

'The fire needs a match,' she said, in what seemed to her to be a quite astoundingly normal and even voice.

He dumped the bag on the table, his bundle on the floor and fished in his waistcoat pocket. Rachel heard the scratch of a match and saw the glow of flame.

He straightened and turned, watching her.

Rachel felt the sudden and all but overwhelming rise of something close to hysterical laughter. If the man had come as a lover, which she supposed in simple terms had been the invitation her letter had extended, he was hardly putting himself out to fulfil the role. He'd not smiled since he'd seen her; the infuriating face with its flat-planed, foreign, gipsy cast was closed and shuttered against her.

Kili stood, anxious, poised, just within the door. She took a step towards her master. Gideon, not looking at her, gestured sharply, and unwilling she lay, nose on paws, eyes wide and unblinking upon him.

'Do you treat all your women like that?' It was not coquettish – far from it, it was plain question, with a good, crisp edge of asperity.

She saw the faint, answering glint of amusement on his face. He shook his head. 'You should know it.'

Something in the voice arrested her. A hesitancy? Some slight, unacknowledged uncertainty? She could not be sure. Cold and windblown, she was still in her heavy woollen coat. She shoved her hands into her pockets and moved closer to the fire. Closer to him. He reached for her, took her arm, drew her to him, turning her so that he could study her face in the light.

And then she saw it in his eyes, behind the sternly disciplined lines of his face. Uncertainty, raw question, the fear of hurt, of rejection. Gideon Best was no more superhuman, no more invulnerable than anyone else. God alone knew how much it had cost him to come. And now, the die cast, he was afraid.

The realization was the undoing of her. She reached her arms about his neck, leaned against him cradling his head gently, pulling his face down to hers. 'Gideon,' she said, softly, upon his mouth. 'Gideon, Gideon, Gideon.'

For a moment it seemed he might resist her. Then his arms tightened about her and he kissed her back, for a long time and very thoroughly. The tide lifted about them, inevitable, irresistible. Her coat slid from her shoulders to the floor, unnoticed.

The bedroom was an icebox, and dark.

'Put the light on,' she said. 'The little lamp by the bed. I want to see you.'

The light glowed upon exotic silks, an illusion of warmth. 'I'm cold,' she said, laughing suddenly, lifting her arms.

He covered her, warmed her, loved her, fiercely and not gently; still afraid. The primitive commitment made, the wildness ebbing, they lay, limbs and bedclothes tangled, no longer cold. She shifted, making herself more comfortable. His arms tightened about her, holding her to him. In the sitting room the fire crackled.

She tilted her head on his shoulder to look at him, traced the lines of his face with her finger. 'What were you saying?' she asked. 'Just now? While we were making love?'

He said nothing.

Her finger reached his lips. 'Outlandish language. You'll have to teach it to me. I'm not having you saying things I can't understand.' She laughed a little, softly. 'I daresay we can do that very satisfactorily in English.'

His labourer's hand, calloused and strong, yet gentle as a woman's as it touched her, cradled her head against him.

They lay in silence for a long time. Then, 'Are we mad?' she asked.

His grunt could have meant anything. She extricated herself from his arms, rolled up onto her elbow, leaning above him. 'One thing you're going to have to learn.' She laid her finger upon his long mouth, insinuating it between his lips. 'To answer me! To talk! I'm not going to spend my life –' she hesitated, covered the blunder with a laugh, '– with someone who refuses to string two words together. I might even – God help us all! – insist that you manage to call me by my given name now and then. Go on. Try it.'

His eyes, that had been half-closed and sleepy, opened wide, focused intently upon hers. 'Rachel,' he said, very quietly. And then again, 'Rachel.'

She nibbled her lip and took a breath.

Kili, stationed watchfully by the door, sighed heavily and shifted stance.

'Well?' Her voice had changed, all lightness gone. 'Are we mad?'

'Perhaps.'

'I said – in the letter – not to come if you weren't prepared to stay.' She hesitated, ran her finger down the side of his face. 'Will you stay?'

'Yes.'

'Why?'

He did not answer.

'Gideon? Why?'

Very faintly he smiled. 'I'll tell you when I know.'

She shook her head. 'Not good enough.'

He moved easily, taking her with him, pinning her beneath him. 'It'll have to be. For now.'

He loved her again, less urgently this time, with space and time for tenderness and for laughter.

They lay comfortably and in silence for a long time, the vivid silken eiderdown wrapped about them.

'Are you asleep?' she asked at last, very quietly.

'No.'

She rolled over, lifted her head, looking at him. The sloe eyes opened, watching her. Against the pale satin of her pillows his skin looked darker than ever. 'Frills don't suit you,' she said.

He smiled, teeth gleaming. 'They do you.'

She rolled back, stretched like a cat. 'I'm starving.'

The grin widened.

'You?'

'Yes.'

'What would you like – egg and bacon or bacon and egg?'

He contemplated the choice seriously. 'Bacon and egg.'

She slid out from under the warm eiderdown, slipped a thin dressing gown on, shivering. 'God, it's cold. Where are the matches? I'll light the gas fire.'

'Now, she thinks of it.'

She bent to kiss the point of his chin. 'I didn't think we needed it before. Jolly handy, actually. If we can keep this up just think how much we'll save on gas bills.'

She wriggled away from his grasping hands, lit the fire, crossed the living room, went into the small, muddled kitchen, picking up the bag of groceries on the way. Whistling cheerfully she lit the gas ring, reached for the bag containing the bacon.

The smallest of sounds made her turn.

Kili stood by the open door watching her, one paw poised, dark and shining eyes lifted, flagged tail wagging tentatively.

Rachel surveyed the little dog resignedly. 'Don't tell me,' she said, 'I suppose you're hungry too?' She reached for another couple of rashers.

'There'd be more bacon,' she said a little while later as she deposited the tray containing two plates of bacon and eggs and a couple of doorsteps of bread and butter unceremoniously on the bed, 'if that little beast of yours hadn't just hogged most of it. Wasn't it St Bernard who coined the phrase, "Love me love my dog?"'

He was sitting up, knees bent, arms crossed upon them, his dark torso naked, his straight black hair flopping untidily over his eyes.

He lifted his head. 'And could you?'

Too smart for him by half she smiled with lucent sweetness and handed him his plate. 'I'll tell you when I know.'

The cabin was full of flowers. A champagne bucket, the ice melting, stood empty upon the small table.

'Well, Hugo m'boy –', Sir James extended a hand, '– good luck, and good hunting. Keep the old flag flying on the island, eh?'

'I certainly shall, sir.' Hugo glanced about him. The small cabin was packed with people. Philippa was nowhere to be seen.

'Give my love to your charming mother. We'll be over to see you all next year, no doubt.'

'I'll tell her, sir.'

Fiona's husband moved away. His place was taken by the slender, colourful figure Hugo had done his best to avoid all day. 'Hugo.' Rachel kissed him, eyes mischievous, earrings swinging, glinting in the light. 'There. I haven't done that for ages.'

'Rachel –'

She smiled with amused and friendly malice. 'Don't worry. I shall contain my heartbreak. I shan't cast myself from the bridge, or try to seduce you or anything like that.' The bright eyes teased him. He felt a faint and disconcerting echo ring in his blood, quickly suppressed. He looked around again.

'Philippa went up on deck to get some air,' Rachel said. 'Don't worry. She'll come back.' And this time, in her face and her voice the warmth was pure affection, unclouded happiness for him and for herself.

Tongue-tied he looked at her. He had heard rumours, of course, all sorts of rumours, from romantic stories of gipsy lovers to far more cruel judgements, harshly delivered. Friends who had come to see them off had, he noticed, turned from her flamboyant figure when she had entered the cabin. He had seen too, and admired as always, the challenging lift of her head, the gleaming, derisory contempt of the smile she had aimed at them like a spear. Fiona, on the other hand, had made straight for her, arms outstretched, laughter in her face. 'Rachel! It's been just ages!' Openly she had hugged her, taken her by the arm, led her to where Sir James, face fiery, had waited to greet her, less enthusiastically it must be admitted, but warmly nevertheless. If rumour did not lie – and Hugo strongly suspected that it did not – and Rachel was living in sin with a man who had once been Sir James Paget's gamekeeper, neither Sir James nor his wife seemed about to hold it against her.

That said, Gideon was not here.

'You're alone?' he asked, gently.

Her eyes were absolutely direct. 'Of course. I wouldn't inflict this lot on Gideon. They'd bore him to tears. Present company excepted, of course.'

Hugo, remembering the intimidating Gideon, took private leave to doubt that, but said nothing.

Rachel put her arm about his neck and kissed him again. Her perfume, so well remembered, drifted about him, evocative and tempting. He stepped back. She let him. 'Hugo – be happy. And look after Flip. She's the best.'

'Yes. I know. I'm a very lucky man.'

'Hugo, lad – got a minute?' Philippa's stepfather was waving to him from across the cabin. Hugo half turned, glanced back, and Rachel had slipped away from him.

As she had, he thought, a little rueful still, so often before.

She stood in the narrow doorway, hand lifted. As he watched, she blew him a swift kiss and disappeared.

A succession of unsettling emotions jangled for a moment within him, to be followed, gratifyingly quickly, by something that could only be identified as relief. He glanced at the clock. Half an hour. In half an hour they would all be gone. Soon after that the ship would slip anchor and slide out into the Solent on the start of her voyage.

And he and Philippa, man and wife, would be alone and heading for their new home.

'Hugo?'

'Coming.'

Philippa drew the wrap tighter about her shoulders against the chill breeze and leaned against the rail, watching the activity on the quayside. Crowds of people came and went up the steep gangplank – officers of the ship, passengers, well-wishers, messengers delivering gifts and flowers.

Beyond the happy bustle of the pleasure ship's departure the more sombre docklands stretched; towering cranes, grimy warehouses, rust-marked, oil-stained, battered working ships. Busy tugs puttered to and fro, tooting officiously.

She remembered it all, from childhood. Remembered the sounds and the smells, the feel of a working dock.

She remembered her mother, for whom just such a setting had been cradle and nursery. Sally Smith would have recognized this scene.

'Flip?'

She jumped. So lost had she been she had not heard his approach.

Toby smiled, handed her a jacket. 'Are you all right? Daphne saw you go. She sent me after you with this.'

They both smiled without comment at the characteristic Daphne-ness of that action.

Philippa allowed him to slip the jacket over her shoulders, turned back to the rail. 'I was just thinking, that's all.'

He waited, watching her.

'About – my mother. The docks – they reminded me –' She glanced at him. As a child he had shared this background of her mother's. This, and much more. Never to her knowledge, in adulthood, had he spoken about it.

'Yes.' His voice was even, utterly unemotional. 'Docks are much the same everywhere, aren't they?' Narrow, grimy streets. Dirt. Poverty; above all poverty.

'You remember her favourite hymn?' Philippa hummed a snatch of tune. 'Jerusalem. That was what they all wanted, wasn't it? To build Jerusalem, in England's green and pleasant land.'

'It's a pretty thought.'

She looked at him sharply then, her ear caught by the caustic edge to the words. 'You don't think they ever will?'

Toby shrugged. 'Unemployment? Depression? Oh, it's a green and pleasant land, all right; but only if you're on the right side of the fence.'

'You are.'

He turned her to face him, brushed a strand of windblown hair from her eyes. 'Yes, I am. Now. And I'm going to stay there. Now what about you?'

'What about me?'

'All this retrospection? You aren't having second thoughts? It's a bit late if you are – I seem to remember a wedding ceremony this morning? And a certain amount of effort that went into the achieving of same?' He was gently teasing, his eyes very bright, his hair as windblown as her own.

She leaned against him for a moment, hugging him tight. 'Oh, of course not! Don't be silly! It's just – a funny feeling, that's all. Perhaps you never really look at somewhere until it's time to leave it?'

He laughed. 'Oh, come on, now – that's altogether too deep for me, young Flip –'

'All ashore that's going ashore –' A bell rang, distantly.

'We should go back down,' Toby said. 'The others will be looking for us.'

'Yes.' She stayed close to him for a moment, her head leaning against his chest. Then, suddenly, she stood away, slipped her arm into his. 'Right. Off we go. The farewells are said.'

They made their way back down to the cabin. As they approached the door Philippa asked, suddenly. 'What do you think of Rachel's –' she hesitated, '– arrangement?'

She felt him stiffen beside her. 'It's none of my business,' he said.

'Well, of course it isn't,' she said with a touch of her usual practicality. 'It's none of any of our businesses. I never said it was. But you must have an opinion?'

He did not reply. He saw no reason to disclose that his opinion had already been expressed once that day, forcefully – and as forcefully rebutted. The sting of Rachel's tongue was still with him.

She stopped outside the cabin door, from which the sound of laughter and conversation still issued, and perforce he stopped beside her. She cocked her head to one side, studying him with serious brown eyes. 'You never did like Gideon, did you?'

'No.'

'Why not?'

He shrugged, exasperated. 'For heaven's sake, Flip – how do I know? I just don't like the man that's all. It happens.'

'Mm.' She studied him for a moment longer. 'It's probably because you're so very much alike,' she said. 'There but for the grace of God and all that. It must be pretty uncomfortable. But honestly, Toby, I don't think you should take it out on poor Gideon.' And turned to disappear back into the mêlée.

Toby stood looking after her for a long moment, his face a picture of astonishment.

'All ashore that's going ashore! All ashore that's going ashore! Going ashore, sir? Better get a move on or you'll find yourself in Lisbon.' The steward rapped sharply on the open cabin door. 'All ashore, please. All ashore!'

They stood at the rail and watched the dockside and its thinning crowds, handkerchiefs and scarves still waving, recede into the shadowed light of the winter's afternoon. Multicoloured streamers drifted in the churned and dirty wake of the huge liner as, light-bedecked and gleaming she was manoeuvred away from the dock and out into open water. Philippa Fellafield stood beside her husband, her hand in his, both tucked into his greatcoat pocket. They stood in silence.

The ship's siren sounded once, twice in salute. A renewed ripple of high-flung handkerchiefs answered the sound and then the movement died as the space between travellers and well-wishers widened to an unbridgeable void.

There had been no member of the Fellafield family on the quayside, to wave a friendly handkerchief, to offer a farewell wish, even, perhaps to shed the odd tear.

Philippa glanced up at Hugo. He sensed it and looked at her. They smiled together.

'Let's go down,' Hugo said. 'There's nothing more to be seen up here.' He bent to kiss her, firmly. 'And, Mrs Fellafield junior, let me remind you that we've lots and lots of time to fill before we get to Lisbon. Tell me –' He kissed her again. Twice, and very thoroughly. 'Can you think of some pleasant way to pass it?'